THE SLAVER WANTED THEM DEAD

The vid-screen bloomed into life, swiftly resolving into the slaver Corean's perfect face. "You," she said, loathing distorting her voice. "You. I should have killed you the first moment I saw you."

"Probably so," Ruiz said, in as agreeable a voice as he could manage.

"I don't know why I ever thought you pretty," she said. "You're a worthless creature. I'll never make such a mistake again." She jerked at some control, just out of sight, and to Ruiz's horror, the airboat staggered and swooped in response.

The others woke, made various sounds of fright, and clutched at their restraining straps.

Ruiz looked out and saw that the boat was no longer heading for the pass through the blue mountains, but was instead rushing toward a sheer cliff.

He stared out at the onrushing stone as the boat accelerated. From the corner of his eye he could see an avid look on Corean's face, as if she hoped the communicator would survive the impact long enough for her to take a leisurely delight in Ruiz's destruction. . . .

THE EMPEROR OF EVERYTHING

RAY ALDRIDGE

BANTAM BOOKS
NEW YORK · TORONTO · LONDON · SYDNEY · AUCKLAND

THE EMPEROR OF EVERYTHING

A BANTAM SPECTRA BOOK / FEBRUARY 1992

ISBN 0-553-29491-1

Published simultaneously in the United States and Canada

*Bantam Books are published by Bantam Books, a division of Bantam
Doubleday Dell Publishing Group, Inc. Its trademark, consisting of the
words "Bantam Books" and the portrayal of a rooster, is Registered in
U.S. Patent and Trademark Office and in other countries. Marca
Registrada. Bantam Books, 666 Fifth Avenue, New York, New York
10103.*

Printed in the United States of America

RAD   0 9 8 7 6 5 4 3 2 1

Can you ride
the horses of the heart
by some sacrificial art
or the keenness of your wits?
No.
See the blood on the bits.

—Carved on the gatepost of the
Celadon Wind, a SeaStack fabularium

CHAPTER 1

THE stolen airboat followed its preprogrammed course, flying ten meters above the pink veldt of Sook, toward the distant blue mountains.

Ruiz Aw watched the control panel. All seemed to be well; the engines hummed, the compass was steady, the communit was blessedly silent. His Pharaohan passengers had fallen asleep, exhausted by the previous night's violent events. He turned and regarded them. He took particular pleasure in watching Nisa, who slept with her head tipped to the side, a strand of black glossy hair caught in the corner of her rich mouth. Three Pharaohan men with tattooed faces slept in the other acceleration seats; a fourth sat chained in the hold below, still wearing his explosive slave collar and suffering from culture-shift psychosis.

Ruiz felt an odd mixture of cheerful lassitude and anticipatory terror.

On the one hand, he was putting distance between himself and the slaver Corean Heiclaro, which was very good. On the other hand, he expected her to call the boat presently —and that was very bad. She would be expecting to speak with her lieutenant, an ancient cyborged pirate named Marmo, whom Ruiz had disabled and dumped from the boat as they fled across the veldt, or to Banessa, her giant enforcer, whom Ruiz had killed in the course of capturing the boat.

Corean would soon be very angry with Ruiz, and Corean was a person whose rages were to be feared. Ruiz had seen her dispose of substandard slaves with no more emotion than an ordinary person would display at the uprooting of a weed.

Still, his fortunes had undeniably improved. The previous night he'd been a prisoner in the airboat's hold, tethered among his fellow slaves. This morning his neck was pleasantly unconstricted. Even though he couldn't alter the boat's course, he *could* adjust its speed, and he was almost certain that he could cause it to land if an alternative means of escape presented itself. He believed that he had disabled the boat's remote handling circuits, so that Corean couldn't regain control—though he couldn't be sure, since the boat was equipped with an unfamiliar biomech guidance system.

TIME PASSED AND the communit remained quiescent. Ruiz gradually relaxed. The blue mountains grew closer, and it became obvious that they were headed for a notch between two craggy peaks.

He had almost surrendered to a cautious optimism by the time the communit lit up and sounded a soft chime. Terror returned immediately, even though he was almost sure that the boat was unequipped with a remote destruct. Almost.

He had considered and rejected the idea of attempting to conceal his capture of the boat. He could have disabled the video and degraded the voice transmission, but he assumed Marmo and Corean employed some code phrase to establish identity under such circumstances. By immediately confronting the slaver with his deed, he thought it possible she might be usefully startled.

Ruiz reached out with a trembling finger, touched the channel-open switch.

The vidscreen bloomed into life, a swirl of primary colors that swiftly resolved into Corean's perfect face. For a long instant she stared into the pickup, motionless, apparently stunned to see Ruiz Aw looking back at her. Her wonderful eyes widened slightly, her skin went pale, and then her mouth writhed. "You," she said, loathing distorting her voice. "You. I should have killed you the first moment I saw you."

"Probably so," Ruiz said, in as agreeable a voice as he could manage.

"I don't know why I ever thought you pretty," she said. "You're a worthless creature. I'll never make such a mistake again."

"Probably not," Ruiz said, and sighed. Corean owned a face designed by one of the pangalac worlds' greatest lineamentors; even the ugly emotions struggling across those marvelous features couldn't wholly conceal the artist's brilliant work. There was, Ruiz thought, something terribly perverse about a woman so lovely that he couldn't help admiring her, even when she was wishing him a painful death.

She regained control. "Where is Marmo?"

"Somewhere on the veldt."

"Dead?"

"I don't know," Ruiz answered, and smiled with as much charm as he could muster. "Does he bounce?"

She turned whiter, and for an instant her eyes burned incandescently. She muttered a Dobravit curse under her breath.

Ruiz waited, wondering if he dared provoke her further. Why not? "But Banessa's dead, if that helps. I strangled her with this." He held up the explosive-collar controller by its ribbon.

She laughed, though there was no trace of humor in that harsh sound. "I'd have liked to see that . . . but I think you must be lying, Ruiz Aw. She was a mountain, too strong even for you. How could any unaugmented person best her? You're tricky. I'll remember that when I have you back." She jerked at some control, just out of sight, and to Ruiz's horror, the airboat staggered and swooped in response.

The others woke, made various sounds of fright, and clutched at their restraining straps.

Flomel, the Pharaohan conjuror, shouted in a voice breaking with panic, "Lady Corean! I had nothing to do with it, I'd have warned your henchmen, had I known what this wild beast was up to."

Ruiz glanced over his shoulder, saw Dolmaero whack Flomel across the mouth with a meaty hand. "Shut up," said Dolmaero calmly. The conjuror stared at the Guildmaster, shocked speechless by this insubordination.

Ruiz gave his attention to the controls. They were still dead, but he was momentarily pleased to see that they didn't respond accurately to Corean's attempts to redirect the boat. It wobbled to the left, away from the arrow-straight course they had been pursuing, but it showed no sign of reversing directions, as was apparently her intent.

In the vidscreen Corean's face reflected several emotions: triumph, then puzzlement, then frustration. She swore again, wrenched at her remotes again, which only served to produce a more pronounced drift to the left and a sickening motion, a combination of pitch and roll that had the other passengers moaning.

Ruiz looked out and saw that the boat was no longer heading for the pass through the blue mountains, but was instead rushing toward a sheer cliff. He grabbed at the velocity yoke, slowing the boat until it hung in the air over a talus slope, still shimmying with the eccentric motion Corean had given it.

"Make it stop," Nisa said, in a small careful voice.

Corean had apparently heard, because an ugly smile floated on her lips. "He can't," she said. The boat jerked and shuddered, then darted forward, directly at the cliffside. "If I can't have you back, then I'll have to do the best I can."

Ruiz waggled the yoke, but now the boat seemed completely out of control. He stared out at the onrushing stone as the boat accelerated. From the corner of his eye he could see an avid look on Corean's perfect face, as if she hoped the communicator would survive the impact long enough for her to take a leisurely delight in Ruiz's destruction.

For an instant his mind was empty, and then he saw a ruined body in the wreckage of the boat. Not his. Nisa's.

He pushed the image from his mind's eye. For some reason, he thought of poor mad Kroel, once a master conjuror of Pharaoh.

With the thought came an impulse, and he acted on it instantly. He raised the collar controller, which he had previously set to Kroel's resonance. He'd intended to use the sedative ject if Kroel became dangerously agitated; now he thumbed the detonator switch.

A dull thump came from the hold, and the note of the engines changed, shrieking up the scale, louder and higher, until they seized with a final shuddering crunch—and the boat was filled with silence. Ruiz clutched at the arms of his chair and hoped for the best.

Just before the boat dropped and hit the talus, Ruiz glanced down at Corean's image in the vidscreen. The slaver was watching him with a luminous intensity, and Ruiz thought she had never looked more beautiful and more terrible.

CHAPTER 2

By great good luck the airboat struck the talus slope in a nose-up attitude, pancaking into the loose detritus and bouncing up toward the base of the cliff. The initial impact almost tore Ruiz loose from his chair, but he managed to hang on. He hoped the others had braced themselves, but in any case, the acceleration webbing would protect them as long as the boat remained intact.

The boat slid upward, raising a cloud of dust, hull screeching against the rubble of the slope. It slowed, crunched into the ledge at the top of the slope, and stopped.

For a moment the boat rocked unsteadily, and Ruiz feared it might roll back down. He wondered how far the slope dropped. Had the slope ended at the top of another precipice, which then had dropped into a deep valley? He couldn't quite remember; all his attention had been concentrated on Corean and her vengeful face.

But then the boat became still. Ruiz could hear nothing but the retching sounds Flomel was making. The vidscreen was a dead gray, and the control board was dark.

"Well," Ruiz said. "We're still lucky." He turned to look at the others.

Nisa clutched at the webbing, her face pale and serious.

Molnekh smiled crookedly and pulled the hem of his tunic away from Flomel, who was making a mess. Dolmaero was impassive, staring out the port.

Flomel gained control of his stomach. "One day you'll be sorry, casteless one," he said, gulping air. "Now you've wrecked the Lady Corean's miraculous vessel and we're stranded in the wilderness."

Ruiz sighed. "Flomel, must you be so devoted an idiot? Don't you understand that Corean was trying to smash us into that cliff?" He pointed out the forward viewscreen at the dark sandstone.

Flomel glared at him. "Nonsense. It's your meddling that's at fault. If not for your meddling, we'd still be traveling safely and comfortably toward our goal. If you think I don't see through you and your lies, then you greatly underestimate me."

"Don't worry, I don't underestimate you. But I'll agree that in one respect things would be better, had I not 'meddled,'" Ruiz said wearily. "You'd still be safely tethered in the cargo hold."

A short silence ensued. "Speaking of the cargo hold, what of Kroel," Dolmaero asked, a bit hoarsely.

Ruiz shrugged. "I'm sorry," he said, but none of the others seemed to understand his meaning. "Kroel is dead."

"But, how do you know?" asked Molnekh, looking stricken.

Ruiz stood. "I killed him. I couldn't think of any other way to save us."

THE EMERGENCY LOCK was sufficiently intact that Ruiz and Dolmaero were able to manually crank it open. The others fled past Kroel's headless corpse, but Dolmaero lingered with Ruiz for a moment, staring at the small jagged hole in the engine compartment bulkhead, torn open when Ruiz had detonated Kroel's collar. Dolmaero turned his gaze to Ruiz. "How did you think to do this?"

"I don't know. A lucky whim. For us, anyway—though I suppose Kroel would be dead with the rest of us, otherwise, so he's no worse off. Here, help me with these food packs. The boat carried enough food for another day, but there are fewer of us now, so it should last several days, with care."

Dolmaero hung the packs from one broad shoulder.

"Kroel wouldn't have lived much longer, anyway. His soul had already fled." He shrugged and turned away. "You're an odd man, Ruiz Aw—though I hope you'll take no offense at my saying so. You kill your enemies as easily as another man might swat bloodbugs. Then you regret the death of poor Kroel, who meant nothing to you. But I fear for your remarkable luck. Can it last?"

"We only have to get off Sook. If my luck lasts that long I won't ask any more of it."

OUTSIDE, RUIZ EXAMINED his little group of survivors. They clustered around the airlock, all wearing unhappy faces, except for Nisa. Ruiz's susceptibility to her beauty had been responsible for most of his recent difficulties . . . but there were compensations. He took a moment to admire her smooth pale skin, her great dark eyes, her long black hair, thick and soft and glowing with coppery highlights, and her graceful long-limbed body. Her loveliness complemented a quick intelligence and an admirably strong character.

He smiled at her. She gave him a sweet melting look in return, at which Flomel scowled and made a grunt of disgust.

Ruiz considered Flomel, a stringy middle-aged man with a hard face and a self-important manner. The tattoos of a senior conjuror were prominent on his shaven skull. Flomel had been as much a prisoner as the others, but unshakable arrogance compelled him to regard his captivity as a form of protective custody. He had yet to be convinced that Corean had intended to sell his troupe to the highest bidder.

Ruiz judged him a dangerous man, and he was certain that Flomel was hatching some treachery. Ruiz shook his head. What was wrong with him that he could not simply kill the conjuror, as common sense dictated?

Molnekh stood beside Flomel, looking about curiously. He was tall, gangly, and thin to the point of emaciation. Molnekh also wore the tattoos of a conjuror, and had assisted Flomel in performing the masterful illusion-plays that had made the phoenix troupes of Pharaoh so valuable in the pangalac worlds. Ruiz felt a certain admiration for Molnekh, with his optimistic acceptance of his changed circumstances. He couldn't help contrasting Molnekh's resilience with the fatal brittleness of Kroel, who had been reduced to comatose panic by the strangeness of Sook.

Finally there was Dolmaero, a stout somber man, tattooed in the spiky red and green patterns of a Guildmaster. He had been the leader of the troupe's supporting crew—the dozens of scene setters, animal trainers, gowners, carpenters, surgeons, and other specialists whose expertise beneath the stage made possible the conjurors' miraculous tricks. His position was subordinate to the conjurors, on Pharaoh . . . but on this new world he was evolving toward a more dominant role. Dolmaero took his responsibilities to his people seriously, Ruiz thought, and his was a supple, clever mind. When Corean's catchboat had scooped up both the phoenix troupe and Ruiz Aw from the harsh world of Pharaoh, Ruiz had believed his disguise a near-perfect one. But Dolmaero had been the first to notice that Ruiz was not a Pharaohan.

Dolmaero had never attempted to use this knowledge against Ruiz, and Ruiz was still grateful. He felt a degree of cautious friendship for the Guildmaster, despite their disparate origins—and despite the risks inherent in friendships formed under such precarious circumstances.

Dolmaero's brooding eyes fixed on Ruiz. "You seem cheerful; I envy you your light heart. Too many questions burden mine."

Ruiz regarded Dolmaero uneasily. In Nisa's case, affection ruled him—but his responsibilities to the other prisoners seemed less well defined. Perhaps, however, he owed Dolmaero some degree of explanation. "I'll tell you what I can," he said to Dolmaero. "What do you want to know?"

Dolmaero sighed. "I fear I don't know enough about our situation even to ask the right questions. Still . . . where did Corean mean to send us, before you killed her giant henchwoman and disabled the machine man? Do you know?"

"Yes." The subject filled Ruiz with unpleasant sensations —a crawling sensation along his spine, a queasiness in his stomach, a sudden film of sweat on his forehead. In the depths of his mind, the death net twitched, reminded him that it would kill him if he fell into the tentacles of the Gencha. He shuddered. "Yes. Corean was sending us to the Gencha, so that we might be made safe."

"Made safe?" Dolmaero looked dubious, as if he felt certain that Ruiz Aw could never be rendered harmless.

"The Gencha . . . they're aliens, much stranger than the Pung who ran the slave pen. They're repulsive creatures, but that's not the reason I fear them. They've devoted centuries to the study of human mentation. They know us too well; they can make a person do or be anything."

"And for us?"

"The process is sometimes called deconstruction. If we're taken down into the Gencha enclave, they'll tear down our minds and rebuild them in a form that would make us perfect slaves. Our primary loyalty would no longer be to our *selves*, but to Corean—or to whoever purchased us from her."

"It sounds complicated," Molnekh said. "Surely there are less troublesome ways of controlling slaves. On Pharaoh we manage well enough. If a slave is rebellious, we crucify him, or stake him out in the waste, or use him in an unsanctified Expiation. The other slaves watch and learn."

Ruiz frowned. Sometimes he forgot that the others came from a primitive client world, that their cultural matrix was alien. He found it especially disturbing that Nisa was nodding her lovely head, apparently finding Molnekh's statement reasonable and obvious.

But then it occurred to him that his own ethical standards were more theoretical than actual. At the thought, he was suddenly quite depressed. He might find the idea of crucifying slaves barbaric; still, Ruiz Aw destroyed innocent lives in the course of every job he did. Many had died since his arrival on Pharaoh, beginning with the Watcher on the Worldwall, whom he'd been forced to kill. Then Denklar the innkeeper, Relia the doxy, Rontleses the coercer—their deaths stained his hands. And after his capture and transport to Sook, the list of his victims grew too long to count. Sometimes Ruiz Aw saw himself as a sort of random merciless plague, constantly mutating, incurable.

Something must have shown in his face, because Nisa spoke, voice full of concern. "What is it, Ruiz? Perhaps this new way is kinder, but on Pharaoh we don't have the means to rebuild minds."

"Kinder?" Ruiz laughed bitterly. "No. The Gencha build human-shaped puppets—they're no longer real people. The Gencha would make me into a flesh machine. And the worst thing is, I wouldn't even know it; I'd think I was still the same person. But if one day my owner told me to open my belly and drape my guts over the shrubbery, I'd think it was a perfectly reasonable request and I'd do it happily. Even then I wouldn't know that I'd lost my self."

A silence ensued, as each considered the ugly picture Ruiz had painted. Even Flomel, who had studiously ignored the conversation, looked shaken.

After a while, Dolmaero looked up. He rubbed his heavy jaw, scratched his tattooed head. "Well," he began hesitantly. "I mean no disrespect, but I can't understand why, if the Gencha can do as you say . . . why they don't rule the human universe. Or do they?"

Ruiz was once again surprised by the Guildmaster's grasp of the situation. "A good question, Dolmaero. The Gencha don't do this thing easily—the effort of fully deconstructing a human substantially decreases the Gench's vitality, and recovery is lengthy and somewhat uncertain. They can perform smaller mental modifications with much less damage to their health."

It occurred to Ruiz to wonder how Corean was able to arrange for the processing of five slaves such as he and his companions were—and why she would be willing to pay the astronomical fees such services surely demanded. He found, however, that it was difficult for him to consider any matter connected with the Gencha—it made his head hurt.

Then he was distracted by dark memories. He recalled the Art League factor on Dilvermoon who had hired him for this job . . . and then the League-owned Gench who had installed the death net and mission-imperative compulsion in his own mind. He discovered to his surprise that he had at some point reached a decision: He would never again permit his mind to be tampered with. It occurred to Ruiz Aw that he might have to find a new profession, in the event he survived his present difficulties. *A remote possibility,* he thought, and put the notion away.

"Also," Ruiz continued, "the Gencha are a nontechnical race—they appear unable or unwilling to design machines to augment their abilities. Otherwise they might indeed control the pangalac worlds. Oh, occasionally a particularly ambitious Gench gains substantial power by converting a few influential humans. None has ever consolidated its position successfully. Partly luck, I suppose, but mostly it's because the Gencha as a species don't seem to be interested in power for its own sake. Finally, there are very few Gencha—and most of them are prisoners."

"Very valuable prisoners, so I would suppose, if they can be forced to do their work at their captor's behest," said Dolmaero.

"Yes. Very valuable." Ruiz was forced once again to consider an unpalatable truth: The Art League had sent him not to identify those who had been poaching valuable slaves from the League's client world of Pharaoh, but to lead the League to an enclave of Gencha on Sook.

RUIZ GLANCED DOWNSLOPE, verified that the tumble of loose stone ended in a sheer drop, and shuddered.

Dolmaero followed his glance, smiled. "More luck. I must remember to stay close to you, Ruiz Aw."

Ruiz sighed. "The luck comes and goes, Guildmaster. We're far from safe yet."

"What do you think we should do?" Dolmaero leaned forward attentively.

Flomel spoke in testy tones. "We must rely on the Lady Corean's mercy. She'll surely understand that we had nothing to do with the casteless slayer's outrages. She'll soon be here to rescue us from this bizarre place."

Ruiz laughed, astounded. Even the other Pharaohans were watching Flomel with wide eyes, as if he were some odd menagerie beast, trained to perform eccentric tricks.

Dolmaero only shook his head.

"Flomel, Flomel," said Molnekh. "This is no moment for jests; besides, you were never a great joker. The Lady Corean's mercy strikes me as unreliable. Don't you remember her 'mercy' to Casmin, your favorite enforcer? She cut his throat and burned him to a cinder."

"I think Flomel's too stupid to learn," said Nisa. "He's like Kroel, only he hides it better." She looked at Flomel with vindictive eyes. "He'll end up just like Kroel, with any luck."

Flomel purpled, knotted his hands into fists. For a moment Ruiz thought Flomel might strike Nisa, and he swayed forward, filled with a hot impulse to commit violence. Here was an opportunity to be done with the treacherous conjuror; his fingers ached with the urge to snap Flomel's thin neck.

Flomel looked into his eyes and stumbled back, suddenly pale.

Ruiz took a deep breath, and by degrees relaxed the snarl that had frozen on his face.

The others were watching him with frightened eyes. Even Nisa had drawn away, as if suddenly unsure of him. His heart twinged, and he managed a smile.

Her responding smile was genuine, if a bit cautious, for which he could not blame her. She would need to be mad or utterly foolish to trust him entirely . . . and she was neither.

"Well," he said, in a somewhat shaky voice. "You may wait here for Corean, if you wish, Master Flomel. She'll be here in two days, or a little less. Yonder ledge will make a roof for you, but we can spare you no food." He smiled a different smile. "Still, I can almost guarantee you won't die of hunger."

Flomel looked down. "Guildmaster," he said in a low voice. "What do you advise."

Dolmaero answered reluctantly, "I think Ruiz Aw is our only hope, Master Flomel. We're babes here, in a wilderness full of banebears. I think we should accompany him as long as he will permit it."

"I must accept your advice, then," muttered Flomel.

Ruiz was disappointed.

He examined the weapons he had salvaged from the wreck. He wore, clipped to his belt, Marmo's splinter gun—the only really effective weapon they possessed. From Banessa's collection of archaic weapons he had taken an antique stiletto, a heavy two-edged dagger, a small lady's kris with a garter sheath, and a short solid-brass club with a spiked head. The giant woman had owned more powerful weapons: a graser, a brace of seeker-stingers—but like many personal weapons, they were designed to function only under their owner's control. He'd jettisoned them along with her body.

He gave the dagger to Dolmaero, who handled it as though he had no idea what to do with it. Ruiz recalled that there had been no wars on Pharaoh for many generations. He would have to remember not to expect too much of the Guildmaster, should they meet with hostilities before they escaped from Sook.

"Carry it through your belt, Guildmaster," Ruiz instructed Dolmaero. "No, like this; you'll probably want to avoid castration, should you stumble."

Ruiz handed the sheathed kris to Nisa.

"And how shall I wear this?" she asked.

"I'll show you." Ruiz knelt and pushed up the hem of her tunic, enjoying the silky texture of her skin. When he'd fastened the garter that held the kris to the outside of her thigh, he had to force himself to take his hands away. Desire made his head swim for a moment. He realized he was still at the mercy of those reckless romantic impulses that the bootleg minddiver Nacker had afflicted him with.

He handed the club to Molnekh. "I wish we had a better choice of weapons," he said.

"No matter," said Molnekh, swishing the club enthusiastically back and forth. "We'll make do."

Ruiz pulled up the sleeve of his tunic and bound the stiletto to the inside of his forearm with a length of sturdy cloth.

Flomel edged forward. "Where's mine?" he asked.

Ruiz turned to him, surprised at Flomel's audacity. "Sorry. But surely you need nothing sharper than your wits."

Flomel opened his mouth, as if he meant to argue, then snapped it shut and contented himself with a dark glare.

"Now," Ruiz said. "Here's what we must do."

IT WAS A pity, Ruiz told them, that the boat's power system had been irreparably damaged and that the turret ruptor was therefore useless. Otherwise, they might do well to wait here and arrange an ambush for Corean when she came, as she certainly would.

He explained his plan to the Pharaohans—they would walk over the pass, and hope to come across some habitation or at least a promising track. Then they'd try to reach a launch ring and get off Sook.

Ruiz was deliberately vague about what might happen to the Pharaohans after that; he didn't know. He wanted to give Nisa the opportunity to stay with him if she wanted to; he could afford to buy her from the Art League. The others could escape to the pangalac worlds with his blessing, or he might be able to arrange to have them returned to Pharaoh—though the League would insist on removing their memories before they would be released on their home world.

The Pharaohans seemed no more eager to ask about their eventual fate than Ruiz was to discuss it, though Dolmaero looked as if he were full of questions that weren't quite ripe yet. Ruiz was grateful for the respite.

Ruiz distributed the food packs equitably. Only Flomel grumbled over his load; the others accepted their packs cheerfully enough. He gave Flomel a hard look, and the conjuror subsided.

Into the food packs Ruiz jammed a few more useful items: three of the self-inflating tents, a water jug for each traveler, and insulated rain capes.

Finally he took one of the self-securing leashes by which they had all been tethered the night before. Flomel looked at him and showed his teeth in a grimace of disgust.

THE SUN WAS hot on Ruiz's back as the five of them toiled up toward the pass, but a chill wind blew down the mountainside, making him shiver occasionally. They had scrambled across the talus slope and found a rough path leading in the direction of the notch through the mountains. It showed little sign of recent use, and Ruiz wasn't optimistic that they'd soon come across anything resembling civilization. Still, he was as happy as he'd been since he'd landed on Pharaoh. He was free, except for the mission-imperative that still pushed him, and the death net that waited in the abyss of his mind. As long as he could stay free, the death net would remain quiescent. Only if he were helplessly captured by enemies of the League and in imminent danger of dying or divulging League secrets would the net kill him and send his recent memories to League headquarters on Dilvermoon.

Ruiz forced himself to optimism. All he had to do was to launch a message torp to the League, detailing his discoveries: the location and identity of the poacher who had been stealing slaves from Pharaoh—and the fact that an enclave of rogue Gencha existed on Sook. And when he'd done that, the net and the mission-imperative would evaporate from his mind, and he would be truly free.

He gave himself to the pleasurable contemplation of Nisa's smooth strong legs as she climbed the path just ahead of him.

•   •   •

AT THE TOP of the pass they paused, and Ruiz looked out
over the country on the other side of the mountains. The
foothills were much greener, and the dense forest beyond
indicated that this was the moist side of the range. In the far
distance, another range lifted misty peaks. The broad valley
between them seemed to stretch forever in both directions.

To his delight, Ruiz could see a straight line striking
down the center of the valley, parallel to the mountains,
perhaps thirty kilometers away. It was too far away to positively identify, but it looked like a highway cut through the
forest, on which might travel vehicles fast enough to get
them away to a hiding spot before Corean arrived.

"It's like my father's gardens," said Nisa, who stood
close beside him. "Where do they get all the water?"

Ruiz smiled at her. "It falls from the sky here, all the
time. Or at least often enough that the trees grow without
tending."

She turned an unbelieving glance at him. "Of course,"
she said in tolerant tones, as though she was certain he
teased her.

"No, really," he said. "Wait, you'll see." As he spoke, he
noticed that dark roiling clouds were building to the north.
"In fact, we'd better hurry along, before we get washed
away."

Flomel sat down. "I must rest. And it's time to eat."

Ruiz sighed. "I tire of you, Master Flomel. I cannot leave
you here; you would surely tell Corean where we've gone,
long before she finished killing you. So, either come along
without further complaint, or I must end your life. I can do
it without pain."

Flomel stood quickly. "I'll go," he said sullenly.

"Are you sure?" Ruiz asked gently. "I fear our association must end badly for one of us. And there are worse
places to die." He made a gesture that took in the broad sky,
the green country beyond, the clean wind that blew up the
pass. "And worse ways."

"No," said Flomel with more enthusiasm. "I'll go."

CHAPTER 3

T HE path, though steep, seemed in better condition on
this side of the pass, and they made good progress.
By the time the sun was halfway down the afternoon
sky, they had descended to the wooded foothills, where the
trees were tall and ancient. Ruiz set a fast pace, but apart
from the occasional mutter from Flomel, no one com-
plained. As they walked down the path, the day grew
darker, and soon the sun was hidden behind the clouds, and
the light further dimmed by the branches of the trees that
overhung the way. The Pharaohans drew closer together,
made uneasy by this unnatural exuberance of greenery. Pharaoh's one habitable plateau was such a dry barren place
that only the richest and most powerful Pharaohans could
afford to maintain gardens.

"What sort of folk could live in such a strange place,"
asked Nisa in hushed tones.

"I don't know. All kinds, probably, like everywhere
else." Ruiz spoke in a distracted voice. He felt something of
the others' uneasiness. The forest was dense enough that it
offered ample opportunity for ambush.

Nisa took his distraction as a rebuke and drew away, for
which he was sorry.

Despite Ruiz's anxiety, nothing sprang at them from the undergrowth. No missiles flew at them, no nets dropped, no traps sprang. But by the time the light began to fall toward twilight, his troops were footsore and slow, except for Molnekh, who seemed as fresh as he had at the outset of their trek. His frail-looking body apparently disguised a hearty constitution.

They passed into a belt of up-tilted limestone strata. Here and there breakdowns had formed caves; just ahead a fairly capacious one opened just off the trail. The roof projected sufficiently to keep off the rain that threatened, but the cave was too shallow to attract large predators. Soot stains on the gray ceiling showed where other travelers had camped under the overhang, but none of the signs of use seemed recent, and Ruiz decided to call a halt. He was pinning all his hope on the highway he'd seen from the pass. They would reach it in the morning, and stumbling down the path in darkness would save little time, or at any rate not enough to risk the possibility of broken ankles and night-roving beasts.

Flomel stared gloomily at the shelter. "This is where we must spend the night? This damp hole?"

Ruiz grunted. "Be grateful you're not still at the pass. That you have a need for shelter," he said. His dislike of the conjuror had grown more intense over the last few days. It wasn't just that Flomel had arranged Nisa's brief death in the first phoenix play, or that he would have cheerfully killed her again at Corean's behest. Dolmaero and Molnekh were equally culpable; none of the Pharaohans saw any great immorality in the brutality of the phoenix play, not even Nisa, who in an attempt to avoid a second death had once ripped a pair of sewing shears through Flomel's guts. No, Flomel was an innocent product of his primitive culture, just as Ruiz Aw was a product of his own hypercivilized one.

But Flomel saw other human beings only in terms of their usefulness to Flomel.

Ruiz frowned, struck by an unpleasant notion. Was Flomel so different from himself? *Yes, of course,* he told himself fiercely. *Otherwise I'd just kill the little snake and rest easier.*

He shook himself; that was developing into a disquieting line of thought.

He directed the other men to set up the tents under the

overhang, while he and Nisa gathered wood for a fire. He was reasonably certain that Corean wouldn't catch up with them until late the next day, and so a fire would be a fairly safe luxury.

Several seasons had apparently come and gone since the last traveler had visited the shelter; there was plenty of wood within sight of the shelter. But they moved far enough away for a private conversation.

Nisa bent close to Ruiz as he snapped dry twigs from a small deadfall, and he caught the clean scent of her hair. He smiled and drew a deep breath. She turned to look at him through the dark veil of her hair. "Have I angered you?" she asked. Her voice was almost truculent.

"No, of course not," he said. "Have I angered you?"

She smiled at his serious tone, and her face became cheerful. "No, not really. But you've been different, since you captured the boat."

"I suppose so." Ruiz set the deadfall across two boulders, and used his boots to snap its trunk into usable sections. "It's because I'm working at my trade, and not just waiting for an opportunity to act. Though . . . waiting with you was as sweet a pastime as I've ever known."

Her smile grew warmer, and her eyes shown with held-back tears. "I'm happy to hear that, Ruiz Aw. Though perhaps I shame myself to say so. No . . . that's wrong. I'm a princess, but I'm sure you're a prince in your own lands."

He patted her hand. "I grew up a slave."

Her eyes widened. "Then the princes in your land must be mighty indeed."

He laughed. "I know of few especially mighty ones. In the pangalac worlds, persons of any station, even slaves, may make themselves kings and queens, if that is their desire —and if they can out-climb and out-fight and out-scheme all the other would-be rulers. There are many candidates, very many."

"Your lands aren't so different from mine." She seemed a bit wistful, as if she had hoped that the wider universe was a happier and more just place. She straightened up with the armload of wood she had collected. "Well. You said you were working at your trade. What might that be?"

Ruiz shrugged. "It's a simple one; staying alive. I hope to be a success for a few more days, long enough to get us away from Sook."

She looked at him quizzically, lovely head tipped to the side appraisingly. "My confidence in your prospects grows daily. Will we share a tent tonight?"

"If that's your wish." He felt a sweet unfamiliar glow.

"That's my wish, yes," she said, and bumped him playfully with one round hip.

LATER, WITH A low fire casting an orange light on the stone overhead, the five of them ate in silence. Looking at Dolmaero's broad face, Ruiz saw that the Guildmaster had evolved more questions.

"What?" Ruiz asked.

"You will not be offended?" Dolmaero raised cautious eyes to Ruiz's.

"No, speak freely." Sometimes it saddened Ruiz that he seemed to inflict fear on everyone he met. Of course, Dolmaero had seen Ruiz perform terrible violence—so he could hardly blame Dolmaero for being wary.

Dolmaero sighed and looked down. "I must trust to your restraint, then." For a long moment the Guildmaster was silent, staring into the fire. "I would ask you to tell me the truth about yourself, and about Pharaoh. Who are you, really? And what are we? And what have you to do with us?"

Ruiz was unprepared for such direct questions. His first impulse, born of a lifetime of subterfuge, was to lie as reassuringly as possible—he told himself that he must still protect his secrets, or risk triggering the death net. The meddling of Nacker the bootleg minddiver, and the near trigger after his attempted escape from Corean's slave pens, had weakened the net somewhat . . . but if Corean recaptured him in such a way that he was helpless, the net would fire, and he would die. If the Gencha took him, the net would fire. If any other enemy of the League held him helpless, the net would fire.

It struck him that telling the Pharaohans the truth was no great threat, compared to these other likelihoods. After all, before any of them could be returned to Pharaoh they would be mindwiped.

He felt a sudden overwhelming weariness with deception. Caution evaporated. "Are you certain you wish to know these things?"

Dolmaero nodded heavily. Molnekh wore his usual look

of bright-eyed amiable curiosity. Flomel curled his lip and feigned indifference.

"Please tell us, Ruiz Aw," asked Nisa.

So he did.

HE EXPLAINED, WITH some hesitation, that he was a free-lance enforcer, a man whose profession involved inflicting pain, stimulating fear, committing atrocities. No one seemed surprised, not even Nisa. Ruiz was a little taken aback by her easy acceptance of this ugly truth. *Never forget,* he told himself. *She comes from an alien society, however human she may be genetically.* Somehow the concept lacked force; perhaps he didn't care what she was, as long as she was Nisa.

He explained that he had been hired to sniff out a poacher who was stealing valuable Pharaohan slaves. Despite his sudden distaste for deception, he was careful not to mention the League, and he described his commission and employers in deliberately ambiguous terms. The League was unpopular on Sook—since it was one of the strongest multistellar entities, and had an effective police arm. He couldn't risk one of the Pharaohans dropping the League's name in the presence of a local.

But even so, a truthful picture of Pharaoh's status began to emerge. This information seemed less palatable to his listeners.

"Please," said Dolmaero. "Explain further. Pharaoh is owned? Like a catapple plantation?"

"Something like that," Ruiz said.

"But what do the pangalacs want from us? Gold? Snake oil?"

"Some oil is exported," Ruiz said. "But mainly, the wealth of Pharaoh is in its conjurors. That's why Corean stole your troupe from Bidderum. She would have one day sold your people to some collector of theatrical oddities, for a great deal of pangalac credit."

Dolmaero looked wryly amused. "So we're cattle? Or dancing banebears?"

"Oh, no. On the pangalac worlds the institution of slavery is restricted by many humane rules. It's very unlikely you'd have been mistreated, had you been taken by a legitimate pangalac organization. Now Corean . . . she might have sold you to some wildworld monster—who can say?"

Molnekh looked bewildered and said nothing.

Nisa turned away and spoke in a low voice. "I always thought that Pharaoh belonged to my father."

Of all the reactions, Flomel's was the strangest. A look of malevolent defiant pride came into his eyes, though his face maintained its expression of ostentatious disinterest. He seemed to glare at Ruiz with a different, more submissive degree of hatred. The look on the conjuror's face made Ruiz's skin crawl.

"How long have we been owned?" asked Dolmaero.

"Many generations. Soon after your people developed conjuring into a high art."

Nisa made a muffled sound of woe. Ruiz touched her shoulder. "What is it?"

"Nothing. It's just . . . I remember, not so long ago, though now it seems a lifetime past, when I stood on my father's terrace above the city, and drank a toast to my ancestors. The ones who first traveled about Pharaoh, performing their rough tricks. The ones whose cleverness had given me such a good life. And now I see that they made me a slave. . . ."

"No," he said. "It isn't all bad. You haven't had a major war since you became a client world. Three hundred years ago there was a plague that might have killed three quarters of your population; the owners stopped it before it started."

She put her face in her hands. "My father's hunting dirgos are content; they no longer remember what it was like to freely roam the wastes. They get meat twice a day, and the huntsman sees that they get enough exercise. It's good, I suppose."

Ruiz could find no comforting words to speak. He put his arm around her, pulled her close. She resisted for a moment, then turned her face to his chest.

Dolmaero spoke again, though this time he seemed to speak more to himself than to Ruiz. "I must find a way to get back to the troupe, someday. I must try to take them home; I'm responsible for them, you understand. Most of them didn't seek glory or transfiguration; they worked to feed their families. Tell me, Ruiz. Now that the conjurors are gone, what will Corean do with the ones who are left?"

Ruiz shook his head. "I don't know, Guildmaster." He couldn't see what use the depressing truth would be to Dolmaero. In all likelihood, Corean would simply euthanize the others, if she became convinced that she would never recapture the conjurors. What good was a conjuring troupe without conjurors?

A little time passed, and the fire burned low, until only a few red coals sputtered in the ashes. The night air was chill and damp, and Ruiz became very conscious of Nisa's warmth against him. He found himself wishing that he could be frozen in time, that he could rest like this forever, that somehow the arc of his life could be arrested here and now, before it plunged down to the painful ending that probably waited for him a day or two down the line. He had managed all day to put from his mind the impossibility that they could escape Corean on foot, the improbability that the highway would be traveled by anyone willing to give transport to a ragged group like his.

All his life, he had possessed a talent for putting away thoughts he did not wish to think, a talent that had served him well in his violent pursuits; now he could not seem to do it. He looked down at Nisa's dark head. Perhaps she had become too precious to him, but if so, there was nothing he wished to do about it.

Dolmaero stirred. "Another question, if you'll permit, and then I must retire—or I won't be able to walk very far tomorrow."

Ruiz nodded.

"Then tell me . . . what are we to you that you should help us as you have? I know you are fond of the Noble Person . . . this is written in your face. But the rest of us? Forgive me for saying so, but you don't seem the sort of person who often performs capricious acts of charity."

Ruiz was also fond of Dolmaero, and was growing to like Molnekh's cheerful energetic personality. Still, Dolmaero was essentially correct. Why had he undertaken to rescue the others?

He made a successful rationalization. "I expect your help in return."

Dolmaero spread his hands. "But what can we do? We're not trained in violence, we know nothing of this world."

Ruiz considered. "Here's the first thing: We must set a watch, so that one of us is always awake. I don't know what predators live in these woods, or what sort of people. In any case, we mustn't be taken by surprise. So . . . Molnekh, perhaps you'll stand the first watch?"

"Of course," said the skinny mage, beaming.

Ruiz looked up. He saw that the threatening clouds had blown away, and that patches of starry sky showed through the branches overhead. "See that bright star?" He pointed to an opening in the canopy. "When it hangs above the white-barked tree, call me for my watch. I'll call Dolmaero, who will call Nisa."

"And what shall I do?" sneered Flomel.

Ruiz pushed Nisa gently away and got to his feet. He picked up the self-securing leash he'd brought from the wrecked airboat. "Come with me, Master Flomel. I'll tuck you in."

Flomel followed him slowly to the tent farthest from the fire. "Must you hobble me like an untrained striderbeast?"

Ruiz set the leash, activated its mechanism, watched it corkscrew its taproot into the stone. "I must, until you're better trained."

"I know I've spoken roughly to you, but I've done you no real harm. Why do you so distrust me?" Flomel smiled a crooked smile, an expression of alarming duplicity, even in the dim light.

Ruiz snugged the leash around Flomel's neck, sealed it. "Instinct, let us say."

"I've learned much this night, Ruiz Aw. How may I earn your trust?" The smile trembled on Flomel's thin mouth.

Ruiz laughed. "At the moment, I have difficulty with the concept. Perhaps you'll think of something." He tugged at the leash, found it secure. "Good night."

MOLNEKH HAD TAKEN his post at the side of the shelter and stood motionless against the gray stone. He was hard to spot in the darkness, and Ruiz felt a degree of approval. Molnekh was intelligent and adaptable; he might actually be of some help.

Dolmaero had gone to bed, and only Nisa remained by the dead fire, huddled over, arms clasping her legs to her chest. He went to her, lifted her to her feet. "We should rest," he said.

She looked up at him with a curiously unreadable expression, and for a moment he thought she would tell him she no longer wished him to share her tent. He could hardly blame her, considering the unpleasant things he had revealed about her world and about her life.

But then she took his hand and led him to the tent.

THEY LAY PRESSED together, bodies touching from head to toe. Though there was no passion in their embrace, Nisa clung to Ruiz tightly, apparently taking comfort in his closeness.

Unexpectedly, Ruiz was comforted too. He found it good just to hold her, to feel her heart beating against him. Her scent, her warm breath, the tickling touch of her hair; all these were pleasures more than adequate to the moment.

After a while her breathing grew regular, and she slept— but Ruiz felt no such urge. Who knew when, if ever, he would come across this species of delight again?

Two hours passed in a long sweet instant.

WHEN MOLNEKH CAME to call him for his watch, Ruiz felt a deep pang of regret. He unwrapped himself from Nisa's arms as carefully as he could, hoping not to wake her. She stirred, made drowsy wordless sounds, then seemed to settle back into sleep.

Outside, a low ground mist lay knee-deep beneath the trees. The forest was almost unnaturally quiet, except for the snores coming from Dolmaero's tent.

"Everything's well?" Ruiz whispered to Molnekh.

Molnekh nodded, showing a flash of white teeth in the darkness. "I can say this much: Nothing has happened. Is that good?"

Ruiz grinned back. "Time will tell, mage."

Molnekh chuckled. "I'm tremendously reassured, Ruiz Aw." He reached out one skeletal hand, laid it on Ruiz's shoulder. "We all have great faith in your skills. Even Flomel, though his admiration is unwilling and pains him." Molnekh chuckled again, then seemed to grow serious. "Our lives are in your hands, but all things considered, I feel sure matters could be worse."

Ruiz was oddly moved. "I hope you're right, Master Molnekh. We'll do our best. Who knows, it may be enough."

Molnekh patted his shoulder again, then turned away

and crawled into Dolmaero's tent. The snores stopped for a moment, then resumed.

Ruiz found a comfortable seat on a jumble of fallen stone, just outside the shelter. He settled himself for a long night. He felt no urge to sleep, and Dolmaero, the oldest and heaviest of them, would need all his strength to keep up tomorrow.

And if he had no other gift for Nisa, at least he could give her a few extra hours of sleep. He tried not to believe that this was her last night.

WHEN RUIZ LEFT the tent, Nisa woke. She reached for the comfort of sleep, but it didn't immediately return. Uneasy thoughts crowded into her mind, as if they'd been waiting for an opportunity to catch her alone.

She thought of Ayam, Corean's hermaphrodite slave, whose incautious decision to rape Nisa had provided Ruiz Aw with an opportunity to capture the airboat. She still ached where it had thrust itself into her, but the pain was fading. She remembered the terrible silent manner in which Ruiz had drawn the creature from her tent and throttled it, and the memory gave her a keen vindictive delight. It had died with such ambiguous surprise on its strange face, as if it couldn't help finding some sort of perverse fulfillment in its own death.

Ruiz Aw. Such an odd man, such a perplexing tangle of mysteries. Tonight in the tent, he had known without words that, this once, she wanted just his comforting presence, his arms around her, and nothing more.

Not, she thought, that there was anything wrong with his lovemaking. In fact, never had she bedded with so skillful a lover. He was both fierce and tender, he seemed to know the ways her body wanted to be touched better than she did, he seemed to be able to sense the tempo of her passion perfectly. In bed, his mouth, usually so hard, became soft; his beautiful hands, those slayer's hands, touched her gently when gentleness was what she wanted and gripped her strongly when the time was right for strength.

His fervor would be almost frightening, did it not bring her such overwhelming pleasure. She sensed in his lovemaking the same intensity she had seen in his face when he was killing his enemies—a thought both terrifying and fascinating.

Her memories of Ruiz Aw had strayed into uncomfortable areas, so she forced herself to think of the coming day. What new sights would she see, what marvelous things that had never existed on Pharaoh?

Then a quiver of anxiety went through her. And what new miracle would Ruiz perform, to keep them safe from Corean? Nisa had come to have an almost-fatalistic confidence in Ruiz; she refused to consider the possibility that Corean would best him, despite all the advantages that the slaver possessed: airboats, terrible weapons, monstrous henchmen.

No, she thought, growing drowsy again, Ruiz would manage, somehow. Her mind emptied, and then she slept.

After a while she dreamed.

THE DREAM BEGAN well. She was once again Nisa, favored daughter of the King; once again she had all her pleasures: her bondservants, her gracious apartment in the palace, her books and games—and the adoration of everyone who knew her. She rested in a bower, gazing out at her father's cool green gardens, wearing her favorite dress, a long high-waisted gown with vast butterfly sleeves, sewn from pale blue Hellsilk and spangled with tiny glitterlizard scales.

It was as if the past weeks had never happened. Her imprisonment, her painful role in the phoenix play and her death in the final act, her resurrection and capture by aliens, her strange attachment to the slayer Ruiz. All, all, a dream-memory, fading fast.

She forced away the tiny voice that whispered that *this* was the dream, and it fell silent.

Now she was moving through her father's polished halls, drifting light as a thistle, with that glorious ease that comes in dreams. The dear familiar scenes floated past her dream eyes. The porcelain floor tiles that she had played on as a child, with their thousand subtle shades of ivory. The fountains she had bathed in. The shady rooms in which she had dallied with her lovers—sometimes the sons and daughters of noble houses, other times joyfolk from the public square.

A brief darkness fell over the dream, until she found herself on her favorite terrace, above all but the highest towers of the palace. The sun shone brilliantly on the city, and she felt a sense of grateful wonder. All this was hers, the palace, the great city, the vastness of Pharaoh beyond the walls. All hers to command.

She felt an exultation that made her giddy; she was so light with joy that when she spread her arms she was unsurprised to find the sleeves of her gown transformed into huge wings.

She rose up, soaring above everything, her movements swift as thought, inhumanly graceful.

The palace grew small beneath her and the sun grew fiercer, but she rushed upward, faster and faster, until it seemed that her wings trailed fire and she had become a comet, trailing glory.

An uneasiness came over her, too late. She discovered that she had passed the sun, and its dwindling warmth no longer reached her. Pharaoh was a grain of sand, lost in the void.

She looked up. Above her was a glassy black ceiling, a smooth arc that seemed to have no beginning and no end. She tried to slow herself, lest her delicate body be smashed against this barrier, but still she rose.

Finally a tiny round opening appeared in the otherwise featureless surface. An awful truth came to her; she saw that Pharaoh and everyone in it existed in a monstrous glass jar —and that she was rushing into its neck. Was it stoppered?

She brushed the slick walls painlessly, slid upward, slowing as the bottle's neck narrowed and her body made firmer contact with the glass.

Finally she stuck, arms reaching upward, feet kicking furiously. *No!* she shouted soundlessly. She fought to get higher, clawing at the glass. Her wings were tearing, and this *did* hurt her, terribly, but she ignored the pain and struggled on. She moved a tiny bit, then a bit more. She had a sudden horrible sensation that the black tunnel was about to squeeze shut and crush her life away. She made a last muscle-tearing spasmodic effort.

And pulled herself to the top of the bottle, where she clung to the lip, and looked out across the starry wastes. Her wings were bloody tatters of agony, the stars were cold meaningless fires, impossibly far away.

She was terrified, but it was an oddly joyful terror, and at that moment she didn't want to wake up.

RUIZ SAT MOTIONLESS for the remainder of the night, submerged in his thoughts, giving only a small part of his attention to the silent forest. He could see little hope for their survival, unless the highway they would reach tomorrow was a busy one, traveled by beings of remarkable confidence or naivete. Who else would stop to help them?

When Corean arrived, she would no doubt be equipped with mechanical sniffers, or some sort of trailing beast—these were standard tools used by all successful slavers. Depending on the efficiency of Corean's sniffers, she would catch up to them tomorrow afternoon or the next morning —if Ruiz failed to find swift transportation away from the area.

Ruiz looked up through the canopy, saw bright stars, and the gleam of the Shard orbital platforms. Had it rained, as it had earlier promised to, the sniffers would have been slowed.

He worried at the problem, but could find no purchase on its slippery shell. He might attempt an ambush; he had the splinter gun. But Corean would doubtless be armed with heavier weapons. If her Mocrassar bondwarrior had finished its molt and was with Corean, confronting the slaver was hopeless, even if she were foolish enough to engage him at close range.

No, everything depended on finding transportation, which was to say everything depended on luck. This intransigent reality made him grind his teeth in frustration. He had always been lucky, but he had always been careful to put no faith in luck.

Never to need luck: that was the secret of being lucky. Now he needed it.

When gray light began to seep through the treetops, a few big raindrops fell, plopping into the leafy forest floor. Then they stopped.

CHAPTER 4

Ruiz hurried the others through the morning's necessities: breakfast, packing, stretching sore muscles. Dolmaero seemed somewhat refreshed by his slumber, but he went up to Ruiz and spoke in mildly truculent tones. "Why did you not call me for my watch?"

"I wasn't sleepy," Ruiz answered. "Why should we both suffer."

"Well, next time, call me. I can do my part."

"I know," Ruiz said, lowering his voice to a confidential whisper. "In fact, I have a job for you today. I'll ask you to keep a close eye on Flomel. Nisa will watch him too, but she may not be strong enough to stop him if he takes a notion to do something foolish."

Dolmaero nodded. "As you say. It's odd. There was a time when the troupe was everything to me . . . and despite Flomel's unpleasant aspects, I thought him a great man. He was such a wonderful conjuror." Dolmaero sighed. "But times change, and now I see that I was a fool."

"No, no. You weren't a fool, Guildmaster—you were like everyone else, doing the best you could with what you knew."

"Perhaps . . . kind of you to say so, anyway." Dolmaero returned to his packing.

THE PATH WAS broader and smoother now, and they made good time. For a while Ruiz treated himself to the pleasure of walking hand in hand with Nisa, following the others. He felt a bit silly, like an overage schoolboy, but Nisa apparently saw nothing undignified in such affectionate gestures. Her hand clasped his tightly; occasionally she turned her lovely face up to him and gave him a smile.

By midmorning, they began to pass evidence of recent use: plastic food wrappers, discarded articles of clothing, small heaps of charcoal where fires had been built. Ruiz forced himself into a higher level of alertness. He released Nisa's hand, called a halt.

"We'll have to be more careful now," he told the others. "I'm going to run ahead and see if the way is clear. You follow at a slower pace. If you hear or see something you don't understand or that seems dangerous—or if you meet with anyone—get off the path and hide in the forest."

Ruiz looked at Flomel, saw the sly expression he wore. "Above all, don't let Flomel get away." He took the leash out, fastened it to Flomel's neck, and gave the other end to Dolmaero. "And if he attempts to cry out or otherwise attract attention, kill him as quickly and quietly as possible. Can you manage that?"

Dolmaero nodded, face somber. He fingered the dagger he carried in his sash. "You may rely on me, Ruiz Aw."

Flomel's expression wavered between outrage and disbelief, but he said nothing.

Ruiz bent and brushed his lips against Nisa's and whispered in her ear so that only she could hear. "Watch them all."

Then he ran away down the path.

WHEN HE WAS several hundred meters ahead, he slowed to a more cautious pace. The forest was unchanged, though the path had become a broad promenade, paved with ochre bricks.

He began to pass stone benches with fancifully carved legs and backs, and it occurred to him that the path functioned as someone's picnic ground. But he met no picnickers, though he hoped earnestly to—preferably picnickers with a high-speed airboat, armored and bristling with weaponry. He laughed at himself. He might as well wish for his picnickers to also be too abysmally stupid to use any of the security technology such a vessel would carry.

No, what he needed was picnickers with, say, five motorized bicycles.

The path looped through the woods in graceful sweeps, and Ruiz would have cut across, had the undergrowth not been so dense. Because of the path's curvature, he could see only a short distance ahead. There was an unidentifiable change in the air, and a feeling of imminence touched him. He began to think that the highway junction must be near, and he became even more cautious, keeping to the shadiest side of the path, alert for any sign that he was not alone.

Ruiz came around the last curve and discovered that his hoped-for "highway" was actually a canal.

The path terminated in a sunny clearing, in which stood an elevated landing built of shiny pink granite, over which rose a decorative gateway—two columns in the form of attenuated weasels, supporting an arched lintel carved in the likeness of two winged reptiles, toothy snouts kissing in the center. Here and there striped poles rose above the landing, still carrying ragged scraps of faded cloth, apparently left from a time when the landing had been covered with a festive canopy.

The immediate impression was of long disuse, and Ruiz's heart sank.

He approached the landing slowly, still alert, but with a growing sense of futility. The scattering of recent trash on the path had raised his hopes, but the landing's air of abandonment had dampened them.

He climbed the steps and went across the landing to the canal. The canal itself seemed to be in perfect repair. It had two narrow channels, separated by a strip of monocrete. The still black water had an unpleasant oily quality, but no debris blocked the channels—hopeful evidence that the canal was still in occasional use. He looked to the left. The canal cut south through the trees in a perfectly straight line, and though the branches formed a tunnel over the canal, none of them hung low enough to impede the progress of a barge. It appeared they were trimmed on a regular schedule.

Ruiz went to the verge of the canal, and peered over the monocrete curb. Repulsor strips were set into the side, just above the waterline, an indication that the canal was maintained by folk of a fairly high-tech level. No growth fouled the canal sides, another indication of advanced engineering.

He sat on the curb and considered his options. Was there time to build a raft? Perhaps—he could use the splinter gun to fell trees, though that would severely deplete its power cell. But what then? When Corean arrived, her sniffers would lead her to the canal, and she wouldn't have to go far to catch up to them. Besides, it was doubtful they could pole the raft at a significantly greater speed than they could walk.

Maybe they could confuse the trail—go down the canal a couple of hours and kick Flomel off the raft, run him into the woods to divert the sniffers. No—without a good deal of luck—and an improbably degree of incompetence on Corean's part—that would be no more than a brief delaying tactic. All their scent-signatures were surely on file in Corean's computers and accessible to her sniffers. She would either ignore Flomel, or split off a portion of her forces to catch him.

Idly, he flipped a twig into the dark water. It lay there for an instant, and then he felt a high-frequency vibration in the curb. He jumped up and stood back, but not before he saw the twig shatter and then dissolve in a swirling pool of foam. The vibration ceased.

He abandoned the idea of a raft, as well as several barely formed ideas about using the canal as a hiding place.

He walked a few paces south along the curb and saw that there was ample concealment away from the landing. It would be no trouble to jump to the deck of a passing barge from here, if the barge wasn't moving too fast and wasn't defended with automatic weaponry or too many guards.

As this thought passed through his mind, he heard the mutter of an engine and looked north, to see a barge moving sedately toward him in the near channel. He stepped back into a clump of bushes and waited.

As it came closer, he saw that it apparently carried no passengers or crew. In fact, it seemed to be an automated cargo carrier, heavily armored against pilferage, but showing no obvious armament. Its back was featureless steel, rounded at the topsides.

It seemed perfect. When it drew abreast of his hiding

place and he had still seen no defenses, he accepted the risk and leaped aboard. The barge was moving deceptively fast, and he stumbled before catching his balance.

Nothing struck him down, to his astonishment.

He turned and looked at the landing, receding behind him, the trees closing in around the waterway. *Safe,* he thought. With any luck, Corean would never catch him—her sniffers would have to search both banks of the canal, which they would do at a speed that in all likelihood would be slower than the speed with which he was now fleeing. If the barge didn't carry him into a fatally hostile situation, he'd survive.

The glow of happiness he felt faded almost instantly.

Nisa. And the others, but mainly: Nisa. The sunny landing had become just a bright spot in the shadowy tunnel of green. *No, don't be foolish,* he told himself. They'd had no chance before—what had changed? If he got off the barge, who knew when another might happen along? It could be days. Or weeks. Long before that, his hide would be decorating Corean's apartment.

But there was Nisa. He couldn't be sure what Corean would do to Nisa and the other escapees, but it wouldn't be pleasant. In his mind's eye he could see the others reaching the landing, to find him gone. What would they think had happened? Flomel would know, he was sure—this was exactly the sort of thing Flomel would do, if he got the chance.

He sighed and turned to leap back to the bank. He saw a space between the trees and jumped—and as he did, the mission-imperative rose up in his mind and shrieked that he was doing the wrong thing.

He almost fell into the canal, but he made the bank and fell rolling. The mission-imperative hurt him terribly. It couldn't kill him, as the death net could—but it could hurt him. What it was saying, in wordless waves of pain, was: "Ruiz Aw, you have deviated from the accomplishment of the mission you promised to perform for the Art League."

Ruiz lay sprawled, shuddering with pain, teeth clenched on a scream, until the mission-imperative ceased its punishment. After a time he sat up, still shaky. *Never again,* he promised himself. Never again would he allow anyone to tamper with his mind, to install another's agenda in place of his own.

When he was strong enough, he stood and began walking the bank, back to the landing.

THE OTHERS HAD arrived when he reached the clearing. They stood in a tight apprehensive knot at the foot of the landing, looking about uncertainly. They didn't see him immediately.

He paused behind the last clump of concealing brambles and watched for a moment. Dolmaero's broad face showed a mixture of anxiety and disillusionment. Molnekh glanced about, looking blandly alert. Flomel, still tethered to the leash Dolmaero held, wore a face full of malevolent triumph.

Nisa stood slightly apart from the others, and she seemed to be striving for calm and confidence.

She's been defending me, he thought, and his heart melted, just a little.

Ruiz stepped out and they jumped.

"Hello," he said.

He took a malicious pleasure in watching Flomel's face fall, but the light in Nisa's face was a far better reward.

"We feared for you," said Dolmaero with a rare cautious smile.

Molnekh grinned, an oddly macabre expression in that skeletal face. "Oh, certainly we did—but perhaps we felt a bit of anxiety about our own selves."

Ruiz laughed. "Nonsense. We're all far too brave for such emotions."

Nisa hugged him. "I wasn't worried," she said.

"You're too optimistic, Noble Person," Ruiz said, in what must have been an odd tone, for she looked confused momentarily.

"Well, thank you. Anyway, this may be good luck," Ruiz continued, indicating the canal.

"What is it?" Molnekh asked. The Pharaohan came from a world in which water was far too rare and precious to leave open to the air.

"It's a 'canal,'" he said, using the pangalac word. "It's a low-energy transport system. Things called 'barges' float along it, propelled by internal engines or pushed by barges specially designed for that purpose."

"It seems an oddly complicated system, in a place where

one may as easily soar through the air," remarked Dol-maero, as if he couldn't quite believe in such an eccentric concept.

"Perhaps," said Ruiz. "But it works reliably, uses little energy, and provides a safe and picturesque means of travel. For example, we wouldn't have crashed into a mountainside, had we traveled by barge."

"A point," Dolmaero conceded.

"And how do we summon one of these barges?" de-manded Flomel.

Ruiz smiled a bit sadly. "You've cut to the heart of our present difficulty, I fear. We have no means of calling up a barge—we must hope that one happens by before Corean catches up with us."

Flomel snorted contemptuously. The others looked stricken, except for Nisa, who perhaps had come to rely too greatly on Ruiz's luck.

"It's not so bad," Ruiz said. "One passed through just a few minutes ago. I rode it a short distance, to see if it was feasible."

"So that's where you were?" Dolmaero looked just the smallest bit skeptical, and Ruiz realized: *He knows me better than any of the others, even Nisa.*

"Yes. The barges move rapidly, but not so fast that we won't be able to jump aboard—provided that their decks are undefended, as the last one was."

"Meanwhile, what shall we do? Shall we eat? It's lunch-time." Molnekh looked cheerfully famished.

"Why not?"

THEY SAT ON the landing's steps and ate the last of Core-an's food. Ruiz tried to clear his mind of the unpleasant-nesses that, it seemed, must soon occur. He had no reasonable hope that another barge would pass through be-fore Corean caught up with them; still, why deny the sweet-ness of the moment. The sun was warm on his back, and Nisa sat close to him, her thigh pressed comfortably against his. It was possible that Corean would not arrive until to-morrow morning—if not, he hoped to enjoy another night in Nisa's arms. It seemed a worthwhile way of spending his last night.

No! He mustn't accept, he mustn't give up. Cold rationality would be of little use at this point; an entirely rational being in his position would have long ago perished.

He examined the landing with an eye to ambush. He had the splinter gun. He could hide the others in the bushes. He could tie Flomel to one of the landing's poles, a sacrificial goat. Maybe Corean would assume Flomel to be excess baggage left behind when they fled, and stop to question him. Who could tell; perhaps Corean would be foolish enough to emerge from her boat unarmored, and he could potshot her. He looked up at the carved gate. If Corean's craft approached the clearing at a low level, as would be the case if she was using mech sniffers, Ruiz might be able to hide atop the lintel, in the wingfolds of one of the granite reptiles.

Well, it was a plan, though not a terribly good one. Still, it was far better than supine acceptance.

Ruiz finished his lunch and leaned back against the warm stone. Suppose another barge actually did arrive. How would he get everyone aboard? The barges apparently moved at a fairly high speed. Ruiz might be able to run fast enough to keep up with one for a short distance but none of the others seemed that quick. They'd have one chance to jump aboard; anyone who missed would be left behind. Flomel would try to be a problem; if he dragged his feet, he might slow one of them disastrously.

The others had finished their lunch and were sitting in a silent group on the other side of the landing steps, looking about aimlessly.

Ruiz stood. "Come," he said. "Let's discuss strategy."

The others rose. Dolmaero tugged Flomel to his feet; the mage now regarded the Guildmaster with the same virulent hatred he directed at Ruiz.

"To the canalside," said Ruiz.

When they all stood on the bank, Ruiz spoke. "The problem is more complex than it looks. The barges move rapidly, and we will have but one chance to board—supposing that the barges are uncrewed and undefended, as the last one was. Also, we don't know which way the barge will be coming. If it's going south, that would be best, since we are on this bank. However, if it's going north, it will travel in the far channel."

"How will we reach it?" asked Dolmaero.

"A good question. I have a plan; it may work." Ruiz glanced at the trees on the north side of the clearing. He selected an overhanging branch about the diameter of Flomel's neck, pulled the splinter gun out, and fired a burst. The spinning wires cut through the wood and dropped the branch into the canal, where it shuddered and disintegrated.

Molnekh stepped cautiously back from the verge. "I'd been hoping for a bath," he said wryly.

Ruiz smiled and shrugged. "Inadvisable." He turned to Flomel. "I must warn you now, Master Flomel. If you're in any way obstructive, I'll have to use the gun; I can't let Corean catch you, as richly as you deserve that fate."

Flomel swallowed, eyes wide. "I understand." For the moment the mage seemed subdued and tractable.

"Anyway," Ruiz continued. "If we see a northbound barge, I'll try to drop a tree across the first channel, which we must all scramble over before the barge reaches the landing. Then we must distribute ourselves along the bank, for reasons that will be obvious. I'll jump on first, so I can help catch you. Then Nisa, followed by Dolmaero, then Flomel, then Molnekh. This is the technique you must use: Before the barge reaches you, you must run as fast as you can in the direction the barge is moving. When it reaches you, run a little faster and jump aboard. With any luck, none of us will break an ankle."

"There's that word again," said Dolmaero—but he was smiling.

"I'm afraid so," said Ruiz.

THE PHARAOHAN MEN settled in the shadow of the gate to wait. Dolmaero and Molnekh made an effort to restore their stubbly heads to a decently shaven state, using the dagger Ruiz had given Dolmaero. They took turns scraping at each other's scalp, the scraper working industriously, the scrapee making terrible faces as the not-very-sharp knife did its damage.

After a while, they reluctantly agreed to shave Flomel, and Ruiz thought to detect a certain pleasure in Molnekh's homely face as he inflicted pain on the senior mage.

But finally all were restored to a socially acceptable condition, their scalp tattoos glowing in the sunlight.

Ruiz had decided to let his hair grow out, since his disguise as a Pharaohan snake oil peddler was thoroughly compromised—and already there was a fine black nap obscuring his fading tattoos.

A silence fell over the clearing. The only sound Ruiz could hear was the slight click and rattle that came from Molnekh and Flomel, who were doing dexterity exercises, passing small stones and twigs through their agile fingers. Ruiz found this an oddly touching exhibition of faith. It wasn't terribly likely that the mages would ever practice their art again, even if they succeeded in escaping Sook—yet they remained devoted to their craft.

After a time even these sounds ceased, and the breeze went as light as a sigh. In this deeper silence, Ruiz heard the faint splash of dripping water.

He turned his head. It seemed to him that the sound originated from the north edge of the clearing, where a faint path led into the forest.

"Wait here," he said to Nisa. "Call out if you hear or see anything—especially if a barge comes."

He went into the forest, following the path. Less than fifty meters beyond the edge of the clearing, he came to a bower.

A fountain dripped a slow trickle of cool water over a bronze statue of some graceful browsing creature. It had a head much like an Old Earth deer, delicate and fey, but it had six long, powerful legs. The fountain fed a clear shallow pool surrounded by a low coping of pink granite. At the back of the pool the overflow slid glistening over a watergate into a tiny stream that meandered off toward the canal.

Ruiz sat for a moment on the coping, trailing his fingers through the water. He shut his eyes. For the minute he sat there, his mind was blessedly empty.

He went back to the others and told them about the fountain. He turned to Nisa and said, "Would you like to bathe? You must be ready to abandon your bath instantly, should a barge come—even if it means boarding naked and dripping."

Nisa smiled delightedly. "Oh yes. I'll be ready to leap out, I promise . . . but it would be so good to be clean."

"All right. The Noble Person will bathe first, then the rest can take a turn."

She was undressing as the two of them walked down the path, handing her garments to him as fast as she could pull them off. By the time they reached the pool, she was running ahead, naked and lovely. She splashed into the pool and sank down into the cool water with a sigh of contentment.

"Oh, this is so wonderful," she said. "I stink of the pens, of Ayam, of the potions the philterers filled me with before we boarded the boat." She scooped up handfuls of silvery sand from the pool's bottom and began to scrub vigorously.

Ruiz watched for a while, filling his eyes with her, which she didn't seem to mind—in fact, her movements took on something of that flirtatious languor that he had found so compelling when she had bathed for the first time in the slave pen, the day they had become lovers. But now the circumstances were different, and while her body delighted his eyes as much as it had on that other day, he was too taut with anxiety to respond as he had then.

After a bit, he knelt by the outlet and scrubbed her clothes clean in the flow, as best he could, and then wrung them out and spread them on low-growing bushes to dry.

She smiled as though he had committed an entertaining eccentricity. "Thank you, Ruiz."

He shrugged. "You're welcome. Perhaps you'd do the same for me when I bathe."

For a moment she seemed to regard his remark as an insult. Her nostrils flared, and she opened her mouth as though to utter some stern reproof. But then she saw that he was smiling, and her annoyance seemed to evaporate, and she laughed. "Why not? I must have a new trade in this new world, since I'm no longer a princess. Maybe I'll be a washerwoman."

"You'll be the most beautiful washerwoman on Sook," he said.

"Do you think so? Yet you don't join me."

"I wish I could, but what if a barge appeared at an awkward moment? If I were forced to suddenly choose between salvation and consummation, I fear I might be indecisive."

"Oh," she said, but her eyes were shining. "Well, at least I'll be sweeter tonight than I was last night."

"You were sweet enough for me last night," he said.

When she was done, he stripped and scrubbed off as quickly as he could. From the corner of his eye, he watched her slosh his clothes about inexpertly in the little brook. When he put them on, they were soaking wet and not much cleaner than before, but he thanked her solemnly.

The Pharaohan men scurried toward the fountain as

Ruiz and Nisa left the bower. Ruiz admonished them to be ready for swift action, and left them to their ablutions.

RUIZ SPENT THE rest of the afternoon on the bank, listening for a barge, but giving most of his attention to Nisa, who sat beside him, leaning against his shoulder. She spoke of her former life on Pharaoh, as she had done during the days they spent imprisoned in Corean's apartments, but Ruiz detected a difference in her attitudes. Before, she had recounted the wonders of her father's palace with great pride. Now her recollections were apparently diminished by the new knowledge she had acquired—it was as if she looked back through the wrong end of a telescope, so that everything she remembered was smaller and grubbier, compared to the things she'd seen since her capture. And yet . . . her wistful affection for the things she had lost was more obvious than ever, as though she no longer took for granted those familiar pleasures.

As the time passed and the sun dropped lower in the sky and no barges appeared, Ruiz became increasingly tense. Finally he decided he must prepare for the worst. If Corean had made the best possible time, she might well arrive within the hour.

He called the others over. "Listen," he said. "There's a chance that Corean may get here before the sun goes down. If not, we'll be safe for the night—remember, the Shards permit no high-speed night travel on Sook. But . . . if she does arrive, we'll have to be ready.

"I'm going to hide on top of the gate. I may get a clear shot. In any case, if Corean comes you'll be on your own—run into the woods and try to get away."

He sent Dolmaero and Flomel to the south side of the clearing. "You watch and listen—if you see or hear anything coming, shout. If Flomel gives trouble, pitch him in the canal."

He gathered Nisa to him, held her tight, kissed her. "You and Molnekh watch from the north."

She hugged him with all her strength, then went off without another word.

When the others were in place, he climbed the gate. He had some difficulty with the smooth granite, but the carving was sufficiently deep to provide a few handholds and footholds. He reached the lintel, then eased himself into the crevice between the reptile's body and folded wing. He was high enough to see over most of the treetops; perhaps he would spot Corean's airboat in time to give the others enough warning to scatter into the woods.

Ruiz Aw tried to find a comfortable perch, but was only partly successful. He was as ready as he could be. He tried not to think of anything but the satisfaction he would take in killing Corean.

CHAPTER 5

Ruiz Aw's emotions ran along a steep curve. At first they plummeted into fatalistic despair, as he waited for Corean's airboat. But as the sun dropped toward the horizon and she did not come, his hopes flared up brightly. One more night; was that too ambitious a favor to ask of his luck? He began to believe it might not be.

He was so involved in this fantasy of delayed destruction that he didn't react for a moment when Molnekh shouted.

"What?" he yelled back.

"Something's coming!" The tone of Molnekh's shout wasn't entirely joyful, however.

Ruiz took one last look up toward the pass. No sign of Corean. He crawled out of his hiding spot, to discover that his legs had gone a bit numb from his uncomfortable perch.

He reached the ground without falling and hobbled toward Molnekh and Nisa at his best speed.

COREAN PACED THE control blister of the survey sled she'd borrowed from her starboat. "Can you push this thing no faster?" she demanded of the creature who sat at the controls.

The pilot turned to her, opened his catlike mouth in a parody of a smile. "Yess, misstresss. We can go fasster. If the Shardss are watching, as they alwayss are, we can become a lovely flaming comet for about, oh, ssix hundred meterss. But then I fear we'll sstop." His eyes glittered with appreciation for his own wit.

She made no answer—she had learned to accept Lensh's sarcasm as the price of his service to her. Apparently such insolence was a hard-wired part of his enhanced feline-based brain—not even the Gencha could root it out, without impairing Lensh's intelligence and effectiveness.

Of course she knew that the Shards were watching. Sook's alien owners enforced their peculiar rules with astonishing rigor. They prohibited certain modes of travel, large warships, large military units, nuclear weaponry, and many other useful elements of modern warfare. From their orbital platforms, they punished transgressors instantly and severely.

Occasionally this was inconvenient. On the other hand, were it not for the Shards and their unreasonable proscriptions, the pangalac worlds would long ago have exterminated the criminal enterprises that now flourished so vigorously on Sook.

"Patience," Corean said to herself.

Beneath the sled, the pink veldt flowed past. The blue mountains where Ruiz Aw had wrecked her airboat were still only a smudge against the horizon—and the sun was very low. They would never get there by dark, and the survey sled was unequipped for the slow ground-level travel the Shards allowed after dark. She would be forced to land, and so Ruiz Aw would have to wait until the morning for his reward.

For a while Corean lost herself in pleasant visions of what she might do to that troublesome person. Ruiz had stolen her boat and several of her most valuable slaves, had killed two of her most useful henchmen, had almost murdered poor Marmo. Marmo was in the cargo bay now, being attended by Lensh's littermate, Fensh. A medical limpet was busy healing the scraps of flesh that remained to him, and Fensh was directing a repair mech in the replacement of Marmo's damaged mechanisms. Corean cursed herself for a sentimental fool. If she hadn't stopped to pick up Marmo's wrecked chassis, and then had to backtrack to find his missing power cell, she'd have reached the wreck well before dark.

At the back of the cabin, the Mocrassar shifted, its claws clicking on the plastic deck. Fresh from the molting cell, its stink was particularly vile, but Corean had long ago learned to ignore the odor. It was, after all, the stink of wealth—no one but the very rich possessed Mocrassar bondwarriors.

She descended to the cargo bay, where Marmo lay clamped in a repair frame. The lower half of the cyborg's face showed pale sweat-beaded flesh, but he had regained consciousness and a faint smile trembled on his thin lips. "How are you doing?" Corean asked curtly.

"Much better, thank you," Marmo answered.

Corean sniffed. Her feelings toward the old pirate were ambiguous. He had been with her for a long time, he was the closest thing to a friend she possessed, he had always found ways to be useful. On the other hand, he must have committed some act of incompetence. How else could Ruiz Aw have managed to take the boat?

"What happened, Marmo?" She strove to contain her annoyance.

The cyborg's oculars shifted focus with a tiny whine, as if he were no longer looking at Corean, but at some memory. "He bested me. I know nothing of what happened to Ayam and Banessa, except that they must both be dead."

"Yes." Corean had found the giantess's vast corpse and Ayam's smaller remains, covered with gorged carrion birds, near the place where she had recovered Marmo's power cell. "Can't you be more specific?"

"It was Ayam's watch, just after midnight. I was in the control blister, Banessa in her cabin. The next thing I knew, Ruiz Aw jumped through the hatch, grinning like a demon, whirling some primitive weapon at me. I got off a burst—I carried a splinter gun—but somehow I missed and the chains snapped tight around me. I was helpless for a moment, then Ruiz Aw fired some chemical-energy ballistic weapon at me, which knocked the gun out of my hand." Marmo drew a deep breath. "It went downhill from there, and soon I was on my back and Ruiz Aw was sawing through my neck with a dull knife. He gave me no choice but to cooperate."

"You might have chosen to die—rather than betray me."

Marmo sighed. "Perhaps. But I must tell you, I don't

think it would have helped much. The man is not entirely human. Are you certain you wish to pursue him? It might be more trouble than it's worth."

Corean stared at him. What was wrong with the old monster? In his pirate days, he must have suffered more grievous defeats—the scarce flesh that still clung to his mechanisms testified to terrible wounds. What was Ruiz Aw but a clever trickster with good reflexes?

"Well," Marmo said. "Never mind—if you must have him, I'll help, as always. But let us take a vow not to underestimate him again, and to be very very careful."

"Marmo," she said. "He's hurt me badly, in many ways. I must inflict greater pain on him, before I can be happy again. Do you understand?"

"Yes, Corean," he said in the faintest of whispers.

RUIZ AW REACHED the bank where Nisa and Molnekh stood, and looked north.

"What is it, Ruiz?" asked Nisa.

He wasn't quite sure. There seemed to be a flotilla of barges approaching, but they shouldn't have been so clearly visible at that distance. He squinted against the shine that reflected from the water, and waited.

A moment later he saw that the barges carried high eccentric superstructures, large strange faces, perhaps the forms of animals. They looked a bit like floats in a parade.

"Wait here," he told them. "If you see me get aboard, then you get ready to jump on. If something happens to me, run away." He set off toward the approaching barges at his best speed.

A few seconds later he was only fifty meters from the leading barge, and he darted off the bank into a concealing tangle of vines.

There was too much to see in the moments he had to make a decision. There were six barges, all somewhat longer than the cargo carrier that had earlier passed, and with higher topsides. The sculptural forms welded to their otherwise featureless decks were disturbing, even frightening. At the prows were the handsome elongated faces of beautiful men and women, far too large for the crouching human figures into which they merged—as if megalocephalic steel giants knelt on the decks of the barges. The faces displayed expressions of detached delight—wide eyes, cool smiles. The sculptures had been anodized in rich primary colors, and the sexual characteristics of the figures were exaggerated; breasts were massive pendulous billows splayed across the deck from gunwale to gunwale, penises were great veined tree trunks, running the length of the decks and curving up under the figures' chins. Great swaying chains ran from heavy belts at the figures' waists to the gunwales on either side.

But he saw no evidence that the decks were otherwise crewed. The first barge passed in a rush of foam; Ruiz observed two standard security locks set into the topsides, fore and aft. He saw no evidence of automated weaponry—which meant nothing much.

The second barge was gone. Ruiz dared delay no further. When the third barge drew even with him, he jumped from concealment and ran alongside for a dozen steps. He could barely keep up; the others would have to be helped. He veered toward the bank, leaped, landed successfully on the deck grating.

Nothing destroyed him, and he shouted for the others to be ready. The barge approached the landing swiftly.

He heard Dolmaero calling, getting the others into the positions he'd planned, and felt a rush of gratitude for the Guildmaster's competence.

Nisa was running alongside, and he caught her as she jumped, keeping her from sprawling. He set her on her feet and turned, just in time to catch Dolmaero's outstretched arm as the Guildmaster missed his footing and started to fall toward the water. Dolmaero's weight threatened to jerk Ruiz from his feet, but he heaved with all his strength and drew him, floundering on his belly, onto the deck.

Before he could set and turn around, Flomel hit him, grabbing at his splinter gun as he bounced off Ruiz's left side. Rage blinded Ruiz. He crouched and whirled, bringing up his arm and bunching his fist into a heavy ball. He struck Flomel's forehead at full extension. The conjuror flew back, smashed loose-limbed into a great steel thigh, spilled bonelessly to the deck—but the gun he had somehow reached bounced off the deck and twinkled into the canal.

Molnekh appeared at Ruiz's side; apparently he was much more agile than the others. He started to reach out toward Ruiz, but then looked at his face and cringed away,

raising his hands protectively. "Be calm," he squeaked.
"The damage is done, and Flomel has paid for it."

"Paid for it?" Ruiz said, struggling for control. "If he's
dead, he got off easy."

Nisa knelt beside the mage, who indeed looked like a
corpse. "He's breathing. Let's throw him in the canal," she
said, her face paper-white except for two red spots at her
cheeks.

Her expression was single-mindedly feral, and somehow
it shocked Ruiz from his rage. He wondered if he looked like
that—though surely his hard face was more practiced at
ferocity than her smooth young one. "No," said Ruiz.
"Leave him alone. If he lives, I'm going to sell him to the
first slaver I meet. If ever a man deserved to be a slave,
Flomel does."

RUIZ DIRECTED HIS flock to stay put until he had examined the barge for dangers. Dolmaero nodded somberly.
Nisa patted him gently. Molnekh was busy tugging Flomel
into a more comfortable position and didn't look up.

He roamed about the deck for a few minutes, finding no
obvious security devices, no hatches other than the two
locks set into the barge's topsides. Though it had not been
apparent from the bank, the barge was designed to provide
deck passengers with a degree of comfort. In the various
nooks and crannies of the steel statues were a number of
seats, upholstered in red softstone. Under the arch formed
by the figure's penis and drooping testicles was a luxurious
circular pit equipped with a padded floor—Ruiz would have
been amused, had his mood not been so dark. The loss of the
splinter gun had dealt their chances of survival a severe
blow. How could he have been so careless? Granted, Flomel
had made a lifework of having fast hands—few hands were
so deft as those belonging to the conjurors of Pharaoh. Still,
Ruiz blamed himself bitterly.

On the far side of the figure was a spiral staircase, leading
to the statue's back. Ruiz ascended cautiously, but found the
upper deck as unpopulated as the lower. Here were rows of
seats, arranged like an excursion boat's. Forward, a gangway
led up to a small observation pulpit atop the figure's cra-
nium.

Nowhere did he see any access to the interior of the barge.

He stood for a while on the pulpit, leaning on the polished rail, gazing down the tunnel of trees through which they traveled. The sun must be nearly down; the light had that golden impermanence that accompanies the longest shadows of the day. He felt a deep weariness that had nothing to do with physical exhaustion. The bedrock to which he had anchored his life seemed to be shifting; he no longer seemed capable of following the maxims that had for so long successfully guided him. For example: One must kill one's enemies as soon as conveniently possible. He should have killed Flomel long before, of course—he should do so right now. And he would, as soon as he had overcome this temporary—surely it was only temporary—distaste for murder.

But even more basic to his existence was this rule: Give no loyalty to anyone. And he had violated this rule a dozen times since the moment he had first seen Nisa.

He was afraid. It was a kind of fear he had not felt in more years than he could remember. He lowered his head to his arms. If he hadn't so thoroughly forgotten how, over all those hard years, he might have cried.

RUIZ CAUGHT A flicker of movement from the corner of his eye and whipped up his head. Above the broad rump of the leading barge's statue, someone peered at him through a railing. After a moment the person hesitantly stood up. Ruiz saw a thin old man dressed in dirty tatters that might once have been magnificent. The old man showed a lean vulpine face, a wildly tangled mane of white hair, and large pale eyes. His expression was cautiously friendly, as if he had no idea who Ruiz might be, but didn't want to risk offending anyone.

They stared at each for a moment, then the old man raised a fragile hand and waved, a gesture so slight that it might only have been the tremble of age.

Ruiz waved back, with only a little less restraint.

Two other people appeared to each side of the old man. One was a young girl wearing rags similar to the old man's, though cleaner. Her face was round and unremarkable, but she smiled with what appeared to be genuine friendliness.

The other was a large young man, wearing a drab unisuit,

such as might be bought in the cheap emporiums of a thousand worlds. He had a wide coarse-featured face and an air of confident stupidity. He ostentatiously shouldered the old man aside, once he decided it was safe—and then he glared at Ruiz with bovine truculence.

Ruiz laughed silently, then waved again, this time with cheerful enthusiasm. The young man's mouth sagged open with perplexity, then clamped shut with annoyance.

Ruiz turned away, somewhat reassured by the presence of these other hitchhikers—for such they obviously were. Perhaps they were as thoroughly ignorant as Ruiz of the dangers of their situation—but in any case, their survival was at least a hopeful sign.

He went to the aft end of the observation deck and stared at the rest of the barges, but if they also carried passengers, none were visible.

He felt an unwilling fascination as he looked at the great steel face of the trailing barge. It was a woman with huge heavy-lidded eyes, high sculpted cheekbones, and cascading hair. Her mouth was just a bit too full, as though distended from some internal pressure. The proportion and detail were exquisite, very different in style from the crude exaggeration of the body. The bodies were laughable; this face was compellingly erotic.

He went back down to the lower deck, where Flomel was moaning and showing signs of recovery. Molnekh was bathing away the blood where Ruiz's fist had split the skin on Flomel's forehead, and he looked up at Ruiz with a slightly ambiguous expression. "His skull may be cracked, but it doesn't seem to be broken," Molnekh said in a tone that neither approved nor censured.

"I don't care," Ruiz said flatly. "If he lives, I must make you responsible for his conduct—no one else is sufficiently quick."

"Yes," Molnekh said. "Flomel has always had nimble fingers. I'm sorry he lost the weapon, Ruiz Aw."

"Well, here's his leash, Molnekh. I'll seal it to his neck, so. Here is the other end, and the seal. If you must leave him, loop the leash around some object too sturdy to be persuaded, and seal it. Do you understand?"

"I'll be his keeper, Ruiz Aw." Molnekh suddenly regained his usual look of expectant cheer.

"Good. Now, there is no more food, but we all still have

our water bottles, and empty bellies won't kill us for a day or two. The main thing is: We're getting farther away from Corean with every minute, which is better than the best food, in my view."

Only Molnekh looked momentarily doubtful.

Ruiz told the others of his discoveries and surmises, and directed Molnekh and Dolmaero to wait in the padded pit, where they might make Flomel comfortable, if they wished. He stood up and took Nisa's hand. "Be alert," he told the men. "Call out if you see anything strange."

Nisa giggled and Ruiz followed her gaze to the enormous phallus that thrust the length of the barge. "Well," he amended. "Anything strange and dangerous."

"It looks dangerous enough to me," she said. "What sort of folk worship such odd idols?"

"I don't know," he admitted. "I imagine we'll find out, but not, I hope, until we're well away from Corean."

Then he led her up to the observation deck, to a bench at the back, where they sat together in companionable silence until the sun had gone down and the night had arrived.

CHAPTER 6

WITH the advent of full darkness, the barge lit up
with millions of tiny lights. Beads of soft glowing
color clustered thickly along every edge, and
dusted every surface of the statues. It occurred to Ruiz that
the barges would be a wonderful sight, seen from the canalside. He wondered if anyone watched.

Nisa nestled into his shoulder. "I can hardly bring myself
to believe in this," she murmured. "And you? Are you sure
this isn't all some fever dream? Or perhaps we've fallen into
one of those goblin tales that nannies tell to frighten bad
children."

"Do you think so?" he asked.

"Perhaps."

"If this is a goblin tale, what must we do?"

"I was never bad," she said, and laughed. "Well, once in
a great while. Anyway, the hero always knows exactly what
to do; he never bothers to ask the princess he rescues what
she thinks he should do."

Ruiz sighed. "I'm not a very satisfactory hero, then."

"Oh, no," she said, and touched his face. "You're a fine
hero." She raised her mouth to his, kissed him gently. Her
lips had a soft clinging quality, like ripe fragrant fruit, sticky

with sweetness but somehow electric—his mouth tingled where she had kissed him.

It came to Ruiz that they now had more privacy than they had enjoyed in days. He kissed her again, more urgently, and felt her tongue flicker along his lips. He found that he was breathing hard, and his heart thumped.

She pushed him away, slowly, and he released her. Her eyes seemed a bit glazed, her lips were puffy. She looked at him for a long motionless moment, then, still looking into his eyes, she lay back on the bench.

He wondered if it was safe, to so distract himself. He decided he didn't care, though some ancient scarred part of himself was horrified at this carelessness.

He touched her knee lightly with trembling fingers. Her face relaxed, and she turned her gaze up to the starlight. He pushed up her tunic, slowly, admiring the texture of her skin, the strong beautiful muscles of her thighs. He unfastened the garter that held her little knife and dropped it to the deck.

As his hands moved higher, she sighed and let her thighs fall open. He knelt beside her and kissed her knee, and then trailed kisses up the inside of her thigh, until she gasped and lifted her hips to meet his mouth.

A long time later she knelt on the bench, naked, clutching the railing, damp tendrils of hair tangled across her lovely back, head thrown back, moaning in time to his thrusts. His hands gripped her hip bones, and he looked down at the upside-down heart shape formed by her buttocks and slender waist, marveling at her beauty.

He increased the tempo of his movements and she bucked against him, her voice hoarse and ragged.

Just before they came for the last time that night, he looked up and saw the huge perfect face of the trailing barge. Perhaps it was only the delirium of the moment, but in that moment he had the overwhelming sensation that the face watched their coupling and that the eyes glowed with a strange intensity, as if it approved of the heat between Ruiz and Nisa. There was some great perversity in that gaze, but at the same time it seemed a fiercely erotic regard, and Ruiz surrendered to it, shuddering, pushing himself as deeply into Nisa's body as he could, pouring himself into her in wave after wave of joy. She thrashed beneath him, cried out wordlessly, reached back to claw at his hips, to pull him deeper yet.

AFTER, THEY LAY on the bench together. Ruiz had pulled their discarded clothing over them, to hold in the heat they had generated, and then had given himself entirely to delightful sensation. He found an almost-suffocating pleasure in the tiny movements of her sweat-slick flesh against his. He was intensely aware of the subtleties of her body where it touched his: the softness of her breasts, the slightly different pressure of her nipples against his chest, the feathery touch of her hair, the coarser hair and the slippery warmth where she held his thigh between hers.

It came to him that something about her lovemaking had been different. The reserve he had sensed in her, that first time in the bathing pool—the reserve that seemed to define the act as a casual exchange of pleasure—was gone.

She had given herself without restraint. He wondered what had changed.

WHEN FINALLY THEY began to speak, at first it was of inconsequential things: the softness of the night air, the beauty of the stars as they slipped through the passing branches of the trees, the relaxing throb of the barge's engines.

Nisa propped herself on her elbow and stroked his chest idly. "Did you know that women on Pharaoh bear children when they wish? Every month, when they're done bleeding, they take a tea of dalafrea root—and then, until they bleed again, they may take pleasure without consequence. Do pangalac women do the same?"

Ruiz was unprepared for her question and spoke without thought. "They have other ways; so do pangalac men. But you needn't worry, Nisa. When you were captured, the doctors gave you this." He touched the skin at the back of her left arm, where a tiny contraceptive implant made a barely detectable bump.

She fingered the little hard spot curiously. "Ah," she said in a voice of sad discovery. "To keep the slaves in salable condition?"

He nodded, sorry for his tactlessness. He pulled her

closer and she made no resistance. "It's easily removed," he said. "Whenever you wish."

A silence fell between them.

Finally she spoke again in a breathless whisper. "I've never asked you this, but I've wondered. Back in your pangalac worlds, is there a woman who wishes you were there? Would you rather be there with her?"

"No," he answered. "No one." He grinned. "I admit: I'd rather be there than here, but I wouldn't wish to change companions." It was true. He was going to have to stop wondering what was *wrong* with him.

He knew what was wrong with him. "No, I wouldn't want to be with anyone else," he said. *Even,* he thought, *if it means I'll never get home.*

"Oh," she said, and somehow managed to feel even softer against him.

Long peaceful minutes slipped away.

HE HOVERED IN that pleasant interval between wakefulness and sleep until he heard Molnekh cry out.

"Ruiz Aw!"

He jerked upright, almost spilling Nisa to the deck.

Molnekh shouted his name again, but there was no overtone of panic to the skinny mage's voice, so Ruiz took the time to dress before he went to the ladder. "Wait here," he told Nisa, who was obviously still sleepy. She nodded, stretched entrancingly, and bent to gather her clothes.

Ruiz climbed down the ladder and trotted forward to the place where Molnekh and Dolmaero stood. He found them staring down at something on the deck.

When Ruiz looked, he was astonished to see a stainless-steel tray, bearing several glass flagons, two loaves of crusty bread, a wheel of cheese, a basket overflowing with small golden grapes, a small green porcelain vase with three red flowers. To one side was a stack of plastic cups and a dispenser full of paper napkins.

"Where did it come from?" Ruiz asked.

Dolmaero shrugged. "I don't know. I've been getting up and walking about the barge—my legs get cramped. A few minutes ago, it wasn't here. Now it is. I called Molnekh; he called you."

Ruiz turned to Molnekh. "And Flomel?"

"Securely tied," Molnekh said. "But recovering—his complaints are incessant. His head hurts, he's sore all over, his dignity is fatally injured, he's hungry."

"Too bad," said Ruiz absently. He looked again at the deck, could find no seams, no hatch through which the food might have appeared.

His own stomach rumbled, sending him an uncomfortable message. They were all hungry. Was the food safe? He picked up a flagon, unstoppered it, sniffed. Wine.

"This is what you must do," he told Molnekh. "Take Flomel a flagon, bread and cheese, a handful of grapes. Tell him we've already eaten; does he want any? If he asks where the food came from, tell him I discovered a cache of picnic goodies on the upper deck and broke into it."

Molnekh nodded. "He'll believe it. And if he survives his meal?"

"We'll all eat."

THEY ALL ATE, and the mysterious food did them no harm. Ruiz and Nisa again went to the upper deck, where Nisa leaned against the rail and watched the passing forest. Ruiz sat beside her and tried to puzzle out the meaning of their odd circumstances.

What were the possibilities? The simplest explanation—that they traveled with generous and benevolent hermits—seemed a farfetched absurdity. Why would hermits travel in such extravagant style? And if their habit was to provide free food, wine, and excursions to the general public, why were the barges not thronged with guests?

Were the barges simply traps of some sort, designed to capture the naive and footloose? Then they were remarkably ineffective, for such elaborate traps—as far as he could tell, the barges had caught only eight vagabonds, and five of those by the merest chance. Still, that explanation seemed most logical to him.

It occurred to him that he could test that theory by seeing if the barge would allow him to jump off. Not tonight—in the dark he'd find it difficult to avoid splattering himself on a tree trunk. Perhaps in the morning he could try.

Of course, if they came upon any sort of civilization, they would all debark, if that proved possible.

"Are you sleepy?" Nisa asked.

"A little," he said, surprised to find it true.

"Then tonight, you sleep first, and I'll watch."

He turned and pressed his cheek against her elegant hip. "Yes," he said.

TO HIS VAST surprise, he did sleep, deeply, lying on the bench with his head pillowed in Nisa's lap.

He may even have dreamed, though from long habit, he immediately suppressed the impulse to remember his dream when Nisa shook him awake. He surged from sleep and sat up, shaking his head. Had it been a pleasant dream, for once? He would never know.

The light was gray and cold and the air had a fragile daybreak chill in it. Ruiz was astonished to find the night gone; he had never meant to sleep so long. He stood up, looked out at the passing forest.

Nisa shifted awkwardly, as though her muscles were sore. "I wanted to let you sleep a bit longer," she said. "But I heard Dolmaero call."

"What's wrong?"

"Nothing serious, I'd guess—he didn't sound alarmed. Perhaps it's breakfast." She stretched, then rubbed her back and winced.

He touched her cheek. "You should have moved my head. You made a soft bed, but you shouldn't have made yourself stiff for my comfort."

She laughed and pushed his hand away playfully. "You made yourself stiff for my comfort," she said. "I want to do what I can. How many things have you done for me? I've lost count. But what have I done for you?"

"Much," he said, and meant it.

IT WAS INDEED breakfast—another tray sat on the deck. It held a plate heaped with still-hot muffins, a white bowl filled with pale blue hard-boiled eggs, jars of purple jelly and honey, a huge jug of some frothy pink juice.

Dolmaero stood beside it, looking vaguely triumphant. Molnekh looked ravenous.

"One mystery is solved," announced Dolmaero.

"Oh?" said Ruiz.

Dolmaero pointed up at the statue's belly. "It came from

there. The metal opened, the tray descended—hung from a thin rod. The tray reached the deck, the rod withdrew, the metal was as before."

" 'How' is explained, but not 'why,' " Molnekh pointed out. "But I'm not complaining. Who'd have thought such things could happen? For desperate fugitives, we're doing well."

"Possibly," said Ruiz. "In any case, we might as well eat before the muffins get cold." He picked up the tray. "Is Flomel well secured?"

"Of course," answered Molnekh in injured tones. "I carry out your instructions meticulously."

"In that case, let's go to the upper deck, where the view is better, and we won't have to listen to Flomel's whining," Ruiz said.

COREAN CURSED, AND kicked at the remnants of Kroel's head, an ill-considered action that left a stain on her armored foot and prompted a longer burst of invective. The cargo hold of her damaged airboat stank of death and burned insulation—and of the Mocrassar, who stood by the lock in a watchful posture.

Marmo floated forward on his repaired chassis and examined the hole in the engine compartment wall. "Vast luck," he muttered darkly. "Have you considered the possibility that he's just too lucky."

"None of your foolish pirate superstitions, Marmo." Corean turned a wrathful gaze on Marmo. "Instead, you might start formulating useful advice—since that's what I pay you for."

"Indeed." But he said no more then.

She went to the lock and signaled to Fensh to bring the repair mech from the survey sled. She ordered the Moc to remove Kroel's remains. As the great insectoid carried the body out, she shook her head violently. "He's done me a great harm financially. Now the phoenix troupe is broken, and who knows if the boat is repairable."

"On the other hand," Marmo said, "you were going to smash the boat into the cliff, until he prevented you."

She looked at Marmo thoughtfully, eyes cold. "Good of you to remind me, Marmo. I'm certainly glad I scraped you off the veldt, so that you could assist me in this manner."

"Sorry," he said in a subdued voice.

She nodded. "I'm going to give Fensh an hour to make an assessment. If he can repair the boat, I'll leave him here with his brother. He can bring the boat when it's ready; we may need the armament."

"All Ruiz Aw has is the splinter gun and a few pigstickers."

"Nevertheless. Now, since he may have contrived booby traps, you will explore the remainder of the boat. When it's safe, call me."

BY THE TIME they'd eaten their fill, the light was strong, and it had become apparent that the forest was changing. They saw occasional brushy clearings, and the trees were of more recent growth, as though the forest had been logged in the last hundred years or so.

"Look," said Nisa. "Is it a road?"

"So it seems." Ruiz studied the opening in the trees as it passed. A small landing abutted the canal. It lacked the ornamental features of the landing from which they had boarded the barge, but it was built of the same shiny pink granite. "Perhaps we should think about leaving—the road looks recently used. Maybe we're near some town where we can get better transport."

"Maybe not," said Molnekh, rubbing his belly. "And I have no objection to the accommodations."

"Oh?" Ruiz lifted his eyebrow. "Did you know that it's the custom on many worlds to provide a condemned criminal with a fine meal just before his execution?"

"It goes differently on Pharaoh," Molnekh said, but he looked shaken.

"Besides," Ruiz continued. "Corean will understand that we have embarked on this voyage. She'll catch up with us soon; before noon, if she's clever enough to overfly the canal before she sets her sniffers on us."

"She is not stupid," said Dolmaero glumly.

"No."

Ruiz considered that it might be time to see if disembarkation was possible. He rose, leaned over the rail, and looked ahead, hoping to see a fairly clear area for his experiment.

He was startled to see another landing drawing near, and

even more startled to see a large group of people standing on the quayside. He pulled his head back, turned to tell the others, and felt the barge slow.

"What is it?" asked Dolmaero.

"I don't know." Ruiz had no idea what to do. Until they were threatened, it might be a bad idea to show hostility. "We'll have to wait and see. I suppose."

By now the others had seen the landing, and there were no more questions.

They slowed to a drift. The barge drew even with the landing and they looked down at the crowd. It seemed to be divided between a large number of old people shrouded in what appeared to be black mourning cloaks, and a smaller group of almost-naked youngsters wearing colorful wisps of silk. The old folks wore grim faces; the young ones seemed to be celebrating some happy event—but no one looked up at Ruiz.

The focus of the sorrow or felicitations appeared to be a young couple who stood together on the bank. They were beautiful, in an unformed youthful way; they were obviously the handsomest couple in the festive portion of the gathering. They wore identical expressions of resolute anticipation —though Ruiz thought he detected a good deal of anxiety beneath that surface. Otherwise, they were naked, except for beauty paint and hair ribbons.

The barge bearing Ruiz and his people slid past; then all the barges stopped. The boy and girl stepped aboard, and, holding hands, turned and waved to the crowd. The old folks watched them stonily; the others clapped and cheered.

The young couple disappeared behind the statue's vast breasts.

The barges began moving again with a slight jerk, and the landing receded. Just before it disappeared behind them, Ruiz saw the old people begin to file away, and the young ones lie down on the grass in twos and threes.

Nisa colored and turned away. "How strange," she said. "Why would they wish to do that so publicly?"

Ruiz shrugged. "Another mystery." The whole spectacle had made him even more uneasy about their benefactors—it had the flavor of a decadent religious rite. Unsettling thoughts circulated through his mind. Were they captives of one of the numerous outlawed cults that infested Sook?

Some of those practiced extremely unpleasant sacraments. It was, he thought, time to see if they could leave the barge.

He turned to the others. "If we can, we should try to leave. I'm going to see if I can jump off. If I succeed, follow."

Molnekh frowned. "I'm not sure Flomel is that strong yet."

Ruiz shrugged. "He can't stay. Make sure he jumps quickly, one way or the other."

"As you say, Ruiz Aw."

"Be careful," said Nisa, her expression solemn.

Ruiz led them to the lower deck, where Molnekh untied Flomel and prodded him to the waist of the barge. Flomel glared at Ruiz with equal amounts of hatred and fear, baring his teeth in a defiant grin.

Ruiz ignored him, stepped to the gunwale, gathered himself. Just before he threw himself outward, a bell-like voice sounded in his head. *No*, it said calmly.

He couldn't arrest his movement completely, but the voice startled him sufficiently that he didn't hit the barge's containment field with as much force as he otherwise might have.

Still, the impact jarred the voice from his head. The field flared a brilliant yellow.

He rebounded to the deck, falling into a nearly unconscious heap.

The next instant he felt Flomel land on his back, punching at him. "Now's our chance!" Flomel shrieked. "Help me kill him."

Then Flomel's weight disappeared. Ruiz rolled to his feet, and saw Flomel curled up against the figure's knee, clutching his ribs, gasping.

Dolmaero was hopping up and down, holding his foot, grimacing with pain.

Ruiz grasped the situation quickly, though he was still dizzy from his encounter with the containment field. He nodded to Dolmaero. "Thanks, Guildmaster. There's a trick to kicking villains."

"So I see," said Dolmaero, setting his foot down gingerly and wincing.

"How is it?"

"Not broken, I think. . . ."

"Good."

Molnekh, looking somewhat less cheerful than usual, fastened the leash to Flomel, heaved him to his feet, and marched him back to the pit.

"Are *you* all right, Ruiz?" asked Nisa.

"More or less. But I'm afraid our cruise isn't over."

CHAPTER 7

COREAN lifted the survey sled from the slope where her damaged airboat lay, leaving Lensh and Fensh behind. Lensh waved up at her cheerfully and crawled back under the boat.

"Are you happier now?" Marmo asked.

Corean glared at him. "It'll take them three days to fix the boat, if they work harder than I expect them to."

"But at least it's repairable."

"That's something, I suppose." She flew toward the pass, covering in a few minutes the distance that Ruiz had taken hours to walk.

"What's the worst case? If he's reached the canal, he may have caught a barge, but the barges are slow. He can't have reached SeaStack yet, if he went south—and where else could he find high-speed transport? If he went north, the sniffers will catch him long before he reaches the IceGate launch rings."

Corean was still sullen. "You make it sound so simple."

"Isn't it?"

"I used to think so, but he's a slippery snake." Her mouth quirked downward, and she fell into a silence.

Finally Marmo spoke again. "Such a sour expression! If

you don't stop abusing your face, you'll lose it. Didn't it cost more than a dozen airboats?"

"It's guaranteed for a hundred years," she said—but she smiled with artificial brilliance, then smoothed her hands delicately over her cheeks. "Do you really think it might go bad?"

"No," he said. "I was just teasing."

She laughed, and the hard line of her mouth relaxed a little.

She frowned again when they reached the landing. "They've been here," she said.

Marmo peered through the armorglass. "Send out the Moc first. It's a good place for an ambush."

"I will . . . but they're gone. I feel it."

"Perhaps."

A few minutes later they stood on the landing, looking at a heap of empty food wrappers.

"I wonder how long they've been gone," she said, looking at her sniffers—two tall, spidery mechs equipped with olfactory analyzers and trank guns. One went striding off to the north and one went south.

"Maybe they didn't catch a barge; maybe the sniffers will catch them a few miles down the bank."

"Sure," Corean said scornfully.

The sniffers soon returned unsuccessfully, unable to pick up a scent. She was unsurprised. She raised the survey craft and drove it arrowing south. "It's a couple of days to Sea-Stack, even by the fastest barge," she said. "We'll take a quick run that way first. If we don't see him, we'll go north. If we can't spot him from the air, we'll come back here and set the sniffers."

"A good plan," Marmo said agreeably.

RUIZ HELD HIS aching head, while Nisa rubbed gently at his neck. That pleasant sensation couldn't completely distract him from the unhappy reality of their situation. They were the prisoners of unknown beings. They traveled toward an unknown destination, to face an unknown fate.

On the far side of the upper deck, in low voices, Molnekh and Dolmaero discussed the possible motives of their captors.

Dolmaero took a gloomy view. "They're slavers; what

else? In the wider universe, it seems that all are either slaves or slavekeepers."

"Would slavers feed us so well? Would you go to so much trouble to ensure the comfort of your slaves? Well, perhaps *you* would, Guildmaster, but you're not typical."

Molnekh was overly influenced by the culinary evidence, in Ruiz's opinion.

Dolmaero shook his head. "Perhaps it's no trouble at all. Many things I regarded as impossible seem to be easy here: flying, raising the dead. . . . Perhaps, for these folk, hot muffins and fresh-squeezed juice are as easy to provide as stale bread and water."

"It's a possibility," Molnekh said, looking unconvinced.

Ruiz ignored them and studied the forest. It grew increasingly less wild, interrupted more frequently with cutover tracts, cultivated fields, manicured pastures. Occasionally they passed habitations. Many were crude huts, some were hunting lodges built elegantly of wood and stone, and once they passed a palazzo built of some glistening blue ceramic material, all slender spires and graceful flying buttresses.

"What is it?" Nisa asked.

"A wealthy house," he answered absently. Just the place, he thought, to steal a good airboat. A bitter useless pang of regret touched him. Soon Corean would catch up to them, and then what would happen? Even if the containment field operated in both directions, Corean probably carried weapons powerful enough to breach it—certainly her Moc did.

The afternoon passed slowly. After a while, Dolmaero and Molnekh lost interest in their discussion. Molnekh went below to wait for the next meal to arrive, and Dolmaero sat stolidly, staring at the passing sights.

Ruiz felt a sense of dismal failure, and he could think of nothing to say to Nisa. She seemed not to take his silence badly, and he was grateful for her quiet company. He tried to think of a course of action, but nothing came to him, not even the most farfetched of ideas. He wondered if he had at last exhausted his ingenuity—a profoundly depressing possibility.

Finally, he was drawn from his dark mood by a change in the atmosphere, a feeling of imminence, a shift in the movement of the air. He heard an odd sound, like wind moaning through a tunnel. The forest ahead seemed to grow lighter, as if they approached a huge clearing.

Ruiz got up and went forward to the observation pulpit, followed by Nisa.

They were standing together when the forest ended and they emerged into sunlight and space.

His heart fell and lifted in one violent swoop.

"Oh. Oh," whispered Nisa. "What . . . ?"

Ruiz drew a deep breath. "The locals call it the Edge."

"You know where we are, then?"

"I think so."

The barges moved now through a barren rocky zone. Ahead, the world seemed to end, replaced by pale blue sky. The canal continued out into empty air, a long dark finger of still water, leading nowhere, apparently supported by nothing but the monocrete banks.

The barges began to slow, but it was obvious that at their present rate of deceleration, the barges would never stop before they reached the edge. The wind howled, blowing straight up past the lip of the cliff.

Nisa clutched at him. "Are we going to die?"

"Probably not just yet," Ruiz said hopefully. He was craning his neck, trying to get a glimpse of what lay below the cliff.

The barges slowed a little more, and the first one floated out into space. Nothing happened to it, and he felt Nisa relax slightly. Then the barge directly in front passed the lip of the cliff, also without dire consequence.

When their turn came, Ruiz saw what he expected to see.

Perhaps a thousand meters down and twenty kilometers away across a flat coastal plain a vast cluster of bizarre shapes twisted from the bright ocean far into the sky. They looked like nothing else in the known worlds, misshapen skyscrapers, or horrifically attenuated mountains—sometimes narrower at the base than at the top.

From this distance it was impossible to grasp the scale of these structures.

"What in the world. . . . How can so much water exist? It *is* water, isn't it? And those . . . are they buildings?" Nisa's eyes were wide.

"It's water, though not the kind you can drink. The place is called SeaStack."

She looked at him. "You've been there?"

"Several times."

"What manner of place is it?"

Ruiz sighed. "It's a city, of a sort. Or a thousand different cities. But mainly it's where star pirates are born, and where they go to die."

BY THE TIME the last barge had slid out into nothingness, Molnekh had come pounding up the ladder, pale with terror. Still, Ruiz noted with approval that Molnekh was able to move. Dolmaero clutched at the rail, face frozen and shining with sweat; he looked, for the first time since Ruiz had known him, incapacitated. Perhaps he was afraid of heights.

Looking back at the cliff edge they had passed, Ruiz felt a quiver of the same fear. The slab of black basalt seemed to drop away forever, and the plain was so far below that it didn't seem real—a panorama in a misty painting.

He took Nisa's hand and joined the others. "Don't be afraid," he said.

"Oh, of course not," Molnekh said, leaning cautiously over the rail. Apparently he was sufficiently in command of himself to be capable of sarcasm.

Ruiz grinned. "No, really. This is a device called a lock, unless I'm fatally mistaken. We'll be gently lowered to the plain, where we'll resume our journey."

"Truly?" Molnekh shook himself, attempted a smile.

Just then the barges, which had been motionless, shuddered and began to drop.

Dolmaero shrieked, then looked embarrassed. He unlocked his hands from the rail. "Startled me," he explained, but he looked a little calmer, now that they were no longer so dreadfully exposed.

The sides of the lock were the same gray monocrete that had formed the banks during their journey. As they dropped, the skinny rectangle of bright sky at the top of the lock rapidly grew smaller, and the barge's lights came on.

By that soft illumination, Ruiz noticed that the lock walls were marked by graffiti, apparently burned into the obdurate monocrete with energy weapons. The graffiti were in the main vertical, in script stretched by the speed of the vandal's passage. Many were the usual clutter of names and dates, but others were longer messages. Most of these were in unfamiliar languages and alphabets, but near the bottom of the great shaft, Ruiz saw one he could read.

Abandon hope, all ye who cannot swim, it said, and Ruiz laughed.

They came to a stop, the barges surging and rolling.

"I don't know which is worse," Dolmaero said. "Hanging from the sky or being buried alive."

A moment passed, then a great door levered up and the barges moved out into the sunshine.

The air was suddenly oppressive—fifteen degrees warmer and saturated with humidity.

Ruiz could smell the sea, and the stink of decay that always blew from SeaStack.

THEY MOVED NOW across long-cultivated fields, broken by occasional marshes and meandering streams. Here were a number of great manor houses, but the styles varied widely. Some were built in aggressively archaic forms, and in the fields surrounding these, overseers watched gangs of archetypical peasants labor in the mire. Other manors were confections of glass and metal, and the fields were full of gleaming mechs.

"What are they?" asked Nisa.

"The mechs? Just machines."

"Why aren't all the fields worked by mechs?" asked Dolmaero. "Surely they're more efficient than slaves?"

"Yes, they are—but these are hobby farms," said Ruiz.

Dolmaero seemed puzzled.

Ruiz tried to explain. "In the pangalac worlds, little food is grown—most of it is manufactured from elemental matter. These farmers are either hobbyists, or cater to the luxury trade."

Dolmaero shook his head. "So these farms are the property of rich folk, who play at farming? Very strange."

"Yes—well, rich pirates, which isn't exactly the same thing."

"And what is a pirate?"

"You've met one," Ruiz said. "Remember Marmo? He was once a pirate, until he retired to a gentler trade. Pirates are thieves, kidnappers, murderers; their arena is the void."

Dolmaero rubbed his chin thoughtfully. "They are then in the same line of work as yourself?"

Ruiz was taken aback. "One might say so, I suppose." He scratched his head. "But I commit my depredations under a commission from a legally registered business entity; perhaps that makes a difference."

"Oh, surely. I meant no offense." Dolmaero looked wryly skeptical.

Ruiz shrugged, and the conversation lagged.

The sun beat down, the air was breathless, and after a while, they all went to the lower deck, to find shady places under the belly of the statue.

IT WAS LATE afternoon before Corean caught up to them. Ruiz and Nisa sat together at the taffrail, gazing out at the flat landscape. The spires of SeaStack had drawn close enough to tower menacingly over them, and Ruiz had begun to hope that they would reach the city before Corean found them.

Then Corean's sled swooped past, ten meters off the ground, fifty meters out. It veered around and burned past again, and Ruiz imagined he could see Corean's dark hair through the armorglass bubble.

He jerked Nisa to her feet and ran for the pit, where they might get some protection. As he ran, he shouted for the others, who tumbled into the pit just moments after he and Nisa arrived.

"It's Corean, I'm afraid," Ruiz said.

Flomel tugged at his leash and fixed Ruiz with red eyes. "Now you'll get what's coming to you, casteless one," he said, gloating.

COREAN LAUGHED WITH genuine pleasure. "Wonderful," she said. She had seen Ruiz Aw and his Pharaohan slut running to hide under the testicles of the grotesque statue atop the barge. "You saw them?"

"Yes," answered Marmo. "Do you recognize the barges? I wonder who they belong to."

"No . . . but what does it matter? What should we fear from creatures who decorate their craft with such leering monstrosities? They must be primitives."

"Possibly."

She laughed again. "Though you must admit, Ruiz Aw's hiding place is strikingly appropriate."

Marmo made a noncommittal noise.

"Well," she said. "Let's see if they're stupid enough to surrender. If I can get the Pharaohans back in one piece, I can still salvage something from this fiasco."

She slowed her sled until it paced the barge and activated a loudhailer.

"RUIZ AW! I see you; no point in hiding. Come out empty-handed, and we'll put this unpleasant episode behind us." Corean's amplified voice was light and easy.

Ruiz peeked over the rim of the pit. The survey sled floated a mere twenty meters off the port gunwale; if only he had a ruptor, or even a heavy portable graser. . . .

"Come now . . . I admit to being hasty, before. I was very glad you managed to shut down the boat before my little fit of temper resulted in an unhappy accident. My people tell me the damage is not so bad."

A moment passed, then she resumed her persuasions. "I was hasty in sending you to the Gencha. Clearly your cleverness is too valuable a commodity to risk so foolishly. Now I understand what an enhancement to my business you'd be, truly I do. We'd make such a formidable team.

"You won't come out? Well, I don't blame you for not trusting me. I want to make amends, truly. The Pharaohans belong to me; send them out and you can go your way, no hard feelings—though I hope you'll change your mind and enter my service someday."

The sled withdrew a short distance. Flomel was smiling, as if he actually expected Ruiz to release him into Corean's custody. Ruiz was tempted to; Flomel deserved it richly.

"What next?" asked Dolmaero.

"She'll talk some more; then she'll start shooting. I don't think she's stupid enough or crazy enough to come on board after us—she'll content herself with cutting us to pieces from a distance."

Nisa clung to him with both arms, eyes shut tight.

Flomel gasped. "You won't let us go? Why? Why? You insist that we die with you?"

Ruiz sighed. "The others are free to turn themselves

over, but you and I, Flomel, we must live or die together. Besides, the barge won't let us go."

Molnekh shivered. "I'm not brave enough to risk her kindness, anyway. Guildmaster?"

"Nor am I."

Ruiz felt a black resentment against the slaver—not so much because she was about to kill him; he had never expected to die in bed. No, he hated her because she was stealing a life he might have spent with Nisa. He pulled her close and concentrated on the precious sensations of the moment: the touch of her body against his, her scent, the sound of her breathing. He succeeded in shutting away the thoughts of what might have been.

Corean spoke again, and now her voice was ragged with anger and anticipation. "All right. Keep the woman—my parting gift to you. But send out the others. You know they're my property!

"You won't?" A long moment passed, then the survey sled's weapons pod swiveled and its muzzles twinkled.

Ruiz pressed Nisa to the floor of the pit, covering her with his body. The barge's containment field flared brilliantly as the projectiles struck and an earsplitting screech assaulted them.

The attack ceased for a moment, and Ruiz felt the vibration of machinery, transmitted through the deck. He raised his eyes cautiously, and saw yellow fire lance out from the barge and touch Corean's sled. It tilted and wheeled away, staggering through the air in short uncertain arcs. It crossed several fencerows before plunging into a small bog.

Ruiz was on his feet, watching, fists clenched. With all his heart he hoped for a secondary explosion; it didn't come.

Soon the wreckage was lost to view behind them. On the barge, several impressive arrays of energy weapons rotated their barrels up and sank back into the deck, which closed seamlessly over them.

"Damn!" he said, caught between uncertainty and the elation of survival.

"What is it?" shouted Dolmaero, who still crouched in the pit with the others.

Ruiz sat heavily on the edge of the pit. "We're safe, for a time. But I'm afraid Corean may still be alive."

•   •

THE AFTERNOON MOVED toward sundown, and another dinner appeared. This time Ruiz was watching, hoping for an opportunity to penetrate the barge's interior. But the platter descended from a closed-off recess, big enough to hold the platter and nothing else.

Near dusk the barges neared the border between the freeheld lands of the coastal plain and the city of SeaStack. A customs fortress squatted above the canal, a fat armored spider of a building supported on delicate curving pylons.

"What is that?" asked Dolmaero.

"Customs. They won't bother us." The pirate lords who controlled most of the activities in SeaStack cared little who entered their watery city—newcomers were fair game, valued for what goods and skills they might bring. But the lords were much less easy about allowing folk to leave Sea-Stack . . . who knew what treasures they might try to steal away?

In fact, as their barge passed under the base of the customs fortress, they saw, in the outgoing channel, a small rusty barge tied up to one of the several inspection piers. Its crew stood facing a wall, hands on heads, watched by armed guards. Dozens of uniformed inspectors swarmed over the barge, waving detectors, prying up the barge's plating, burning probe holes here and there.

Their barges weren't stopped, as Ruiz had predicted, though as they moved out into the sunlight again at the far end of the fortress, several hard-looking men came out onto an overhanging balcony and gestured ambiguously at them. The pirates spoke together in soft voices, laughing softly, then went back into the fortress.

FINALLY THEY PASSED through a tidegate, out into the labyrinthine waters of SeaStack. Overhead, the towers twisted up into the darkening sky, blotting out most of it. The origins of the stacks seemed even less imaginable, seen up close. In places they rose from constructed bases, or at least shaped metal shone through the crust of age that covered everything. In other places, they seemed wholly natural in their random upward growth, stone and dirt and ancient trees hanging from the terraces that overhung the channels. The bases of the towers were riddled with caves and entryways, some at water level and some higher, some lit by brilliant security lights, others dark and forbidding.

The others stared, openmouthed. The craft that plied the scummy waters ranged from battered junks with painted sails and slave-powered sweeps, to the newest skimmers and needleboats. The people were as motley as their craft, representing every human variant. An occasional alien drew gasps of astonishment from the Pharaohans, who had seen few aliens during their stay in the slave compound.

Ruiz concentrated on remembering the route they took into the heart of SeaStack, and on trying to relate the landmarks to his memories of the pirate city.

CHAPTER 8

COREAN cursed, a low, bitter, monotonous stream. She hung upside down from the acceleration webbing, unable to see out because of the mud and vegetation plastered across the sled's armorglass bubble.

The craft shifted and subsided slightly. She cut short the curses. Time for that later, after she had somehow prevented the sled from sinking into the bog.

She slapped at the webbing releases, and fell sprawling onto the ceiling. The sled lurched again, and she felt a touch of fear. How deep was the bog?

She examined herself, waggled her limbs. She discovered no broken bones—though she ached everywhere.

She crawled to an upside-down flight panel, and peered at the readouts. She cursed again. The sled was dead; the blast that had grazed it had thoroughly fried the power and control systems.

She heard a clicking rattle and looked around. Marmo was carefully easing himself to an upright position.

"Are you functional?" she asked.

"I believe so," he replied. "How is the Moc?"

"Don't know." She got up and picked her way across the ceiling, back toward the cargo bay. When she pulled herself up through the hatch, she saw the Moc, standing by the burst-open lock. One midarm hung by a thread of chitin.

The insectoid bondwarrior seemed otherwise undamaged, and the midarm would regenerate—though the injury cut its firepower in half, since its midarms carried implanted energy weapons.

It swiveled its head to look at her, and she saw from the nervous rasping movements of its mandibles that it was preparing for combat. It bowed its head, a lightning flicker of movement, and bit off the encumbering remnant of its arm.

"What is it?" Corean moved to the lock and cautiously peered out through a crevice. She saw, beyond the cattails that bordered the bog, a line of peasant guardsmen staring at the sled. They wore plumed hats and carried archaic weapons: pikes, harquebusses, crossbows. Behind them an armored individual sat an elegant mech charger. The armor imitated steel plate, but Corean was certain it was of more advanced design, since it seemed not to weigh heavily on its wearer. The rider wore an ornate broadsword in a sling across the back. The charger, looking something like a steel horse with claws instead of hooves, seemed equipped with more potent armament; two blackened orifices opened in its breastplate.

Corean narrowed her eyes. Bad enough that she was stranded in the middle of a mudhole—all she needed now was an irate local squire.

The armored person rose in the stirrups and called out. "You in the sled! Come out, hands empty and in plain sight."

"Oh, sure," she said in a low voice. She settled her helmet on her head, flipped down the visor, and checked the toggles that held the collarpiece securely to the rest of her armor.

"Last chance," shouted the squire. Moments passed, and then flame coughed from the charger's breast.

A spinner charge hit the lock and fragmented, sending a hail of glass slivers into the bay. The Moc jerked, then looked at her. The slivers had shredded its doublet, but bounced off its carapace, which was as dense as the armor she wore. One of its great compound eyes had taken a grazing hit, and thick yellow fluid welled from the wound.

Corean bared her teeth. The peasants were moving forward, sinking knee-deep in the mire, raising their harquebusses. "First," she said, "kill the rider. Then the others."

The Moc nodded, and blurred into movement, hitting the lock and crashing it open. It was past the peasants before they had time to react. It took a diagonal veer, so as to avoid the charger's armament. The charger was very quick, however, and whirled to protect its rider before the Moc had quite cleared the bog. It fired again, but the Moc had already gone into an evasive movement pattern, so that the spinner missed. It detonated in midair, killing half of the guardsmen and maiming the rest.

Corean took her usual satisfaction in watching the Moc at its work, though the battle was decided in the first second. The Moc sprang, tearing the rider's head off with a rip of its remaining midlimb. It continued the motion until its energy tube pointed down into the charger's barrel. It triggered a short burst of energy, burning out the charger's interior mechanism, freezing it instantly—and then the Moc was on its way back to finish the surviving peasants.

It was, she thought, a wonderful thing to own such an irresistible juggernaut of destruction. She remembered the time she had ordered the Moc to spare Ruiz Aw. *Such foolishness.* She would never be so soft again; when next Ruiz Aw fell into her hands, he would die quickly. Or maybe not; maybe he would live for a long time, but wish he could die quickly. Yes . . . that would be better.

Marmo came to stand next to her, and looked out at the Moc standing immobile among mangled bodies. "What's this?"

"Local bog owner, who objected to our landing without permission."

"Ah. What now?"

She shrugged. "Lensh and Fensh will follow when they can. We could try for the manor house, but it's probably defended heavily—if we hadn't had the Moc, the squire would have taken us. These retired pirates have a lot of enemies—this one was well armed, despite his playacting with the guardsmen."

"Best to wait here and hope the squire has no friends to avenge him, then." He leaned out and examined the surroundings. "The bog seems shallow enough that we won't disappear into it."

Corean nodded. "Yes. Let's sit tight. A dreary wait—but

it'll pass. I'll spend the time considering how best to make Ruiz Aw suffer for his sins."

Marmo looked at her curiously. "He'll be in SeaStack by now. He'll probably be long gone by the time we get moving again."

She glared at him. "No! I will have him again—I refuse to believe that he can escape me. Besides, how would he get past the pirates' screening probes? Would they allow such a dangerous creature aboard one of their shuttles?"

"He fooled you," Marmo pointed out.

She snarled wordlessly, then spoke in a deadly monotone. "Yes. But the matter has gone beyond business now. And have you forgotten? He knows about the Gencha. What if he somehow finds out that it's not just a few rogues, what if he finds out what's really going on, and spreads the word through SeaStack? We'll be ruined, and one of the pirate lords will take the Gencha. We must be sure he's dead."

"I see," said Marmo. If he had forebodings, he kept them to himself.

WITH FULL DARK, only a few dim lightstrips illuminated the barges—just enough for safety. Ruiz noted that their captors had chosen dull discretion over the spectacular display of the night before, and he applauded their caution.

In SeaStack, wise beings attracted no unnecessary attention.

The night brought no relief from the heat, and Ruiz tried to ignore the rivulets of sweat that trickled down his body. The air must feel even stranger to the Pharaohans, he thought. They had spent their lives on a hot planet, but one with negligible humidity. Dolmaero seemed particularly affected; he mopped constantly at his broad face and his breathing had an unhealthy rasp. Ruiz hoped he wasn't getting sick.

"It's so tall," Nisa said, craning her neck to look up at a particularly high and twisty spire. The lower terraces, which began a hundred meters above the water, were strung with tiny green and blue pinlights. From these terraces a festive murmur drifted down, composed of an odd staccato music, laughter, and occasional screams of delight. Apparently a celebration was in progress, or perhaps the dwellers in this particular seastack sold entertainment.

Ruiz felt a stab of envy for the celebrants, and more than a little pity for himself. He contrasted his sad little group with the apparently carefree people above. The comparison made Ruiz's situation seem even more intensely unfair.

To distract himself, he began to tell Nisa about SeaStack. "It's even bigger than it looks—SeaStack is. Most of its habitats are below sea level—many of the folk who live in Sea-Stack have never seen the sun."

Dolmaero spoke up. "So you've been here, Ruiz? How much do you know about it? Do you have friends here, or allies?"

Ruiz laughed. "No one knows very much about Sea-Stack, not even those who live here. I may have met a few locals, one time or another, but even if we were free to seek them out, we might not find them. And if we did, they'd have no reason to help us." There were doubtless a number of League agents in SeaStack, he thought, but they would be in extremely deep cover, impossible to contact. The great pirate lords who controlled SeaStack were the League's bitterest enemies; any League agent who fell into their merciless hands could expect a miserable death at best.

He could think of only one person in SeaStack who might be persuaded to assist them, but Ruiz was reluctant to consider that possibility. That individual was hardly a friend, and he would be an ally only if his circumstances required such an alliance, or if Ruiz could force him to help.

Ruiz began to regret his openness with the Pharaohans. Were one of them to tell the wrong person all about Ruiz Aw, serious difficulties might arise. He'd had his attack of candor at a moment when he'd been almost certain that he wouldn't survive another day; still, he'd been ludicrously incautious.

"So," Dolmaero said. "You still have no idea who the barges belong to? Or what they want with us?"

Ruiz shrugged.

"I have a feeling it's nothing too terrible," said Nisa, surprisingly. Indeed, in the semidarkness, her face seemed unclouded by fear or uncertainty, and Ruiz wished he could be so optimistic.

Dolmaero shook his head doubtfully. "Has anything happened to us on this world that is not terrible?"

"Oh, yes," answered Nisa.

"What?" asked Dolmaero in a challenging voice.

"Hot muffins," said Molnekh, showing his large teeth in a grin.

"My resurrection," said Nisa. "And there *have* been other nice happenings." She looked meaningfully at Ruiz, and he felt his heart quiver pleasantly.

Dolmaero grunted noncommittally, but his eyes twinkled, and Ruiz saw that the rigors of the journey hadn't worn away all of the stout Guildmaster's good humor.

"I can tell you a little more about SeaStack," Ruiz offered.

"Please," said Dolmaero.

"All right. Have you wondered how it was built?"

"Yes."

"So does everyone else. When humans first arrived on Sook, SeaStack was already here, though inhabited only by animals and a few devolved aliens. The early explorers thought the spires were natural formations, until they found the first doors. The stacks are hollow, for the most part, but divided into millions of levels, corridors, shafts. No one knows how deep they go, but they tell stories of habitats two kilometers or more below sea level."

"Who made them?" Dolmaero's eyes were wide with wonder.

"No one knows that either, but I've heard several theories. Shall I tell you my favorite? Some say they're junked starships, stripped and left here before the land subsided, a few million years ago."

"Whose starships? The Shards?"

Ruiz shrugged. "Unlikely. Their tech level is unremarkable. No one builds starships that big. Maybe they were built by whoever the Shards took Sook from—though that was probably too recent an event."

No one spoke again for a while, and their faces were somber.

Perhaps, Ruiz thought, the talk of measureless eons had oppressed them. The first time he had visited SeaStack, he'd felt the same diminishment.

THE NOTE OF the barge's engines changed subtly. Directly ahead was a narrow gate at the foot of one of the smaller spires. In keeping with the decorative theme of the barges, the gateposts were tall phalli.

When they were a little closer, Ruiz saw that a low relief of intertwined copulating figures swirled around the posts.

Low red lights illuminated the dark water within.

Apparently they had arrived at their destination.

THE BARGES ENTERED a lagoon between steep cliffs of black alloy, drifted to a stop alongside broad metal ledges. The only sound was the scrape of the hulls against the landing, and Ruiz tried to force himself to a higher level of alertness.

Mooring posts rose from the landing with a whine of hidden motors. Toggles extended from the barges and locked to the posts.

In a moment all was still.

"What now?" asked Dolmaero.

Ruiz shook his head. "Who knows? Molnekh, go get Flomel. We should be ready."

Molnekh nodded and hurried aft.

Ruiz took Nisa's hand. She squeezed his hand and rested her head against his shoulder.

They waited.

A series of clicks sounded from the alloy wall directly in front of their barge; similar sounds echoed along the landing. With pneumatic sighs, a series of narrow blast doors levered up, one opposite each barge.

Almost immediately, folk began to leave the barges and enter the doors. From the trailing barge came the pretty young couple; from the barge just ahead came the three mismatched vagabonds. From the leading barge came a half-dozen people, cloaked in concealing white gowns.

Ruiz looked at their door. Blue lightstrips revealed a metal corridor, which curved into dimness after ten meters.

"Should we go?" asked Dolmaero hoarsely.

Ruiz studied the moorage. The surrounding vertical walls offered no handholds; they could not climb out. Nor could they swim to freedom. Despite the jocular graffiti at the Edge, no one with any sense swam unprotected in Sea-Stack's murky waters. Besides disease, poisons, hazardous currents, submerged machinery—there were the many scavengers that lived on the refuse discarded by SeaStack's inhabitants. The most terrifying of these were the margars, great armored reptiles big enough to swallow a small boat in one gulp—but there were countless others, ranging in size down to the tiny brainborers that infested the sewage outfalls and waste-heat exchangers.

What would happen if they stayed aboard? Ruiz sighed. He was pessimistic. Probably the barges would be fumigated for vermin—which they might well be considered, if they refused to leave.

"Let's go," he said, reluctantly.

THEY FILED OFF the barge, Ruiz leading. He disengaged his hand reluctantly from Nisa's—best to be ready to act. Behind her came Molnekh, leading Flomel, who cringed and rolled his eyes. Dolmaero brought up the rear, walking with slow dignity.

Ruiz paused for a moment before entering the doorway, to confirm that no other exits offered escape, then he shook himself and went in.

The corridor curved to the right and descended at a gentle incline. Their steps echoed strangely as they trooped along. After a bit, Ruiz realized that they were following a spiraling path into the roots of the spire.

Other than the blue lightstrips, the corridor was featureless, the floor free of dust, and the walls polished to a high shine. Clean cool air sighed from concealed ventilators; otherwise the silence was complete.

The corridor abruptly ended in a broad high-ceilinged hall. A serving mech waited for them there, its chassis a simple unmarked ovoid. It stood motionless until they had all entered the hall, then it spoke in clear unaccented lingua pangalac.

"Your rooms are prepared," it said.

"What does it say?" asked Dolmaero.

"Apparently we're expected," Ruiz replied in Pharaohan. "We're to have rooms."

"Or cells," muttered Dolmaero pessimistically.

"Perhaps."

"Come," said the mech, and inclined its chassis.

It led them to the first of a dozen doors. "Yours," it said to Ruiz.

The door swung open silently. Ruiz debated the wisdom of acceptance. He glanced about. No security devices were visible, but he had no doubt that they existed—their captors seemed fond of hidden weaponry. He sighed. What choice did he have? He started to lead Nisa inside, but a manipulator extended from the mech and barred her from entering.

"Each must be alone for now," it said.

Ruiz teetered on the edge of attacking the mech, but controlled the impulse. He smiled encouragingly at Nisa, lifted her hand, and kissed it gently. "It says we must have separate accommodations, Nisa. I think we should obey, for now. Be alert, and remember: There's always a way out, if we can be clever enough." Ruiz turned to Molnekh. "You'll have to release Flomel, I suppose. We'll rely on our hosts to control him."

He turned again to Nisa, filled his eyes with her.

Then he went inside and the door locked behind him.

HIS CELL WAS a small apartment, equipped with all the necessities and most of the luxuries a pangalac person might require. The walls shone with soft white light, the floor was of warm, slightly resilient softstone. A suspensor lounge occupied one corner. Across from it was a plush levichair, floating before a dark holotank. An autochef's stainless-steel louvers filled a recess in the far wall, just above a dining ledge.

Ruiz jumped when a door to his left slid open. Inside, a warm light beckoned, and he heard a splash of water in the shower enclosure.

He shrugged and went in to get cleaned up.

Later, wrapped in the soft robe the valet slot had delivered when he was finished, he sat in the levichair, studying the holotank. He was strangely reluctant to activate it. After all, he might learn something unwelcome from his captors, who obviously expected him to make use of the tank.

"Ah, well," he said finally. Then, "Activate."

The tank bloomed with random color for an instant, then organized swiftly into the scaled-down image of an uncannily handsome man.

He had a narrow fine-boned face and luminous green eyes. He smiled in a professionally friendly manner and spoke in a smooth baritone. "Welcome, seeker," he said. "Shall we introduce ourselves? My name is Hemerthe Ro'diamde. And yours?"

Ruiz saw little point in claiming an alias—the others would quickly prove him a liar. "Ruiz Aw."

"An interesting name. You're of Old Earth stock?"

"I've been told as much. Who can say for sure?"

Hemerthe smiled again. "True. We thought to seed the stars, but there have always been many fine vigorous weeds among us."

Ruiz was having difficulty following the thought. "I suppose," he said. "Will you tell me who you are, and where we are?"

Hemerthe widened his eyes in dramatized surprise. "You don't know? Why then did you board the Life-Seeker?"

Ruiz assumed he referred to the barge. "It was somewhat of an emergency—no other transport was available, and we were fleeing for our lives."

"Ah." Hemerthe's face smoothed out as he digested the information. "You did not, then, intend to seek refuge with us?"

Ruiz's curiosity was piqued. "Refuge?" They needed refuge, if the cost was not too high.

"This is the purpose of the Life-Seekers, to bring to us those who hope to be worthy of refuge."

That sounded less promising, as though there might be tests of "worthiness." "I see," said Ruiz, though he did not.

"Good. To return to your questions, I am the autonomous revenant of one of our prime founders, who departed his embodied life almost sixteen hundred years ago. And this is Deepheart, where immortal love defeats eternal death."

This speech was delivered with well-projected fervor; it had the ring of an oft-repeated motto. Ruiz searched his memory for anything related to a cult called Deepheart. Nothing definite emerged, but the name tickled at something in the depths. Sooner or later he would remember.

"Perhaps," Ruiz said, "you might be more specific?"

"Perhaps," answered Hemerthe tolerantly. "But first the Joined must discuss the meaning of your presence, and our response."

"Might I ask what sort of responses you might consider?"

Hemerthe smiled. "They vary widely. We might throw you to the margars who swim the lagoon's depths, or sell you to the slave pound uplevel. That's the usual fate of those found unworthy—which discourages the frivolous from crowding the Life-Seekers."

"Oh."

"Or, you might be offered refuge." Hemerthe was abruptly serious. "You have a certain hard beauty—if your mind matches your flesh, you may find a place among us."

Ruiz wondered if his smile had gone somewhat sour. "There are no other options?"

Hemerthe shook his head. "Rarely."

"Oh."

Hemerthe was suddenly brisk. "You may wish to assist us in making the others of your party comfortable. Their language is not immediately identifiable; can you help?"

"They're natives of Pharaoh; they speak the major dialect," said Ruiz, and gave the coordinates of the system.

"Thank you. We'll acquire an adaptor module in a few minutes; our datastream is well connected."

"Good," said Ruiz, in a hollow voice.

"Yes, a good start," said Hemerthe. "Now, sleep, recuperate, luxuriate. Prove to us that you can enjoy these simple pleasures."

Ruiz nodded.

Just before he turned to a cloud of glowing confetti and faded away, Hemerthe winked at Ruiz and said, "I was just teasing you, about the margars."

NISA ALSO TOOK advantage of the shower and the robe, but she had no idea what function the holotank served, so she ignored it until it chimed and filled with misty color.

The woman whose image condensed in the tank smiled reassuringly at Nisa. "Don't be afraid," she said in a soft clear voice.

"I'm not," said Nisa. To her surprise, she discovered that she was telling the truth. Was she becoming inured to wonders?

"Fine." It seemed to Nisa that the woman was as striking as Corean, in a different way. Her body, clothed in a clinging silky gown, was fuller, its contours more lushly female. She appeared to be somewhat older than Corean, and her smooth oval face had a time-polished beauty, a quality of confident experience—the sort of beauty, Nisa thought, that a face as perfect as Corean's would never gain. Nisa wondered how old the woman actually was.

"My name is Repenthe," said the woman. "What is yours?"

"Nisa."

"A pretty name. It suits you." The woman smiled, with what seemed genuine warmth. "You'll have questions. We've already talked to Ruiz Aw, who must be your leader. We understand that you boarded the Life-Seeker by mistake; we'll consider your status carefully. Meanwhile, I'm here to help you. Call on me anytime, by speaking the word *activate*."

Nisa thought. "Can you tell me who you are, and why you send out the barges? That's what you do, isn't it?"

"Yes; how perceptive of you. We send out the Life-Seekers to expand the breadth and strength of love available in Deepheart—which is the name of this place, our community."

"I don't understand."

"Not yet. But you will. Perhaps there will be refuge here for you—you are lovely, and we have evidence that you can love."

"Excuse me?" Nisa was having difficulty following the meaning of Repenthe's words.

Repenthe laughed. "Watch."

She faded away magically, and was replaced by darkness and the sparkle of tiny lights.

Nisa watched for several seconds, before she understood that the holotank was showing her a scene from the night before, when she and Ruiz had made love on the barge. She watched, trying to decide how she felt. Part of her was outraged—she had regarded those moments as private, as belonging only to her and Ruiz. But her body remembered the sweetness, and reacted. She felt her heart thump a little more strongly, felt desire simmer to life. She was compelled to admire the grace with which Ruiz touched her; there was nothing awkward in his movements—nor in hers, as if the intensity of the act had somehow lifted them beyond the inevitable small clumsinesses of lesser passions.

When the recording ended and the woman reappeared, Nisa felt a sharp stab of loss, which must have shown on her face.

"No, don't worry," said Repenthe. "Our tradition is that

seekers must rest alone on their first night in Deepheart, so you cannot go to him. But all will be well. I feel it strongly, Nisa. Two such lovers will surely find a place in Deepheart."

Nisa could think of nothing to say. She was pulled between anger and embarrassment—and distracted by remembered lust. She wondered if there was any way to make the woman go away, even though she should probably be formulating questions.

As if she had read Nisa's mind, Repenthe smiled and said, "Sleep now; then call me when you need me."

RUIZ RESTED UNEASILY, and woke to the smell of breakfast wafting from the autochef.

He ate slowly. He was buttering a last muffin when the holotank chimed.

The woman was tall and slender; her face had a delicate strength that made her beautiful despite the irregularity of her features. "Hello, Ruiz Aw," she said, as if they were old acquaintances.

"Hello. Who are you?" asked Ruiz.

She laughed, showing charmingly crooked teeth. "Don't you recognize me? I'm Hemerthe, of course."

Abruptly, Ruiz seized the memory connected to Deepheart, dragged it struggling to the surface of his mind. Now he knew where they were, and what the dwellers here wanted of them. *It could,* he thought, *be worse.*

"Ah," she said. "You *do* know of us."

"Yes, I think so."

"Good, good. Then you won't come to judgment in ignorance."

Ruiz seemed to be losing the thread again. "Judgment?"

"Follow the mech when it comes for you," said Hemerthe, and dissolved.

THE MECH PAUSED at the next door. When it slid back, Nisa stepped out. She saw Ruiz and rushed to him.

"A strange place," she whispered, holding tight.

"True," he said, smoothing his hand over her glossy hair.

Dolmaero joined them, then Molnekh and Flomel.

"How was your night, Guildmaster?" asked Ruiz.

"Tolerable." Dolmaero seemed pale and uncertain; Ruiz again wondered about his health.

"The food was excellent," said Molnekh, grinning.

Flomel had regained some of his former assurance; he said nothing, but Ruiz could see that his hatreds had lost none of their virulence.

They followed the mech through more featureless corridors.

Dolmaero paced along at Ruiz's side. "What have you learned, Ruiz Aw?" he asked.

"A bit. I remembered a little about this place, Deepheart, and those who dwell here. They call themselves the Sharers."

Dolmaero pursed his lips. "High-sounding . . . but indefinite. What do others call them?"

Ruiz smiled. "Several things . . . but most commonly, they're known as the Fuckheads."

"Indelicate," said Dolmaero. "What does it mean—in this context?"

"Yes, what *does* that mean, Ruiz?" Nisa gave him a little shake.

Ruiz considered how best to explain. "Well . . . these are folk who have deified sexual adventure. It's hard to explain briefly, but they claim to believe that the highest human purpose is to give and receive sexual pleasure. All their laws and institutions are aimed at promoting this belief."

Nisa shrugged. "I've known people like that. What's different about these Fuckheads?" Her expression seemed to say that she saw nothing so dreadful in such a belief.

Ruiz was a little taken aback, but he persevered in his explanation. "They go to great lengths to promote the diversity of their experiences—they believe that human beings are designed to take the greatest pleasure with new lovers, so they contrive ways to maximize the novelty of their couplings."

"They still don't seem so unusual," said Nisa.

Dolmaero looked faintly repulsed. "Then they do not form permanent bonds? They spend every night with a different lover?"

"Oh, it's stranger than that," Ruiz said.

They looked puzzled.

"They spend every night with a new lover—and also in a new body."

"How can that be?" asked Dolmaero.

"They have the means to switch personalities from body to body—as easily as you'd change your clothes. It greatly increases the sexual variety available to them. But they're always looking for new recruits, because . . ." Ruiz hesitated. How much should he tell them? "They never die—their minds live as long as they care to, so they must find new lovers somewhere, so as to avoid excessive repetition. Eternity's long."

They looked stricken. "Don't they ever grow old? Have accidents?" Nisa seemed overwhelmed by the thought; her eyes were wide with shock.

He took a deep breath. "In the pangalac worlds, people live as long as they can afford to—the wealthy could live forever, if they wished. And if the Sharers lose a body to some mischance, they can replace it with a brainwiped body from the slave market, or a mind-suppressed clone."

Nisa seemed to struggle with some tangential thought. Eventually she spoke in a small voice. "And you, Ruiz? How old are you?"

Ruiz cursed himself for failing to see the personal implications of his revelations. "I'm a little older than I look," he said gently.

No one spoke for a long time after that, as if they were having difficulty digesting these startling ideas.

CHAPTER 9

EVENTUALLY they reached a great hall. At the bottom of a broad ramp was a circular stage, occupied by a half-dozen strikingly handsome men and women, who waited in high-backed levichairs. Concentric semicircles of seats marched up into a darkness behind the stage. Only the first row was occupied—by the other travelers from the barges.

Ruiz and his group were the last to arrive. When they were seated, the woman who today was called Hemerthe rose to speak.

"Welcome, seekers," she said with a smile and a look that seemed to focus on each of them for a moment. "Today we'll discover how you may serve Deepheart. We must exercise discrimination; eternity is infinite in time, but not space. Some of you will be chosen to join us in eternity. Others will surrender their freedom to defray our expenses. In either case, you will contribute to the grandest experiment in the history of desire."

Cold comfort for those not chosen, thought Ruiz.

"So, without further delay, let us begin." She gestured, and a mech guided an autogurn down the ramp. On it squatted a Gench—perhaps the most moribund one Ruiz had ever seen. Its sensory tufts were dry and crumbling, its eye-spots were frozen in a random jumble. Its shapeless wrinkled body resembled a paper bag of moldy trash. Wires and tubes connected it to the autogurn, and on the gurn's lower tray, machinery clicked and bubbled. Trailing the autogurn were two security mechs, equipped with padded manipulators and catch-nooses.

"What is it, the creature?" whispered Nisa, voice full of disgust.

"Remember the Gencha I told you about? That is one, although it's certainly not a very healthy one."

"Do they plan to take our minds, then?" asked Dolmaero.

"I think not," replied Ruiz. "It seems too decrepit to survive a single such effort."

The three vagabonds from the next barge were seated to Flomel's left. The large young man glared at Ruiz. "Shut up," he said. "There should be no gabbling at this important moment."

Ruiz eyed him calmly. "You're right, no doubt," he said politely. "My apologies."

The young man thrust out his chin, looking pleased.

The Gench paused before the first of the white-robed seekers, and a thin tendril reached out from the Gench and touched the seeker's forehead. The man jerked, became rigid.

On the platform, the judges gathered around a podium dataslate. They murmured together, pointing at the slate and shaking their heads. A minute passed, then Hemerthe spoke. "I'm sorry," she said. "Your body is flawless, but your mind is superficial, inflexible, disengaged from your passions. You are ambitious, but not committed." She motioned, and the security mechs took the man by the arms and led him away.

The evaluations continued. Of the six in white, only two were accepted. The others were taken away in silence; apparently they adhered to a stoic code.

The Gench reached the plump young woman in the ragged finery. She turned up her face for the Gench's touch with a clear-eyed innocence that Ruiz found unsettling.

This time the judges took a long time to reach their decision. Finally Hemerthe stepped forward. "We're sorry, truly —this was a hard decision," she said. "Your body is imperfect, but bodies may be enhanced without difficulty. The trouble lies in your mind. You are passionate, you are intelligent, you have enthusiasm and the urge to excel. Your deficit is this: You have never been beautiful, you have not learned the lessons of adoration."

She lowered her head and waited for the mechs to take her. But Hemerthe wasn't finished. "Still, you're such promising material that we cannot simply sell you in the slave market. This we will do instead: We will make you beautiful and return you to your home. When you think you have learned what you must learn, come to us again, if you wish."

When the mechs came to lead her away, she clutched at the fox-faced old man's hand for a moment, then went, teary-eyed and smiling.

The old man was next. The judges' conference was short and Hemerthe's pronouncement definite. "You are one of ours," she said.

The large young man was judged in similar swift fashion, but not positively. "You're a joyless lout," said Hemerthe. "I wonder at your temerity, to present yourself to us."

He sat in shock for a moment. But when the mechs seized him in their padded clamps, he struggled and shouted out. "But you took the old man—that dried-out relic, who hasn't been stiff in more years than he can remember."

Contempt glowed in Hemerthe's elegant face. "Do you imagine that one's capacity to love depends on the health of one's glands? His body can be made new; your mind will never rise above its present brutish level."

The mechs dragged him away, cursing and flailing.

The judges disposed of the beautiful young couple quickly, but more gently. Hemerthe told them that they were too young, and had led lives of excessive comfort. "Still, should you someday escape or receive manumission, return to us. You may need nothing more than the experiences you will have as slaves to make you fit to join us."

They took it bravely, Ruiz thought—and they appeared to take Hemerthe's advice seriously. They *were* young.

The Gench touched Flomel, who jerked away and then fell limp as the Gench seized his nervous system.

The judges seemed to recoil in revulsion, faces stiff with suppressed reaction. "No," said Hemerthe, without explaining. "But we will wait a bit before we send you to the block

—the circumstances of your group are unusual—you did not volunteer for eternity."

Flomel shuddered and gasped when the Gench released him.

It moved on to Molnekh.

"No," said Hemerthe again—but this time she spoke in good humor. "Your passions are different from ours. If instead of Deepheart this were Deepstomach, you would be our king."

To Ruiz's surprise, the judges conferred at length over Dolmaero. But finally Hemerthe, shaking her head unhappily, pronounced him unfit.

"You were a beautiful young man, and could be so again, and you have the mind and spirit to dwell among us, but your loyalty is already given . . . and you cannot take it back."

Nisa clutched at Ruiz's arm as the Gench moved toward her, eyes wide with fear. Ruiz patted her hand. "Don't be afraid," he said. "It's painless and soon over."

The tendril sank into her forehead and she froze.

The judges crowded close to the readout slate, smiling and whispering among themselves.

"There's no doubt with this one," said Hemerthe, after lingering over the data. "She's very well suited to eternity. She has always been beautiful, a creature of sensuality. Her cultural matrix is fascinatingly alien. And she has the depth of one who has died a death. Delicious. We must have her."

Ruiz felt a bleak mixture of relief and loss. Surely, her existence in Deepheart would be better than the other possibilities that she faced—far better than her original fate, which was to play the phoenix for Flomel's conjuring troupe until she had died too many times. Better than dying with Ruiz in some SeaStack dungeon. Better than standing on the block in the slave market, to be auctioned off to some downlevel harlotry.

But she would no longer be his. And he was certain she was capable of a wider life, that Nisa possessed more important talents than her enthusiasm in bed. Would it not be a form of bondage, to spend the eons rutting in Deepheart? No matter how much pleasure it brought, might there not come an emptiness, finally?

The Gench withdrew its tendril from Nisa and came toward Ruiz. He felt the cold sting as it penetrated his skull, and then nothing.

WHEN HE AWOKE, it was a slow painful process. He struggled toward consciousness, as though he swam up through some dark viscous substance.

He opened his eyes and saw that he had been returned to his apartment/holding cell. Hemerthe sat beside him, a look of grave concern on her elegant features.

"You didn't tell us you were League," she said.

He coughed and cleared his throat. "I'm freelance. Contracted." The weakness of his voice frightened him.

"In any case, we almost killed you. The old Gench disturbed the mission-imperative, and it claims it triggered the death net. For some reason it stabilized before it went critical. You're lucky to be alive—and I have no explanation for your survival."

Ruiz coughed again. "I'm wearing it down," he said.

Incomprehension masked her. "Whatever. At any rate, we want you. You and the woman."

"Why would you want me?"

Hemerthe looked at him oddly. "You don't know? You have no introspection? You have a strange and rich mind, Ruiz Aw. We have nothing in Deepheart like you. You're a sensualist and a stoic, a libertine and a Spartan. You make love and deal death with equal facility. You are that most intriguing of candidates, a genuine mystery.

"Some of us fear you; these would have destroyed you while you recovered. They say you will loose a cancer of nihilism among us that will eat away our collective soul. But most of us are eager to learn from you. Come to us and you will never be alone again."

"No," said Ruiz.

"No? The alternative is slavery."

"I've been a slave. It's a temporary condition, for me."

Hemerthe became agitated. "We cannot force you to join us—then you would be a cancer indeed. Can we bargain with you?"

"I have things I must do."

"The mission-imperative? We can deal with that. The Gench is too feeble to remove the net, it claims, but it can clean away the mission-imperative—and then the net will gradually break down."

"It's not just that," Ruiz said. He felt a sudden flood of terror, which he strove to conceal. To stay down here in Deepheart forever, with nothing but the endlessly repeated pleasures of impersonal sex . . . it suddenly seemed to him a horror. What must it be like, to be buried alive in a grave of eager flesh? "I have other responsibilities."

"What are they? I tell you now, the woman must stay. She may protest initially, but our reading of her character assures us that she will soon adjust—and be one of us. You might be able to resist our persuasions; you're much older and harder than she is. But she won't."

"I'm not so sure."

"No matter," said Hemerthe. "She must stay. But it's you we most desire. Tell me why you object so much. Many risk slavery to come to us, but you reject us without hesitation. Why?"

Ruiz sat up, feeling a little stronger. "Perhaps I cannot submit myself to only one pleasure. The prospect seems tedious—to do the same thing always."

"Oh, you misunderstand us. Do you think we spend all our time in bed? No; we humans are not so vital; we would soon grow ill. We have other interests, like anyone else. We have the standard entertainments: vid, emotigogue, psychskew drugs. Hobbies are popular. I myself breed flamefish; also I make traditional porcelains—though I must admit, my bodies vary in aptitude and dexterity, so that the quality of my work varies and sometimes I'm frustrated. Still, one day we all will learn to make porcelain, as my spirit circulates through all our bodies."

"That's very nice," Ruiz said, "but I fear I would feel diminished. . . ."

"No, no. It's obvious you do not understand us at all. Please listen; you cannot know what it's like," she said. Her face lit, and her gaze had an inward quality. "I know, you imagine that what we seek is the small hardwired thrill that comes of copulation with a stranger. I know what they call us, above. The Fuckheads; correct? No, it's so much more than that. You must trust me; the sensation builds, through body after body—you penetrate and are penetrated, you tangle your flesh with his, then hers, and then another, and another, until you begin to feel what we prize above all, a consuming identity with all the other great souls, a sense that you have loved the universe, or as much of it as is possible for a human being to encompass. You cannot know what it is like." She glowed, and against his will Ruiz was moved by the intensity of her emotion.

"Yes," he said. "But . . ."

Abruptly her mood shifted. She seemed angry; she bared her perfect teeth and spoke in a harsh voice. "We can make you wish you had joined us. We could sell you to a downlevel bloodstadium. There you might live forever, too, but you will kill and be killed every day. Wouldn't you rather love and be loved?"

Ruiz said nothing.

"Or," she continued, "we can hurt the ones you care about. We can sell your friends into hard lives. But if you come to us, we'll set them free."

Ruiz shrugged. "Free? Alone and naive in SeaStack? Not much of a bribe; how long would they last?"

She drew a deep breath and regained control. "I'm sorry," she said. "I spoke in anger, foolishly. We would do nothing so vengeful, if you did not join us. We're civilized people. Still, the SeaStack slave market is an open one, and the bloodstadia would bid heavily on you; so I would guess."

Ruiz could think of nothing to say. He considered his prospects. If he did not stay, if he somehow escaped and thrust himself out into the brutal world of SeaStack and attempted to fight his way home, would he survive? Unlikely. Even so, the prospect of immuring himself in Deepheart's eternal sexual frenzy was a dreadful one.

Above all, he thought, in Deepheart he would lose forever that special connection he had found with Nisa. Once in a thousand years he might lie with her, if they both dwelled in Deepheart, but it was unlikely they would ever again be together in the flesh they wore now.

He tried to explain. "Have you ever noticed that there are great differences between people who have lived everywhere, who have walked the soil of a dozen worlds and the pavements of a hundred cities, and the folk who were born in the house their grandparents were born in, who spend all their lives in one place?

"The city folk," he said, "they're clever and versatile and adaptable, and often the stay-at-homes envy them their breadth of experience. But there are advantages to staying in one place forever, too. The setting takes on an importance, a depth, that it never has for the travelers . . . and in that stability, people can come to know themselves more deeply. Sometimes they can think larger thoughts. Do you understand what I'm saying?"

She smiled. "An interesting analogy, to be sure. I think I know what you're saying, and why you might feel that way —but it's hard to keep them down on the farm. You are no bucolic, after all; how many strange worlds have you walked? Though I'll admit it; few human beings are as intimately connected to their bodies as you are to yours—that's one reason we want you so badly. We can learn much from you. But at least, I'm pleased to see that your objections are based on more than just blind fear."

An idea came to him. A chilly revulsion resided in it, but he forced himself to consider it anyway.

"Perhaps we can make a deal," he said.

She smiled and hugged him. "I hope so. What do you propose?"

He drew back slightly from her embrace, but she didn't appear to notice. "I'd have to discuss it with Nisa first, before I can formulate my offer. Will you arrange it?"

She looked at him with suddenly cautious eyes. "There will be no opportunity for escape, Ruiz. We know your capabilities; we've taken stringent precautions."

He shook his head. "You mistake me."

"And we must watch you constantly. There will be no privacy."

"I understand," he said.

THE MECH LET her into his apartment and closed the door, leaving them alone.

Nisa threw herself into his arms. "I thought you had died," she whispered, arms tight around him. "When the monster touched you, you threw yourself back, and your face was someone else's. The monster fell off its cart and shrieked. When they took you away, you didn't seem to be breathing."

He pressed her to him, oblivious to the spycells that surely watched. "I'm all right. Are you?"

"I'm fine. They've treated me well. My rooms aren't as

nice as the ones Corean kept me in, but I won't complain."
She giggled.

He led her to the couch. "Sit with me. I must ask your
opinion of a plan."

She looked surprised, as if she'd never expected to be
asked for counsel. "Heroes never ask the princesses what to
do."

"This is no goblin tale, Nisa," he said, smiling. "But first,
tell me. Have they explained what life would be like here?"

"Yes," she said, looking down. "They have."

"And how do you feel about staying?" Ruiz asked this
with a sudden trembling uncertainty, though he strove to
keep his voice calm. Suppose she wanted to stay?

She tilted her head and looked up at him. "I must explain
something to you, Ruiz. On Pharaoh, I lived for the pleasures of the flesh; I kept slaves whose sole purpose was to
bed me expertly, on the nights when I couldn't find anyone
more exciting."

His heart grew heavy and he looked away.

"But," she continued, "things are different now. Had the
Sharers come to me then, I'd have gone gladly to them.
Now, no. I have you." She laid her hand against his cheek.
"I do, don't I?"

"Yes," he said gratefully.

"They explained to me, Ruiz. I would never be with you
again in the way we are now. Our bodies would go to other
minds, and our minds to other bodies. I would lose you,
wouldn't I?"

"In a way. But you would be safe here—Corean would
never find you."

She drew back from him slightly. "You want me to consider this seriously?"

He nodded.

Nisa sighed and stood up. She walked to the autochef and
operated it expertly. When she came back, she carried two
beakers of a pale yellow wine. "Here," she said, offering one
to Ruiz.

She sat and sipped her wine for five minutes, staring at
the wall, ignoring Ruiz.

Finally she turned to him and spoke in a careful voice.
"Let me ask you: If we escape Sook, will you take me with
you to your home? Will you let me be your companion, for
as long as we both are satisfied with each other's company?"

Her face seemed utterly composed.

"Yes," he answered. He felt a sudden uncomplicated joy.

"Then I do not wish to stay here." A lovely intimate smile curved her mouth.

"You understand that there are many dangers yet? That we may be captured by Corean, or by other enemies?"

"Of course," she said, a little scornful. "Do you think me so unobservant? I *have* noticed that you attract difficulties. Still . . . you've so far survived them, which must mean something."

"Perhaps. Well then, here is the proposal I will make to the Sharers."

He told her his idea. First she was puzzled. When he explained it so that she grasped its essence, she shivered. "It's so strange, Ruiz. So strange. Can you trust them to act honorably?"

"I hope so. I've already done so, in fact; they're listening to us right now."

"Oh."

They sat together in comfortable silence for a few minutes. "I've noticed something," she said. "You haven't called them Fuckheads in a while."

HEMERTHE STOOD BEFORE them. "You realize, of course, that we had already considered this possibility. In a way, you offer us nothing that we could not take without your permission."

"That's not entirely true," said Ruiz. "Your Gench will have told you that my mind is heavily self-circuited. Many areas of memory are locked down; if you simply take a copy of my mind and clone a body to hold it, you'll be faced with the same difficulty you now have. You wish my willing participation, or so you claim."

Hemerthe drew a deep breath. "Then let me see if I have this right. You two will permit us to take an impression of your total personality matrices, and will freely donate clonable cells. You, Ruiz will undertake to unlock the inaccessible areas of your mind, so that your replicant will be completely open to us."

"I make no guarantees that my replicant will be any happier about staying," said Ruiz.

"I understand. We're not worried. It's the self-protective

aspects of your mind that we were most concerned about—otherwise you're perfect. But what do you demand in exchange?"

"When the procedure is complete, you'll release us: Nisa, Dolmaero, Molnekh, and me. You will provide us a boat in good operating condition and personal weapons. You will remove the mission-imperative from my mind. You will buy the slave Flomel from me at a fair market price—and he's valuable, a conjuror from Pharaoh. Finally, you'll give my friends a datasoak, so that they can learn the pangalac trade language. They speak only Pharaohan now, which would sabotage any chance they might have to survive in SeaStack, if something happens to me."

Hemerthe laughed. "It seems you value yourself highly, Ruiz Aw. But apparently you trust us to keep our bargains."

Ruiz shrugged, feeling a sickly helplessness. "I can find no alternative to trust. I'm afraid I've grown unresourceful in my old age."

Hemerthe patted his shoulder. "No. Your instincts are still sound. We will agree to your terms; they are small things to us."

Gradually, Ruiz began to feel a bit better. After a long while, he asked, from a rare urge to make polite conversation: "How long before the new Ruiz and the new Nisa will walk in Deepheart?"

Hemerthe grew animated and prideful. "Oh, we have the best tech this side of Dilvermoon. We grow the cells in dispersion, and then use nanomanipulators to construct the body, cell by cell. None of that primitive embryo-acceleration for us. How long? A week, ten days at the most. A few days more to embed the personality."

This information gave Ruiz an odd chill. "Then I must leave immediately."

THE FOUR OF them stood on the landing, in the steamy SeaStack sunlight. Tied fore and aft to the mooring rings was a low sleek boat, powered by a silent magnetic propulsor. Its cockpit was covered by an armorglass bubble, now raised.

Dolmaero studied the boat with puzzled eyes. "I confess, Ruiz, I find this latest development even more astonishing than your capture of Corean's airboat. How in the world did you win our freedom?"

Ruiz shrugged uncomfortably. "I sold a bit of myself. And a bit of Nisa. And all of Flomel." In the safety pocket of his new unisuit was a cylinder of Dilvermoon currency, fourteen hundred paper-thin iridium wafers. An energy tube was strapped to his forearm under the sleeve, operated by implanted muscle sensors. He wore a splinter gun at his belt, carried a tiny pepperbox graser tucked into each of his high boots. Here and there about his clothing he had hidden other weapons: knives, a stun rod, a monoline garrote.

"Which part of you and Nisa did you sell," asked Dolmaero.

"A part that doesn't show," Ruiz answered shortly. Nisa squeezed his hand.

"Ah." Dolmaero drew back slightly, as if in apprehension. "Well, the new language you bought for us is a remarkable thing. I find myself thinking thoughts that had never occurred to me before."

"Me too," said Molnekh. "It's not a comfortable feeling, Ruiz Aw—but I suppose you had a good reason?"

Ruiz turned to Molnekh. "If somehow I should be unable to interpret for you, how would you manage?"

Molnekh rubbed his chin. "I hate to even consider the notion. We yokels, here on this weird world without Ruiz Aw's protection? No, I can't imagine such a disaster."

"Nor I," said Dolmaero.

Ruiz smiled. "Well, time to go," he said. He stepped down to the speedboat's deck. The boat rocked, sending ripples across the still black waters of the moorage. "Come," he said, raising his hand to help Nisa aboard. "Let's get moving, before the Sharers change their minds."

When Dolmaero and Molnekh were seated in the aft bench, and Nisa was secured beside Ruiz, he pressed the toggle that lowered the bubble. The control slate lit, and a faint hum came from the propulsor. He touched another switch, and the mooring lines retracted.

He took the yoke and the boat powered away from the landing, leaving a frothing silver wake.

When they were outside, heading into the twisting channels, Nisa shivered, looking back at the carved gateposts. "It's such an odd feeling, Ruiz. To think that our second selves will live forever in Deepheart, doing things that I cannot quite imagine. . . . It's upsetting and yet . . . we two will live forever, in a way."

Ruiz nodded, already preoccupied by his plans. He had tried to put away the speculations that now disturbed Nisa. His mind still felt raw, and somehow less well connected to the world, as if some crucial disintegration had occurred when he had released the locked-down areas. He felt a little out of control, as though his thoughts were no longer entirely his servants, as though they no longer obeyed the boundaries he had always placed around them. His mind seemed, as it had not in so many years, to be unknown territory. Perhaps, he thought, it was partly because the weight of the mission-imperative was gone, leaving him a little light-headed and unfocused.

Whenever his attention strayed, and he began to imagine the clones slowly developing in their gestation tanks, he shifted his thoughts to other matters.

Nisa spoke again. "It's strange, Ruiz. I wonder if what I feel now is anything like the way that peasants feel, when they must sell their children to the slavetaker or let them starve."

There was such a forlorn tone in her voice that he put his arm around her and pulled her close. "We made a hard choice, but it's done. Who knows; their lives may be far sweeter than ours."

CHAPTER 10

B Y the time Lensh and Fensh found Corean, two days
after the crash, she was thoroughly sick: of the bog,
of her companions, of the stink of death that soaked
through every rent in the sled's hull, of the sour odor of her
own unwashed body.

The airboat approached cautiously, and though she was
pleased to see that the feline brothers were showing signs of
prudence, she was also impatient to be done with the bog.
No one had molested them and she had seen no sign of life
around the manor house . . . but who knew when the survivors, if they existed, might muster sufficient courage to try
to avenge their losses.

"Hurry," she shouted, waving from the broken lock. But
the brothers circled the site once more, apparently scanning
for booby traps, before they landed the boat at the edge of
the bog, a fastidious distance from the carrion scattered
about in front of the sled.

Without waiting for Marmo and the Moc, Corean
stepped out and began to wade through the thigh-deep mire.
She arrived at the boat's lock, just as Lensh cracked open
the armor and stuck his short-muzzled head out.

His eyewhiskers rose quizzically. "You seem the worse for wear, mistress."

She snarled wordlessly at him, and shoved past, bound for the closest hygiene station. She wanted a shower, more than anything but Ruiz Aw's death.

When she discovered that the brothers had yet to fix the boat's ruptured plumbing, her anger filled the boat, so that no one dared speak, not even the brothers, who ordinarily refused to be intimidated by her displeasure.

"Where to, mistress," asked Fensh, finally. "Home?"

She turned unbelieving eyes on him. "Are you mad? Home? No, to SeaStack, as fast as you can."

RUIZ DROVE THROUGH the less-traveled channels of Sea-Stack, following a dimly remembered route. The channels grew increasingly deserted. They met with none of the common hazards of SeaStack: junior pirates practicing their future trade, press gangs for the pirate fleets, lunatics seeking violent entertainment.

The others had nothing to say, which left Ruiz free to formulate—and then discard—plan after plan. The difficulties were many. The launch rings of SeaStack were controlled by the pirate lords, who exercised a rigorous security. If Ruiz attempted to buy passage on an upbound shuttle, all sorts of uncomfortable questions would be asked. *Who are you? What were you doing on Sook? Are you in any way connected with the Art League, or with any other supra-system legal entity?* Their brainpeel tech would undoubtedly be better than Corean's; naive to assume that he could fool them. And what if Corean were to broadcast a reward for their capture? That was not an unusual tactic for slavers seeking escaped property.

The only other launch rings in SeaStack were owned by various alien embassies, who were if anything more paranoid than the pirates.

If they were allowed to leave the city, they might attempt a coastwise journey, west to the Camphoc Protectorate, where a mercantile center and associated launch complex existed. But such a voyage would be dangerous; though some local commerce moved along that route, it was preyed on by pirate trainees in search of on-the-job experience.

They might attempt to steal an airboat, which would convey them to any of a thousand neutral launch rings—but in SeaStack thievery was a way of life, and anything as valuable as an airboat would be elaborately protected. And leaving would still be problematical.

Several overland routes suggested themselves, but they all had their particular hazards—and Corean might more easily find them, outside the protective complexity of SeaStack's warrens.

Ruiz shook his head wearily. He needed help, as much as he feared the risks implicit in such assistance. He knew of only one place in SeaStack he might look for help—but he would certainly be asked to pay a price for it. He hoped it wouldn't be too high.

He tried to stop thinking, to give himself to the simple enjoyment of his new freedom. Who knew how long it would last? Gradually he succeeded.

An hour later they pulled under a low broad archway, which spelled out, in letters of wrought iron, "The Diamond Bob Pens." Inside was an anchorage crowded with a variety of boats, from armored gunboats to sleek speedneedles to ragged wood-hulled junks.

Ruiz turned to the others. "Do you trust me?" he asked.

Nisa smiled. "Of course."

"Why not?" said Molnekh, and then he shrugged.

After a time, Dolmaero nodded cautiously.

"Good," said Ruiz. He gestured toward the landing at the innermost wall of the anchorage. Two security mechs stood sentry on each side of a heavy blast door, now closed. "I need to leave you all in a safe place, while I go and try to arrange passage offworld. This is the only such place I could think of."

"What is it, Ruiz?" asked Nisa.

"It's a slave pen," he answered. "It caters to transient dealers who need a place to keep their stock while they make more permanent arrangements."

Their faces fell. "Oh," said Nisa in a small voice.

"Please," he said. "Don't be afraid. No one will harm you here, and even if Corean locates you, she'd have to raise an army to get you out. These pens are sanctioned by the pirate lords; she'd have to be insane to antagonize them."

"She *is* insane, Ruiz," said Nisa.

"Not *that* insane," he said, and thought: *Or so we must hope.*

A moment of uneasy silence passed, and then Dolmaero spoke. "And what will happen to us, if you do not return?"

"That's a possibility for which I have no solution." The procedure followed by the pen was to keep the merchandise until the prepaid fee was exhausted—and then, after a short grace period, to sell the stock in the open market.

"Is it possible you'll not return?" Dolmaero spoke with reluctant determination.

"Anything can happen," said Ruiz. "But truly, Dolmaero, I don't know what else to do. You don't understand what a dangerous place SeaStack is; you wouldn't survive a day unprotected. There are hotels, but their security is a joke—Corean would have no trouble locating and recapturing you, if I left you there. I'll deposit sufficient funds for a week's maintenance; I'll surely be back before that."

"I believe you," Dolmaero said heavily. "But I'm worried. To have no control at all over one's fate . . . it's not a happy feeling. Still, I suppose that even in the worst case, we'll be in no worse condition than we were when Corean had us."

"Can't I go with you?" asked Nisa.

"I'm sorry. I'll probably meet with trouble; I'll be more likely to deal with it successfully if I don't have to worry about protecting you."

She dropped her gaze. "I understand," she said.

The speedboat drifted toward the landing. "I must ask you all to play the appropriate roles. Speak when spoken to, keep your eyes down, look defeated. Will you do this?" Ruiz looked at each in turn; they nodded. He looked especially long at Nisa, then, concealing the movement beneath the boat's dashboard, squeezed her hand gently. He dared make no other gesture of affection. They were doubtless being watched by the pen's security monitors.

"Above all, say nothing that the monitors might interpret as inappropriate for slaves. Be consistent and you'll be safe."

The boat touched the landing and attached its mooring linkages. Ruiz drew his splinter gun and made herding gestures. "Out!" he shouted. "All out now!"

The Pharaohans debarked onto the wharf, shoulders sagging believably, faces slack with misery. Ruiz followed, springing nimbly out and pushing them toward the personnel lock set into the wall next to the blast door.

The mechs watched them without interest, stunrods

lifted in casual readiness. The lock slid open and they were inside.

A long steel corridor, dimly lit, stretched away into darkness. At ten-meter intervals, flashing signs pointed down side corridors. The signs indicated the quality of accommodations and the availability of vacancies in that area of the pens. At five-meter intervals, surveillance cameras and automatic weapons pods scanned the corridors.

"It's self-service," Ruiz said. He moved his group down the main corridor for several hundred meters, until they had passed beyond the minimum-service section of the pen.

The lights were brighter and more frequent, the floor was covered with soft carpet, and soothing music began to play from hidden speakers. But the weapons pods were still in evidence.

Ruiz turned down a side corridor and found three adjacent cubicles. He ushered Dolmaero and Molnekh into the first two, pressing his palm to the green touchplate of the identifier, then offering his eye to the red retina lens. He dropped a half-dozen Dilvermoon currency wafers in each slot.

Lastly, he opened the door to Nisa's cubicle. She went inside meekly, but then she turned and stood looking at him, hands clasped, eyes huge. She didn't smile.

When he pressed the door closure, he felt a wound open in his heart. He struggled with a dreadful feeling that he had just seen her for the last time. *No,* he thought. *It'll be all right.*

But his hopeful thoughts had a cold insubstantial texture.

COREAN REACHED SEASTACK just before dark. She sent Fensh up to man the ruptor turret; SeaStack was a dangerous place, even for folk in an armored airboat.

As they crossed the invisible border between the coastal plain with its manors and follies, into the thick air of SeaStack, they were hailed by a pirate gunboat, which swooped toward them out of the setting sun and ordered them to heave to.

Fuming at the delay, she told Lensh to comply.

The gunboat slid alongside, all its weapons banks aimed at their flank. The vid chimed and she punched the activate stud.

A scarred old face stared out at her. "Identify yourself," the pirate said languidly.

"Corean Heiclaro and crew." She stared back truculently —she had never before been interfered with on her infrequent trips to the pirate city.

"Business in SeaStack?"

"Business," she snapped.

"Ah," said the pirate, smiling a wintry smile. "Well, I see by my dataslate that you're not unknown here in SeaStack— if you're who you say you are. So you may pass."

"How gracious of you."

Now he laughed, as if she were a rude but not very bright child. "I must warn you, we cannot be so gracious if you attempt to leave SeaStack. Conditions are presently unsettled—all departing visitors are subject to brainpeel. Are you certain your business here is compellingly urgent, Corean Heiclaro?"

She snarled and clicked off the vid.

"*Are* we certain, Corean?" asked Marmo.

She didn't bother to reply.

"Where shall we stay?" asked Lensh from the pilot's seat.

"Take us to the Jolly Roger. We may as well plot our revenge in comfort."

"Excellent choice!" exclaimed Lensh, licking his furry chops.

The Jolly Roger was a hostelry patronized by wealthy pirates and their offworld clients, who might include folk on Sook to ransom kidnapped loved ones, or mercantilists in SeaStack to buy pirated cargoes, or mediafolk there to interview famous marauders for the vid conglomerates. It had a reputation for reasonable safety, as long as patrons maintained their own stringent security.

They left the airboat in a locked, heavily hardened revetment. Corean ordered Fensh to remain on board, to his irritation—but she was taking no chances.

Their suite was satisfactory; with separate bedrooms for all of them, and a separate entryway where the Moc might be sealed away from sight and the worst of its odor.

After her shower, Corean felt a return of confidence and a slight lessening of urgency. She lounged on a large divan, wrapped in a warm robe, while Lensh expertly combed out her hair.

"What now?" asked Marmo.

"In the morning, we'll visit the slave markets. Ruiz Aw will have sold the others by now; he'll need cash, and they hamper his flexibility."

Marmo made a skeptical sound. "Are you sure? When he took the boat, I got the very strong impression he valued the woman." Marmo rubbed at his neck, as if remembering the touch of Ruiz's knife.

"Nonsense. He'll get rid of them—it's what I'd do, and he's not so different from me."

RUIZ DROVE THE boat at its highest speed, westward through the dark labyrinth at the heart of SeaStack. The night concealed him, and turned the waterways into dimly lit canyons, traveled only by other unlighted vessels. Several times Ruiz avoided collisions only at the last instant. He began to worry that his concentration was faltering.

He had hoped that in hiding the Pharaohans in as safe a place as he could find, he would feel a release from the weight of responsibility that had descended on him since he had arrived on Sook. But in fact he felt the burden more heavily than before. He could not completely clear his mind; he kept foreseeing dreadful possible futures. In his mind's eye, he saw Nisa waiting in her cubicle as the days passed . . . until one day the guards came to take her to the market. He wondered if she would be angry with him, if he died before he could return for her. He hoped so—it would be easier for her if she could fix her bitterness on him.

He shook his head violently. Maudlin useless thoughts. He felt a sudden fierce annoyance with himself. If he couldn't focus his energies any better than that, he deserved failure.

The anger washed through him in waves, cleansing away all those soft emotions that were of no use to Ruiz Aw now —leaving in their place nothing but a cold hard knot of purpose.

NISA SAT ON her thin mattress and wistfully remembered the luxurious apartment she had enjoyed in Deepheart. Her present accommodations didn't delight her. The cubicle walls were barren steel. A single overhead glowplate shed a harsh light on the few furnishings: a straight-backed chair, a dry cleansing stall in one corner, a screened toilet in the other, a food hopper and water tap next to a small mirror. Another locked door was set into the rear wall. Above the mirror was a flatscreen vid—a few minutes before, an androgynous face had appeared in the screen and explained the room's facilities, then informed her that twice a day she would be permitted to exit her room through the back door, to mingle with her fellow prisoners for a supervised social period.

She looked at herself in the mirror, and in that still beautiful but slightly haggard young woman found it difficult to recognize Nisa the favored daughter of the King. What had changed? The eyes were deeper, somehow, as if they had seen more strangeness than a person of her station should ever be expected to endure. The mouth was as soft and lush as before, surely—though something about it looked bruised, and the curvature was ambiguous, neither a smile nor a frown.

She thought about Ruiz Aw, that oddly wonderful man. Did she indeed trust him, as she had claimed when he asked her? He was such an enigma; sometimes she thought that his motives were mysterious even to himself.

"Just like everyone else," she said out loud. "Nothing so remarkable about that."

An ugly suspicion had crossed her mind more than once since she had stood looking into his hard expressionless face, as the door to her cell closed. Each time she thrust it away from her, ashamed; still, it wouldn't go away. What if Ruiz had chosen this way of getting rid of her and the others?

"No!" She would not believe it.

Not yet.

RUIZ SLOWED THE boat, and picked his way through the corroding remnants of some ancient girderwork. Blackened metal snags rose from the oily water, thrusting jaggedly into the night mists. He was in the decaying center of SeaStack, where its most depraved and least fashionable denizens laired. The stacks here were in bad condition, some half-collapsed into the sea, others leaning together, supporting each other in precarious stability. Almost no lights showed above the water, though occasionally the boat slid across a patch of sickly luminescence shining up from the depths.

Ruiz looked for landmarks, trying to match his memory of his last visit here with the confusing shapes he moved through.

There! That snag; its outline vaguely reminiscent of a man crucified upside down—he remembered that. He turned the boat toward a low tangle of rusting beams and saw the opening where he expected it.

He passed under a rough arch of skeletal alloy beams, into an anchorage occupied only by an armored gunboat, its gleaming hull half-submerged, moored to a snag.

He swung the boat and circled the airboat, admiring its bulbous engine pods, its three dorsally mounted graser turrets, its midships row of missile launchers. If only he had the equipment to disable the boat's security system, his troubles would be over. But that was wishful thinking, he reminded himself. If the boat belonged to Publius, as he suspected, it would be protected by cunning wards indeed.

He sighed and let his boat drift toward the makeshift dock at the innermost edge of the anchorage. He could only hope that Publius still controlled the stack, and that his creatures would allow Ruiz to enter unmolested. Perhaps they would mistake him for a customer—in a way, he *was* a customer.

The boat kissed the dock with a small clang of metal, and Ruiz stood up. He raised the boat's armorglass bubble and set its security monitors. He was painfully aware of the boat's inadequacies in that respect, but he had no time to upgrade its alarms and traps. The first competent thief who happened along would steal his boat—he could only trust that it wouldn't matter—one way or another.

He chained the boat to the dock, and trotted off into the cave-riddled darkness beyond the anchorage, looking for the monster-maker.

PUBLIUS'S LABYRINTH WAS as eerie as ever. The walls were carved of ancient meltstone, a rusty black veined with thin ribbons of some murky crimson glass. The low ceilings supported a patchy growth of luminescent moss, which shed an uncertain blue light on the dank floor, its pools of stagnant water and slime-slick stone.

Ruiz moved as silently as he could, ears straining for any evidence that one of Publius's monsters lurked in a nearby passage. But at first all he heard was the drip of water, and very faintly the rumble of vast engines deep below. Still, he carried the splinter gun in one hand and kept his energy tube ready.

As he penetrated farther into the labyrinth, the passages grew narrower, the junctions more numerous and confusing, the light dimmer. He hoped he hadn't forgotten the safest route; it had been a long time since his last visit.

In some places the luminescent moss had died out entirely, and Ruiz moved through the velvet blackness with exquisite caution, fearing with every step that he might put his foot down on something that would bite it off. He began to hear unpleasant sounds: faraway roars, the pad of heavy feet, the sigh of things breathing in the darkness. None of the sounds necessarily meant anything dire; the labyrinth had erratic acoustics, and it was possible that none of Publius's monsters were close to him.

He began to feel oppressed by the weight of the stack above him; to worry that it might choose this moment to yield to gravity. He knew it was an irrational fear; the stack had stood at its present precarious angle for a million years.

The air was hot and steamy, thick with stinks. As he went deeper he more frequently came across small heaps of carrion rotting here and there along the corridors—unsuccessful monsters, or the remains of other visitors, perhaps. Fresh droppings were a continual hazard; Ruiz could ill afford slippery boots.

He was beginning to wish that a monster would appear, so that he could stop anticipating and *act*.

When the thing came rushing out of the side passage, he realized what a foolish wish that had been.

It was tall and muscularly slender, with a vaguely humanoid torso and the head of a long-jawed reptile. Its arms were oddly articulated, with too many joints, but its claws were long and sharp, and it leaped toward Ruiz, arms reaching out to tear at him.

He snapped up the splinter gun and squeezed off a burst that tore diagonally across its chest. It fell forward, still intent on grabbing Ruiz, but he ducked under its arm and dodged to the side.

The splinters must have severed its spine, because it could only drag itself after Ruiz, scrabbling with its claws for purchase on the floor. It tried to speak, cursing or praying. The half-formed words were almost understandable.

Feeling a little sick, Ruiz put another burst between its yellow eyes. It died slowly; after he had left it behind, he could still hear the slow scrabble of its claws, the scrape of its scaly limbs against the stone.

He tried not to think about what he himself might become if Publius was in a bad mood, as he often was. Ruiz had no great claim on Publius's charity, if indeed it existed. He could only hope that the monster-maker would be willing to grant him a favor, or to sell him one at a price he could afford.

He had never understood Publius's devotion to his lunatic art—Publius appeared to be human, but Ruiz couldn't imagine what it must be like to live inside Publius's head. And the last time Ruiz had seen Publius, the monster-maker had entertained himself by telling Ruiz what interesting creatures he might carve from the raw material of Ruiz's body.

Ruiz shuddered. Until this instant, he had forgotten just how much he detested and feared his old comrade-in-arms.

COREAN COULD NOT sleep, so she sat up in her luxurious bed and ordered Lensh to bring her a flagon of soporific-laced hot milk and a plate of butter cookies. While she waited for the drug to take effect, she occupied herself by running the bedroom holotank through the offerings on the public slave market, beginning with the merchandise to be offered the following day.

She first assumed that Ruiz Aw would be sufficiently clever to offer his wares under false names and provenances, to prevent her from tracing the offerings before he had sold them and gone his way. So she set up the search parameters to select for lowtech Hardworld inhabitants with performance art skills. She was sure that Ruiz would be unable to resist the temptation to get a good price for his prizes, and if he sold them as unskilled primitives, he'd get next to nothing for the men—though the woman would bring a decent price from the downlevel harlotries.

The open market in SeaStack was vast, however, and she paged through a hundred images and stat sheets without success—every slaver in SeaStack seemed to be overstocked on primitive performers: raindancers from Pueblo, flame-singers from Hell II, beastbreakers from Silverdollar, passionplayers from GoldenEye.

Her eyelids were drooping, and she'd seen only a fraction of the catalog. Just before she gave up, she decided to see if for once Ruiz Aw had been stupid. This time she searched with a single new screening parameter: merchandise originating on Pharaoh. Instantly, the hard arrogant face of Flomel appeared in the holotank, gazing disdainfully at nothing.

She clapped her hands in delight, and read the stat sheet. When she reached the ownership line, she frowned. An entity called Deepheart Corporation now owned Flomel—Ruiz Aw had been unnaturally quick again. Still, she would enter a preemptive bid on Flomel, and tomorrow she would wring him dry of any useful information. She tapped the transfer codes into her dataslate, and was rewarded by seeing the ownership line ripple and display her name.

Thus encouraged, she continued her search, and was surprised to find no mention of the others. Was Marmo right, after all? Had Ruiz again done the utterly unpredictable, and set his companions free? Or even more inexplicably, was Ruiz continuing to protect them?

No. She shook her head in vigorous denial. He couldn't possibly be that foolish, and so she would soon regain her property.

And then she would find Ruiz Aw.

CHAPTER 11

RUIZ was very close to the center of Publius's labyrinth now. He had taken a hundred turns, walked
for kilometers. He had seen no other monsters, and
now he no longer expected to encounter any; the monster-
maker used his failures to patrol the outer passages of the
maze, thus discouraging uninvited visitors. But he prohibited these creatures from returning to the laboratories where
they'd been born, so as not to repulse the paying customers
who came to see his marvels.

The lighting had improved; the moss was supplemented
now by an occasional glowplate, and the floors were cleaner
and drier. Ruiz began to worry about his reception. Would
Publius even agree to see him—or would he simply have
Ruiz ejected or killed? He became so involved in this unhappy speculation that he was a little slow to notice the
oncoming shuffle of many feet, and he almost collided with a
party of merchants, who were evidently just leaving the inner sanctum with their purchases.

He slipped into a dark side passage, just an instant before
the point guard came around a curve. He stepped to the wall
and became still.

They did not see him, and he was unimpressed with the

party's vigilance—he could have effortlessly killed the half-dozen guards and taken their merchandise, which was carried in two large cloth-shrouded cages, by eight sweating litter bearers. The three merchants were Grasicians in elaborate pink bell-suits, wearing fashionable jeweled masks and carrying pomanders against the stench of the corridors.

Ruiz wondered what horrors they had bought from Publius.

When they were gone, he went on, and shortly reached the high-ceilinged rotunda at the center of the labyrinth.

The lighting here was mercilessly bright, and a trio of Dirm bondguards waited at Publius's security lock, a monocrete and armor structure over the elevator that would carry Ruiz down into Publius's domain.

They instantly aimed heavy grasers at Ruiz's chest. He stopped, raised his arms, displayed his empty hands, then clasped his hands atop his head. "I'm here to see Publius," he called, and waited.

"Name?" demanded one Dirm.

"Ruiz Aw."

"Purpose of visit?"

"Business."

At the mention of business, the Dirms relaxed fractionally. The one who had spoken to Ruiz whispered into a lapel communicator.

After a moment, it raised its weapon and gestured for Ruiz to approach, but the others' aim never wavered.

The first Dirm slung its graser when Ruiz reached him, and expertly patted him down, relieving Ruiz efficiently of most of his arsenal of personal weapons. Then it used an odor analyzer/detector to deprive him of the rest.

When it was satisfied that he was as innocuous as possible, it stepped back and said, "You may reclaim your possessions on your return."

Ruiz fervently hoped he would return—and that he would return wearing the same shape that he now wore. But all he said was "Thank you."

It nodded and pressed a switch on its controller armlet. The armored blast door slid aside, then the decorative grill of the elevator. Ruiz stepped inside, and watched the grill slide shut. The gleaming palladium filigree suddenly resolved into a montage of howling faces, almost human faces, stretched into bizarre shapes by terror.

Ruiz shivered, and wondered if he had been wise to seek out Publius.

But it was too late, so he concentrated on refining his story as he dropped swiftly down into the roots of the stack. He seemed to fall forever, and he began to worry that Publius planned to dump him into the unexplored levels below his laboratories.

The elevator decelerated violently enough to make Ruiz's knees buckle a little—probably a little joke. Publius had an eccentric and relentless sense of humor.

The doors slid aside, to reveal Publius standing in the foyer with arms spread in welcome. Or he thought it must be Publius, though the body Publius wore was unfamiliar— a tall lean body with a supercilious aristocratic face. Surely it was Publius; who else had that uniquely demented gleam in his eye?

"Ruiz," shouted Publius gladly. "Can it be? My old friend, come to visit me at long last?"

Ruiz stepped cautiously from the elevator. "Publius?"

"Who else?"

Ruiz allowed Publius to fling his arms around him, and managed a brief embrace in return. Publius apparently didn't notice his lack of enthusiasm; he held Ruiz by the shoulders and examined him, eyebrows jiggling up and down with curiosity.

"Still beautiful, I see," he said to Ruiz approvingly. "You're wasted as a leg-breaker for the League. I always tell you this, I know, but I'll tell you again: find a way to become notorious, then sell your clones. You'd be a rich body-source in no time. I'd buy one myself, make a pretty snakeweasel of you, sell you to some wealthy old woman for a lapdog."

Ruiz swallowed his revulsion. "I'm not a League contractor anymore, Publius."

Publius laughed, a low-pitched sound, oddly reminiscent of water draining into a sewer. "Oh, sure. Don't worry. I'd never tell anyone you're League—though I don't blame you for being cautious—this *is* SeaStack, after all."

"No, truly," said Ruiz. "I'll never work for them again."

"Oh? I'm astonished—an adrenaline addict like you, swearing off murder and pillage and high wages? What in the world has happened? Are you dying? Have you fallen in love?"

"Don't be silly," said Ruiz, straining for conviction.

"You're right, you're right. What could I have been thinking of?" Publius laughed again. "You're the famous Ruiz Aw, a paragon of mindless self-sufficiency, never tempted by the softer things of life, ruthlessly devoted to your own intermittently flexible code of ethics." There was a sour undertone to Publius's voice now, and Ruiz feared that he was remembering their time on Line, when Ruiz had deserted the cadre of freelance emancipators commanded by Publius.

"Ah . . ." said Ruiz, grasping for a diversion. "How have you been?"

"Well might you ask," shouted Publius in a booming voice. "How long has it been since the last time you came crawling to blackmail me into doing you yet another favor? Thirty years? Forty? Much has happened, my art has flowered, my fortunes have waxed, my power is substantially enhanced, though not enough, never enough." Publius had discarded his pose of good humor, and his ugly essence shone through his new flesh. "But what's that to you, eh? What do you want of me now, Ruiz Aw? Old friend."

"Nothing too elaborate, Publius," said Ruiz. He strove to show no fear or resentment, though he was terrified.

"No? I'm astonished. So, what is this 'nothing too elaborate'? And what can you pay for it?"

Ruiz took a deep breath. "I need transport up to the Shard platforms, for myself and three slaves. I can pay a fair price."

Publius made an airy gesture of dismissal. "Nothing more than that? The simplest thing!" His face writhed into a mask of disbelief. "Are you mad? What makes you think I could do such a thing for you. The pirate lords are currently in the grip of a massive paranoiac hysteria; did you not know this? My customers fume in their hostelries, unable to leave, and their goods stink up the place until the customers are driven to try to return them. I've had to kill a baker's dozen of complainers in the last twomonth alone—can't have them tarnishing my reputation."

"I hadn't realized," said Ruiz dismally.

"Just got into town, eh? Well, how grand that you thought of me first. Come, come . . . we'll tour the labs and talk." Publius pasted a grotesquely sly look on his face and winked, apparently finished with his brief rant. "Things are never so bad as they might become, eh?"

He put his arm around Ruiz's shoulders, and tugged him from the foyer, into a world of white tiles, stainless steel, and horror.

Publius's laboratories were extensive, covering thousands of square meters—and always teeming with activity. The monster-maker's creative passion was only matched by his lust for wealth; the two drives conspired to push the labs to their maximum output. It always astonished Ruiz that the pangalac worlds' appetite for monsters could keep pace with Publius's mania for production—it was another illustration of the ungraspable immensity of the universe and the unknowable diversity of the countless folk who crowded it.

Publius led him past a railed-off pit arena, in the depths of which dozens of stocky ursine warriors hacked and stabbed at each other with long knives—snarling, white fangs gleaming, inhumanly quick. "Elimination trials," Publius said, by way of explanation. "We started with over two hundred experimental scions. In another day or so, the best will emerge—though we'll run the trial a few more times, to eliminate the possibility of flukes. But they'll do well for some berserker prince on a rich Hardworld, won't they?" He beamed in a parody of fatherly pride. "They'll have to wear muzzles, perhaps, but nothing's perfect. On the other hand . . . you're good with a pigsticker, aren't you, Ruiz? You wouldn't last two seconds against the feeblest of these."

Against a great support column was a bank of upright vitro tanks, their contents concealed by a screen. Publius paused here and slid the screen up, revealing three adult humans, two men and a woman. These had the puffy formlessness that characterized tank-grown clones, before they were decanted and conditioned, but Ruiz could see that they would be handsome. All of them had Publius's coloring, and suddenly Ruiz realized what they were.

"Yes," said Publius. "They're me. Insurance. If I ever go, they'll be decanted and set at each other. The strongest one gets my identity."

Ruiz was horrified. What if they decided to cooperate? Could the universe survive a triad of Publiuses?

Technicians scurried past, shoulders hunched and eyes down, as if they feared their employer as much as Ruiz did.

They passed a series of one-way windowed cubicles, each

containing a different variety of joyperson. Some of them seemed to be no more than human men and women, their somatypes modified toward some animal standard. There was a slender languid lizard girl, who groomed her eyescales with a long forked tongue. In the next cell was a young boy with a face like a mastiff, his body muscular and bowlegged. They passed an armless woman with a bald shapeless head, her soft white skin glistening with mucus. An androgynous creature stroked feathery antennae; it had a segmented thorax and a tubular proboscis curled on its chest.

But others were much stranger. They appeared to partake of the characteristics of aliens for which no analogue existed on Old Earth—though Ruiz knew that their genetic material derived primarily from human DNA. Publius was a purist in that way. He averted his gaze from latticed tentacles, stony silicoid carapaces, pulsing masses of stringy yellow fiber. There was even a lumpy creature covered with Gench sensor tufts, gasping through trilateral mouth slits. The symmetry was maintained with three plump breasts, three vaginas.

The Gench-like creature made him shudder, and a wave of disorientation passed over him. He felt the death net stir . . . and then stabilize. He had avoided thinking about the Gencha since his arrival in SeaStack, apparently for good reason. He wondered how many more near misses he could stand, before either the net decayed or he lost interest in survival.

"Samples. See anything you'd like to try?" Publius slapped him on the back, laughed his strange bubbling laugh. "No, no, I'm teasing you; I know you're a devoted prude."

They passed surgeries, in which white-coated technicians operated lamarckers, carving cloned bodies into new shapes. Other spaces held DNA keyboards, where Publius's employees created new races of monsters, for clients who were willing to pay extra for reproductive functionality. Banks of half-gestated clones floated in clear nutrient baths, autogurneys trundled back and forth, some carrying grotesque corpses, others bearing anesthetized monsters in various stages of completion.

And over all, thick enough to gag Ruiz, was the special stink he associated with Publius and his works, a miasma of organic stenches and chemical wafts, of riotous life and casual death, of creativity and dread.

Finally they reached the apartments Publius used when in residence at his laboratories, and they passed from frenetic activity into silent isolation.

Publius slid the lock shut, and turned to Ruiz, a look of weary contempt blooming on his face.

"So, will you threaten me again? Will you never grow tired of hanging over my head, a ruination waiting to strike me? You cannot live forever; have you no mercy?"

Ruiz adopted a humble tone of voice. "You gave me no choice, Publius. If I failed to take precautions, you would instantly destroy me. I regret as much as you do that you confided your origins to me—had you not, you wouldn't hate me so virulently, and I wouldn't be forced to threaten you."

Long ago, over a campfire on Line, a badly wounded and delirious Publius had told Ruiz his greatest secret—that he had been born in a Dilvermoon Holding Ark and was not, as he had claimed, the bastard of a noble Jahworld family. Ruiz had never completely understood the intensity with which Publius defended his pretentions, but he had realized their importance to Publius when the monster-maker tried to murder him, years later. In self-preservation, he had filed a posthumous memorandum, which would be broadcast over the public datastreams, in the event of his death or disappearance.

In later years, he had begun to worry that Publius had lived with the possibility of exposure for so long that it no longer gave Ruiz any leverage over him. "Truly, I wish you could convince me that my precautions are unnecessary."

Publius grunted. He moved across the rug-covered floor of his public room, and took glasses and a decanter from a cabinet. He poured, offered a snifter of pale lilac liquor to Ruiz. "Well, at least you can drink with me without fear of poisoning. Few can, eh?"

Ruiz nodded and sipped.

"I'm such a bad boy," said Publius, sitting on a deep-cushioned sofa and gesturing Ruiz to a nearby chair. "Now: escape. Where's your expensive little starboat? The Vigia, isn't it? My memory is a wonder!"

"Hidden on a faraway world. I arrived on Sook a stowaway."

"Somehow that seems appropriate," said Publius. His eyes had lost some of their customary fey brilliance; he seemed a more ordinary man, for the moment. "And what was your mission, if it's no great secret?"

Ruiz shrugged. "Not anymore. I was hired to sniff out a poacher on a League Hardworld."

"And did you succeed? No, a foolish question, eh? You never fail, do you?"

"I know who the poacher is," said Ruiz.

"You see, I was right." Publius took a mouthful of liquor and swilled it around noisily before swallowing. "So, let us suppose you get up to the Shard platforms—you then plan to take commercial transport?"

"Yes."

"Ah. Well, as I said, the pirate lords are hysterical, at the moment. They've apparently stumbled across a big secret. . . . They don't know what to do about it. Some argue for destruction, others for exploitation. Does it surprise you to learn that I know the secret too?"

Ruiz shook his head.

Publius laughed his odd laugh. "Nothing about me surprises you, does it? Perhaps that's why I don't squash you like the insignificant bug you are; you help me to maintain a certain perspective. I'm going to exploit the secret, of course, if I can get my hands on it. Tell me, how does this sound: Emperor Publius, the Emperor of Everything?"

Ruiz hardly knew what to say. "What's the secret?" he asked, finally.

Publius giggled. "Why, it's a *secret*; didn't you hear me?"

"Oh."

Publius adopted a businesslike expression. "Now, I don't say it's impossible to leave SeaStack now, but it's exceedingly difficult. Expensive. Dangerous. I might be able to help you—but you must perform a service for me first. No, don't bother to wave your terrible revelation at me. I no longer care; I've outgrown my origins by so vast a margin that it no longer matters what they were." Publius smiled a rapacious smile. "Such a promising omen, that you should arrive after all these years, just as I need someone exactly like you."

Ruiz grew suddenly weak with apprehension. "What," he croaked, "do you want me to do?"

"The simplest thing, for a slayer like you," Publius said. "I want you to kill a man."

IN THE MORNING, Corean took Lensh and Marmo into
SeaStack's major auction pit—the proctors refused to allow
the Moc inside, so she left it outside the security lock.

Flomel was being kept in one of the small independent
pens adjacent to the pit, so she went there first, satisfied the
ident processor that she was Flomel's new owner, and
opened the door to Flomel's holding cell.

The conjuror was sitting on his narrow bunk, shoulders
slumped in dejection, when the door moved aside. He
glanced up, saw Corean.

A range of unexpected emotions slid across his face. She
had expected to see terror and abasement, instead he appeared first astonished, then delighted.

"Noble Lady!" he said in glad tones. "I knew you would
come."

Corean was a bit taken aback. Either Flomel was much
cleverer than she had supposed, or he had absolutely no
grasp of the situation. In either case, she was willing to play
along. "Did you?"

"Oh, yes. I knew you wouldn't abandon me. The others
were corrupted by that snake oil vagrant, but not me. I
know Ruiz Aw for what he is, a casteless slayer, a thief, a
troublemaker. I knew my faith would be rewarded . . .
and here you are."

Corean smiled. She was willing to accept his cooperation,
though she had intended to punish Flomel—if not for any
part he might have taken in the theft of her boat, then for his
simple presence when the deed occurred. But she could be
flexible, she could defer his punishment. She sat beside
Flomel, patted his knee. "Tell me all about it," she said.

COREAN REQUIRED ALL her meager store of patience to
listen to Flomel's account. The conjuror's recollections in-
cluded constant references to the outrages perpetrated on his
dignity. Several times Corean had to interrupt before Flomel
entirely lost the thread of his narrative. He seemed unable to
grasp that she was uninterested in his personal feelings, but
she summoned all the forebearance she possessed, and continued to smile and nod sympathetically at appropriate
points.

When Flomel told about the judging in Deepheart, her interest quickened.

"He flailed about, convulsing and drooling in a most vulgar manner," said Flomel. "There he revealed his low origins again. Perhaps he's dead; he was very still when they took him out, and his face was a bit blue."

"Wait," she said. "Try to remember—did they rush him out, or was it a leisurely process?"

Flomel frowned. "What difference would that make?"

She ran out of tolerance. She shot out a hand and gripped Flomel by the throat, squeezed with the augmented muscles of her slender fingers. He tried to speak, could only wheeze. He half raised his hands, as if to claw at her, and she clamped down a little tighter, so that his eyes bulged. "You," she said, "are my property. You do not ask me for explanations. Do you understand?"

He nodded painfully. She eased the pressure on his throat slightly. "So, tell," she said.

"Fast," he gasped. "They took him out quickly."

She released him, and stood. "Then he's probably still alive. I think I would feel it if he died—we're connected now, somehow. Perhaps it's my need for satisfaction. . . . What else, Flomel?"

He rubbed at his throat and coughed. "There's not much else to tell, Lady. They took me to my room, and in the morning brought me to this place. I didn't see the others again, and you're the first person I've seen here."

She turned away from him and spoke musingly to Marmo. "I wonder . . . is he still in Deepheart? What did you find out about them, Marmo?"

"I spent last night hooked into the datastream, but useful information is difficult to come by. They're a self-development corporation, chartered on Dilvermoon but entirely contained within their facility here. They espouse a cult of sexual diversity. . . ."

"I'm not interested in their philosophy, Marmo. What I want to know is: How well defended is their facility? How difficult to infiltrate?"

Marmo was silent for a moment. "Recall what I said about useful information. But I can infer a probability: They are well defended. In the nearly two thousand standard years since the present facilities were completed, the datastream records no successful hostile incursions into

Deepheart. This is somewhat surprising, since they are reputedly a very wealthy corporation; presumably they would attract the avarice of the pirate lords."

"Discouraging," said Corean, thinking. She refused to accept that Ruiz had found a hiding place where she could not reach him. "But we must do what we can, eh, Marmo? Come, let's visit a friend."

She turned to Lensh. "Collar the mage and take him to a suitable holding pen; Diamond Bob's has a good reputation. Then meet us back at the hotel."

RUIZ LEANED BACK, set his goblet carefully aside. "I'm not an assassin," he said.

"Oh?" said Publius, bright-eyed. "Since when?"

"I've never been an assassin."

"Oh, of course not, of course not. But you were always willing to kill anything that got in the way of your job, whatever it might be. Tell me, how many corpses have you left behind this trip out?"

Ruiz had no answer.

Publius laughed in a jolly manner. "You see? What difference does one corpse more or less make? Eh? And I assure you, he's a very evil man, almost as evil as I am—he deserves killing almost as much as I do. Help me out, and I'll get you offplanet, no matter what it takes, money or time or blood. But if you won't do this little favor for me, I'll take you and chop you up and make toys out of your pieces. I'm tired of worrying about your foolish little blackmail; a man like you will eventually perish, probably sooner rather than later, so why not get it over with? In a hundred years, who will care? Not I."

Ruiz tensed his muscles and prepared to leap at Publius. The monster-maker had once been formidable, but perhaps his skills had deteriorated, perhaps Ruiz could subdue him, could hold him hostage until he had escaped the laboratories.

Publius raised his hand in an odd gesture, and stunner muzzles slid from the wall behind him, pointed at Ruiz. "Don't be silly, old friend—and please, don't make me wonder if you consider me so stupid as to sit and chat with you, protected by nothing but your famous goodwill. I must tell you, I'd be terribly insulted, if I ever imagined you thought such a thing. And you know what a temper I have."

Ruiz sagged back in his chair. A feeling of futility came over him; what had he expected? That he would walk in and Publius would help him, out of the nonexistent goodness of his monstrous heart? Foolish, foolish.

"Who is the man?" Ruiz asked.

Publius stood gracefully and beckoned. "Come. I'll show him to you."

RUIZ STOOD WITH Publius, looking into an observation cell. He saw a man of medium height and build, dressed in a moderately fashionable unisuit. His face was unremarkable, even-featured, neither plump nor thin. His hair was an indeterminate color, neither brown nor blond, cut in a conventional style. He sat in a comfortable chair, face almost expressionless, except for a subtle quality of alertness. Ruiz wondered if he was a spy of some sort—he looked the part to perfection.

"Who is he?" Ruiz asked.

"His name is Alonzo Yubere."

Ruiz was puzzled. "Why would you require my assistance? There he sits; why not just kill him yourself?"

Publius smiled and malicious delight spread over his face. "Oh, it's not *this* Alonzo Yubere I want you to kill. No, no. It's the other Alonzo Yubere, the one who controls the secret. You know, the secret that's so inflamed the pirates."

Ruiz assumed a look of bland indifference.

"You see, *this* Yubere is actually an old servant of mine, torn down and rebuilt in this undistinguished form. Alas, poor Hedrin—he served me well, but I had greater need of his body than he did. I long ago had Hedrin Genched, by the way. Everyone needs at least one henchman he can trust. So his loyalty, even in this new form, is absolute."

"Ah," said Ruiz noncommittally.

"Do you begin to understand? It's an old idea, of course —replace the key person with a duplicate who belongs to you. But you know how tediously exact ident procedures can be these days, so it isn't often tried anymore, and is less often successful. And Yubere is the most careful of men; his ident data was very difficult to come by. But," said Publius, holding out his hands and wiggling the fingers, "my virtuosity with flesh and spirit has become prodigious, more than adequate to the task, and Hedrin has become Yubere, in every aspect but his basic loyalties."

"I see. Still, why not simply buy an assassin in the market?"

Publius clapped him on the shoulder. "That was my plan, until you appeared on my doorstep, as if by magic. And who am I to sneer at Fate's gifts? Besides, I have vast faith in your skills; if it's possible to get to Yubere, you're definitely the one who can do it."

CHAPTER 12

OREAN fumed. Bad enough that Alonzo Yubere had made her wait, worse that he refused to meet with her face-to-face. She was insulted . . . and worried.

His nondescript face stared calmly from the holotank. "Matters are unsettled, Corean. Somehow the pirate lords have learned our secret—or enough of it to make them froth at the mouth. I've been threatened, and even my Gencha are restive. They're not stupid creatures, you know. Just unworldly."

Corean was stunned. "Oh no."

"Oh yes. You wouldn't know how they found out, would you?"

"Don't be absurd," she snapped. "You have dozens of other clients, any of whom could have leaked it." But she was very uneasy. Had Ruiz Aw somehow divined that she had been sending him and the others to SeaStack for their treatment? Maybe. But that wasn't the central element of the secret she shared with Yubere, and the other slavers in his organization. "Do the lords know about the machine?"

Yubere's lips writhed. "Best not to mention such things, even here," he admonished. "No, I think not. They know only that an unnatural number of Genched slaves have recently appeared on the market, and they suppose that someone has a pack of unregistered Gencha hidden in their basement. That's enough to drive them mad with avarice, as it is. They've made a connection with me, unfortunately. I may be forced to flee; you should be prepared to."

Corean drew a deep breath. "I have unfinished business here. It's your business too, so you'd do well to help me. That group of Pharaohan conjurors I was shipping to you for processing, do you recall? They escaped, and one of them knows I was sending him to the Gencha. And he's not a Pharaohan, he's a pangalac, a freelance enforcer . . . and a very capable individual. The longer he stays alive, the more chances he'll have to pass along what he knows."

Yubere leaned closer, his face suddenly keen. "What *does* he know?"

"Not a great deal—just that he and the others were to be processed. They escaped before the boat reached SeaStack, so he probably doesn't know that the Gencha are here. But he's clever; I don't want to give him too much time to think about it."

"What do you want of me?"

"I need a slayer. A very good slayer, someone who specializes in difficult infiltrations. And best if you can give me a Genched slayer, so there'd be no possibility of disloyalty."

Yubere sat back, so that the tank's focus dissolved and his face became a random pattern of primary color. He said nothing for a bit, and Corean became impatient.

"Well? Will you help?"

His face came back into focus; his eyes were luminous and Corean could almost see gears spinning in the facile mind behind those eyes. "Yes, of course. I have exactly the man you need. Leave your cyborg and your Moc; follow the mech I send. We'll take a look at your slayer, and you can have him immediately, if you like."

THE MECH TOOK Corean to an elaborate security lock set into an ancient bulkhead. Once inside, she was searched, scanned, and deprived of all her external weapons. Finally the mech locked a neutralizer around her hand; if she tried to use the sonic knife built into her index finger, she would only succeed in blowing her hand off.

At the other end of the lock Alonzo Yubere waited for her, his unremarkable features composed, his hands folded across his stomach. "Come," he said, and walked down the corridor.

She had never been in his stronghold before, and she looked about, frankly curious. The walls of the corridor were brushed stainless alloy, bright and clean and unadorned. The ceiling was a continuous glowpanel, the floor spongy gray tile. She fancied she could smell the decaying-earthworm stink of the Gencha who lived somewhere below, but if so, it was very faint.

They came to a series of observation rooms. Each had a one-way glass across the width of the room, and as they passed, she glanced in, taking note of the properties her fellow slavers and competitors were having processed. She saw several items which excited her avarice and her envy, but Yubere moved briskly along, so she didn't have time for a more leisurely examination.

One of the properties in particular caught her eye. They went by that window so quickly that she couldn't be absolutely sure of the prisoner's identity, but she was almost certain she had seen Ivant Tildoreamors, one of the more powerful pirate lords, renowned for his ruthlessness and cruel sense of humor. She maintained the same look of innocent curiosity, but her thoughts were racing. Was Yubere Genching the pirate lords? Very dangerous, she thought, but audacious and ambitious.

At the end of the corridor was an elevator, into which Yubere led her. The door shut, and the cage dropped. For a moment Corean was touched by a cold finger of fear. She glanced at Yubere's impassive face. Was he taking her to the Gench, had he decided at last to make her safe? No, no—the process required several days of preparation before it could be done, and her people would know that something was wrong if she did not return shortly. They could not rescue her from Yubere's stronghold, of course, but they could spread the word of his betrayal to the other slavers in Yubere's organization, who would surely destroy him before he could destroy their autonomy. Yubere would have considered all this . . . so she was safe.

But she wondered why none of this had occurred to her, before she'd allowed herself to be taken into his stronghold. Was her passion for revenge strong enough to overshadow her defensive instincts? Perhaps, but there were other reasons—good practical reasons—why Ruiz Aw needed to be dead.

The elevator jarred to a halt, and they stepped off into another and darker world. Here the walls were of some gray alloy, lumpy and showing slagged ripples, as if damaged by some ancient conflagration. Rivulets of dirty water ran down the metal; in places minerals had been deposited in masses of glittering white crystals. A single faded glowtube, fastened in uneven loops to one wall, cast a bluish light.

"Are we in the Gencha enclave?" asked Corean. The stink was stronger here.

Yubere shook his head. "No—that's *much* farther down, Corean."

"How far down does this stack go?"

"No one knows. Oh, maybe the Gencha know, but they won't tell."

His matter-of-fact words made her uneasy. Somehow, she had envisioned a different situation—she had assumed that Yubere kept his Gencha in tidy little cages, obedient to his whims. The realization that Yubere was not entirely in charge sent apprehensive shivers down her back. She wondered what else she didn't know.

"How many of them *are* there?" she asked.

"I don't know that either, Corean."

"How can that be?"

He stopped abruptly. "You don't understand my relationship with them, do you?"

She began to be angry. "Apparently not."

He gripped her arm tightly. "Apparently not, eh? I don't control them; I'm just a middleman. I don't even furnish their guards . . . did you know that they have hundreds of people down there, folk who've lived in the enclave for who knows how many centuries? They're not human anymore, how could they be?" He spoke with such hot-eyed distraction that her annoyance mutated into a stronger uneasiness. "No, not human but they will make it very difficult for the pirate lords to take the enclave, no matter how many soldiers they send down there. They're not human, those people; they would be no better than a Gench at doing my job. So the Gencha, they use me as a go-between, an intermediary with the human city of SeaStack. They don't trust their ability to deal with the city, but they feel sufficient congruency with me. They trust me."

At that moment, with his face thrust close to hers, and some strange compound of desperation and pride glittering in his flat eyes, Yubere looked believably alien.

"I see," she said.

He released her and jerked away, walking fast. "No, you don't. Still, they do as I ask, they pay me by using their grand machine to make our puppets for us, so never complain."

She hurried to keep up. "I'm not complaining," she said in a subdued voice. "But . . . what are they doing down there?"

His voice had a curious lightness. "They say they are Becoming. What they are Becoming, I cannot guess. Gods, perhaps, or demons."

THESE WERE YUBERE'S dungeons, she eventually understood. They began to pass doorways blocked with painfields and bars. From some of those dark mouths came the rattle of chains, moans, curses. Yubere's enemies?

When they reached their destination, she was growing tired, and oppressed by the antiquity of the dungeons. She felt the great mass of the stack over her head as a physical weight, pressing her down toward the Gencha enclave and its unpleasant mysteries. She found that her curiosity was also exhausted; all she wanted was to get her slayer and be gone.

Yubere touched a switch, and the cell lit up.

A man lay in a muscle-stimulator, eyes closed, body jerking and bunching as the machine exercised his body. His skin was stretched tight over a massive musculature; no fat masked the striated tissue. His face seemed ordinary enough, perhaps a bit small for that impressive body, but she saw something disturbing in it. She still had not decided what it was that had that effect, when Yubere spoke. "My brother Remint."

Then she saw the resemblance, and wondered why she had not immediately noticed it.

"He was once my most valuable and trusted lieutenant," said Yubere, almost dreamily. "Oh, what a pair we were— my intellect and his perfect murderous strength. But he lost his way, he allowed his imagination to betray his intellect. He turned traitor. I've saved him for special jobs, since the day he finished his processing—his first assignment was to destroy his fellow conspirators, which he did with admirable efficiency. I order him to maintain his skills, to be ready to serve. I keep him here not to imprison him, of course—what would be the point of that—but to protect him from his enemies, who are many and persistent."

"How competent is he?"

Yubere glanced at her; he seemed a little annoyed. "There never was a slayer to match Remint. Only an unlikely stroke of fortune saved me from him, and delivered him to my vengeance."

"So he is unlucky?" She recalled what Marmo had said about Ruiz Aw's luck.

"Only that once," said Yubere. "It was then, in fact, that I knew that I was a being of destiny." For a moment he glowed, he even smiled—the first smile she had ever seen on his face.

He touched the switch again, and the bars slid aside, the painfield dimmed and faded away. "Remint," Yubere said. "I need you."

Remint shut off the machine and unstrapped himself. He slid out of its embrace and came toward them. He moved with a graceful economy that reminded her a bit of Ruiz Aw. His expression was distant, heavy with restrained power, taut with arrested violence—and suddenly she accepted Yubere's evaluation of his brother's abilities.

Remint stopped a pace away from his brother, and hatred made his face hideous.

"Yes," said Yubere to Corean. "He still hates me—but he must serve me. Oh, of course the hatred is as synthetic as everything else that fills his head, but it feels as hot as ever, to him. And the synthetic humiliation he suffers when he must serve me . . . well, it's the best the Gencha could do, which after all is quite satisfactory."

Yubere looked up at his brother with an oddly affectionate pride. "What an engine of destruction Remint is, Corean. Did you know, he once killed a Moc in unarmed combat? It's true the Moc was old, and suffering from a degenerative chitin disease—but still, a formidable feat. And he is much stronger now; reengineered bone and tripled muscle fiber. Monomesh embedded in his skin. Other enhancements. I think now he might even best your Moc, terrible as it is. . . . Anyway. Remint, you must obey this woman as you would me; unless of course she orders you to do something detrimental to my interests. But you already understand that, don't you, brother—now and forevermore?"

Corean repressed a shudder. She had always considered Alonzo Yubere a passionless calculating man—how wrong she had been.

Only after she had taken Remint away did it occur to her to wonder what scheme or act of Yubere had caused Remint to turn against his brother.

FLOMEL FOUND HIS new quarters no more satisfactory than his last—it was, after all, little more than a cell.

When the back door opened, and the woman in the vidscreen told him to go out and socialize with his fellow slaves, he went gladly.

He moved through the door and found himself in a vast high-ceilinged room. Little knots of people stood about, talking. Others copulated in upholstered niches along the wall, or sat at tables playing board games. Flomel curled his lip in distaste. What a frivolous people the pangalacs were—or maybe it was their slaves who were frivolous. On Pharaoh the slaves were not notably serious-minded. Probably it was the same in the wider universe.

He walked among the other prisoners, avoiding eye contact and studiously ignoring the vulgar activities of the folk in the wall niches.

Suddenly he stiffened, unable to believe his eyes. Dolmaero, Nisa, and Molnekh sat at a small table, drinking from tall glasses and watching the other slaves.

His first impulse was to rush gladly up to them, to greet them like long-lost friends, but then he remembered the way they had cooperated in the abuses the casteless slayer had inflicted on him. A rage rose up in Flomel, and he clenched his fists. For a moment he wanted to rush at them, to destroy them with his hands. Ruiz Aw was nowhere to be seen; they were unprotected. But then he controlled himself. He could be patient; soon Corean would come for him, and until then he could make himself valuable to her by learning what he could. Corean would punish them, he had no doubt.

He composed himself, pasted a glad smile on his face, and rushed up to them, shouting out a cheerful greeting.

NISA LIFTED HER head at his shout and saw Flomel, who wore a crooked smile of such naked falsity that a chill shivered down her backbone.

"Dolmaero! Molnekh! How good to see you." He widened that obscene smile. "And you too, Nisa, of course. Where is your gallant snake oil man?"

She could not force herself to speak. Flomel's sudden unlooked-for appearance seemed an evil portent.

But Dolmaero answered for her, in a guardedly polite manner. "We don't know, Master Flomel. He left us here, to find a buyer for us—or so he said. But, what an unexpected coincidence, to find you here too."

"Yes, I'm astonished," said Flomel. He drew up a chair and sat down uninvited. "So, he has abandoned you to your fate," he said, triumph flickering across his face, to be instantly replaced by an almost-convincing expression of sympathetic commiseration.

"I fear so," said Dolmaero glumly, and Nisa was moved to admiration for his thespian skills. Perhaps the Guildmaster should have been a conjuror—certainly he acted his part more convincingly than Flomel did his. On the other hand, perhaps Flomel's hatred for Ruiz Aw was far too huge for him to entirely contain it. Dolmaero was acting from a cooler and more calculated impulse.

"Well, I never trusted his generosity—and you'll remember how he rewarded my caution? He's a bad one, and I'm relieved to see that you've come to share my opinion—though I'm sad to see us all come to such an end," said Flomel in a voice ringing with insincerity.

Nisa had to control her urge to defend Ruiz; she clamped her lips shut and nodded jerkily.

Flomel laid a comforting hand on her shoulder, and she struggled not to shudder. "This disappointment must be particularly difficult for you, dear," he said with a condescending smile.

Dolmaero must have sensed her distress, because he spoke quickly, as if to distract Flomel from the vindication he was so obviously savoring. "And what of you, Master Flomel? How did you come to be here?"

A brief confusion passed across Flomel's face, then cleared. Nisa thought: *He's decided which lie to tell.*

"It was a somewhat obscure process, Guildmaster—I admit to puzzlement. The ones who held us all took me to another and less pleasant pen, where apparently I was purchased by some great person of the city, who sent his creature to bring me here. A strange creature, who walked like a man, but had the face and mannerisms of a house cat. Very odd. What will happen to me now? I have no inkling." Flomel appeared to reflect on his mysterious circumstances, then gave a philosophical shrug of his shoulders. "Well, we're far from old Pharaoh. Things are very different here, eh, Molnekh?" He gave the skinny mage a good-natured dig in the ribs with his elbow.

Molnekh's answering smile was somewhat sickly, but Flomel appeared not to notice. Flomel continued his musings. "We must adapt, it seems. So you believe that Ruiz Aw has yet to sell you? Perhaps he won't, perhaps he intends to return for you at some later date, and keep the promises he made to you—when he needed your help. Is it possible?" A slyness flickered in Flomel's eyes, and Nisa decided he was testing them, to see if any remnant of loyalty to Ruiz remained in them.

Dolmaero shook his head sadly. "I'm afraid not. It seems we misjudged him. It now appears he was nothing more than a convincing liar." He glanced at Nisa; she saw that he was asking for her help in convincing Flomel.

Nisa managed a nod of agreement. Perhaps Flomel would take her silence for an incapacitating rage, and not see on whom it was focused.

Flomel laughed, a cruel sound of satisfaction. It suddenly occurred to Nisa that Flomel had a secret from which he took great pleasure, and she wondered what unpleasant consequences his secret would have for them.

"TELL ME," SAID Ruiz. "What difficulties do you foresee in reaching Yubere?"

They had returned from the cell with the false Alonzo Yubere walking behind them in calm obedience. Now the three of them sat in Publius's rooms, again sipping the lilac cordial. The presence of the ringer made Ruiz acutely uncomfortable, though he told himself that it was no different than keeping company with a semiautonomous mech. But mechs didn't drink sweet liquor, smacking their lips after each sip. Mechs didn't watch him with clear guileless eyes, apparently eager to be helpful. Mechs didn't breathe, no heart beat in their metal breasts, their brains were cold crystal, not warm flesh. Ruiz had never been so close to a person who had undergone the Gench processing—at least not to his knowledge—and the ringer's presence seemed to disrupt the smooth flow of reality. What did that human-shaped inhuman creature feel; were his feelings so different from the things that everyone else felt? If not, what did that say about the validity, or even the verifiability, of Ruiz's existence?

Publius nodded at the false Yubere. "Alonzo can tell you all about his circumstances—though he's not quite sure of some important details. Most regrettably, these include the defenses of Yubere's stronghold, which are almost sure to be more formidable than we expect."

Ruiz shook himself, dragged himself back from his unproductive musings. "I'd like to discuss other important details, first. I don't want to seem untrusting . . . but in fact I am. How do I know you'll keep your bargain, if I succeed in replacing Yubere with your puppet?"

Publius shook his head in mock sorrow, though his mouth kept trembling toward a fey smile. "Ruiz, Ruiz. You surprise me. We're such old and devoted comrades. How could you suspect me of duplicity?"

This seemed so eccentrically rhetorical a question that Ruiz could think of no appropriate reply.

Publius laughed. "All right. Well, let me see. . . . What assurances would comfort you?"

"At present, my imagination fails me," said Ruiz dryly. "Let's discuss your proposal in greater detail; perhaps something will come to me."

"Fair enough," said Publius in a good-humored voice. "This essentially is the plan: You will penetrate Yubere's stronghold, taking along my Yubere. Once inside, you'll locate and dispose of the real Yubere, see that my man is securely installed, and leave. What could be simpler, what could be cleaner?"

"Forgive my suspicious nature, but . . . what's to keep you from disposing of the real Ruiz Aw, after his work is done?"

Publius raised his eyebrows. "Loyalty? Gratitude?"

"Insufficient," said Ruiz. "However . . . back to your plan. How do you propose we get into the stronghold?"

"Ah! Here I've already done much of your work. My people have located a partially sealed-off ingress, only a few hundred meters below the waterline. Our best analysis—old charts, one of Yubere's former prisoners, and, most indisputably, identifiable waste discharged through an adjacent out-pump—indicates that the ingress connects to the lowest levels of Yubere's holdings—though we can't be absolutely sure. You might have to do a bit of exploring, to find your way into his space—but I have confidence in you."

Ruiz had less confidence. "Supposing I get inside. What then?"

Publius nodded at the false Yubere, who set his snifter aside and leaned forward, an earnest look on his unremarkable face. "I've concentrated the majority of my security forces in the upper and most accessible levels of the stronghold, as you might expect. They consist, as far as I know, of a half squad of SeedCorp-trained shock troops, a dozen or so killmechs manufactured recently by Violencia-Muramasa, and a semisapient surveillance network installed four years ago by Clearlight Robotics. The design of the upper level secured accesses is along conventional lines, so far as I know —top-level reception area with holosim negotiation facilities, state-of-the-art security locks, and cross-channeled baffled elevator shafts. Pretty much impregnable, without the use of heavy weapons—and of course the use of weapons heavy enough to breach my defenses would bring swift reaction from the Shards."

"I only wish my own defenses were so formidable," said Publius. "But continue."

The puppet nodded. "Then on the second level are barracks for my troops and mechanisms. Below that, my living quarters—also heavily defended, though less rigorously than topside. Then a level of labs and holding areas where I do my work."

"And what might that be?" asked Ruiz.

Before the false Yubere could answer, Publius spoke up. "No need to go into that, Alonzo."

A spasm of mindlessness twitched over the puppet's face, was almost instantly gone. Watching, Ruiz felt a mixture of horror and morbid curiosity. It was as if the puppet had suffered a tiny disconnection from the fabric of the moment, had briefly existed in another reality.

But he mustn't allow himself to be distracted, Ruiz decided. "No. I need to know more than you're telling me. Besides, won't I see what he's up to when I come up through that level. Your attitude worries me, Publius. It's almost as though you don't expect me to survive."

Publius stared malevolently at Ruiz. Finally he spoke in a grudging voice. "Oh, as you wish. Tell him, Alonzo."

The puppet smiled genially. "I make reliable people. Or to put it another way, I make people reliable."

A long slow moment passed, while Ruiz's brain processed this data, while his mind was painlessly blank—and then understanding roared in. *Oh, no,* thought Ruiz. *This is where the Gencha are, this is where Corean was sending us. This is where the League wanted me to die.* The death net groaned and shuddered in the blackness at the bottom of his mind—but this time he felt its crumbling structure rupture and tear. He was for a measureless time suspended between life and death, only dimly aware of the puppet chattering on, of Publius watching him with startled concern, of the chair that held him, of the air he could no longer breathe—of the essence of himself, slipping away. His inner voice shrieked wordless warnings; he swayed and his eyes rolled up, so that all he could see was a ruddy darkness, and the stars of experience shooting across that warm nothingness.

Then it was over, and Publius was pressing him back into his chair, holding an injector in one manicured hand.

"No!" shouted Ruiz. He shoved Publius away and the monster-maker, caught by surprise, went stumbling back. "I'm all right."

Publius held the injector ready. "You had me worried—I thought Yubere had run a ringer in on me—beat me to the slice." He still looked undecided. "That look you had . . . it speaks to me of Gencha work."

"It was Gencha work," Ruiz said. "A death net." He wiped at the sudden sweat beaded on his brow. He looked into himself, waiting for the weight of the net, but it was gone.

And he was still alive.

Publius was looking at him as if he had just made a sour joke. "Of course," he sneered. "So why are you still alive?"

Ruiz laughed, a sound of shaky delight. "I wore it down, I guess. But enough of that—what lies under Yubere's labs?"

The puppet answered as though nothing had happened. "My dungeons."

"And below that?"

"Unknown," interrupted Publius, before the puppet could speak. Ruiz had the definite impression that the puppet had been about to say something else, but it was pointless to press it. On the instant the puppet's master had spoken, the puppet's reality had changed—now the ringer believed what Publius had asserted. "In any case," Publius continued, "the ingress you'll use connects to the level of the dungeons, we think . . . so the unexplored depths of the stack are irrelevant to your mission."

"So you say."

"Yes, I do," said Publius smugly.

"Let me get this straight. You intend that I should dive down—how many meters?"

"Six hundred and thirty-six," said the puppet helpfully, eliciting a displeased glare from Publius.

"I should dive down six hundred meters, fighting off the margars and the brainborers, pry open a sealed ingress, break into Yubere's dungeon, fight my way up to his labs— or worse, his residential level—all the time dragging your ringer with me, kill Yubere, see that the ringer is functioning properly, and get away clean. Do I have it right?"

"Exactly right, Ruiz Aw, old friend."

"Oh fine."

Publius snorted. "You put the worst possible face on everything—I'm astonished that you've survived in your profession as long as you have. Murder and pillage are inappropriate vocations for realists. But I've already made many of the arrangements. I have a sonar-transparent submersible ready to go—it has a clamp-on repair bay, so you won't even get wet when you break in. You can draw on my funds to hire mercenaries, within reason—the sub holds only eight crew and passengers. Your weapons budget will be generous. What more could you want?"

"A way of preventing you from sticking a knife in my back, in the unlikely event I succeed."

Publius sighed. "I'm open to suggestions, Ruiz."

Ruiz sipped at the lilac liquor. "It's a matter that requires serious thought. Let me return to my own lodgings and I'll consider."

Publius smiled and shook his head. "Don't be silly, Ruiz. I can't let you out of my control now—you're gravid with dangerous information. I'll have a suite prepared for you here, and you're welcome to brainstorm to your heart's content, or at least until tomorrow." His expression darkened and he directed a worried look at the puppet. "The pirate lords are growing restive; who knows how much longer they'll delay moving against Yubere. They don't know exactly how he's connected with the secret, and of course it's difficult for them to make any sort of concerted effort . . . but they're working themselves up to it."

Something about this last bothered Ruiz. "What makes you think your Yubere would do better against the lords than the real one would?"

"Perceptive question, Ruiz," said Publius, sounding a bit displeased. "I don't know why I even try to fool you. Well, I'll say only that I can call on resources that the real Yubere cannot—and don't ask me to elaborate."

Ruiz felt strangely weakened, out of control, bewildered —he could only dimly perceive the mechanisms so obviously grinding away beneath the surface Publius had presented to him. As he considered this, he grew resentful. He looked at the monster-maker and only with great difficulty did he conceal the disgust that flooded through him.

"Well," he finally said. He made his voice light and fixed a disarming smile on his face. "I hope you'll put me up in decent style, Emperor Publius. We who are about to die could use a good night's sleep."

CHAPTER 13

OREAN took her assassin back to the Jolly Roger in silence. Marmo, who had waited for her in Yubere's negotiation facility, spoke to her only in monosyllables, and if she hadn't believed that Marmo had long ago worn out his store of such human emotions, Corean might have thought Remint had frightened the old cyborg.

When they reached their rooms, Lensh seemed openly distressed by the slayer's ominous presence; his feline features constantly wavered between cringing disapproval and outrage.

She found Yubere's brother more than a little intimidating herself, so much so that she couldn't be very irritated with the reactions of the others.

She directed Remint to a corner ottoman, where he sat quietly, staring into space, a machine waiting for its instructions.

Her most urgent need then was a bath. Perhaps she only imagined it, but she still smelled the subtle Gench taint she had noticed in Yubere's stronghold, as if those alien molecules were clinging to her with unnatural tenacity.

She lingered in the warm bath, thinking aimless thoughts.

She noticed the slight dryness of her perfect skin, her need for a manicure. After a while she rubbed a soapy sponge across her breasts, and she became aware of a dull sexual ache. She had, after all, been away from her various erotic pets for several days now; her growing frustration was natural enough. Perhaps she would send out for a brace of joyfolk later; the Jolly Roger kept several well-regarded catering firms under contract. She considered summoning Lensh to service her immediately, but as a lover he was uninteresting. Like most folk with substantial feline DNA adulteration, Lensh tended to mate in a brief, brutal, matter-of-fact manner—which at the moment held no appeal for Corean.

For a moment she considered the slayer—how would it be to lie in such inhumanly strong arms? She dismissed the notion with a tiny shiver. She was feeling unadventurous tonight—unusual for her.

Something turned her thoughts to Ruiz Aw. A perversely wishful mood came over her, so that she lay back in a swirl of sweet-scented heat, and remembered how much she had once lusted for Ruiz Aw's handsome flesh.

She cupped her hands around her small breasts, and stroked her thumbs across the soap-slick points of her nipples. After the Moc had almost killed Ruiz, she had sent him to the rooms where she was keeping the Pharaohan woman. Those rooms were equipped with the standard surveillance cameras, of course, and she recalled the times she had watched the two of them rutting in the woman's silk-covered bed.

Corean slid her hands down her belly, and her fingers moved in a languid rhythm. Ruiz Aw had been lovely to watch, and the woman too—Corean had looked forward so much to having them . . . until the woman had half killed a valuable property, until Ruiz Aw had stolen her boat and cargo. She had desired them both fiercely. She had put off the moment of consummation, so that the anticipation might sweeten her pleasure. She had waited just a bit too long.

But they'd been so pretty, Ruiz and the Pharaohan—the two bodies entwined, pleasing each other in all the ways a man and woman could.

Images of their artful couplings filled her memory, and her fingers moved more quickly.

For all her rage, she still wanted him. If by some miracle Remint had at that instant brought Ruiz into her bathroom, she would have made him satisfy her, over and over. She arched her back, so that her pelvis rose from the water. She threw her head back, and felt the first clenching spasms begin.

She thought: and then, when Ruiz Aw's strength was all gone, she would make him die.

She came, shuddering with the culmination of that joyful fantasy.

LATER, COMPOSED AND cold with determination, Corean went in to instruct her slayer in his task.

"Listen, Remint," she said. "There is a man called Ruiz Aw who is my enemy. He is a dangerous man with dangerous knowledge. We believe he is still here in SeaStack. It is your job to seek him out and render him helpless. You must adhere to these priorities: Ideally, you will bring him to me alive. Failing that, you must kill him and bring me his head or other indisputable evidence of his death. Do you understand?"

Remint nodded once, a sharp decisive gesture. The intensity of his attention was almost unnerving, Corean thought. But she continued. "There are other and somewhat less urgent elements to your task. Three slaves belonging to me were stolen by Ruiz Aw. I want them back, if recapturing them will not jeopardize your most important task: the capture or killing of Ruiz Aw."

She waited for a fairly long time, before she realized that he wasn't going to ask any questions unprompted.

"What do you need to know to begin your work?" she asked.

It was as if some powerful engine started spinning behind his stony eyes; they flared with purpose and, to her surprise, something approximating intelligence. "First," he said. "Tell me everything you know or surmise about this man."

RUIZ PACED SLOWLY back and forth across the thick carpet in the suite Publius had conducted him to. "I keep it for impressing merchant princes," Publius had said with an expansive gesture that took in the various luxurious appointments. "Call if you need anything." He had waited a moment for a response, then shrugged and left.

Ruiz had hardly noticed; he was too busy trying to think of some way to ensure his continued existence. How could he avoid doing Publius's dirty work? He attempted to review his alternatives, but was depressed to discover that he could find none. Publius had him, and somehow he was certain that Publius wasn't bluffing when he said he didn't care anymore about the scrap of information Ruiz held against him. Escape from Publius seemed unlikely. After all, Publius had great respect for his violent skills; presumably he had taken adequate precautions against any attempt Ruiz might make to fly the coop.

For hours, Ruiz wrestled with the problem. Obviously Publius did not intend for him to long survive his mission— that much Ruiz could take for granted. But what possible leverage could he develop to use against Publius?

He considered the potential sources of leverage.

Honorable folk could be bound by promises; Publius would promise him everything and it would mean nothing.

He was in no position to employ fear; Publius would laugh at his threats, and rightly so.

Could he somehow use the dribble of information Publius had divulged? The idea had possibilities, but he was morosely certain that Publius would never let him near a datastream terminal—the one in his suite had been hurriedly removed by two of the monster-maker's technicians. And to whom could he confide his damaging story, who would keep it safe until and unless Ruiz failed to return? His only friends on Sook were locked up in a slave pen. It occurred to him that he should have spent a little more time on devising a safe place for them to hide. But at the time, he had been sure that Corean would be hot on his trail—and the matter had seemed urgent.

Greed seemed the best possibility. How could he divert the torrent of Publius's greed into a useful channel, use it to drive the turbines of Ruiz's own purposes?

He shook his head, as if to shake loose the cobwebs of distraction. He sat down and stretched overly tight muscles. Now was a time for clear thinking, if ever there was one. He took a deep breath, composed himself.

First, what did Publius value? His reputation was evidently not as important to Publius as it once had been. His labs, of course, but Ruiz could see no way to hold that huge facility hostage without assistance. His monsters, his employees? No . . . Publius had often declared that no one in the universe is irreplaceable—except, of course, Publius.

What else, then? Was there some essential core to Publius's business that Ruiz could affect single-handed?

He wondered: Did Publius own a Gench? The more he considered the idea, the more likely it seemed. The puppet Publius proposed to substitute for Alonzo Yubere had undergone deconstruction; had it happened in Publius's own labs? Possibly. If so, was Publius sufficiently eager for Ruiz's services to risk the Gench as a hostage? *I suppose,* Ruiz thought, *it depends on how much of a gambler Publius is, and on how he rates my chances of success.* Presumably Publius hoped to gain access to a larger number of Gencha, if he supplanted Yubere—but if Ruiz failed, Publius would have no Gencha at all. Maybe Publius owned two Gencha—he was probably wealthy enough.

If so, perhaps he would consent to risk one of them.

It didn't seem enough. What else could he ask for, especially if, as was probable, Publius refused to give him a Gench?

Nothing came to him. He pounded his fists against his forehead, in panicky frustration. What could he do? There must be something; he refused to believe that he was no more than a tool that Publius could pick up, use, and discard. Besides, others depended on him, and on his resourcefulness.

Much as he tried to focus all his attention on the problem of controlling Publius, distracting thoughts kept creeping into his mind.

And all of them concerned Nisa.

Eventually, he dimmed the lights and lay on the bed and forced his body to relax. Perhaps he was too tired to be clever, he thought, and so he willed himself toward sleep.

REMINT INTERROGATED COREAN to exhaustion, and the process revealed how little she really knew about Ruiz Aw. She found the process unpleasant, but Remint was relentless, and she could not order him to desist without blunting his effectiveness.

What in fact did she know about Ruiz Aw? She knew

how he looked, how he moved, how he sounded. She knew
that he was a skillful slayer, ruthlessly decisive. To some
extent she understood the basis for his almost-pathological
self-confidence—or what appeared to be self-confidence. She
knew he could be charming. He was an excellent liar, and
she was beginning to believe that he had lied to her under
the probe . . . and that he was much more than a freelance
slave poacher. How could anyone as effective as Ruiz Aw
exist in such obscure circumstances?

Who was he, really . . . and why had he chosen to inflict himself on her?

The trend of Remint's investigations veered to the matter
of Ruiz Aw's affiliations. Remint asked a hundred questions
about Ruiz's first escape attempt through the marinarium
belonging to Corean's neighbor, the Farelord Preall.

Eventually Corean grew impatient, and asked, "Do you
think he had help? Do you think he's part of a hostile organization?"

Remint sat back and did not answer immediately.

"Well?" she demanded.

"He had no help; such is my opinion, based on feeble
data. He is simply very good, and very lucky."

Corean looked at the slayer curiously. "You believe in
luck? Strange. How can that be?"

Remint shrugged. "How else do you explain the hidden
mechanisms of the universe? The fate that spared my
brother and destroyed me?" He seemed uninterested in the
matter; it was simply an illustrative example, and Corean
felt a chilly unease. "In answer to your second question, I
believe he was sent by some organization, though perhaps
not one specifically hostile to you. He may be a League
agent—since they own the world where you've been poaching slaves."

Corean was horrified. "But, he carried no death net! How
could he have been League."

Remint assumed a didactic tone. "In the first place, not
all League agents carry the net; this notion is a carefully
nurtured myth, designed by the League to intimidate their
enemies. In the second place, the nets can be successfully
tampered with—not removed, but slowed. From your description of the events at the launch ring, I think it conceiv-
able that Ruiz Aw suffered a partially triggered net at that
time.

"But all this is beside the point. Ruiz Aw is presently operating without any outside assistance, in my opinion.

"Now," said Remint, regaining that lambent intensity. "Tell me about the other slaves he escaped with."

So she did. He allowed her no privacy, he wanted to know everything, including her plans for Ruiz and the Pharaohan woman Nisa. As she described what she now perceived as her mindless lust, Remint betrayed no sign of disapproval or scorn or titillation, which further reinforced his inhumanity.

Then he asked her about Flomel, and what the mage had told her of Ruiz Aw's activities since the escape. Then he asked Marmo about Deepheart, and Marmo silently handed the slayer a charged dataslate showing the results of Marmo's earlier search of the datastream.

Hours later, he abruptly stopped asking questions. He sat back and a veil seemed to fall over his face—it was as if he had stepped out of his body and gone elsewhere.

Corean waited with what equanimity she could summon, but another hour passed before Remint spoke again.

And all he said was: "I see."

A vast annoyance filled Corean. "So what now, mighty Remint? What will you do with all the weighty conclusions you've reached?"

He looked at her, expressionless. "I've reached no conclusions," he said.

"No? Well then, what's your plan? Will you organize an attack on Deepheart?"

"Premature," said Remint. "First I must interview your slave Flomel."

"Why? I've told you everything he knows about Ruiz."

"No, you've told me everything he told you about Ruiz. It's unlikely that these are identical bodies of knowledge."

"Go, then," she said, getting up and moving toward her bedroom. "Lensh will take you to the pen."

As it almost always was, Ruiz's sleep was dreamless, but his mind must have continued to chew at the problem of controlling Publius, because when he woke, it was with a glimmer of a plan.

He tapped at the flatscreen communit; it came to life. One of Publius's more subtle monsters appeared, a woman with a curiously elongated body. Her eyes had large violet pupils surrounded glowing red sclera. It was Ruiz's theory that each of Publius's monsters contained an equal portion of grotesqueness; this one evidently carried most of her strangeness within.

"Yes?" she said.

"I'd like to see Publius now," Ruiz said.

"I'll send a guide. Publius left orders that you were to be brought to him without delay, whenever you requested it."

The guide was an eel-thin woman with gray elastic skin and the face of a predatory fish. She wore a bubbler over her gills and spoke through a vocalizer. "Come with me," she ordered, and said nothing else.

PUBLIUS WAS WORKING in his personal lab, bent over a microsurgery unit. An infant lay anesthetized on a tray, the skin on one side of its face peeled back; Publius was carving at the baby's facial musculature, using resonating laser pinbeams.

Ruiz choked back his revulsion and waited until Publius finished and turned the closing over to the machine.

"I do a little freehand work, from time to time," said Publius. "It keeps me from becoming overly dependent on the tech, keeps my fingers bloody, so to speak."

"Let's talk about this job you want me to do," said Ruiz.

"Certainly. Have you devised a way of reinforcing my promises?" Publius seemed vastly amused, as if he was certain that no matter how clever Ruiz was, Publius would be able to thwart him.

"Not a completely satisfactory one. But first, tell me how exactly you intend to get me offworld."

Publius shrugged. "I'd intended to retain my flexibility, Ruiz. You know me, a creature of opportunity. I'll do whatever seems best, at the time."

Ruiz gave him a wry look. "Unsatisfactory. I must ask you to be more specific, Publius."

Publius drummed his fingers impatiently on the infant's gurney. "All right, all right, if you must be so compulsively suspicious, I'll tell you what I had in mind—though I must say your attitude is rather unfriendly."

Ruiz laughed sourly. What could he answer?

"When you return, Ruiz, crowned with success, I propose to cash in a favor owed to me by one of the pirate lords. He will transport you to one of the Shard platforms, where you can get commercial transport back to Dilvermoon."

Ruiz frowned. "So, now I must trust not only you but some starpirate? I'm not reassured."

Publius made an exasperated sound. "Really, you try my patience with your endless suspicions. Well then, if you cannot trust me, I will offer to wear madcollars with you, and accompany you up to the platform and into Shard jurisdiction."

Ruiz had not expected Publius to make so bold a suggestion. Madcollars were a fairly effective trucial technology. Two persons forced to devise a way to trust each other for short periods would each don explosive collars, which could be activated by an impulse from the hand controllers each held. However, if one wearer lost his head or otherwise perished, the other's collar would instantly explode. They were equipped with volitional filters, so that they could not be activated against the wearer's will. Once the collars were locked on, they could only be removed by mutual consent. Their major limitation was that they were short-range devices; distance or the interposition of a suitably massive object rendered them useless.

"You would wear them with me now?" Ruiz asked.

"Don't be ridiculous. I have great faith in your skills— you know this—but you are after all undertaking a very dangerous piece of work."

"Ah," said Ruiz. "So the problem remains—how can I trust you until I've done the job?"

Publius shrugged. "It's your problem, Ruiz. Didn't your night of scheming birth any plans?"

"I'm not sure. Tell me, do you own a Gench?"

Publius's face curdled slightly, as though he had bitten into an astringent fruit. "Yes. What of it?"

"More than one?"

"Yes, yes. Three, in fact, though one is almost moribund and one barely trained."

"Ah. Excellent," said Ruiz, feeling a slight degree of hope. "Then here is my proposal: Allow one of your Gench to accompany me, wearing a madcollar with me. I'll rely on your cupidity; even *you* aren't rich enough to throw away a Gench. When we return, I'll unlock the Gench as soon as you're locked with me, and everyone will be safe and happy."

"Absurd!" barked Publius. "Why would I risk so major a portion of my fortune?" His face filled with a snarling anger, but as Ruiz had hoped, a duplicitous gleam flickered behind his eyes.

"Because you have such great faith in my skills."

Publius fumed and shouted for fifteen minutes, but in the end, he agreed to lend Ruiz his youngest and least valuable Gench.

And Ruiz was thankful that Publius's vast arrogance had caused him to underestimate Ruiz's subtlety.

WHEN LENSH RETURNED with Remint from their visit to Flomel in the pen, the pilot seemed to have gotten over his initial fear.

"Good news," he called, bouncing into the suite. "Guess who we found?"

Remint stepped forward swiftly and took Lensh by the arm, gave him a shake that rattled his teeth. "Shut up, beast," he said. "I will inform; this is how I choose to perform my duties." There was no emotion in that pronouncement, just a cold intensity.

Corean shivered, but she kept her face as expressionless as Remint's. "What did you find?"

"We found your other slaves," said Remint. "I conclude that Ruiz Aw is no longer in Deepheart; your slave Flomel made statements that support this conclusion."

Corean couldn't help smiling. "Good news, indeed. And what did Flomel say?"

"He reports that the others are convinced that Ruiz Aw has abandoned them to the slave market. My assessment is that this is likely."

"I was right," Corean said to Marmo. "You see, he's a lot like me . . . but I'm far more intelligent. How should we proceed?"

Remint regarded her stonily. "My hypothesis is that he is unlikely to return for his profits; no doubt he has made arrangements to receive his funds remotely, if at all. Unless I can obtain access to the others—so that I can put them under brainpeel—or unless we can coerce the pen into cooperation, the trail ends there."

Corean sat on the couch and looked up at Remint. "I don't think we can get the pen to help us—their business depends on their reputation for incorruptibility. So, we'll take the others. Let's buy them, though it galls me to pay out good money for things I already own."

Remint gave his head a single negative shake. "Not possible. Ruiz Aw has placed a hold order on them for a week—I checked with the management."

Marmo stirred. "Perhaps he intends to return for them, after all."

"Unlikely," said Remint. "Probably he hopes to thwart our investigations until the trail has grown cold."

"Yes, that's it," said Corean. "So, we must take them from the pen by force."

Marmo floated forward and protested. "Corean! You'll bring the pirate lords down on us. Your passion for revenge is out of hand; please, come to your senses!"

Corean turned to him and spoke in a deadly voice. "Marmo, you don't understand the issues here. The matter has gone far beyond personal vengeance now; our survival is at stake. Remint, see to it."

He nodded, and turned to leave. "Come, Lensh," he said. "We must hire some firewood; we will need decoys."

Lensh turned pleading eyes to Corean, but she looked back impassively. He hung his head and left.

SIX HOURS LATER, Remint returned, leading the four dazed Pharaohans, who were chained together in a coffle. Flomel looked up with haunted eyes, recognized her, and cried out. "Lady Corean. I'm so happy to see you. Can you get me out of these chains. Your man was most disrespectful."

Remint backhanded Flomel, and the sound of the blow was shockingly loud. Flomel fell back, mouth bloody and eyes huge.

He handed the leash to Corean. "Shall I see to renting a brainpeeler now?" he asked.

"Yes," she said. "But be careful with the peeler—I don't want them damaged. Where's Lensh?"

"He allowed himself to be captured by the pen security forces. I killed him before they could take him away."

●   ●   ●

WHEN REMINT WAS through with the brainpeeler, the
Pharaohans were led away to a cage set up in one of the
guest bedrooms. Remint came to Corean and made his report.

"We were both wrong, in my judgment," he said. "Ruiz
Aw intends to return for them. He told them he was putting
them in as safe a place as he could find, that he would find
transport for all of them offplanet. They're not entirely convinced that he will return—not even the woman is completely sure of him—but I don't doubt he will be back for
them." Remint paused, then spoke on. "Ruiz Aw has become infected with soft feelings. They will be his downfall,
as they were mine."

Corean studied his expressionless face, fascinated and repulsed. Remint betrayed no scorn or self-pity; apparently his
brother had permitted Remint to keep no human feelings
except the hatred he bore Yubere.

"What do you advise?" she asked.

"I left misleading clues at the pen; these will allow us to
be traced to a remote location. I will keep this location under surveillance." Remint drew back his sleeve, to reveal a
small flatscreen vid strapped to his massive wrist. "When
the pirate lords arrive, I will permit them to continue down
a false trail. When Ruiz Aw traces us, I will attempt to
capture or kill him."

Corean nodded, impressed by Remint's scheme. "A reasonable plan. How long must we wait?"

"He put a one-week prepaid hold on them. Therefore we
should wait no more than six days, as he left them yesterday. He might come for them at any time, but my guess is
that it will take several days, under the worst of circumstances. He'll have no easy time finding a way out of Sea-
Stack, at present."

She laughed delightedly. "Good, good. I should have
time to get them processed at Yubere's before he comes for
them. How nice. You take them to Yubere now, then pursue
your plan."

CHAPTER 14

"WHAT now?" asked Publius.

"Troops," said Ruiz.

Publius nodded agreeably. "You can take your pick of my security barracks."

Ruiz snorted. "Oh, sure. No, you'll have to let me choose my own people. I'd feel insecure, surrounded by your henchmen—and that would reduce my effectiveness. Take me to the Spindinny and bring lots of money."

Publius argued, but without great heat. Eventually he called for a slave collar, which he locked around Ruiz's neck. "I can't risk you giving me the slip before I get you sealed into your sub. You might have an opportunity while we're wandering about the city. I'm sorry to be so suspicious . . . but you started it, Ruiz."

Ruiz settled the collar in place as comfortably as he could. It seemed a great deal heavier than it really was. "Give me a high-necked tunic, at least. The people I want to hire would be unwilling to work for a slave; slaves get sent into hopeless situations more frequently than free folk do."

"As you say."

.   .   .

WHEN THEY EMERGED from the labyrinth, Ruiz saw that his little speedboat had indeed been stolen. He had expected it, and however his job for Publius turned out, he wouldn't be needing the boat, but for some reason it still angered him.

Publius had brought two Dirm bondguards with him, and now these herded Ruiz toward the armored airboat that Ruiz had admired only yesterday—though it seemed as though much more than one day had passed in the monster-maker's stronghold.

Publius was tense and uncommunicative. Ruiz deduced that the monster-maker felt exposed, away from his safe lair. He took a certain pleasure in Publius's discomfort, though he was careful to show none of it.

The Dirm sealed the boat, and one of them took the pilot's seat and drove carefully out of the anchorage. In a few minutes, they were easing into the Spindinny's moorage.

"I'll send Huey here in with you," said Publius, indicating one of the Dirm. "Huey, you're to act as though you belong to Ruiz, unless he tries to get away, in which case you blow his head off. Understood?"

The Dirm nodded solemnly.

Publius held up the controller of Ruiz's collar. "And remember this, Ruiz. I won't hesitate to take your head, if I get even a little nervous. Don't make me nervous."

Ruiz took a deep breath. "Let's go, Huey," he said.

On the other side of the inner lock, Huey returned Ruiz's weapons; no free person would enter the Spindinny unarmed. Then he opened the outer door and they stepped onto the Spindinny's dilapidated dock.

The Spindinny was a joyplex frequented by unaffiliated mercenaries, and it functioned as an unofficial hiring hall. Ruiz and Huey entered, unquestioned by the two killmechs stationed by the doors—apparently they looked dangerous enough to be on legitimate Spindinny business.

Inside, Ruiz was briefly assailed by nostalgia. The air seemed so familiar, thick with the stinks of his trade: sweat, alcohol, smoke, gun oil, ozone. Harsh voices drifted from the various curtained openings along the entryhall. He heard sudden ugly laughter, curses, off-key song, the clink of glasses, the bubble of pipes, sighs, and moans.

He shook his head. It seemed strange to him now that he had ever lived that life . . . though it wasn't so long ago.

"Let's go down to the message room," he said, and Huey followed obediently.

The message room was an island of hygienic technological calm in the steamy depths of the Spindinny, full of chrome and glass and the soft hum of machinery. Ruiz sat at a dataslate and entered his requirements and payscale. When he was done, he rented an interview room and went there to wait for his troops to crawl out of their revels.

Four hours later he had five mercenaries he judged competent, out of almost a hundred applicants. Publius had allowed him six choices, but he was growing discouraged. And he was exhausted; every session with the verifier—the limited brainpeeler he was using to assess the skills of his applicants—had taken a little more out of him. The holomnemonic oceans of the mercenaries who frequented the Spindinny were murky dangerous waters.

His squad so far consisted of: a much-scarred graduate of the downlevel bloodstadia, a cyborged clone of the famous emancipator Nomun, two solemn women from Jahworld who were expert pinbeamers, and a beaster-addict who favored the wolverine persona. The beaster might have been a mistake, Ruiz thought, brought on by exhaustion and frustration with the poor material from which he'd had to choose. The beaster was ferocious, no doubt about it, and skilled at killing—but could he be relied on to control his murderous alter ego in situations calling for more detachment than ferocity? Ruiz was unsure.

While they waited for Ruiz to find his last recruit, the three men played a card game in the corner. The women held hands and watched Ruiz with wide golden eyes.

When he was about to close up and make do with what he'd already found, a familiar figure stumbled into the interview room, a tall gangly individual who wore his silver-plated hair in a stringy ponytail. His lumpy face was embellished with random slashes of blue-green beauty paint, and he was dressed in a worn-out unisuit, decorated with souvenir patches from a number of Dilvermoon tourist attractions.

"I'm not too late, am I?" asked Albany Euphrates, swaying a bit. He peered at Ruiz, took a shaky step forward. "Ruiz? Ruiz Aw? What are you doing in this devil's den?"

"Looking for you," said Ruiz, not altogether facetiously. He couldn't quite contain his delight. Albany was no more saintly than any other person who fought and killed for money—and for the perverse pleasures to be found in violence. But Ruiz had campaigned with Albany on two prior occasions, and had witnessed Albany acting from both loyalty and compassion. These were rare qualities in a freelance slayer. He had formed a cautious friendship with Albany, even though in the second instance, the ill-fated campaign on Line, they had ended up on opposing sides. Albany's major personal weakness was a predilection for the various chemical recreations; at the moment he seemed quite drunk.

"Looking for me," said Albany blearily. "How odd. Well, I'm found. What's the job?"

"Sneak and snuff," said Ruiz.

Albany shook his head doubtfully. "I don't know, Ruiz. I've never been much for the cold blood."

"I know. But this is a worthwhile job. The target needs killing badly—a lot depends on it." And this was no lie, Ruiz thought.

Albany sighed. "Well, if you say so. I don't think you'd mislead me—you were always funny that way."

"Good," said Ruiz. "Let's get you sobered, and then we'll go. It's a rush job."

THEY WERE ALL in the hold of Publius's armored airboat, except for Publius, who had seen the wisdom of Ruiz's suggestion that he not make an appearance. "One of them might recognize you and come down with a fit of moral qualms," Ruiz had said.

Albany was sober, but still a little shaky. The on-board medunit had fitted a perfusor cuff to his arm and was pumping restoratives into him. "So," said Albany. "What's the plan?"

They were on the way to the storage facility where Publius kept his submarine, and Ruiz had a few minutes to go over the plan he'd developed in conference with the false Yubere. He explained how and where they'd break into Yubere's stack. He discussed, though not in horrifying and discouraging detail, the obstacles they might have to deal with on their way up to Yubere's quarters. All of them were experienced in urban warfare and had been trained in the basic maneuvers necessary for such an assault—though Ruiz hoped they could be crafty enough to avoid any pitched battles.

Occasionally one of the mercenaries would ask a question about the target's identity or the stack's location, but Ruiz parried the questions as gracefully as possible. He felt an unwelcome sense of responsibility for the killers he'd hired, especially since Albany had joined them. He was certain that if any of them learned what was going on, Publius would see they didn't survive long enough to spread any inconvenient rumors.

When he was done, he asked for questions. "No one?" he asked, looking around at the stolid faces. "All right. When we get to the depot, you can draw whatever personal weapons you prefer. Albany, you'll be our trap man; you've got a good nose." He nodded at the cyborged clone. "Huxley will run the antisurveillance gear; that's his specialty."

The beaster, whose name was Durban, spoke in his breathless way. "And I?"

"Point walker." Ruiz turned to the ex-gladiator, who claimed no name. "You'll leapfrog with Durban. And you two will flank," he told the women, who called themselves Moh and Chou.

"How 'bout you?" asked Albany. "We seem to be doing everything."

"I wish," said Ruiz. "I'll be herding the nonexpendables."

The stolid faces acquired sour expressions. "Who might they be?" asked Durban the beaster.

Ruiz answered reluctantly. "A Gench and a noncombatant ringer."

Now the faces were turning mulish. "What the hell," said Albany weakly.

Ruiz shrugged. "Well, that's why you're getting the big money. What else can I say?"

"How about: 'If you've changed your mind you can get off at the first stack we come to'?" asked one of the Jahworld women.

"Sorry," said Ruiz, shaking his head. "Your chop is on the contract. Nonperformance gets you sold in the Pit."

"You're a harder man than I remember," said Albany, shaking his head ruefully.

"I have a tougher contract than you do," said Ruiz, thinking of Publius's knife.

·   ·   ·

BEFORE THEY BOARDED the sub, Publius sent Huey to
fetch Ruiz to him. When Ruiz arrived in the command
cabin, Publius was looking out through a large armorglass
port, at the twinkling lights of SeaStack. The cabin was lit
only by a central cluster of dim red glowbulbs, presumably
to accommodate the preferences of the small Gench who
waited in the corner. On a couch at the back of the cabin sat
the false Yubere, smiling his thin unemotional smile. Four
Dirm bondguards stood spaced around the cabin, fingering
their weapons and watching Ruiz alertly.

Publius turned as Ruiz entered, raised a hand in greeting.
"Ah! Ruiz! Are you ready to turn the tides of history?"

"I suppose," said Ruiz doubtfully.

Publius frowned. "Ruiz, you have no sense of the magni-
tude of this moment. That's a shame; I wanted you to feel
the importance of your task. When you succeed, the universe will change forever."

Ruiz was growing weary of Publius's grandiosity, but he
concealed his contempt. "I'm glad you have confidence in
me, Emperor Publius."

Publius was happy again. "Oh, I do. But now, to business." He beckoned, and an immature Gench shuffled across
the floor toward them. "Let me take your slave collar," Publius said.

Ruiz bent his neck, and Publius applied his molecular
key to the collar's lock. "Doesn't that feel better," asked
Publius. "Are you sure you want to wear the madcollar with
my little Gench?"

Ruiz didn't bother to answer.

"Oh, all right." Publius took a metal case from a storage
slot and opened it, to reveal two madcollars. "You'll want to
examine them, I suppose."

Ruiz lifted them from their case and carried them to a
pool of brighter light. He noted that they were of SeedCorp
manufacture, ordinarily a sign of reliability. He checked to
see that their seals were undamaged. He ran both controllers
through their diagnostic sequence, while Publius stood waiting impatiently.

"They seem all right," said Ruiz without great confidence.

"Of course they're all right. What do you take me for?"

"A clever man," said Ruiz.

"Well, of course you're correct," said Publius, mollified. "Get on with it, then."

Ruiz turned to the Gench. "Has Publius explained the arrangement to you?"

One of the Gench's mouth slits trembled, then opened. It spoke in a faint whistling voice. "I am to be a hostage."

"True," said Ruiz. "You understand how the madcollars work?"

"Yes."

"Please verbalize your understanding," said Ruiz.

"If I die, you die. If you die, I die."

"That's right. Also, once the collars are locked on, they can only be removed if we both agree to it."

"I understand perfectly," it said.

"Good. Let's do it, then." Ruiz snapped his collar around his neck, then watched closely as Publius set the collar around the Gench's neckring, securing it with anesthetic staples. Ruiz picked up his controller; the Gench opened another mouth and extended a manipulator to its controller.

They both pressed the appropriate stud, and Ruiz felt his collar click into active mode. Foreboding rushed into him; he thrust it away. He would need all his skills, every fraction of concentration, to perform Publius's task—and then to survive Publius's gratitude.

"Let's go," he said.

THE SUBMARINE DRIFTED silently down through the black SeaStack depths, feeling its way through the murk using passive sonar. Several times Ruiz heard the surging thresh of a margar passing nearby, and the sonar constantly picked up the sounds of smaller life forms, the engines of other, less clandestine subs, and the passage of surface craft. The sonar analyzed the reflectance patterns of these vibrations and constructed a ghostly green image of the stack's underwater wall, projecting it in the holotank. It marked their own position with a red dot, which seemed to crawl down the vast wall at an almost-imperceptible rate. Ruiz watched intently for a while, then satisfied that the sub's autopilot was functioning properly, he went aft through the cramped cargo hold where the slayers sat with their equipment. He beckoned to Albany, who got up and followed him into the private cabin where the Gench and the false Yubere waited.

"You're the trapman, Albany," Ruiz said. "Look at the madcollars and tell me if they're straight."

"I'll see what I can do," said Albany. He began to lay out the probes and analyzers of the trapman's trade.

Half an hour later, he rose from an examination of the Gench's collar, wrinkling his nose against the Gench's stink. "This one is gimmicked," Albany said. "There's a monomolecular film over the receptor port, which would have filtered out the destruct signal. When your boss kills you, the Gench won't die."

Ruiz shook his head. Publius's greed was monumental; he wasn't even willing to sacrifice his little Gench to expunge Ruiz. He felt a bit insulted. He reached up to the overhead and activated a videocam. "Let's make a record of this," he said. "It might come in handy, later. Can you clear the filter?"

"No problem." Albany applied an atomic eroder to the collar, set a timer.

Ruiz addressed the Gench, who received Albany's attentions impassively. "Did you know of this trick?"

"No. But I am a valuable property; it seems logical that my owner would attempt to protect me. Do you plan to inform him that his trick is discovered?"

Ruiz grunted noncommittally. When Albany had pronounced the collar functional, he said, "Do me a favor, Albany. Take the ringer and go forward for a while. Entertain him however you like, but don't bruise him up too much."

Albany took the false Yubere by the arm. The ringer smiled placidly and went without protest. Ruiz shut the pressure door behind them and spun down the lockwheel. He switched off the camera.

"We must confer," he said to the Gench.

NISA, HOLDING HER back straight, sat chained to a bare steel bench in the back of Remint's sled. Beside her, Flomel muttered curses: at her, at Ruiz Aw, at the unkind fate that had led him to this unhappy end.

"Shut up," she finally snapped, wearied by his endless sniveling. "Must you carry on in such a contemptible manner?"

Flomel glared at her. "Slut . . . it's you who should be silent. It's your fault all this happened. The casteless slayer was seduced in Bidderum—thus he threw himself onto the stage and our dooms were sealed. If not for him, we would even now be performing for the princes of the pangalac worlds."

Dolmaero, who sat back to back with Nisa, made a sound of disbelief. "Unlikely, Master Flomel. And our minds would no longer belong to us, had Ruiz Aw not interfered."

"How much longer will they belong to us, anyway?" asked Flomel. "Besides, if I'd never learned that my mind had been remade, why would I care? It doesn't sound so terrible to me."

"It wouldn't," said Molnekh dryly.

"What do you mean by that?" asked Flomel hotly.

"You've always been more devoted to the appearances of things than to their actuality. It served you well when we were conjurors—that was the nature of our art. But now we're slaves." Molnekh seemed grimmer than Nisa had ever known him to be. She realized unhappily how much comfort she had taken from his dependable cheerfulness.

Flomel nattered on, oblivious, pronouncing ever more imaginative curses on Ruiz Aw's head, until Nisa could no longer keep silent.

"You should be ashamed," she said. "Ruiz allowed you to live when the rest of us would have killed you. If he hadn't been merciful, you wouldn't have been able to inform Corean of our whereabouts. We'd still be back at the pens, and Ruiz would have come to take us away from this terrible world."

At that, the massive man who was piloting the boat turned his head and spoke tersely. "You're wrong," Remint said.

"What do you mean?" Nisa said stiffly. Remint was a frightening person; he seemed a stylized icon of destruction, not quite human. In the pen, she had watched him coolly kill dozens of the pen's security troops; he had never displayed any expression but intense concentration.

"Flomel didn't betray you," said Remint. "How do you think we found Flomel?"

"How?" demanded Nisa, feeling a sudden dreadful anticipation.

"Ruiz Aw told us where you were. He hoped to trade

your lives for his, he wanted to bargain with us. But it won't do him any good. We'll find him anyway, so he betrayed you for nothing."

"I don't believe you," said Nisa. She glared at Remint. "You must think we're fools. If Ruiz Aw had sold us to you, you wouldn't have had to blow up the place and fight the guards to get us."

"He didn't sell you to us; he had already sold you elsewhere. Your new owners were stiff-necked folk; they wouldn't put a price on you, so we were forced to act directly." Remint shrugged, and returned to his piloting.

Nisa glared at Remint through a mist of hot tears. But she was no longer absolutely certain he was lying—and there was an aching hole where her heart had been.

RUIZ CONTEMPLATED THE Gench. Like all its kind, it was a repulsive creature in human terms. Its baggy loose-skinned body was covered with weedy tufts of sensory fiber. Three eyespots roamed in a random pattern over its squat head, and it exuded a nauseating odor.

It seemed to be attending him with as much attention as any Gench ever gave to a human who wasn't trying to hurt it.

"Listen carefully," Ruiz said. "Your owner intends to kill you, in order to kill me."

"You will not inform him of the repaired madcollar?"

"Yes, but it will make no difference. He needs to kill me, and he will sacrifice you to do it."

The Gench fluttered its mouth parts, a gesture of skepticism. "I am too valuable a property."

"It's true, you're valuable. But your value will largely disappear if I succeed in my mission."

"How can that be?"

"Because our target, the man we intend to replace, owns a large number of Gencha—so many that your death will represent only a minor loss of capital for Publius."

The Gench became very still. Ruiz waited patiently for it to process this information.

Five minutes later it spoke again. "This is true?"

Ruiz nodded. "You will be able to confirm it as soon as we are inside the stronghold; the pheromones of many Gencha will fill your olfactory organs."

Another five minutes passed. "What must I do to survive?" it finally asked.

Ruiz sat back, feeling a cautious optimism. "Let's consider. I have a suggestion, but it's only a beginning and not a solution. Let's take off the madcollars."

The Gench quivered back, an expression of rejection. "Publius would punish me severely if I do so—he explained this to me at length. You cannot imagine what terrible threats he made."

"Oh, I think I can," said Ruiz. "But you miss the essential logic of the situation. If we do not remove the madcollars, Publius has only to kill you to kill me. If we remove them, he must kill me directly, and may spare you, if it comes to that. Though to be honest with you—I intend to retain you as a hostage, for whatever good that may do me."

"I see."

"I wish you no harm personally. But I do wish to survive."

"This is understandable." The Gench seemed unresentful, but Ruiz cautioned himself to make no groundless anthropomorphic assumptions about the creature.

Ruiz took his madcollar controller from his pocket. "We must press the disengage key simultaneously."

The Gench was motionless; then a slender glutinous tentacle emerged from its second mouth, the tip wrapped around the other controller. "Yes," it said.

They both pressed, the collars made a series of muted clicks and fell away.

Ruiz took a deep breath, rubbed his neck where the collar had chafed it slightly. He wanted to savor that small increase of freedom, but time was slipping away. "How proficient are you in human minddiving?"

"I have only minimal skill as yet. But I will learn, in time."

"There's no more time," Ruiz said harshly. "What do you know about diving a deconstructed person?"

The Gench shuddered. "Difficult to think about it . . . the holomnemonic ocean of such a person is a cold place, bright with unfriendly light."

"What changes are possible in such a person?"

"Without tearing down the personality and rebuilding it? Very few." It shifted uncomfortably. "I lack those skills."

"Other than such an extensive process, which in any case

we don't have time for, what could you do to prevent Publius from making use of his puppet without our cooperation?"

The Gench became still again. Ruiz felt his patience slipping away, but he stifled the impulse to badger the Gench. If he should cause the Gench to succumb to hysteria, he was lost.

After what seemed an endless silence, the Gench spoke uncertainly. "I find this modality difficult. My experience of treachery is almost nonexistent; perhaps I have no aptitude."

"Nonsense," said Ruiz. "You're an intelligent being; no species attains sapience without recourse to treachery. Let me restate the problem: What can we do to make our survival necessary to Publius? Let me suggest a possibility—can you install some sort of blockage in the puppet's perceptual channels, so that he will be unable to respond to Publius's instructions? Could you make the blockage contingent on some stimulus, perhaps a code phrase known only to us?"

The Gench's eyespots ceased their endless circulation, as though it had focused all its energies on the solution Ruiz had proposed.

Finally, when Ruiz had almost decided that the Gench had fallen prey to some self-circuited fugue, it spoke. "It seems at least possible," it said.

Ruiz considered. He no longer wore the collar, so he might now turn around and flee to some dark corner of SeaStack, there to hope to hide from Publius's anger. But he would be in no better position to get off Sook. No, his best hope still lay in gaining leverage over Publius.

Ruiz bounced to his feet. "Let's try," he said, and went forward to fetch the puppet.

CHAPTER 15

THE submarine was approaching its design limit, creaking under the pressure of the black water, when they reached the ancient ingress. Ruiz watched the sonar image in the holotank intently, nudging the craft centimeter by centimeter closer to the stack's vertical wall. The ingress showed as a circular depression, two meters in diameter, crudely blocked with fused metal girders, now shapeless with corrosion.

They touched the wall as gently as Ruiz could manage, but the submarine rang like a bell at the impact. The others watched with anxious faces as he extended the repair chamber, adjusted its mating surfaces to the wall's irregularities, and activated its molecular hooks.

A pump came to life, sounding unnaturally loud. "It'll be a few minutes before we can get into the chamber and start cutting," Ruiz said.

Everyone looked down, a synchronized gesture that made Ruiz wonder if they had all heard the same tales he had—tales about huge voracious monsters that coiled through the uncharted deep grottoes of SeaStack, never rising to the surface. He laughed, prompting the others to glare at him suspiciously.

When the repair chamber was clear, he beckoned to Albany. "You're good with a torch, Albany, so you're elected; I'll use the other one." The two of them squeezed into the chamber, wearing respirators and protective masks, and started cutting away the dripping metal, along the circumference of the ingress. Thick white fumes filled the chamber, and Ruiz's world narrowed down to the glare of the torch and the bright trickle of molten metal that ran from the cut, to be sucked up by the torch's aspirator. He tried not to think of the coming action, the odds against his success. He succeeded in forcing away those thoughts—but he couldn't entirely forget about Nisa, waiting for him in the pen, who would probably never learn the circumstances of his death, should he fail.

After ten minutes, the hiss of Albany's torch changed, acquiring the fluttering note that indicated breakthrough into an airspace. "Stop," said Ruiz, but Albany was already shutting down the torch.

Ruiz fed a finewire aural probe through the thin seam where Albany had broken through, turned up the gain on the amplifier. "Hold your breath," he told Albany.

Nothing. Ruiz listened intently for thirty seconds. He heard only the most obdurate of silences; devoid even of the most basic sounds—the sigh of ventilators, the vibration of generators, the subtly distorted noises of life that usually filtered into even the most remote burrows of the stacks. "Maybe our employer was right," he said, and put the probe away. "Maybe no one knows about this passage."

Albany seemed briefly cheered. "You mean we might live through this?"

"I didn't say that," answered Ruiz—but he smiled and slapped Albany's shoulder. "Let's cut some more."

An hour later they had freed the meter-thick plug that closed the ingress. They forced a thixotropic lubricant into the seam, then welded half a dozen automatic shear jacks to the outer edges and set them into motion.

Slowly, the plug slid inward, groaning. Ruiz donned his weapons.

"Make sure the others are ready—get them in their armor and check to see they've got all their gear," he told Albany, who nodded and went back into the sub.

Ruiz tried to think what else he might do to increase his chances of survival, but nothing came to him. All now seemed to depend on how good Publius's intelligence had been—and on how much good luck remained to Ruiz. He remembered Dolmaero's dour pronouncements on the subject of luck, and smiled. He found that he missed the Guildmaster.

The plug cleared the opening, and the jacks pushed it inward half a meter, just far enough to permit a person to slip past. Air puffed into the repair chamber. Albany sampled it, bent over his meters, then spoke. "Clean enough." He took off his breather, made a sour face. Ruiz took off his mask. The faint stink of Gencha stained the air. He wrinkled his nose, then put on his helmet and lowered the visor.

The rest of his team stood waiting, and Ruiz nodded at Durban the beaster.

"Go," he said.

Durban shouldered eagerly past him. The personamatrix scarab he wore at the base of his skull gave him the reflexive cruelty and decisiveness of his totem. He glanced at Ruiz, bright-eyed and smiling. The wolverine that filled his brain looked out of Durban's human eyes, happy to be going where it might fulfill its vicious impulses.

Durban went through with a supple twist of his body, and Ruiz held his breath, waiting for the sound of ambush, or automated anti-intruder weaponry. But nothing came, and after a moment Durban whispered, "Come."

"Huxley," Ruiz said to the cyborg with the antisurveillance gear. "Get in, set up." Next, Ruiz sent in the scarfaced ex-gladiator and one of the flankers, then gestured at the puppet. The false Yubere smiled his empty smile and went.

Ruiz went back into the sub, checked to see that the controls were adequately locked against tampering, and that the sub's security systems were set to self-destruct should anyone attempt to enter before Ruiz returned. The Gench crouched in the darkest corner, and Ruiz dialed the lights to a softer level. "We'll be back as soon as possible," he told it, and it made a hissing sound of assent.

"If Publius attempts to contact you, you will be much safer if you do not respond," he said.

"I will remember," it said. "At present, you seem more trustworthy than Publius. So far you have been truthful; I detect the scent-signatures of many members of the Real Race."

A shudder of apprehension wavered through Ruiz. "How many?"

"More than I could separate—more than I knew still existed anywhere. I am very young and my knowledge is small, but . . . very many. Perhaps when you return, you will allow me to go to them."

"If conditions permit," Ruiz said.

"I understand."

THE TUNNEL WAS three meters in height. In the helmet lamps his team wore, its rough alloy walls seemed to curve slightly to the left. Ruiz consulted with Albany, who monitored a tiny scattershot radarscreen on his forearm. "What do you see?" asked Ruiz.

"No activity in my range," said Albany, brow furrowed in concentration. "I get dropouts every thirty-three meters —must be adits of some sort, without doors."

Ruiz set his people in motion—the beaster in front, the flankers drifting back and forth in a reciprocating pattern, the nameless gladiator trailing well back. He held the false Yubere's leash; just ahead of him walked Huxley the cyborg with his antisurveillance gear. Just behind Ruiz, Albany trudged along under his load of detectors.

"Helmet mikes only, minimum range," said Ruiz. "Be stealthy, everyone."

Seven pairs of eyes gleamed at him from the dark; each pair but one carried some unique message: anticipation, curiosity, fear.

The puppet seemed impossibly placid.

Ruiz looked back at Albany. "You're the navigator," he said.

"Let's trot," said Albany. "I'll let you know when we're lost."

THEY FOLLOWED THE empty tunnel for several kilometers, and Albany confirmed Ruiz's impression that they were rising slightly. "That's the right way, boss," he said. "Isn't it?"

"I guess," Ruiz said. They were following a navigation bead provided by Publius; its telltales blinked green in Albany's dataslate.

At regular intervals they passed open doorways, edged by ovals of some silvery alloy. At the first of these, Durban had paused for a moment, then dropped to his belly and risked a peek over the threshold. "Empty storeroom," he said, and went on. So far all the doorways had proven similarly innocuous.

At the three-and-a-half-kilometer mark, Albany froze in midstep. "Activity," he whispered, and the rest of the team stopped abruptly. "I'm getting just a taste of electromagnetics . . . some sort of ranging pulse, maybe."

Huxley tapped at his dataslate. "Not enough to go on," the cyborg said in a grating bass. "I need to get closer."

Ruiz considered, then called in one of the pinbeamers. "Chou, you and Durban convoy Huxley and Albany forward, till they get a better shape of what's coming up. Be quiet—don't use the helmet comms outside the fifty-meter range."

She nodded, and the four of them slid into the gloom. In a few moments they disappeared around the curve of the tunnel. For a dozen heartbeats longer Ruiz could make out the reflection of their helmet lamps, and then there was nothing but darkness ahead.

RUIZ WAITED, THE puppet's leash in one hand, a plasma projector in the other. The remaining pinbeamer crouched against the tunnel wall fifteen meters ahead, the gladiator waited even farther behind them, just inside a storeroom doorway.

"We have a little privacy," said the false Yubere. "Perhaps you'll tell me what the Gench did to me. Publius said nothing to me about any additional modifications."

"Publius doesn't tell you everything, apparently."

"No, of course not. Still it seems strange. Are you sure it wasn't your idea?"

"If it was, would I tell you?"

The puppet's face twisted, just for an instant. "Dangerous even to tease me about such things," the false Yubere said, in a voice that was suddenly dark and wild, as if another person spoke from his body.

Ruiz gave the puppet a speculative stare. What was this? Was the puppet—and thus Yubere—not so bland a creature as Publius had led him to believe?

"Sorry," said Ruiz. "Of course I acted on Publius's instructions. Would I dare to defy such a potent monster? Who is that brave, or foolish?"

The puppet's face resumed its mask of disengaged cheerfulness. "As you say. Well, another matter, then. Why must you keep me on this leash? Surely you know I wouldn't defy Publius's instructions."

"It makes me feel better," said Ruiz. "Besides, it's clear already that he gave different orders to me than he gave to you."

HALF AN HOUR later, Ruiz heard Albany's whisper through the comm. "Come."

Albany was alone when they reached him a few minutes later. "I left the others to keep an eye on developments," Albany said. There was a jagged undertone to his voice. "Do we have to do this, boss?"

Ruiz nodded. "What did you find?"

"Weird stuff. Weird. What is it with you and the Gencha? You seem to be going out of your way to rub up against them."

In fact Ruiz had noticed the slow strengthening of the Gencha stink, as they walked.

"Never mind that, Albany," he snapped. "What did you find?"

Albany sighed. "So don't pay any attention to me; see if I care. Well, we found a great big hole in the stack. This tunnel ends there, like the big hole ate right through it when whatever made the big hole happened. The hole is about a hundred fifty meters across, roughly cylindrical, with lots of other tunnels above and below this one. A spiral tramway goes around the walls, avoiding the tunnels—it looks to be pretty recent construction. The hole goes up almost half a kilometer, according to my radar, but it goes down a lot farther—three kilometers. But I can tell you this: It stinks like the whole Gencha race lives at the bottom of it."

"What was the activity you detected?"

Albany shook his head. "Don't know—it dropped off when we got a little closer. My guess is that it was the tram —a car going up or down."

"Surveillance activity?"

"Huxley says not. Is he any good?"

Ruiz ignored the question. The pit hadn't figured in Publius's briefing; apparently Publius's data on Yubere's stronghold was imperfect. He hoped that the navigation bead wasn't useless.

He turned to the puppet. "What is it?"

The puppet shook his head amiably. "I seem to have forgotten about this. How odd, to be surprised by such a major feature in my own house." He looked genuinely bemused, though only for an instant.

"Can we get to the tram track?" asked Ruiz.

"Passes twenty meters under our tunnel, spirals around the pit wall and passes sixty meters above the tunnel," said Albany. "But you can see for yourself; we're almost there. There's a useful level of ambient light in the pit, if you want to switch off your helmet light."

As soon as Ruiz killed his light, he noticed a soft red light at the end of the tunnel. His stomach jumped, and he felt a sweat break on his forehead.

"Oh yeah," said Albany.

The red glow was the hue preferred by the Gencha who had installed his death net and mission-imperative. He felt a phantom shift in his mind, as if ghosts of those constructs still existed somewhere in him. An odd lassitude welled up in him; he fought it down, bludgeoned it with his purpose.

They reached the end of the tunnel, where the others lay on their bellies. The cyborg had extended several probes into the pit; he appeared to be fishing with invisible line. Chou the pinbeamer was well back from the edge, her face pressed to the tunnel floor. Durban seemed a compressed spring of destruction, waiting to uncoil. He gave Ruiz a feral glance as Ruiz crawled up beside him.

"Cut back your personaskein," ordered Ruiz. Durban gave him a wordless snarl, an inhuman expression . . . but then he reached up to his neck and adjusted the skein.

The beaster might turn out to be a liability, Ruiz thought, just before he looked out over the pit.

The walls seemed to be the source of that disturbing bloody light, and he wondered at the extravagance of Alonzo Yubere, to so illuminate this vast hole. Judging the man from his puppet, he'd never have expected such a flair for the dramatic.

The tramway was a single rail, held away from the slagged-over surface of the pit by webwork brackets; its

metal showed the brightness of frequent use. It spiraled endlessly down into the pit, its delicate glimmer finally lost
against the glow.

Ruiz edged forward, so that he could look far down into
the pit. A thin mist obscured the depths, catching and con-
centrating the light so that it seemed a great gloomy red eye
looked up at Ruiz from the bottom of the world.

"Something's falling fast," said the cyborg, who hastily
retracted his probes.

Ruiz looked up. A dot resolved into the tiny figure of a
person, falling in a boneless tumble. An instant later Ruiz
saw that it was a woman, her face obscured by long dark
hair, streaming in the wind of her descent.

Then she dropped past, somewhat closer to the far side of
the pit than to Ruiz, so that he never got a clear look at her.
She disappeared soundlessly into the red depths.

He was shaken by a sudden illogical conviction that he
had just seen Nisa falling to her death. *No, no. . . . She was
safe, back in the pen.* He cursed himself for his foolishness.
The universe was full of slender black-haired women; it was
supreme arrogance to believe that this one was in any way
connected to Ruiz Aw.

"Feeding the Gencha," said Albany.

"I guess so," said Ruiz in a somewhat shaky voice. The
Gencha were carrion feeders, able to assimilate the decay
products of almost any hydrocarbon-based life. He didn't
want to think what it must be like at the bottom of the pit.
This is just like a goblin tale, Nisa, he thought, and then
somehow he was able to put aside his horror and apprehension. *The hero always rescues the princess,* he told himself.

The cyborg extended his probes and lowered a sensor to
the track. He studied the output, then proffered a datacable
to Albany, who plugged it into his own array of detectors.

"Hey," said Albany. "I think someone's coming down
the slow way."

Huxley reeled in his probes again, and the others dispersed back down the tunnel, so as not to project too obvious an infrared profile.

Ruiz had handed the puppet's leash to one of the
pinbeamers. Now he, Huxley, and Albany were the only
ones remaining at the lip of the tunnel.

A thin singing reached Ruiz's ears. He looked up and
saw the tram far above, descending swiftly, circulating

around the wall of the pit at a speed that stressed the rail enough to produce the sound.

When the tram had descended to a point just above them on the opposite wall, Ruiz peered at it through the tiny photomultiplier telescope that Albany handed him. He saw a bare framework of girders cantilevered out from the rail, sliding on frictionless impellor bushings. Between the ends lay six pallets, to which a half-dozen persons were secured. The passengers' heads lolled with every jolt of the tram; apparently they were anesthetized. A Dirm of gigantic proportions sat at each end of the contrivance, each staring in opposite directions, grasers held ready. Before one of them was a control panel, from which projected various levers and switches. Their alien skulls displayed prominent scars, of a pattern Ruiz recognized.

Albany grunted. "Pithed Dirms," he said. "Your man got the big money, eh?"

Ruiz shrugged. "They wouldn't hire us expensive cutthroats just to snuff a pauper."

"True. Well, we can snip them right off their seats; the real trick will come after we grease them—catching the tram before it gets away. It's moving pretty fast."

"Let's wait until they come back," said Ruiz.

"Well of course." Albany looked mildly insulted. "Do I look like a tourist who's just dying to visit Gencha Wonderland?"

Ruiz smiled. "No. How do you think we should do it?"

Albany rubbed his jaw speculatively. "We got a small problem. The Jahworld sisters are acrophobic—I guess you didn't think that would matter when you probed them. I don't know how much good they're going to do us out there."

Ruiz considered. "If our employer's given us accurate data—aside from the existence of this hole, which he didn't know existed—then we may be able to slip in the target's back door, and we may not need everyone. We'll leave the sisters here in the tunnel to keep our bolthole open."

"Lot of ifs, Ruiz," said Albany.

The tram swept around the side of the pit. Ruiz turned to Huxley. "Get everything you can, scan the contraption for deadman switches, uplinks, antiboarding devices—you know what to look for. I don't know how long a round-trip takes, but when they get back, we'll have to be ready for them."

They waited silently while Huxley worked with his probes. The tram passed beneath them and Ruiz half expected the Dirm to lift their alien heads and see him—but they stared stolidly at nothing.

When they were gone with their cargo of sleeping victims, Ruiz turned to Huxley. "What did you get?"

"I can't be sure I got everything, but . . . there are deadman switches, inductively monitoring the first Dirm's vital signs. No problem there, if Moh or Chou can still shoot. The switches seem inadequately armored—a pinbeam through the central solenoids ought to fuse them open. Stupid design, really—the main uplink transponder seemed to be housed in an impenetrable block of monomol armor, but the remotes are vulnerable."

"What else?"

"There's a random ident uplink, I think. If it works as I assume it does, someone upstairs occasionally calls, and one of them responds. Puts some part of its anatomy in a topological scanner. What do Dirms use for that?"

"Elbow whorls," said Ruiz.

"Ah. Well then, no problem—we'll just keep an elbow handy and hope we recognize the calldown. Then there's an anti-intrusion field—sets off a silent alarm if any unauthorized person tries to board the tram between stops. Fortunately our employer didn't skimp on our gear, and I think I can tune our armor into an invisible resonance with the field —its pattern shift isn't terribly sophisticated."

Albany laughed softly. "Yeah, great, Huxley, what a relief. Otherwise we might have had to give up and go back to our nice little sub. Wouldn't that've been a tragedy?"

Huxley gave Albany a chilly glance, but didn't bother to reply. "Then," he continued, "there seem to be several purely mechanical devices: proximity jects, tanglefoot decking, razor rails. Those are more properly your department, Albany, but they seem to be electronically linked to a central activity monitor—another job for the pinbeamers.

"Then there's some sort of feedback uplink on the tram itself, hooked to a lowtech inertial guidance unit, which probably is designed to report any sudden change in the tram's speed."

"What about the pit itself?" asked Ruiz.

"Nothing, as far as I can tell," said the cyborg, shrugging his metal shoulders. "If we had a week and the right gear, we might be able to scale the wall, if no one came along and noticed us. The rail is hot with detector filaments, though, so we can't just climb the webbing."

"So," said Albany. "Let's see if I can sum up. Our freaked-out sisters got to get steady enough to punch the solenoids, we got to pop the Dirms without losing any elbows, and then we got to get on the thing without slowing it, even though it's moving fast enough to break our legs if we land wrong. Then we got to miss the jects and the razor rails, keep from stepping in the tanglefoot. Then when we get to the top, we'll probably have a reception waiting for us because we missed some detail, or stuck the wrong elbow in the scanner. Stop me anytime, someone."

"I guess I'll go talk to Moh and Chou," said Ruiz. "Meanwhile, figure out how to get on the tram."

Ruiz went back along the tunnel, to where the two Jahworld women huddled in the angle between wall and floor, each clutching her pinbeam, as if deriving some comfort from its heavy glass and metal barrel.

"I'm sorry you're frightened," he said. "But we'll need you when the tram comes back."

"Too deep," said Moh in a voice trembling with strain. "Way too deep. You told us this was going to be a cavecrawl." Her tone was only slightly accusing; her terror seemed to be occupying all her attention.

"I thought it was," said Ruiz. "But it's not; and that's too bad. I'm going to put you two up at the tunnel mouth— you'll have to burn out some gear for us. Can you do it?"

Chou sat up and disengaged herself from the other woman's grip. "We'll give it a shot. But if you think we're going out into that hole, you're wrong."

"No, no, I don't expect that. What good would you be to me there? I'll leave you here to guard our back door, after we get the tram. You wait for us."

Chou's flat broad face cleared. "We'll camp down the tunnel, where we can't see the light or feel the deep."

Ruiz nodded and went back to the lip.

"Go set up the sisters' fire pattern and priorities," he told the cyborg.

MORE THAN AN hour passed before Ruiz heard the rail begin to sing again.

They had used the time to formulate and refine a plan. It depended too much on perfection of execution, Ruiz thought pessimistically, but it was the best he could do. He didn't really believe that he would be able to come up with a better plan if they waited for the tram to make another trip; besides, who knew when that might occur—it might not go down to the Gencha again for a week. And he'd always been luckiest when he improvised quickly.

Ruiz had sent the gladiator, the puppet, and Durban the beaster out along a horizontal crack in the wall that widened sufficiently to hide them, a few meters closer to the rail and perhaps fifty meters farther up—a point from which boarding the tram would be somewhat easier. Ruiz had sealed the puppet's leash to the gladiator's wrist—and told the nameless man that getting the puppet safely on the tram was the most important job.

Ruiz, Albany, Huxley, and the sisters lay on their bellies at the tunnel mouth, rehearsing each other in their roles in the impending attack. The sisters would burn out the deadman solenoids, so those mechanisms would stay locked in the live positions. Albany would try to burn off as many of the physical antiboarding devices as he could. Huxley wasn't notably skilled with long-range weapons, so his job was to get his and Albany's gear aboard undamaged.

Ruiz had taken one of the most difficult tasks for himself —killing the Dirms. Dirms possessed vestigial remote brains distributed through their bodies in a number of locations, a legacy from their overgrown sauroid ancestors. Through an expensive and uncertain process, these vestigial brains could be enhanced with tissue from the Dirm's primary brain, until the alien possessed a form of distributed intelligence that made it almost impossible to instantly disable the creature. Ruiz would have to burn through enough of the Dirm's brains to disable the creature before it could report the attack.

Then, supposing all went well, and Huxley detected no alarms on the tram's uplink, they would all fling themselves into space, tethered by programmable monolastic descenders—special lines that would stretch to absorb the shock of hitting the end of the tether, but not rebound. If Albany's calculations were correct, they would end up dangling two meters over the rail as the tram passed.

They'd have to drop, avoid any of the mantraps Albany might have missed, avoid injury, and not fall off. Then they'd have to catch the puppet, and the other two slayers.

After that they could start wondering what they might find at the top of the pit.

"This ought to be easy," said Albany, grinning ferociously.

Ruiz wasn't very amused. All his life he had thrown himself into situations of uncertain violence, confident that he would survive them, as he always had. It no longer seemed possible for him to enter conflict with the same impersonal monomaniacal intensity that had guarded him for so long, and he wasn't sure what had changed. Perhaps, he thought, it was because he was no longer as indifferent to the possibility of death; now he wanted very badly to live, with a fervor that grew stronger every day.

He wondered how it was he had lived for so many years without noticing that he hadn't cared very much whether he lived or died.

"Wake up, Ruiz," whispered Albany, who nudged him and pointed. The tram was coming up the incline toward them, moving upward somewhat more slowly than it had descended—a heartening development. It carried six passengers, though these weren't anesthetized. They lay on their pallets, looking up empty-eyed. A chill passed through Ruiz —these were obviously deconstructed persons, returning from the Gencha.

Ruiz squinted through the scope of the long-barreled spitter he had carried strapped to his packframe for just such an occasion. The Dirm's scaly face swam into focus, the pithing scar prominent just below the creature's skulltop nostrils. Its moonstone eyes stared dully, as if the redistribution of its intelligence had taken something essential from it.

Ruiz dropped the crosshairs to the Dirm's left shoulder joint; it held the tram's speed yoke in its left hand.

"Now," he said, and fired.

His weapon launched a supersonic needle of frozen gas, which struck the Dirm and thawed explosively.

Before Ruiz could see the damage he had done, he was firing again, at the right shoulder brain, the abdominal brain, the left hip, the left calf. He switched his fire to the

other Dirm, who was reacting to the destruction of its part-
ner, its right hand rising toward an alarm button. Ruiz hit
the right shoulder brain, then before the Dirm could switch
hands, the left shoulder, and on to the other centers.

He was vaguely aware of the spurts of white sparks as the
pinbeamers killed the solenoids, of the darker flash of Albany's graser as he burned away the mechanical devices on
the near side of the tram.

The shooting was over in two seconds.

"Clean so far," Huxley barked. The three of them slung
their weapons and rolled over the lip of the tunnel into the
void.

The fall lasted a timeless instant, until the deceleration
jerked Ruiz upright. He waited until the tram was almost
under him, then slapped the release and dropped the last
two meters. He landed on one of the passengers; it was like
falling into soft sand, it cushioned the impact. He managed
to keep his balance, and jumped toward the first Dirm he
had shot, which was floundering weakly. The spitter had
pulped its joints along with its brains, and it showed no sign
of surviving intelligence.

Ruiz swung the little sonic blade and lopped off the creature's left arm just below its shattered shoulder. He jerked
the arm loose, slashed the Dirm's safety harness, and kicked
the alien over the side.

He turned, to see Albany struggling with the other Dirm,
whom he had apparently not done such a good job with.
Some strength remained in one arm, and it was resisting
Albany's efforts to pry it out of its seat, hissing and swinging
the arm like a club at Albany's head.

Ruiz bounded across the tram and took off the arm with
a slice of the sonic knife. This Dirm retained some of its
sapience, and it stared in bewilderment at the stump of its
arm, as Albany and Ruiz pulled it out of its seat and toppled
it into the pit.

The passengers had begun to react to the attack, had
started to rise from their pallets, faces slowly shifting toward
hostility, as they realized that these ambushers were almost
certainly not allied to their owners.

But their impulse toward attack was cut short by Huxley,
who stitched his splinter gun across them. They fell back
silently, blood welling from the arc described by Huxley's
gun, dead or dying.

"Still clean," said Huxley, consulting the tiny dataslate strapped to his wrist.

An instant later Durban landed on the corpses and rolled, covering his armor in red splashes. Then the gladiator and the puppet hit . . . and matters started to deteriorate.

The gladiator, a heavy man apparently no longer as agile as he must have been during his years in the bloodstadia, stumbled and fell against the razor rail that rimmed the far edge of the tram. He gasped and folded over the rail, which came to life with a high-pitched whine. In an instant its vibrating blades had sliced through his armor and deep into his belly. He struggled to escape the rail's terrible keenness, his legs scrabbling weakly. The rail must have penetrated almost to his spine when he made a last spasmodic effort and slipped over the side.

Ruiz lunged at the puppet, who was still leashed to the gladiator's wrist. The gladiator hit the end of the leash and the puppet slid toward the rail, just before Ruiz landed on the spot he had been. But Albany saw what was happening and grabbed the puppet before he hit the rail, though Albany was twisted awkwardly across the pallets of corpses, his foot hooked precariously under a girder.

"Do something," said Albany hoarsely. "Can't hold them for long."

Ruiz leaped to the rail, stopping just short of the red-dripping blades. The gladiator hung from the leash, while he tried with his other hand to retrieve the intestines that were slipping in gory loops from his belly.

Suddenly he looked up from his task, at Ruiz. His eyes were glazing with shock, but he spoke. "Too slippery, Ruiz."

He wasn't too far gone to react when Ruiz began to saw at the leash with his sonic knife. "No, no, no, no," he said. "Don't want to be Gench food. Don't. No, no, no."

The tough filaments parted reluctantly. The gladiator pleaded. Ruiz kept his eyes fixed on the knife.

He didn't look down, not even when the leash finally parted and the man fell wailing into the pit.

CHAPTER 16

"STILL seems clean," said Huxley, sitting in the middle of the corpses, his detectors spread around him, heedless of the blood that stained his armor. "I was concerned we might find weight sensors, or something else out of the ordinary."

The puppet got to his feet, apparently undisturbed by his near encounter with the razor rails. "In many ways I'm a conventional man," he said calmly.

"Who cares?" asked Albany. "You care, Ruiz?"

"No. Get your gear and clear the rest of the traps, Albany." Ruiz took the end of the leash, took the sealer from his pocket, and attached the end to a girder. "Durban, help me pitch the bodies off."

The beaster looked up, eyes bright with pleasure. He licked a smear of blood from his glove and made an odd purring sound.

"And turn down your skein," Ruiz said.

Durban snarled, and for a moment Ruiz thought he would attack. He felt an answering rage fill his body, and he leaned toward the beaster, knife ready, his mind completely clear, completely purposeful, for the first time in days. The chinks in the beaster's armor seemed to take on a glow in the intensity of Ruiz's regard; he could almost feel the sensation the knife would transmit to his hand when it penetrated Durban's shell and sank into his flesh.

Durban started to rise, lips writhing back to show his teeth. Latent violence stained the ruddy light a darker crimson, and Ruiz felt his anger transmute into a kind of black joy.

The beaster stopped abruptly. Fear and blood lust appeared to struggle for control of his face. He shuddered and dropped his eyes. After a moment he reached up, touched the skein at the back of his neck. Though he didn't look up, Ruiz could sense Durban's returning rationality.

"Good decision," said Albany, who holstered the splinter gun he had held aimed at Durban. "It's generally a bad idea to fuck with Ruiz—even though he might seem like an easygoing fellow."

Ruiz felt his own anger recede, to be replaced by an empty regret. But he switched off the knife and slipped it back into its wrist sheath. "If you max your skein again, I'll cut it off you," he said in a neutral voice.

He and Durban began to pitch the corpses off the tram. The beaster worked with a will, though he still wouldn't meet Ruiz's eyes. Ruiz felt no residue of irritation with him; he was too busy worrying about what they might find at the top of the pit.

They had moved around the pit, to a level just above the tunnel they had jumped from. Ruiz looked through his scope, to see Chou wave and retreat down the tunnel into darkness.

Albany moved about the tram, burning off the remaining proximity jects, tiny mantraps that fired an anesthetic charge at any protoplasm that touched their sensor fields. Albany was using one of the Dirm arms to spring the jects, after which he would apply a pinpoint of energy to fuse the mechanism.

He held the arm aloft. "When we're done with this, I'm going to pitch it to the Gencha. Maybe one of them will eat enough of it to get sick."

Ruiz wondered if any humans lived below, or any Gencha sufficiently worldly to report the sudden rain of food that had fallen from above. There had been nothing he could do about that. The tram would have ground to a stop under the weight of all of them: his slayers, the dead Dirms, and the former passengers. He tried to imagine what it might be like to exist at the bottom of the pit, what sort of person could survive among the great number of Gencha that must fill the caverns below. He couldn't—they would have to be so strange as to no longer be recognizably human.

He went to sit beside Huxley, who had developed a worried frown. "What is it?" Ruiz asked.

"Not sure," said the cyborg, tapping at his dataslate and checking the connections of his sensors. "I'm not getting any of what I should be getting. You'd figure a setup like this, there would be as much security at the top station as on the tram, but I'm not getting much. Actually, I'm not getting anything. Either our party is an overconfident man who expects no trouble from below, or he's got stuff that's too sophisticated for me."

Ruiz looked at the puppet. "Which is it?" he asked.

The false Yubere shrugged. "Like all men, I have my moods and blind spots."

"Whatever that means," said Albany, who had finished his detrapping operations.

The puppet looked at him without expression. "Metaphor and allusion; these are the tools of the supple mind."

"Whatever that means," said Albany. "Ruiz, we're fairly safe now. I don't want to fiddle with the tanglefoot; it would take a lot of my remaining firepower to burn the stuff off. So if you don't mind, we'll all just be careful."

The tanglefoot was a mat that ran around the perimeter of the tram, just outside the razor rails. An incautious foot descending on the mat caused the tanglefoot to fire barbed wires into the foot. Even armor wasn't entirely proof against a mat; some wires would penetrate, enough to discourage lifting the foot. Ruiz had once stepped on tanglefoot, even now he could remember the awful sensations of pulling loose —the barbs ripping through flesh and tendon, the little wet pops as they came through the skin.

"We'll be careful," he said.

The tram rode steadily up the rail, and Ruiz stationed himself at the control panel, ready to press the Dirm's elbow into the scanner cup, should a request come through the short-range communit built into the panel. But the comm's activity light remained dark, and nothing disturbed their progress.

After a while Ruiz relaxed enough to look out at the

walls of the pit, which at this height were even more wormy with interrupted tunnels. From the mouths of some of these openings came signs of life within, soft noises, an occasional flicker of movement, the nose-tingling smells of unfamiliar alien cookery. Ruiz wondered what sort of creatures made their home here so far below the human levels of the stack. According to the data Publius had provided, they were still a long way beneath the lowest levels of Yubere's dungeons.

When humans had arrived on Sook, the planet was populated by a diversity of alien races. Some, reduced to devolved remnants, had been there for eons; others had been more recently marooned.

When the humans had succeeded to domination on Sook, some of those aliens had retreated into the roots of SeaStack.

In any case, none of the pit's inhabitants came to the tunnel mouths to look at them, and Ruiz surmised that the Dirms had entertained themselves by potshotting at the dwellers, a theory that gained credibility when he noticed the recent scars of energy weapons across several of the openings.

The dark roof of the pit drew closer, until Ruiz could see that it was a rough dome, built of scrap alloy beams, chinked with unpolished meltstone. Apparently some titanic weapon had punched a vast hole through the stack in some long-forgotten battle—and then someone had hurriedly repaired the damage. How long ago had that been?

Now he could see the terminus of the tram rail—it passed behind a curved monomol barricade just below the dome's foundation buttresses. The barricade, like the tram, seemed shiny and new compared to its surroundings.

"Let's get set," said Ruiz. "I'll sit one chair, Huxley the other. Albany and Durban on the pallets with Yubere between them. We don't know what to expect, but whatever we find, be quick, get off the tram as fast as you can—and then get behind something hard. Make sure your armor is tight, check your weapons, loosen your muscles."

"Yes, Momma," said Albany.

Ruiz ignored him. "We want to create as little fuss as possible; Huxley, you keep your eye on your sensors, unless you absolutely have to stop to do someone. We need to know right away, the instant word goes up to the target that weasels are in his chickenhouse."

"I'm getting something now," said Huxley. "Not much;

looks like it might be the spill-off radiation from a Konda-class graser. If so, someone up there is carrying a big gun."

Albany looked at Ruiz and shivered elaborately. "Oooh," he whispered. "Getting interesting now, boss. Who do we know can tote a Konda?"

Ruiz shook his head, but suddenly he was assailed by a memory of Corean's big Moc, bounding gracefully through the air, firing its ice gun.

"Have any of you ever danced with a Mocrassar?" he asked.

Albany's eyes widened theatrically. He patted his chest-plate tentatively. "No . . . no. I seem to be alive, so I guess not."

Huxley looked thoughtful. "That might be it, though I don't want to believe it. A Moc, with one big well-shielded graser—hard to beat something like that, if your enemy can afford it. Let's hope it's just a killmech, with sensory pickups too cute for me to detect."

"Four well-prepared humans can sometimes kill a Moc, given a similar tech level," said Ruiz. "We'll probably take casualties, but there's hope."

"Thank you for that inspirational speech, Ruiz Aw," said Albany, still smiling, but looking somewhat pale behind his visor.

The terminal barricade approached rapidly, and Ruiz checked over his weapons one last time. The tram slowed, just as it passed through an automatic blast door that folded shut behind them.

The tram ground to a stop at a platform, empty except for a corridor-car, apparently waiting to take the passengers back to Yubere's stronghold. A long peaceful moment passed, as they started to rise from their various positions. Nothing happened, and Ruiz was starting to hope that they had, miraculously, penetrated Yubere's stronghold without further conflict.

Then the Moc stepped from the mouth of the dark opening at the back of the platform.

IN THE FROZEN instant that passed before the Moc under-stood that it faced enemies, and before his slayers could react to the creature's presence, Ruiz's eyes recorded a number of irrelevant details.

This Moc was somewhat shorter than Corean's, and the paint that decorated it formed less complex patterns, indicating its inferior lineage. It wore no clothing, and its six-limbed body gleamed with fresh healthy chitin. Ruiz noticed no cyborged weapons, such as the energy tubes built into the midlimbs of Corean's Moc—but Yubere's Moc didn't need any such enhancements. This one's midlimbs were fully occupied with a huge graser; ready lights burned green on the weapon's receiver.

The scene erupted into violent movement. The Moc leaped sideways and whipped the graser up.

Ruiz was ready for the Moc's evasive leap, and from the manner in which the Moc held its weapon had guessed correctly at the direction . . . and so he had a chance at survival. He was bounding from his tram chair as he fired his splinter gun, and the shuddering recoil of the weapon spun him onto his back. He managed to maintain his aim through that impromptu tumble, and the hail of spinning wire sleeted against the creature's insectoid head. Most of the wire bounced harmlessly from chitin, but the Moc's great faceted eyes were ruined, reduced to yellow-slimed holes.

It opened its maw and shrieked, a high penetrating sound that carried over the crash of the others' weapons. Ruiz landed awkwardly on the platform and felt something pop in his right shoulder. He ignored the injury and continued to fire, hoping a splinter might ricochet through the Moc's maw into some other sensory channel—even blinded, the thing could fight on effectively, using smell and sound. He rolled, in case the creature decided to fire at the thump he'd made when he landed, and just as he vacated the spot, the big graser turned it into a puddle of molten alloy.

All this took less than a second, and then Albany's graser found the Moc's head and took it off in a puff of evil-smelling smoke. The Moc danced back, its movements almost too quick to follow, the graser firing in a continuous stream, burning holes through the barricade, melting streams of metal from the doorway from which it had emerged.

Finally Albany hit the Moc's graser, and it fell apart in a shower of pink sparks. The Moc flung the smoking pieces aside and continued to whirl about the platform in a random pattern, stamping with its huge lower limbs, slashing with its midlimbs, feeling delicately with its tiny forelimbs at its neck hole, as if looking for its missing head.

"Knees," Ruiz shouted, and concentrated his fire on the Moc's lower limbs.

After what seemed an eternity, but was actually no more than three or four seconds, the Moc lay in a puddle of yellow fluid, still twitching, its limbs lopped off, its thorax chopped into several pieces.

Ruiz got painfully to his feet. His shoulder ached fiercely; soon he might have difficulty in moving it. He wiggled his arm experimentally; it felt like someone had driven a nail between his shoulder blade and his arm. He directed his in-armor medunit to apply a ject of local anesthetic and an anti-inflammatory to the joint. After the tiny sting, the shoulder began immediately to feel better.

Albany was already at the door, peering down the dark corridor. "No reaction yet," he said.

Huxley stood at the edge of the platform, apparently unhurt, peering at his detectors. "Nothing here either," he said.

Ruiz looked at the tram, where the false Yubere still lay, belly down, propped on his elbows, watching the scene with no great interest. He seemed uninjured, and Ruiz sighed with relief.

Unfortunately, Durban the beaster had either stumbled attempting to leave the tram, or had fallen backward from the platform in trying to avoid the sweep of the Moc's graser. He lay on the tanglefoot mat, staring up, eyes blank, jerking as the wires extended their barbs into his torso.

Albany looked at Ruiz. "What now?"

Ruiz stepped over Durban, onto the tram. The beaster looked at him, and it was plain that he was a dying wolverine, cranked all the way down into his hindbrain, what small humanity he once possessed lost forever.

Durban started to lift the splinter gun he still held, but Ruiz kicked it away. Durban snarled and writhed against the grip of the tanglefoot, but he couldn't move his body, and the attempt caused the tanglefoot to fire more wire into his skull. He shuddered and screamed, but only for a second, until Ruiz bent down and triggered a merciful burst into the center of his forehead.

Ruiz helped the puppet up. "Let's go," he said, unsealing the leash. "Mind the tanglefoot."

The puppet jumped nimbly to the platform.

"Where are we?" Ruiz asked.

The puppet shrugged. "I think I'm at the top of my pipeline; don't you think so?"

"So it seems. Tell me, why do you have so few people here? Two Dirm guards, a Moc? That doesn't seem much to guard such a valuable secret."

"*Secret* is the operative term here. The fewer that know a valuable secret, the better—and better yet if they're aliens who have no way of understanding the secret's value."

Ruiz considered the false Yubere. Was there more guile in the puppet's voice, now that they were approaching their goal? That made sense, since the instant the false Yubere took control of the real Yubere's operation, Ruiz would become a liability. Presumably Publius had issued dire orders to his puppet regarding that moment.

He guided the puppet across the platform and gave the leash to Albany. "Sit on him for a minute," he said.

Albany nodded and wrapped the leash around his fist, though his attention remained on the corridor leading away from the platform.

Ruiz went to Huxley, who was wandering about, his detectors extended. "Nothing," Huxley said in wondering tones. "I can't find any sort of surveillance. It's miraculous." Indeed, Huxley's face glowed with a sort of superstitious awe.

"Don't get carried away," said Ruiz. "Remember the Clearlight security network; we know Yubere has it installed throughout the stronghold."

"Then why haven't we come across it yet?"

It was a good question, and Ruiz resolved to consider it. But first he lowered his voice and said to Huxley, "Without being obvious, check the puppet for built-in weapons or comm devices."

"You don't trust our employer?" asked Huxley.

"That's a foolish question," said Ruiz wearily. "Do you trust me?"

"Well . . . yes, in fact." Huxley seemed taken aback by his question. "Albany speaks well of you—and also I'm usually perceptive about such things. We don't expect you to die for us, or anything so melodramatic, but I think you're probably as honorable as anyone in this business can afford to be."

Ruiz sighed.

A minute later Huxley wandered back. "He's got a one-shot pinbeam in his right index finger and a small bomb in his belly."

" 'Small'?"

Huxley shrugged. "Relatively small . . . but I wouldn't want to be within a hundred meters if it pops."

Ruiz considered. He stepped back aboard the tram, and slipped off his packframe. He strapped it to one of the main cross-girders, and tapped at the faceplate of a tamperproof timer. Then he stood and divested himself of the heaviest of his weapons—the sniper gas gun, a midrange graser and its powerpack.

He retained only his knives, his splinter gun, and a rack of light concussion grenades.

Albany raised his eyebrows, giving Ruiz a questioning look.

"Got to be quick," Ruiz explained. "We've got a slippery devil here."

THEY TROTTED ALONG the corridor, Albany fifty paces in the lead, Huxley with the puppet's leash sealed to a harness ring on his armor, Ruiz trailing a hundred paces behind.

Ruiz attempted to keep his attention focused on the moment, on the dimly illuminated metal that formed the walls and floor of the corridor, but after a while, as nothing dire occurred and Huxley detected no evidence of surveillance, his thoughts wandered. It seemed to him that he had been spending a great deal of his life lately walking down empty corridors, bound for events over which he had insufficient control.

He became self-indulgent, which led to philosophical musings of the least useful sort. He began to see himself and his people as maggots wandering through the mineralized veins of some dead steel colossus, frantically searching for some remaining bit of carrion to feed on.

Eventually he was forced to laugh out loud at these pretentious, egocentric fantasies. Huxley glanced back, as if wondering what Ruiz could possibly find amusing under these circumstances. Ruiz smiled at him, which did nothing to allay the cyborg's puzzlement.

"How does it look, Huxley?" asked Ruiz, speaking softly into his helmet mike.

"Still no sign of the Clearlight system. You know, I've developed a theory. Would you care to hear it?"

"Sure."

"Well . . . the target is running a secret operation here —so secret that he needs to keep it from his topside security forces—the SeedCorp shock troops you mentioned. Or, if they're Genched, from his techs and service personnel. And of course, even Genched troops can't be any smarter than they were before their processing; they're as liable to say stupidly revealing things as any real person. Anyway, he fears attack only from above, it looks like, and so maybe we've got a clean conduit right into the heart of his levels."

"I hope you're right," Ruiz said without much conviction.

They trudged on, and shortly Ruiz's attention wavered again. He found himself reviewing pleasant memories of Nisa—her face in the sunlight, her face in the soft colored lights of the barge. When he realized what he was doing, he was frightened. Something deadly might come his way at any moment, and if it caught him mooning over the woman, he would never see her again.

He shook himself, and tried to firmly grasp his mortality and the probability of imminent destruction.

"Stop," whispered Albany. "Come, Ruiz."

Ruiz ran swiftly forward.

Albany knelt at the foot of a ramp that bridged a discontinuity in the tunnel. Apparently the stack had once fractured, displacing the corridors so that one floor was a meter higher than the other.

A high-ceilinged nexus opened on the far side of the break, and bright lights glared down the corridor.

"I think we're just about there," said Albany.

"I believe you're right," said Ruiz. "Let's get Huxley up here—let him fish a little."

Huxley examined the ramp carefully, then climbed it and eased closer to the nexus, extending probes on long monomol rods. Ruiz and Albany hid under the fracture, the puppet sitting next to them, face full of bland unconcern.

Five minutes passed.

Huxley returned, face pale and sweaty behind his visor. "The Clearlight system takes over just beyond the corridor junction. I think I can handle it, but not for very long."

He extended a coiled datacable, plugged it into a receptacle at the hip of Ruiz's armor. He tapped at his dataslate, frowned, tapped some more. "All right," he said. "I can't guarantee how long this ident sequence will fool the system." As he spoke, he plugged into each of the others, fed the data to their armor. "Let's get in quick, before it changes codes and leaves us naked."

"What else did you see?" asked Ruiz.

"Ruptors over the security lock; and it looks well-hardened. I hope Albany's good with explosives, if the puppet can't get us through. Several other corridors feed into the nexus, but according to the nav bead, we have to go through the lock to get to the target."

Ruiz took a deep breath and flexed his injured shoulder to be sure it still functioned adequately. Then he removed the leash from the false Yubere. "Now's your moment," said Ruiz. "Take us inside."

The instant the leash was gone, the puppet seemed to change, to grow a little. "Of course," he said regally. He strode up the ramp as though he owned it already, and the others trailed him in a rough triangular formation, Huxley and Albany immediately behind the puppet, Ruiz at the trailing point.

Ruiz felt terribly vulnerable under the glare of the nexus lights. He forced himself not to look at the ruptor turret that projected from the wall above the security lock, even when the twin barrels depressed to follow him across the floor.

The puppet ignored the turret, and swept up to the lock. Without hesitation, he applied his eye to the scanner, pressed his palm to the lockplate.

To Ruiz's intense relief, the lock's armored doors slid back. They crowded inside; the doors shut, and the far doors opened.

"Come along," said the puppet.

He led the way out of the lock, and into Yubere's living quarters.

JUST INSIDE A Dirm bondguard lounged against the wall. It was just turning toward them, when Ruiz's knife slid into its throat. It died with no more than a small gurgle, and Albany helped Ruiz lower the heavy corpse quietly to the floor.

Ruiz looked at Huxley inquiringly. The cyborg studied his detectors, then shook his head and smiled.

They moved through a large public room, decorated in a rather austere style, with pristine white walls and carpet, sparely furnished with openwork couches carved of some shiny black wood. The effect was curiously unreal, as if they had stepped into some ancient colorless photograph.

A hall full of outre paintings led into the private sectors of the suite. Ruiz passed them without looking, but even from the corners of his eyes, the paintings were disturbing—harsh clashing colors and distorted figures—a madman's vision.

At the end of the hall, a maid came from a linen room, looked up to see them bearing down on her. She gasped and dropped the bundle of towels she carried, and turned as if to flee. But then she seemed to notice that one of the armored men running down the hall was Yubere, and her face filled with confusion.

Ruiz reached her and rapped his fist against her temple, then eased her to the floor.

"Sentimentalist," whispered Albany. "She's probably Genched, she'll rise up and cut your heart out when we leave."

Albany was probably right, Ruiz thought glumly. He resolved to be more decisive with the next servant they met, but they saw no one else before they reached their goal.

CHAPTER 17

THEY found Yubere in his bathtub. His white-tiled
bathroom was unostentatious—not large, and the silver and gold tub wasn't the sort that could seat a
party of three dozen close friends. But it was quite beautiful.
Its comfortably slanted back was inlaid with precious stones
—black opal butterflies flew among jade bamboo stems.

The target was alone, soaping his back with a long-han-
dled brush, when they burst through the door.

He seemed not to be very startled by their sudden entrance. He looked from the weapons pointed at him to the
faces above the barrels, and smiled wistfully.

"You're from Publius, aren't you?" he said. He gazed at
the puppet, as if admiring the fine work Publius had done.
"Clever monster," he said, and sighed. "I should never have
been so greedy as to deal with a thing like Publius."

He looked at Ruiz, and a look of bittersweet astonishment slipped across his face and was gone. Ruiz had the
uncomfortable and illogical sensation that Yubere recognized him. No, no; that was impossible, he told himself.

"Kill him now," said the puppet.

"What are you getting?" Ruiz asked Huxley.

The cyborg shrugged. "Nothing. Weird. No alarms, no sensors, no remote surveillance."

The puppet smiled. "We're a man of destiny, eh, Alonzo. What need have we of the protections lesser men crave?"

"As you say," agreed the real Yubere. He gazed curiously at Ruiz. "What in the world could Publius have promised you to make you come here? You're not Genched; I can tell that much."

Ruiz ignored him; he was dead.

But Yubere spoke again. "I suppose I should take some comfort in the knowledge that you won't long survive me." He began to scrub at his back again, and shut his eyes, a smile of mild gratification lighting his face.

Ruiz triggered a burst that took off the top half of Yubere's head, and spread a symmetrical splash of red across the butterflies and bamboo. He slung the weapon and turned away.

"Cut him up and put him down the recyclers," said Ruiz to Albany. He clung to numb purpose, and resolutely refused to think about what he had just done. He heard the burble of Albany's knife, and then the distinctive sounds that accompanied carving the body into pieces small enough to go down the bathroom recycler.

The puppet's eyes glowed, and he turned to Ruiz as if to congratulate him, and started to extend his hand. Ruiz slapped the hand down on the rim of the tub, and chopped with his sonic knife, splitting the puppet's forefinger and the mechanism of the one-shot pinbeam.

The false Yubere gasped and shuddered, and started to jerk his hand back, then became still, until Ruiz had withdrawn the knife and released his hand.

Blood welled from the puppet's armored glove, dripped to the tiles. He clamped his hand around the injured finger and looked at Ruiz without accusation. "Publius said you were alert." He sighed and took off the glove, examined his mangled finger. He went to a mirrored cabinet and found a self-tending dressing, which he slipped over the wound and activated.

"Well," said the new Yubere. "I'd like to get out of this armor." He opened a tall ebony wardrobe that stood against the far wall, selected an elegant unisuit of dove-gray silk. "Suitable?"

Albany looked up from his bloody work and laughed. "Whatever that means," he said.

"Hurry," said Ruiz.

"We have all the time in the world, now," said Yubere lightly. He shucked off the armor and wiped his thin body with a scented towel, then dressed quickly.

"Wouldn't you like to change too?" asked Yubere. "Aren't you worried someone will wonder why men in armor are wandering around the stronghold?"

Albany laughed again. "He's smarter than that, Yubere." He put the last piece of the old Yubere down the recycler and began to wipe down the tub.

Ruiz nudged Yubere with the barrel of his splinter gun. "Let's go find a comm and make sure the staff accepts you. Huxley, bring your gear. Albany, trail us a few feet, but no shooting unless there's no other way. And, Yubere, no more funny stuff, or Publius's investment will be wasted."

"I'll be careful," said the puppet. "You be careful too."

"A good thought," said Ruiz. "Huxley, spike his bomb, in case we have to kill him."

THE NEW YUBERE led the way to his comm center, moving with a convincing ease. Ruiz dared not aim a weapon at Yubere, for fear that one of Yubere's people would see and react aggressively. He felt a distressing loss of control over the situation, but he needed to establish Yubere's authority.

"When we get there, set up my exit first," he said. "Give us an escort back to the tram."

Yubere looked back curiously. "Don't you want to just go out the top? We're in control here, now?"

Ruiz looked at him wordlessly, and Yubere shrugged easily. "As you wish."

Huxley threw Ruiz a worried glance. He felt impelled to explain, for some reason. "Our employer will be hoping we'll make it that easy for him to get rid of us. He'll be sure to have people topside—but maybe he doesn't have another sub. And on the sub, we'll have the Gench to bargain with."

Huxley looked even more worried. "What made you take employment with such a dire creature, Ruiz?"

"Necessity."

Albany snorted. "Don't let him kid you, Huxley. He likes

this stuff—the more borderline the better, as far as Ruiz Aw is concerned. He's always had that sort of bug up his ass."

Ruiz wanted to deny it, to claim that he had changed, but Albany would only laugh at him.

The comm center was occupied by a tech wearing a black tunic and two Dirm guards—though these were unpithed and wore no armor. As they moved into the room, Ruiz began to calculate angles and priorities. The Dirm to the right seemed somewhat more alert than the other guard, and the tech paid no attention at all.

Yubere walked to the main dataslate, laid a languid hand on the black glass. He tapped it absently, then turned to the nearest Dirm and said, "Kill them."

The Dirm was only starting to bring down its graser when Ruiz's burst chopped across its torso, smashing it back against the wall. Ruiz spun, squeezed off another burst, missing the other Dirm just as it fired; then Albany's graser hissed and cut the guard in half.

Ruiz turned, saw that Huxley was down, his legs twitching feebly, a wisp of steam rising from the hole in his chest. As he took this in, he saw Albany aim at Yubere, a look of murderous rage suffusing his lumpy features.

"No!" barked Ruiz. "We won't kill him yet."

For an instant he thought Albany would do it anyway, and he knew he wouldn't be able to kill Albany before Yubere was dead—his weapon was still pointed at the first Dirm, who wasn't quite dead yet.

But Albany snarled, flicked the graser aside, and vaporized the head of the black-shirted tech, who had finally reacted and was rising from his seat.

Relief shuddered through Ruiz.

Yubere leaned back against the panel. "Well, it was worth a try," he said brightly.

RUIZ STRUGGLED TO maintain a clear mind, though he felt an almost-irresistible impulse to destroy the puppet.

"How can I make the situation clear to you?" he asked Yubere. "If you keep fucking with us, your master's scheme will come to nothing. Didn't you see what I did back at the tram? My pack is full of toroidal explosive." Ruiz looked at the watch embedded in the forearm of his armor. "If we don't get back in twenty-eight minutes, it's going to bring down the dome and choke off the hole."

Yubere snapped upright. His face underwent an instantaneous transformation, from tolerant amusement to taut cold rage. "You'll have to pay a terrible price for your obstructions when Publius catches you," he said through his teeth. His eyes gleamed with an almost-human craziness for a moment, but then he regained control. "Of course, dead is dead, so I suppose I shouldn't blame you for struggling."

"Good for you," said Ruiz. "Now make the arrangements."

Yubere took a deep breath, then spoke terse instructions into the comm. When he was finished, he looked up at Ruiz, completely composed again. "Satisfied?"

"We'll see how it goes," said Ruiz.

Albany knelt beside Huxley, who had become still. "Dead," Albany reported glumly. Ruiz felt a small poignant sadness. Huxley had seemed a fairly decent person, for a freelance slayer, and now he was gone as if he had never existed, his trust proven foolish.

He shook his head—he was indulging in pointless emotions. Each of the beings he had destroyed during this night's work had been as alive as Huxley, and their lives had been just as important, in their own eyes.

As the puppet had said, dead was dead.

Ruiz helped Albany remove Huxley's undamaged detectors, and slung most of the gear from his own armor. "I guess I'll have to do Huxley's job for a while," he said.

Albany stood up wearily. "Yeah. Your army's getting a little thin, Ruiz."

A minute passed, then another brace of Dirm guards entered at a trot and slid to a stop, heads swiveling to take in the carnage. They started to snatch at the grasers they carried slung across their scaly chests, but Yubere spoke sharply. "Wait," he said, raising a peremptory hand. "These are friends—they saved me from a treachery. You are to escort them to the downlevel security lock, then return here to clean up the mess. And see that the comm room is adequately restaffed. Guard the safety of our friends with your lives; we owe them much. And we intend to repay them." A glitter of malevolence returned briefly to Yubere's eyes.

"Thank you," Ruiz said for effect. "Happy to help. By

the way, did you know that life is a stiletto vine that blooms only once?"

When he spoke the code phrase that the Gench had tied into the puppet's volitional network, Yubere slumped slightly, and a light went out of his eyes. He would be unable to make any decision, no matter how small, until Ruiz spoke the counterphrase. He would be unable even to decide to follow Publius's orders. If for some reason Ruiz failed to speak it, Yubere would sit here until he starved, unless his people dared to carry him to a medunit to be fed intravenously.

"Well," said Ruiz. "Good-bye, and good luck."

THE DIRM CONVOYED Ruiz and Albany to the lock, eyes rolling with suppressed panic. They seemed to have accepted the new Yubere's identity without reservation—but they were a credulous species, another reason why they were popular cannon fodder. They bowed Ruiz and Albany into the lock and left at a quick trot.

When the inner door closed, Albany said, "So far so good. What did you do to the puppet?"

"Cut his strings, until we can get away. It gives us a deal point with our employer."

"I wish you'd done it a little sooner."

"I could only do it once. I'm sorry."

Albany shrugged. "Well, it's a tough business, and I know you're sorry. What now?"

"Let's run," Ruiz said, and began to trot back down the long corridor.

THE BITS OF the dismembered Moc were still twitching when they reached the tram platform ten minutes later. Ruiz looked at it and shivered. The face of Durban's corpse had acquired a greasy bluish pallor; the dead eyes still glared, but without heat. Ruiz felt a pang of uncustomary squeamishness at the thought of riding down the tramway with the corpse, but there was no practical way to remove it from the tanglefoot.

Ruiz disarmed the satchel charge and then they stepped carefully aboard the tram. Ruiz sat in the driver's chair. It took him only a moment to decipher the controls and start the tram sliding back down its rail.

To pass the time, he busied himself with Huxley's detectors, getting them set up, ready to sniff out any activity below—just in case some of the alien tunnel dwellers decided to revenge themselves on the tram, or—an unpleasant notion—Publius had arranged some sort of trap for them on their return. It occurred to him that he hadn't explicitly directed the Jahworld sisters to keep a watch down the tunnel, in case a surprise appeared from that direction. It was an uncomfortable feeling. He worried that if such an unfortunate event happened, the sisters would be too preoccupied with their horror of the pit's depths to be paying much attention to what was going on behind them.

Perhaps, he thought, he was being excessively paranoid. On the other hand, Publius, a man with a vast talent for making enemies, was still alive after all these years—which argued for his thoroughness, and deviousness.

The danger was that Publius might kill him without giving Ruiz an opportunity to reveal his meddling with Publius's puppet. Ruiz had to hope after he revealed this perfidy that Publius's avarice would overtop his outrage.

"What's wrong?" Albany asked.

"Probably nothing," Ruiz answered.

"I don't much like the sound of that," said Albany.

Ruiz smiled at him. "I don't blame you for that. I'm sorry to have involved you in such a mess, Albany."

"No you're not," said Albany, but he smiled too.

THE TRIP PASSED without incident, though Ruiz saw more furtive movement at the various openings, as if the dwellers within were curious about the unusual activity on the tramway. No one actually appeared, and Ruiz resisted the temptation to use his scope—he didn't want to seem overly interested in things that weren't any of his business.

When they were only a few hundred meters above the tunnel mouth, Ruiz brought out the scope and looked down and across the pit. He brought the dark opening into focus and saw Chou standing at the very lip, waving cheerfully, helmet visor carelessly open. The scope's resolution was insufficient for Ruiz to make out her expression with exactitude.

Ruiz folded the scope and hung it from his armor. "Shit!" he said.

"What?"

"I think the sisters are dead—and that means Publius is waiting for us. But at least he didn't kill us on sight. He likes to gloat—it's one of his biggest weaknesses, and it'll bring him to grief one of these days. I hope."

Ruiz chewed at his lip, then set his helmet mike for long-range comm. "Publius? Are you listening? If you kill me now, you've lost. I don't buy Chou's act; she and her sister were extreme acrophobes."

A few moments passed; then Chou stepped back and folded up like a doll. "What do you mean, I've lost?" Publius spoke in a taut whisper. "You're mine now, Ruiz. You can't get away. If you go back up, I'll just call my new Yubere and have him intercept you. Or maybe I'll just fire a seeker at you and be done with it—though I'd hate to have my tram damaged."

Ruiz sighed. He'd hoped that the worst was over, but nothing was easy, with Publius—the monster-maker was a match for him in guile, maybe more than a match. He took a deep breath and took out his boot gun, a little pepperbox that fired armor-piercing explosive pellets. He held it to the side of his head, aimed so that if he triggered it, his brain would be reduced to such dissociated pulp that Publius would never be able to sift any memories from it.

Publius's voice filled his helmet. "What a silly person you are. Do you imagine I care whether or not I actually get to carve on you? Or that my little Gench goes pop when you do? I have much bigger fish to fry; I'll just scrape up a few bits and clone you for later amusement."

"That'll be nice," said Ruiz. "But you still don't understand. Have you tried to contact Yubere yet?"

"No," said Publius, his voice betraying just the tiniest degree of uncertainty. "Why? Were you unsuccessful? And if so, why shouldn't I kill you. And by the way, where *is* my Gench?"

Ruiz noted with some satisfaction that Publius had apparently not broken into the sub. "I left it on the sub."

"Oh? Wasn't that incautious of you?"

"Not really. In the first place, how could you think me so stupid as to not understand that one Gench more or less was a matter of indifference to you? In the second place, I'm not wearing your madcollar. In the third place, I used the Gench to gimmick your puppet. Kill me and you'll never get a bit of use out of him, even though he's sitting in his control room, as we speak, in command of the stronghold."

A terribly ominous silence ensued, broken only by the sound of heavy breathing.

Finally Publius spoke, and his voice was full of a cold controlled fury that frightened Ruiz more than all his flamboyant threats had. "Why should I believe you?"

"Call Yubere."

"And if you failed? The real Yubere will learn who acted against him, and even *I* don't care to face Yubere in open war."

"That's a problem, isn't it?" Ruiz struggled to maintain a cool indifferent tone.

More time passed, and the tram slid onward, closer and closer to the tunnel. "What should I do?" asked Albany.

Ruiz cut back the comm to close range, so that he could speak to Albany without Publius hearing. "Nothing. Either he wants whatever he's got cooked up more than he wants to get even—or we're dead. Or worse. You might want to jump, or take off your head with the graser, rather than let Publius take you in restorable condition."

"He's that bad?"

"Worse."

They approached the tunnel, and Ruiz cut the speed, keeping the pepperbox pressed to his head. They glided to a stop directly under the tunnel mouth and waited.

A horrid sound came from the tunnel. It didn't sound like the sort of noise a human being could make; it sounded more like some great predator, a lion, or perhaps some mad monstrous bear. At first Ruiz couldn't identify it, but then he understood that Publius had gotten confirmation and was roaring with rage.

It ceased abruptly. A big killmech with a scarred carapace came to the edge and lowered a cable equipped with magnetic shackles. Ruiz lifted his arm and guided a shackle to his chestplate.

Albany looked at him, his face pale. "Is this a good idea, Ruiz?" His voice was shaky; he seemed to have lost his cheerful bravado in the face of Publius's crazy rage.

"I don't know what choice we have, Albany. Down is the Gencha, up is Yubere's people, who are probably starting to wonder what's wrong with their master. They'll be nervous, and looking for answers we don't have."

"I guess you're right," Albany said dubiously.

"I don't know about that, but I've got a little leverage with Publius, who has his heart set on this scheme of his. I don't think he'll kill us as long as he has hope that it will still work."

Albany looked up at the killmech. "I sure hope this turns out to be worth it." He shackled the cable to his armor, and the killmech began to reel them up.

CHAPTER 18

CHOU lay in a heap, the roughly patched holes in her armor now obvious. The alloy and black plastic device clinging to her back was the corpse-walker Publius had used to animate her body during his attempt to bring them in quietly.

The killmech led them deeper into the tunnel, and they passed Moh's body, huddled into the angle between wall and floor, as if she had died still terrified of the pit.

Publius had established a small camp, well away from the pit and its stinks. Now he sat at his portable picnic table, hunched over his lunch, studying the image in his flatscreen vid. "What did you do to my boy, Ruiz?" he asked in conversational tones. Ruiz looked over his shoulder, to see the new Yubere, standing where they had left him. His face seemed calm, but Ruiz imagined that he could see a trace of some cold abstract anguish in the dull eyes.

"Don't worry; it's not necessarily permanent. All I have to do is tell him the right thing, and he'll be fine." Ruiz's injured shoulder was beginning to ache; he had been foolish enough to hold the pepperbox with his right hand. He already wanted to lower his hand, but Publius had no doubt instructed the killmech to seize him if his aim wavered.

"Ah? Well, that's good news, at least. And what must I do to win your cooperation?"

"Fulfill our bargain."

Publius made an impatient tsking sound. "Troublesome."

Ruiz said nothing; Publius's attitude was hardly a surprise.

Publius sighed. "Well, all right. I know when I'm bested." His eyes glittered, and he looked as treacherous as it was possible for a human being to look. "What shall we do now?"

"Wait here for half an hour, then follow. We'll meet you at the sub, and there we'll put on madcollars." Ruiz's shoulder burned with the pain of holding the pepperbox, and he was afraid that Publius would notice his weakness.

Publius gave him a searching gaze. "You wouldn't be planning any more tricks, would you, Ruiz?"

"If so, it's no more than you deserve," Ruiz said wearily. "But no. I need your help. Keep your word, help me and my slaves get off Sook, and you can proceed with your schemes here unhindered."

Publius drummed his fingers on the table, giving an appearance of careful consideration. Finally he smiled broadly, a horrifying expression. "I'm reassured. It will be as you say. I coupled my sub to your repair chamber; my people are guarding your lock. I'll call and let them know you're coming—and tell them not to bother you." He waved his hand in a dismissive gesture and returned to his lunch.

Ruiz stood for a moment, almost unwilling to believe that Publius would let them go so easily, then he turned and walked off down the tunnel, trailed by Albany.

Albany kept looking over his shoulder until they were well around the curve of the tunnel, and the lights of Publius's camp were lost to view. "You've got odd friends these days," he said.

Ruiz decided it was safe to lower his arm. The pain as he did so made him sway and miss his footing. He stumbled, but Albany caught him under the arm and kept him from falling. "You holed, Ruiz?" Albany asked.

"No," Ruiz said. "I think I separated my shoulder a little when we killed the Moc. The painkiller's wearing off." He instructed the in-suit medunit to give him another ject, and he felt it begin to crawl toward his shoulder again, little clawed feet prickling over his skin.

"That's a relief." Behind his visor, Albany's eyes were huge. "You got me into this. I'm depending on you to get me out of it. What was that about getting you off Sook? Take me too. I've had enough excitement for this century."

"I can't pay you until we get back to Dilvermoon."

"That's fine. If I ever do get back there, I'm going to have my feet welded to the steel. I'm never going to leave again."

Ruiz smiled. "You've said that before."

"This time I mean it," said Albany.

For some reason, Ruiz felt a bit more cheerful, and it wasn't only due to the warm touch of the painkiller.

He set off down the tunnel again at a good pace.

As they neared the lock, Ruiz raised the pepperbox again.

Albany looked at him. "Wait a bit," he said. "Let me rig you an explosive charge inside your helmet, with a mouth switch. It'll be easier for you to handle."

Ruiz stopped, and wondered why he hadn't thought to do that. Albany's trap gear would provide explosives and a remote switch, and the armor would keep Publius's killmech from seizing his weapon in a moment of distraction.

It took Albany only a moment to pat out a thin slab of explosive, wire it, and slip it under Ruiz's helmet. "You want the switch hot, for real?" asked Albany.

"Oh yes," said Ruiz. "I don't want Publius to take me alive, however this turns out."

"Whatever," said Albany, plugging the leads into a squeeze switch. He offered it to Ruiz, who took it and bit down on it, activating the circuit.

"Let's go," Ruiz said through his clenched teeth. He restored the pepperbox to his boot and walked on.

When they were within a hundred meters of the tunnel's end, Ruiz stopped. "Go first," he said. "Tell them I've got a bomb in my hat, just in case Publius told them to grab me if my attention wandered."

Albany smiled. "Would he do a thing like that?" But he trotted away springily, apparently unwearied by the night's exertions.

Ruiz found him waiting by the lock, alone, holding his graser alertly. "Any problems?" asked Ruiz.

"No. There were some very odd-looking persons here,

but I told them to get back into their boat and they went quietly."

Ruiz stepped through into the repair chamber, and saw where Publius's people had cut through the hemispherical shell. Several monstrous faces stared at them through the hole, but said nothing.

Ruiz palmed the sub's lockplate and put his eye to the ident cluster. After a long moment the lock slid aside.

When they were inside, Ruiz tongued the safety selector and took the detonator out of his mouth. His jaws ached, but he felt a sudden uplift of relief.

The Gench waited in the control room, huddled in the corner, its sensory tufts clenched tight. When it recognized Ruiz, it raised its lumpy body slightly and hooted. "You have survived. I am amazed."

"Me too," said Ruiz. "You were wise not to let Publius in."

"I hope never to see him again," said the Gench.

"I wish that could be," said Ruiz regretfully. "But we must invite him aboard, and then hope to control him."

The Gench sank back down and became still.

"I'm not too happy about that either," said Albany. "Why don't we just cut and run, while we have the chance?"

"Do you know a way to get out of SeaStack now?" asked Ruiz.

Albany looked unhappy. "No. The pirate princelings are in a terrible uproar; they're not even letting each other off-planet, at the moment. They've shot down a half-dozen shuttles already."

That was bad news, Ruiz thought. And very strange news; perhaps there was more than simple greed involved. Would the pirates go so far, cripple the commerce that had made them rich, just to catch a few rogue Gencha, no matter how valuable they might be? He filed the thought away for later consideration; Publius was a more pressing problem. "Publius claims he knows a way."

"You believe him?"

Ruiz shrugged. "He's a slippery one, I grant you. But he's as likely as anyone to have the power to help us, and we've got some leverage with him, which we don't have with anyone else who has any power at all."

"I guess," Albany said, but he didn't look very enthusiastic.

Ruiz looked at him, and felt a sudden illogical affection. For all his flaws, Albany was presently the closest thing to a friend that he possessed; he had demonstrated loyalty and faith. Without Albany, Ruiz would have already failed. "I'm sorry I got you into this."

"Ahhh. . . . No, you're not," said Albany. But he smiled and thumped Ruiz on his good shoulder. "Listen, watching the monster at his picnic reminded me that we haven't eaten since yesterday. Can't fight on fumes, true? We have a few minutes before you have to bite the bullet again. Let's see what's here."

Ruiz nodded.

They went back through the converted cargo bay where such a short time ago the rest of Ruiz's assault team had waited. The small place seemed much larger, now that it was empty. Ruiz imagined that insubstantial ghosts still crowded the space, all looking at him with dead accusing eyes. He shuddered, then shrugged off the fancy—if he were to be haunted by the spirits of all those whose deaths he had caused, a stadium would hardly serve to contain them.

The private cabin all the way aft had a simple autochef, which Albany fiddled with until it produced sandwiches filled with spiced meat and chopped pickles. He passed one of these to Ruiz, and tinkered a bit more. The chef produced plastic mugs of steaming broth.

"Not too bad," said Albany, settling back with his mug in one hand and his sandwich in the other. He seemed remarkably at ease. Ruiz attributed it partly to his ignorance of Publius, partly to a mind that was more firmly tuned to the moment than his own. He couldn't help looking forward to the uncertainties to come—and backward at the mistakes of the past.

He thought of Nisa for the first time in hours. Was she well? Had she begun to wonder if he would ever return? Only two days had passed for her, though to him those days had seemed like weeks.

"So," said Albany. "Who are these slaves you're taking with you? Valuable stock?"

"Somewhat," said Ruiz.

"Ah?" Albany seemed to be waiting for Ruiz to elaborate.

Ruiz felt no inclination to do so. A silence formed, and

stretched into minutes, until Albany had finished his sandwich and slurped down the last of the broth.

"Tell me," said Albany. "Why would you burden yourself with 'somewhat' valuable slaves, when—as we both know—you're going to need all your luck just to get yourself off Sook? I sense a mystery here, Ruiz."

Ruiz shrugged.

"Come on, Ruiz. Tell me a little about these folk, while we're waiting for the monster to arrive."

"All right," said Ruiz. "They're from Pharaoh. A conjuror, a commoner, and a princess."

"A Pharaohan conjuror? Worth a good bit, even without a troupe. Why the commoner?"

"The Guildmaster of a famous troupe, which is now dispersed."

"I see. And the princess? What's her claim to value?"

Ruiz fidgeted, and Albany's sharp eyes seemed to see every evidence of his discomfort. "She's quite beautiful," he finally said.

Albany leaned back and snorted dismissively. "Beautiful? What of that? The pangalac worlds are full of beauty; everyone can be as beautiful as they choose to be. Beautiful? On Dilvermoon, ugliness or even simple plainness is so rare that a whore who will accept an intriguing deformity can make a fortune." Albany shook his head and then a slightly malicious curiosity glittered in his eyes. "Oh, no. You don't mean to tell me that you're smitten? What a hideously quaint obsession. I hope you won't tell me that all these folk have died, and probably me too, just because Ruiz Aw—hard Ruiz Aw, ruthless Ruiz Aw, deadly Ruiz Aw—has finally succumbed to true love? Oh, no." He seemed genuinely incensed by the time he finished.

Ruiz glared at him. What to say? If they survived long enough to retrieve Nisa and the others, the truth would become obvious, so what point was there in lying? "Essentially, you are correct," he said in a harsh voice.

Albany's eyes grew very wide, as though he hadn't truly expected this confirmation. His face was still and neutral, unnaturally so. Ruiz wondered if Albany would attack him, so odd was Albany's expression, and he shifted his weight for defense.

But then, surprising him, Albany burst into raucous laughter. "Well then, why not? I thought I had seen suffi-

cient strangeness to burn away all my capacity for surprise
—but I was wrong. It's not so bad a feeling, is it? I mean,
you must be much more surprised than I."

Ruiz thought about it, but concluded that in fact he
wasn't. What did that say about him? How long had he
carried the seeds of the feelings that had finally taken root in
his heart? *Very strange,* he thought.

He was uninclined to share this insight with Albany, who
would either laugh at him again, or become nervous—such
thoughts did not accord with Albany's image of him as an
effective slayer.

But before the silence could become strained, a chime
signaled the arrival of Publius in the sub's lock.

Ruiz looked at Albany. "Remember, Publius is a monster
indeed. Nothing he says can be taken at face value. There
will always be several layers of deviousness beneath anything he proposes. We'll have to exploit our advantage
swiftly, before he comes up with a way to get around us. Be
on your guard—this will be much more dangerous than our
trip into the stronghold."

Albany nodded soberly, and they went back through the
sub to the lock.

RUIZ ALLOWED ALBANY to open the lock, while he remained out of the line of direct fire, in case Publius had
already developed a scheme. But the monster-maker came
in, holding a silver-mounted ebony case over his head. He
was clearly fuming at Albany's disrespectful attitude. He
turned and saw Ruiz, started to take down his hands.

"No," Ruiz barked. "Hands up, and turn away from
me." He aimed a splinter gun at Publius.

Publius purpled, assumed an expression of defiant outrage. Ruiz had an impulse of terrifying power; he abruptly
wanted, very badly, to kill Publius and be done with him—
and with his treacheries. He would find another way to get
off Sook, a way that didn't expose them to the monster-
maker's virulence. They had the sub; they had weapons and
some money; they had a Gench to sell in the SeaStack market. It would be enough; he was sure of it. His finger tight-
ened on the splinter gun's cool trigger, almost involuntarily.

Publius must have seen lethality in his face. He paled and

turned quickly to the bulkhead. Ruiz's finger relaxed marginally.

Albany shut and dogged the lock, took the case. He opened it carefully, after examining it with his detectors. It held two madcollars, elegant objects inlaid with gold and further adorned with large pigeon-blood rubies.

"Keep your grubby little paws off them," said Publius.

Albany set the case down and put his graser to Publius's kidneys. "Let's wilt him a little, what do you say, Ruiz?"

"Maybe we will," said Ruiz thickly. Publius seemed an avatar of all the chaotic brutal lovelessness of the universe, seemed to symbolize all the ugly realities of existence—those relentless failures of humanity that so eternally conspired against happiness and security. His hatred for the monster-maker flared up brightly. He took Publius by his collar and slammed him hard against the bulkhead, jammed his splinter gun under Publius's ear. "Check him," he told Albany.

Albany passed probes over Publius's body, slowly and carefully. He removed a nerve lash from Publius's sleeve, a stun rod from his boot, a pneumatic dart gun from a sheath at the nape of his neck. Albany continued his examination, shifting his detector frequencies in random sequences, muttering to himself. Finally he closed up his probes and nodded to Ruiz.

"He's got sonic knives in his right forefinger and left elbow. He's got a little pinbeam in his sternum. He's got a transceiver in his right mastoid and a vid pickup behind his left eye. He's got a big suicide bomb in his right buttock. That's all I can pick up."

"Spike him," Ruiz ordered.

Albany raised his eyebrows, questioning. "Even the eye?"

"Yes," said Ruiz. "Don't worry about the meat—Publius doesn't. He can always get more."

Publius spluttered. "What do you think you're doing?" he demanded. "You work for me, Ruiz Aw. This is no way to earn a bonus."

Ruiz laughed incredulously. "Go ahead," he told Albany.

Albany shrugged. "If you say so." He got out a surgical laser, applied it to Publius in various spots, severing power leads, disabling sensors. When he was finished, he stepped back and leveled his big graser at the monster-maker. "All yours, Ruiz."

Ruiz spun him around and pressed the splinter gun to Publius's throat, angled up toward the monster-maker's brain. "I really should kill you," he said, and at that moment the idea appealed to him almost irresistibly.

Publius had regained his perpetual air of gracious confidence, and he smiled in what he apparently believed to be a winsome manner. "Now, now. I did nothing you wouldn't have done, in my place."

There was some truth in that—but that was only because Publius was Publius—or so Ruiz told himself. Yes, he'd seized the chance to commit a treachery against Publius—because he knew that Publius would be doing the same. He nodded ruefully.

"Isn't it always the way?" Publius said.

Ruiz shook his head violently. All this musing was dangerously pointless. The universe was as it was, and he must live in it.

"Sit down," he said, and pushed Publius toward a chair.

The monster-maker settled carefully, favoring those portions of his anatomy that Albany had treated. "What shall we do now, Ruiz? I acknowledge myself defeated—I must rely on your sense of fair play and on your desperation to be off Sook. I can still arrange it."

"How do I know?"

Publius shrugged expressively. "Who else can help you? And I'm willing to wear the collars with you. If that isn't sufficient guarantee of my faithfulness, there's the matter of my puppet. At the moment, your life is only slightly less valuable to me than my own."

Ruiz studied the collars, lying in their open case. "I'm impressed by your docility," he said sardonically.

"Well, you're definitely the better man, at present." Publius spoke in a voice of mild reason.

Ruiz looked at Albany. "Fetch the old collars," he said.

Albany nodded, smiling conspiratorially, and went aft.

The faintest hint of alarm showed in Publius's smooth face, and Ruiz enjoyed it disproportionately. He allowed no trace of this wicked delight to show on his face.

Albany returned, bearing the madcollars that Ruiz and the Gench had worn.

Ruiz reached out and took the collar the Gench had worn. "You're right," he said to Publius. "We must be allies for a while. To show you that I'm reconciled to this, I'll take the collar your Gench wore—your delicate nostrils won't have to be offended by the stink."

The alarm in Publius's face increased. "Oh, no," he said. "I won't hear of it. I've brought a much finer pair, far better suited to such stylish gentlemen as we two are."

"Put it on him," said Ruiz.

Publius recoiled, sinking as deeply into the chair as he could. "Don't you trust me in even the tiniest detail?"

"No."

Publius groaned with frustration. "You're a hard man, Ruiz." Albany snapped the collar round his neck, and Ruiz fancied that Publius's confidence had eroded, just a little. He found it a vastly satisfying notion. He donned the Gench's collar, wrinkling his nose against the stench that clung strongly to the metal and plastic of the collar.

Albany handed the controller to Publius, who took it with shaking fingers. Ruiz wondered if perhaps his former collar had been fitted with some additional trap that Publius now feared. Or perhaps it was just that he was discomfitted by the turn of events, which had apparently robbed him of some crucial element of the next betrayal he had designed.

"Activate it, Emperor Publius," Ruiz said, holding up his own controller.

"Ruiz . . ." began Publius in a soft reasonable voice.

"Do it now," said Ruiz. "Or I'll kill you and have done."

Publius opened his mouth, shut it, nodded. They both triggered their controllers, and the collars locked on.

Ruiz clipped the controller to its loop on his collar, and holstered his splinter gun. "Now," he said, "don't you feel better?" He felt the easing of a vast weight; he began to hope that he could deal successfully with the monster-maker.

"Oh, certainly," said Publius glumly. "Certainly."

Back in the shadows, the young Gench stirred, attracting Publius's attention. "How did you persuade it to take its collar off?" Publius asked, peering at the alien.

"It was easy," Ruiz answered. "I told it stories about you."

Publius adopted a sorrowful smile. "Now you're being facetious, Ruiz. Treat me with dignity, at least."

"All right. Go to the comm and tell your sub to withdraw. Please."

Publius rose heavily and went to the comm board. He instructed his people; Ruiz could detect no obviously devious orders, which meant nothing. Publius turned back to Ruiz. "Now what?"

Ruiz was somewhat taken aback by the lack of bluster in Publius—it seemed an unnatural condition, as strange as if the sun should one morning rise in the west. "Now we go to fetch my slaves."

The young Gench trundled forward. "Will you set me free? You said you would, if it was possible."

Ruiz shook his head regretfully. "I'm sorry. I may have further need of your services." He looked speculatively at Publius.

Publius paled. "The creature is untrained; already you may have done irreparable damage to my Yubere. And. . . ." Publius's hand went to his collar, and he became even paler. "And, I will destroy us both, if you attempt to alter my mind."

Ruiz sighed. He had no realistic hope that the young Gench could alter Publius in any but a severely destructive manner—certainly a form of mission-imperative that would leave Publius fully in command of his wits would be far beyond the Gench's undeveloped skills. He would have enjoyed tormenting Publius longer, but if the monster-maker continued to believe that Ruiz's collar was still gimmicked, he might be moved to do something desperate and unexpected. "Let me set you at ease," he said. "We discovered the monomol layer on the Gench's collar, and removed it, before we were able to convince it that it would best serve its own interests by aiding us."

Publius lifted his head, an abrupt predatory movement. "How can I know if any of this is true?"

"Give him this, Albany." Ruiz took out the record cube he'd made during his conversation with the young Gench and tossed it to Albany.

Publius manipulated the cube expertly. The light from the tiny screen flickered on his face, which twisted and trembled with concentration.

Ruiz listened to the small sound of his own voice.

Eventually Publius seemed to be satisfied that Ruiz was telling the truth, and switched off the cube. He smiled, confident again. "I'm reassured, Ruiz."

Ruiz detected a deep foundation of contempt beneath Publius's words. "Good. All I want is to get off Sook. Play fair with me, and you'll get your puppet back. Try to cheat me again, and I'm likely to thwart you, out of simple spite. Remember, neither of us are men who customarily tell everything they know, so restrain your ego, force yourself to practice caution."

"Just as you say, Ruiz." Publius returned to his chair, face smooth and pleasant.

The Gench edged into the brighter light. "Why cannot you let me go then? The monster-maker is subdued and cooperative."

Publius laughed. "Because Ruiz Aw is no better than I am. His promises mean nothing more than mine; he is no more merciful, no more just. You are doomed to disappointment, young Gench, if you trust this man."

"So far he has proven trustworthy," it said. "And he did not promise me my freedom, only said that he would do what he could. It would have been easy for him to lie to me, as you would have done."

The sounds of Publius's sub cutting loose from the repair bubble came through the hull. Ruiz felt a sudden impulse, which he resisted for a while. But it grew stronger. Somehow, he felt that it would be an unforgivable affront to the sources of his luck, whatever they might be, to do exactly as Publius would surely have done in his place. And he might still need a great deal of luck.

Another consideration occurred to him. Here was the only Gench who could restore the false Yubere's functionality. Should Publius somehow regain control of the young Gench, he would no longer need Ruiz and his code-phrase.

"All right," he said to the Gench. "You may go. You probably shouldn't attempt to use the tram—the transport device you'll find at the end of the tunnel—it contains dangerous mechanisms. But Gencha are good climbers, right?"

"Correct," it said in its whispery uninflected voice. It lifted a foot, to display a pattern of rubbery sucker pads.

"Then you must climb down the walls of the pit, avoiding the tram rail and the other tunnels, which may house unfriendly beings. Can you do this? It is very far down to the level where your race dwells."

"I can do this," it said. "I can rest, or even sleep on a vertical face—we are thus adapted."

Ruiz nodded at Albany, who conducted the Gench to the lock and saw it on its way.

Publius sat silently, but a sneer trembled on his mouth.

Ruiz knew what Publius was thinking: that the Gench was still his, since he would soon control the enclave that had belonged to Yubere. Ruiz didn't care. His act of cautious mercy had, oddly enough, made him feel better. And already the air in the sub smelled cleaner.

Ruiz went to the control panel, activated the sonar, and watched the green dot of Publius's sub rising away from the stackwall. He heard the lock clang shut again, and the clatter as Albany dogged it tight.

Albany returned, cast their own vessel off from the stackwall, leaving the repair bubble in place to protect the tunnel from flooding. "Course?" he asked.

Ruiz gave the coordinates for the Diamond Bob Pens, and Albany punched them into the autopilot. The sub shuddered and began its slow rise to the surface.

"Now," Ruiz said. "Let's talk about your pirate friend."

PUBLIUS RAISED HIS hands, made a warding gesture. "Would you winkle all my secrets from me?"

A great weariness was stealing over Ruiz. He hadn't slept for days, he felt, abruptly, slow and vulnerable. He wondered if he still had enough of his strength left to deal with Publius. "Don't start," he said. "I want to know everything, now. If you haven't yet worked out the details of our escape from Sook, then now is the time to begin scheming." Besides, Ruiz thought, any time and energy Publius spent on such a scheme would reduce the time and energy he could devote to tricking Ruiz.

Publius rubbed his chin. "You're determined then to leave Sook?"

"Yes, yes. Have I not said this too many times to count?"

"I could offer alternatives," Publius said brightly. "Wealth beyond your imagination, a secure stronghold in SeaStack, a new body. Many other desirable things. Later, when the crisis among the pirate lords has abated, you'd find it easy to get offworld, if you still wanted to go."

"Please, don't incite me to rage, Publius. In my present state of mind, it might be fatal to both of us. Tell me all about your plan, or let us make one."

Publius shook his head doubtfully. "Do you insist?"

"I do."

"All right. All right. Do you know Ivant Tildoreamors?"

"By reputation." Tildoreamors was one of the bloodier pirate lords, head of a very old family of corsairs, the members of which had troubled the pangalac worlds for many centuries. To him was attributed a single-minded rapacity that was unusual even in SeaStack, where everyone who survived and prospered must be accounted some sort of monster.

"Ah? Well, Ivant owes me a large favor, and I happen to know one of his great secrets, which I now share with you. Ivant maintains a launch ring a hundred kilometers eastward down the coast, and one of his shuttles presently waits there."

Ruiz was skeptical. "East are the FireBarrens. The Blades of Namp allow no infidels to penetrate the Barrens."

"True, in general. However, Ivant supplies the Blades with their sacrament."

"I see. And how will we get there?"

"We'll take a barge, of course."

"Come now, Publius. No bargers in their right minds would go east."

Publius looked pleased with himself; perhaps he enjoyed revealing to Ruiz that he had actually formulated a plan to get them offplanet—an exemplary case of deviousness, when he had obviously never intended that Ruiz survive his visit to Yubere's stronghold. "You're wrong, Ruiz—for once. One barge goes east, twice a year. And the solstice is near."

Ruiz felt a queasy apprehension. "Elaborate."

"Oh, you've guessed what I mean. The Immolators even now prepare for the voyage. We have only to don the appropriate robes, tear our hair, dirty our faces, practice our wailing a bit, and we'll fit right in. My guess is that the pirates will never think to check the Immolators—after all, they go to die, either in the abattoirs of the Blades or among the fires of the Barrens."

"And how do you propose we avoid a similar end?"

"Simple! We wear Tildoreamors's livery under our Immolator robes; when we reach the Barrens, we'll doff the robes and announce ourselves as Ivant's emissaries. We'll carry a few kilos of ganja as tokens of our identity, and deliver the weed to the mullahs. The Blades will conduct us to the shuttle, and we'll be gone!"

Ruiz considered. If Publius were telling the truth, the plan seemed feasible, if uncomfortable. The prospect of sailing several hundred kilometers on a leaky old tub—penned up with several hundred suicidal fanatics—was hardly an appealing one—but compared to the difficulties they had already survived, it seemed not too terrible. *I've led an eccentric life for far too long*, he thought.

He allowed himself to think of Nisa and their pending reunion. An involuntary smile crossed his face.

Publius smiled back, apparently mistaking his expression for approbation. "You like it, eh? I thought you would."

Ruiz frowned. What an odd world Publius must inhabit. To all appearances, the monster-maker had forgotten that he had gone to vast lengths to ensure that he would never need to tell Ruiz of this plan. Did he now expect Ruiz to forget those treacheries and deal with Publius as if he were an ally? Perhaps Publius hoped that the force of his remarkable personality, diligently applied, would cause Ruiz to neglect some essential precaution—but if so the monster-maker would be disappointed. Ruiz could never forget that Publius possessed an unusually supple mind, even if it was an obscenely twisted one.

"It seems at least possible," said Ruiz ambiguously. "Much depends on whether you're telling the truth in all particulars—and we both know how unlikely that is."

Publius assumed an injured look, prompting Ruiz to a bark of almost-hysterical laughter, which he quickly subdued. It wouldn't do to display any weakness before the monster-maker. At present Ruiz held the greater leverage; he was more willing to die than Publius. As soon as Publius divined Ruiz's devotion to Nisa, the balance would shift again.

But he was still looking forward to seeing her again, with an almost-unbearable intensity.

CHAPTER 19

COREAN paced her suite like a newly caged predator, one not yet adapted to the comfort of regular meals and the hateful constraints of her cage. Marmo floated in a dark corner, playing his eternal game against his own coprocessors. The lights of his vidscreen flickered over his half-metal face, and the only sounds were Corean's footsteps and the tap of Marmo's fingers against his dataslate.

Her Moc warrior waited in the entrance hall, motionless. The suite was otherwise empty. After delivering her Pharaohan slaves to Yubere's stronghold, Remint had planned to recruit more slayers to staff the trap he had set for Ruiz; she had received no communication from him for hours.

When the comm's chime finally rang, she jumped and swore floridly. Marmo moved toward the comm panel, but she rushed forward and slapped at the receive sensor.

Remint's cold intense face filled the screen. "I have significant news," he said in his flat voice.

"What?"

"Ruiz Aw has surfaced at the Spindinny; he bought a half-dozen contracts the night before last and then left in a heavily armed gunboat. He had a lot of money to spend, and he got the best to be found there—such as they were. He revealed little of his purposes during these acquisitions, but from questioning his rejects, I deduce that he has undertaken to perform an assassination."

Corean was silent, digesting this information. "Who?" she finally asked.

Remint shrugged. "No truly suggestive data exists, but I believe that the target is unlikely to be you—the skills of the personnel he selected would indicate a target of greater importance, much better protected."

"I see." She found the notion unpalatable; how could Ruiz Aw have so soon dismissed her and gone on to other concerns? She would make him regret his casual disregard of her capabilities and persistence. Oh yes. "Where did he get the money? And the gunboat?"

"In all likelihood, he is working for someone whose resources are more extensive than yours. This may complicate his capture, should he survive his mission." Remint seemed unconcerned; he merely reported a possibility, without attaching any emotion to the concept.

But Corean was instantly enraged by the thought that Ruiz might die before she could heal her wounds with his pain. "What can we do?"

"Little, at this point. I've hired slayers, and placed them at the site of the trap. I've set up a surveillance near the pens. Do you have further instructions?"

"No," she said. "What of my Pharaohans? Did you make the delivery? Were there any difficulties?"

"No difficulties. However, I did not see my brother. Ordinarily he never misses an opportunity to gloat." The impassive face kindled with hatred, becoming for an instant a demonic mask. Then the expression guttered out, as if Remint could not long sustain such ferocity, and he once again became the poised killing machine.

"He has other things on his mind, at present," Corean said.

By THE TIME the sub neared the surface, Publius appeared to have regained all his grandiloquent confidence. "Now we must rendezvous with the gunboat; I will take the controls."

"No," said Ruiz. "Not yet, and perhaps never. I'm familiar with this vessel; aboard your gunboat, in the midst of your crew, I'd find it difficult to relax. So we'll stay below for a while yet."

Publius seemed about to argue, but then he apparently remembered his dignity, and subsided wordlessly.

Running ten meters below the surface, Ruiz sent the sub at its best speed through the winding channels, toward the Diamond Bob Pens.

WHEN THEY ARRIVED, he was forced to surface in order to enter the lagoon. He unshuttered the sub's blast louvers as the murky waters flowed away from the armorglass ports. Immediately he saw that something was wrong. The lagoon was nearly deserted, though a few burned hulks lay awash in the far end. Most of the lights were dark, but several of them had been replaced by jury-rigged glarebulbs, which cast a harsh blue light on the landing and on the phalanx of killmechs that now guarded the entrance. The entrance was a tangle of torn metal around a jagged hole.

Ruiz's heart jumped up and wedged itself into his throat. Something was terribly wrong. He latched up his armor as the sub slammed roughly into the quay. Before the sub had latched itself to the mooring toggles, he was undogging the dorsal hatch.

"Watch him closely," he told Albany. "If he does anything you don't understand immediately, kill him. Don't worry about me—I'll be out of range; besides, I may have just lost my best reason for staying alive. If you hesitate, we'll probably both die anyway, so don't hesitate."

He climbed out. As he was lowering himself down the ladder to the quay, he heard Publius start to say something in a brightly inquisitive voice. He hoped Albany was wise enough to keep his mouth shut.

He landed on the quay and raised his empty hands in a gesture of peaceful intent. The nearest killmech blurred across the landing and seized his wrists in padded clamps. "Your business here?" it asked in an unmodulated mechanical voice. It extruded probes, and inventoried the weapons he carried.

"I have property within," Ruiz said. He noticed that the mech bore the colors of one of the great pirate houses. Glancing about, he saw that most of the lords had sent killmechs to guard the pens. What could have happened?

"Unforeseen events have occurred," said the mech. "Your property may be damaged or unavailable."

Ruiz felt his knees wobble; his muscles threatened to turn to water. "What unforeseen events?"

"We are not authorized to discuss these events. You may retrieve your property if it is available. If not, you must speak with the manager."

It released his wrists and moved aside. He nodded and walked inside, as though in a slow nightmare.

The pens had obviously been the site of a bloody engagement. The corpses of the combatants were gone, but here and there were splashes of brown blood, and everywhere was the smell of recent carnage: an odor of decay, feces, urine, and the persistent reek of discharged energy weapons. Ruiz hurried, faster and faster, until by the time he reached the cells where he had left Nisa and the others, he was running as fast as he could.

The doorways were open and dark, twisted by the same energies that had destroyed the front doors of the pen. Oddly, the doors appeared to have been blasted open from the inside.

He skidded to a stop, gasping for breath, though he shouldn't have been at all taxed by such a short sprint. He could not immediately force himself to enter her room.

An android stepped from the cell where Ruiz had left Dolmaero; it wore the silver and blue uniform of the Diamond Bob Pens. "These were yours?" it demanded.

"Yes," Ruiz answered, in a voice that shook slightly.

The android froze for a moment; apparently it was too primitive a model to be capable of smooth transitions between attitudinal modes. Then it smiled, a grotesquely artificial expression. "Come," it said. "Diamond Bob will want to speak with you." It pointed down the corridor, deeper into the pens.

"Wait," said Ruiz. "Where are my properties?"

"Gone. So sorry. Diamond Bob will discuss the matter at greater length."

Ruiz pushed past the thing into Nisa's cell. It attempted to bar his way, though with no great determination, plucking ineffectually at his armor. "Please," it said. "Diamond Bob urgently requests your attention."

Ruiz ignored it. He roamed around the small room, looking for any indication of Nisa's fate. The door to the common area was also burned open, but carefully, as if the person who had wielded the graser had not wished to injure the person within. Obviously, the attackers had come from the common area, had broken through the cells and gone on out. Had they taken Nisa and the others with them? Inside her room, he found no bloodstains, nor any sign that lethal weapons had been used—and his heart lifted slightly. He imagined that there still lingered a trace of Nisa's scent, under the stinks of the ravaged pen. He picked up her pillow, held it to his armored chest. "When did it happen?" he asked the android, who stood in the doorway, wringing its hands in a mechanical approximation of anxiety.

"Diamond Bob will be happy to make full disclosure," it said. "Please, our customers' satisfaction is our paramount concern. Diamond Bob will try to compensate you for your losses—though you must realize that Diamond Bob has sustained heavy losses also."

Ruiz snarled wordlessly. Diamond Bob had lost nothing so valuable as Ruiz had. But at least there was some evidence that Nisa wasn't dead. Who had taken her. The first thought that came to him was: Corean. Was she really crazy enough to have mounted an assault on the pens? How had she even found the Pharaohans? SeaStack had a number of pens; most of them guarded the identity of their patrons carefully, but none more fiercely than Diamond Bob's. Ruiz shook his head. Perhaps he could learn more from Diamond Bob.

He stepped out into the corridor and saw that four killmechs now blocked him in. They made no threatening movements, but it was clear that he would be required to talk to Diamond Bob, even if he hadn't been eager to do so.

"Let's go," he said to the android.

DIAMOND BOB WASN'T what Ruiz had expected; she was a small tidy woman who affected an appearance of late middle age. Her narrow face was innocent of beauty paint, her nose was long, and her lips thin and colorless. She wore her gray hair in a coil at the back of her neck, drawn so tight as to appear painful.

Her office seemed more like a sitting room from some historic holoplay, a play set in some Old Earth fantasy culture. The light was dim and brown. Dull-green ferns sat on tiny round tables, and the walls were covered with a pattern of faded blue roses. The only jarring note in this ancient decor was a huge gleaming killmech, motionless in the darkest corner—though it wore a lace doily on its polished head and held a yellowing aspidistra in its claws, in an apparent effort to fit in.

Diamond Bob indicated an uncomfortable-looking humpbacked couch, and they sat down together. Ruiz removed his helmet and gloves; he was suddenly conscious of the scuffs and bloodstains on his armor.

She didn't appear to be discomfitted by his appearance. "We have both suffered losses," she said without preamble. She pressed a stemglass of green cordial into his hand. She smiled perfunctorily and then sipped at her own glass. "You gave your name as Ruiz Aw? Isn't that the name of a famous Dilvermoon enforcer? Do you claim to be him?"

"No," he said. "My properties. Who took them?" He set his cordial down untasted.

"Would you prefer tea?" she asked.

"No. Tell me what you know about those who raided your pens."

She took another delicate sip of her drink. "I'd hoped you could help me with that."

"How would I know anything about it?" Ruiz tried to look astonished.

Diamond Bob fixed him with her tiny glittering eyes. "Because I believe that the raid was undertaken for the sole purpose of taking your property."

"What makes you think that?"

"Several things—and my intuition, which is often correct. First, two days ago a clumsy attempt was made to extract your ownerfile from our databanks. Naturally, the attempt failed. Just before that, a notorious slayer visited here, a man named Remint. He interrogated another Pharaohan slave, called Flomel, who had been admitted to the same common area as your properties. Your slaves were Pharaohan, I believe?"

"Yes." Flomel again. Ruiz cursed himself once again for his softness; he should have known better than to let an enemy live. If he ever got another opportunity, he would rectify that mistake. What hideous bad luck . . . that whoever had purchased Flomel from Deepheart had quartered him here.

Diamond Bob drew back slightly, as if Ruiz had allowed something of his anger to reach his face. "Well, to continue: The raiders wore armor, of course, but an analysis of the dimensions and movement patterns of their leader matched the analysis of Remint. Odd that he should take no more effective measures to conceal his identity, isn't it? He didn't even bother to burn the surveillance imagers. It was almost as if he wanted us to know who he was . . . he must be mad, as now the lords—who guarantee the safety of my business—are avid for his blood. Perhaps he *is* mad—my people reported that his affect was very odd during his first visit."

"What can you tell me about this Remint?" Ruiz asked.

"A moment—let me finish my explication."

"Continue." Somehow Ruiz was sure that badgering Diamond Bob would yield little useful information—better to let her tell her story as she chose.

"Thank you," she said dryly. "Finally, and I think most significant, the raiders took your people away alive, and I think they were only interested in your property, though they took several others as well. That was probably an attempt to confuse the issue; the choices seemed random, whereas all your folk were from Pharaoh."

"I see."

"Also," she added, "we've recovered the corpses of two of the other slaves who were taken. Evidently they were carried only a short distance from the pens before someone burned a hole through their heads and dumped them. Fortunately, they weren't terribly valuable, and were insured." She sipped at her cordial, and then poured herself another serving. "So you see, I'm very interested in you . . . and in your enemies." She smiled, again a very remote and abstract expression.

Ruiz realized, belatedly, that he might be in serious trouble. He had been so concerned with controlling the obvious lethality of Publius that he had almost forgotten that Sea-Stack was full of other dangerous folk. "Who else is interested?" he asked.

Her smile widened. "No one, presently. I've withheld some of this from the lords, though of course I had to give them the data regarding Remint—and they've organized a major headhunt throughout SeaStack. If he shows in any of his usual haunts, he'll soon be apprehended."

"When do you plan to tell them about me?"

"Perhaps never," she said. "I can see certain advantages in cleaning up this situation without their help. My reputation has been badly damaged; that will cost me far more than replacing a few dozen dead security people and killmechs. I'm afraid the damage will be permanent, unless I can bring the lords a suitable present; say, Remint's head on a platter."

"Our goals converge, to some extent," Ruiz said cautiously.

"Maybe. Tell me, who would you first suspect of wanting your people—and of being foolish enough to try to take them from me?"

Ruiz considered. The threads of the situation had become so tangled that he could no longer easily follow the one that might benefit him most. He was exhausted and confused; not only could he not see where his advantage lay, he couldn't even decide where the deepest danger lurked. But he tried to gather his thoughts. Diamond Bob was a businessperson. Her interest in apprehending the raiders was obvious and understandable. Why not deal with her on a somewhat straightforward basis?

"If I tell you what I surmise, will you tell me what you can about Remint?"

She nodded.

"All right. As far as I know, my only enemy here—or anyway the only one who knows I'm in SeaStack—is a slaver whom I know as Corean Heiclaro. Do you know of her?" He couldn't mention Publius; he was still dependent on the monster-maker. Any suspicion that fell on Publius would reduce Ruiz's chances of exploiting the monster-maker's connections to escape SeaStack.

"The name isn't immediately familiar," said Diamond Bob. She moved to a rosewood writing desk and tapped at the dataslate inset into the desktop. "No, I find no mention of her in my records. Description?"

Ruiz described Corean as dispassionately as he could—her mannerisms, her slender body, her priceless face. He thought he had kept the hatred from his voice, but Diamond Bob watched him with knowing eyes and a slight smile. When he was finished, she shook her head. "No. She must employ another pen, if she does business in SeaStack—or perhaps she uses a private facility. Or, it may be that she has always dealt with me through underlings. The Pharaohan Flomel was delivered to us by a felinoform who called himself Lensh—and here is another possible connection to Remint. One of the raiders was a catperson. We had almost captured him, when the raider we believe to be Remint took off the cat's head with a graser. Unfortunately, there wasn't enough left to compare the ID with the one who left Flomel here, but I would think they might be the same person.

"Now. Tell me why you think Corean might have something to do with the raid. Why would she want these Pharaohans?"

Ruiz debated whether he should mention the Gencha, but decided that volunteering such volatile information might be foolish, even if Diamond Bob proved trustworthy beyond reasonable expectation.

"They once belonged to her, before I stole them."

"Ah."

"What happened to Flomel?"

She smiled. "He was also taken. We didn't find his body."

Ruiz thought. Corean began to seem the likely motivator behind the raid. If so, she now had regained her phoenix troupe, except for the dead Kroel. But was that financial consideration large enough for her to risk the wrath of the pirate lords? The rational answer was no. Was she rational?

He needed more information. "Tell me what you know of Remint?"

Diamond Bob shrugged. "A few years ago he was the most feared slayer of SeaStack, which is saying quite a lot. He's intelligent, physically gifted, merciless. All manner of myths grew up around his prowess as a killer. Then he seemed to drop from sight. No one with any credibility claimed to have taken his head, so I assumed he had simply grown tired of the profession and retired. It happens. There were reports he'd been seen on Dilvermoon, and on other faraway worlds, but I discount these. Famous people often seem to be everywhere, don't they? I was astonished to hear of his first visit here, when he interviewed Flomel—as far as I know, that was the first verified sighting of Remint in over four years."

"Was he freelance?"

"No, not then. He worked for his brother, a man named Alonzo Yubere. Perhaps you've heard of him; he keeps a stable of Gencha and does personality modifications, mostly for the lords. But it was rumored that the two of them had a falling out, just before Remint disappeared. I think this must be true—Alonzo is an extraordinarily careful man—he'd never attack me unless his survival was threatened, and I can't imagine how those properties could have affected him. Either Remint is operating on his own, or he's working for someone else—such is my guess, for what it's worth."

Ruiz felt a dizzy sense of disorientation. Alonzo Yubere. He had been assembling a theory that involved Corean's thirst for revenge; now that seemed far too simple. There were suddenly too many coincidences.

"Are you well?" asked Diamond Bob. "Do you know Yubere?"

"I . . . met him. Briefly." He was remembering the dark-haired woman who had fallen into the depths of the pit. Gencha food. "Tell me, please: Exactly when did the raid occur?"

"Night before last, oh-three-hundred hours. They were in and out in fifteen minutes—very professional work, in most respects."

Ruiz sat back against the couch, his heart pounding. The woman might have been Nisa; there had been plenty of time for Remint to have delivered the Pharaohans to Yubere before Ruiz had penetrated the stronghold.

Diamond Bob watched him, her shrewd eyes burning with curiosity. "Obviously I have distressed you. Why so?"

Ruiz felt as if he were about to collapse under the pressure of her revelations. He was abruptly a great deal worse than exhausted; his thoughts seemed to run much too slowly for coherence, the beginnings of each thought seemed to fade to formless mist before he could finish it. "Corean was shipping the Pharaohans to Yubere when I stole them from her, or so I believe."

"If she has completed this shipment, would this be fatal to your purposes?"

"Possibly." He tried not to think of Nisa dead, rotting in the corrupt soup at the bottom of the pit. Even if her body was still alive, had she already been processed into a less-than-human creature? What could he do, now? He needed time to think, to analyze his options. And he couldn't be entirely sure that Remint was acting on Corean's behalf. It was at least possible that Publius was behind the snatch; he also had connections with Yubere, and reason to want some additional leverage over Ruiz. Remint might not have made the delivery to Yubere, in any case. He tried to remember the moments he had spent with Yubere, before he'd killed him. Wasn't there something there, something he should take into consideration? Then he recalled the flash of recognition he'd detected in Yubere's face—and at the time discounted. How could Yubere have known anything about him, unless he had been told by either Publius or Corean?

He needed time to think, but was there any time? If Nisa had been taken below to be deconstructed, the process might have already begun. He took a deep breath and tried to clear his head. If she *had* been taken below, it was too late. But if she was still in Yubere's dungeon, then it was likely she would remain there for a while, since the false Yubere was in no condition to order her taken to the Gencha. He would have to act on the assumption that the latter was the case; it followed that he ought to first pursue Remint, in the hope that Nisa had not yet been delivered to Yubere. He would very much like to avoid entering Yubere's stronghold again, since to do so he would probably be forced to release the false Yubere and thus would lose his strongest leverage over Publius.

He rubbed his hands over his face, wishing he were not so terribly tired. "All right," he said. "You need to know who hit you and why—and I need to recover my property. Can you give me a data-excerpt covering Remint: his history, his habits, his customary places, his associates?"

"I can, and I can include the report the lords' forensic people gave me—you may find something useful there, though it was a very clean operation," said Diamond Bob. "But I'll give it to you only if you'll agree to share what you learn with me. I'll pay a fair price for any new data you can add to the file, plus market value for the slaves you lost—and a very good bounty for Remint's head."

"It's a deal," said Ruiz in a ragged voice.

"Good," she said. She rose and took a datawafer from her writing desk and dropped it into his hand. "But I have a caution for you, don't be greedy. Find out what you can, deliver your information to me, get paid, and survive. What you've told me leads me to suspect that Remint is still somehow connected with his brother. Don't make the mistake of dancing with Alonzo Yubere—he plays in a much bigger league than we mere mortals do. Don't attempt to take

Remint's head, unless the odds favor you very heavily. He's a legend, as I've said—a man-shaped demon."

"Probably good advice."

She grinned, an incongruously predatory expression in that neutral gray face. "It is—unless, maybe, you actually *are* Ruiz Aw."

A BRACE OF killmechs escorted Ruiz to the entrance.

Back aboard the sub, he was gratified to see that Albany still held his graser aimed at Publius. He had half expected the situation to have deteriorated even more thoroughly than it already had.

Ruiz took a leash from a storage bin and tossed it to Albany. "Take him back into the cargo hold and attach him to the bench."

Publius leaped up, face shading toward a familiar purple. "This is too much, Ruiz. I'm not your prisoner; we're allies." He threw up his chin, to display the madcollar. "Treat me with the proper respect, or I'll punch our tickets right now. I have my clones; what do I care for this old flesh?" He extended his controller in a trembling hand, his finger hovering over the trigger.

Ruiz was too tired to feel anything but impatience. "Do it, then," he said.

A long moment passed and Ruiz wondered if Publius had by some strange quirk meant what he had said. He still could not bring himself to be very interested in the answer.

Finally Publius snapped his hand down and turned away. The hatred that boiled off his body was an almost-tangible thing, an almost-visible distortion of the air. "No. No, don't let the little man destroy us," he muttered. "More important things must be considered; even dignity must be discarded for a while, if necessary. If we must, if we must. . . ."

He walked ahead of Albany into the hold, and presently Ruiz heard the click of the leash being fastened.

Albany returned and laid down his graser with a sigh of relief. "What now, Ruiz? I see you've got more troubles. Where's your true love?"

"Stolen. I'll explain later." He tried to glare at Albany, but he was just too tired. He decoupled the sub and guided it out of the lagoon, and as soon as it cleared the entrance, he angled it into the depths. He set the autopilot to take them

down to the sub's maximum cruising depth, and then pro-
grammed it to shut down the engines and drift silently with
the sluggish currents at the roots of SeaStack. They'd be as
safe there as anywhere else.

"I need to rest for a couple of hours," Ruiz said. He
fought down his misgivings; Nisa might be lost forever if he
delayed, but in his present condition, he was sure to make
some foolish fatal mistake. "You do too, I know, but we'll
have to take turns. Even with the madcollar and the leash, I
can't bring myself to trust Publius. He's resourceful."

"No doubt about it," said Albany. "While you were
gone, he told me how he was going to be Emperor of Everything. Had me going for it, a little, even if he didn't explain
how it was going to happen. But then I got to thinking how
he probably wasn't the sort to forgive and forget—and I'm a
guy who put a gun to his head."

"I can't fault your logic," said Ruiz. "Look, I'm going to
pass out in the pilot's chair. Wake me in two, and it'll be
your turn."

He prepared a ject of soporifics and vitalizers, then
shucked off his armor. He touched the ject to his arm and
lay back in the chair. His eyes fluttered shut, and he slept.

When he knew that he was dreaming, his first dream-
clouded thought was a sense of gratitude that he wouldn't
remember this. He never had good dreams, never . . . no
matter how promisingly they began.

He was with Nisa at the landing, watching her bathe in
the little fountain. The air had that golden radiance, the
untruthful brilliance that surrounds events remembered
from the perspective of a long lifetime. Already, Ruiz
mused, the dream was wrong; surely that moment was no
more than a few years in the past.

Ruiz watched her with an oddly wistful sense of delight.
She scrubbed at her white skin industriously, using the black
sand from the bottom of the pool, and her pale lovely body
gradually turned pink. She gave him a sweet smile, and the
soft amber light shone in her dark eyes.

Nisa seemed as graceful as the bronze creature who stood
poised in the center of the pool, a six-legged predator, obviously of some coursing species. Its beautiful terrible head
glared blindly; it snarled, exposing long fangs green with the
patina of ages. The dark water that ran down its flanks and
dripped into the pool steamed, as though the day were cold

and the water hot. There was something fascinating about the patterns the water made as it flowed over the bronze, an involving complexity, as the streams diverged and recombined, endlessly. It was almost hypnotic.

After what seemed a very long time, the bronze predator began to seem not quite so graceful. Its limbs were thicker and less cleanly defined, its head a knot of lowering menace. Ruiz tore his gaze away from the ugly thing and looked at Nisa again.

He made a choked sound of horror. While he had been distracted, Nisa had continued her vigorous scrubbing, to hideous effect. Her skin, her wonderful perfect skin was gone, scoured away, exposing the bloody meat beneath. She still smiled at him, but her lips were gone, so that her smile was very wide, long white teeth smeared with red. He saw now that the black sand was really made up of splinters of dark cobalt-blue glass, with which Nisa continued to abrade her flesh.

He could not rise from the coping of the fountain, he could form no words; it was as if his body had turned to stone. He wanted to stop her from continuing her destruction; surely it wasn't yet too late. She still lived and moved; he had brought her back from death once. Why not again? But he couldn't act, he could only watch, as she began to change even more terribly.

She was rotting as she stood, and instead of glass, she bathed in handfuls of maggots, which wriggled into her body and made her flesh pulse with hidden movement. She was dead, long dead, now, and yet she still moved.

Her flesh darkened, liquefied, dripped from her into the pool, which now seemed a sump full of dreadful substances, boiling with virulence.

He expected to see, finally, the clean whiteness of bone, but what he saw instead seemed infinitely worse. As the last of her flesh fell away, he discovered that beneath all had been hidden the bright alloy of a killmech. The thing—he could no longer call it Nisa—moved with quick insectile precision to the center of the fountain and laid its claws on the shoulder of the bronze beast.

With a groan that made Ruiz think of long-locked doors opening, deep under the ground, the beast shifted and then stepped down from its plinth.

Both of them, in a movement that seemed to take hours,

shifted their gaze until they looked at Ruiz. Their glowing red eyes projected an unmechlike hunger.

In a horribly synchronized motion, they took a step toward him, and the killmech raised its arms in a parody of embrace.

He woke screaming, unable to remember what had frightened him so badly.

CHAPTER 20

RUIZ came to himself, covered with greasy sweat, feeling not a great deal better than he had before his rest. He wiped his hands over his face, rubbing at his eyes, waiting for the remaining traces of the dream to fade. He had forgotten the content of the dream already, but he knew it had involved Nisa in some context, and he felt a touch of wistful loss at the thought of her. Sometimes he wished he could remember his dreams, even if they proved unpleasant, as this one evidently had.

Albany had started to move toward Ruiz, but had evidently thought better of it, and now stood still, one hand extended in a gesture of comfort or restraint. "Damn, Ruiz," he said. "You're giving me the crawls. Are you all right?"

"Sure. I'm fine." Ruiz climbed out of the pilot chair and saw that he'd slept almost the full two hours he'd allotted himself. He flexed his injured shoulder and decided that it was healing well, responding to the tissue stimulants the armor's medical limpet had injected.

Albany shook his head. "What a freak show," he said, shaking his head. His face was pale inside the opening of his helmet, and he wasn't smiling.

"Sorry," Ruiz said. "Why don't you take a nap next? I've got a wafer to scan, and some scheming to do." He started to climb into his armor again, wrinkling his nose at the sour stinks that rose from the monomol segments.

For a moment Albany didn't react, then he seemed to relax from some tautness that Ruiz hadn't noticed until he had moved. "Yeah, yeah. I guess I'll do that." He began to strip off his own armor, and Ruiz saw that Albany's hands were trembling.

"What's been happening?" Ruiz asked.

Albany shrugged, and settled into the pilot's chair. "Not much. We're in a west-running current, drifting at a half knot. There was something going on right after you went to sleep, some fuss on the surface, with a lot of active sonar and detector drogues being dropped—someone looking for something. Probably wasn't us, hey?"

"Maybe not," said Ruiz. "Anything else?"

Albany shifted uneasily. "Our former employer . . . he's a firecracker, isn't he? He's been telling me about his art, trying to throw a scare into me. He's succeeded, I have to tell you. I see now why you'd rather be dead than his." He sighed and looked at Ruiz with weary eyes. "Me too. I hope you can control him, Ruiz."

"I think I can," said Ruiz, summoning a confident tone. "If anyone can."

"I guess so." Albany sighed and shut his eyes. A moment later his breathing deepened and he began to snore.

Ruiz stretched, then went to the comm panel and slipped Diamond Bob's wafer into the analyzer slot.

REMINT CALLED AGAIN, shortly after dawn, and woke Corean from an uneasy slumber, in which she had dreamed of ruin and flight. The dreams had been colored by dreadful images from the raving corridors of Dobravit—seepage from her locked-away childhood memories.

Marmo took the call, but Remint insisted he could speak only to Corean. By that time, Corean stood in the doorway, scratching at her sleep-tousled head. When she saw whose face filled the vidscreen, she moved to the comm panel.

"What is it?"

"Another sighting."

"Where?" She was completely awake now, her bad dreams forgotten in the heat of her hatred.

"At the pens. He arrived in a small submersible, went inside for a few minutes, then emerged, reboarded the sub, and left." Remint's expressionless face told her nothing.

"You took him?" She was filled with elation.

"No. We expected him to arrive in a surface vessel—the gunboat—and arranged our subterfuges and devices accordingly. We had no way to strike at him within the pen's lagoon; we had great difficulty in even getting a spymote inside. The pirate lords are incandescent with outrage; they've staffed the pens with numerous killmechs, they search for me everywhere. I fear my usefulness to my brother is permanently diminished." At this digression, something kindled deep behind the slayer's eyes.

"But you're following him? Surely?"

"No. Outside the entrance, the sub dove, before we could get a transponder on it. It descended to a great depth, then went silent, and our detectors were unable to maintain contact."

"You idiot!" Her elation had mutated into sizzling rage. "I ought to cut your throat and feed you to the margars."

Remint seemed unaffected by her outburst. He leaned back and brought a sonic knife into the camera's field of view. He activated the knife and touched the roil of displaced air delicately to his throat. "Do you so order?" As he spoke, the blade bit, just a little, and a flutter of blood ran along the edge of the knife's envelope and spattered the camera's lens with tiny red specks.

"No! No, don't be foolish." She watched him switch the knife off and put it away, apparently unconcerned with the red rivulet that trickled over the corded muscle of his throat. He was, she thought, a creature completely outside her experience, even though she had possessed a number of Genched slaves. None had displayed such frozen intensity; Remint must have been a remarkable man before his deconstruction.

He looked up, his eyes empty of emotion. "Shall I continue?"

"Yes."

"Then: Ruiz Aw is considering what he learned in the pens. My belief is that he will seek me in my once-favorite place, a fabularium in a stack near my brother's stronghold.

Already the pirate lords have visited the Celadon Wind, as the place is called; their agents still infest every room and rathole. He will know this, but my assessment of the man is that he will believe that he can discover some vital information that the lords were too stupid to find. He is an egomaniac, as I once was. We were very much alike, in many ways." His detachment seemed impossible, even for the robot of flesh and bone she knew him to be.

Corean considered. "You're waiting for him there?"

"I hide myself and several slayers in an adjacent joypalace."

She made a decision. "Send me a guide, and I'll join you."

His gaze was cool and full of evaluation. "Your passion may be a liability to my success."

She snarled and said, "Just do it." Then she cut the connection.

She sat back and thought about Ruiz Aw and his inexplicable luck. From somewhere a memory rose to torment her. She remembered that she had wondered aloud about Ruiz Aw, about whether his confidence arose from a foolish ignorance of the dangers of his situation, or whether it came from a strength so overpowering that he truly didn't need to fear her.

A chill came over her, and she shivered involuntarily. No, no, that was ridiculous. Several times she had held his life in her hand, several times she could have snuffed him out effortlessly, and he couldn't have resisted at all.

But still, a tiny voice whispered, deep inside her heart, *but still, Ruiz Aw lives and thwarts you. And ignores you as he goes about his business.*

SEVERAL THREAD BARS appeared on the analyzer's screen, and Ruiz touched the first one, labeled SURVEILLANCE RECORDS. The thread expanded into its nested subjects, and he followed the one that contained the recording of the assault on the pens.

The screen cleared for an instant, and then filled with a slightly grainy image, harshly lit, of a large person in bulky black mirror-armor, who walked quickly through the entrance portal of the pens, accompanied by two smaller figures, also armored. The tagline at the screen's lower right corner said: REMINT Y'YUBERE AND TWO UNKNOWNS.

Ruiz studied this new enemy. He began to feel a little sick. He had never met Remint, but he *knew* him, with a knowledge born of the countless bloody encounters that had forged Ruiz into what he was.

Ruiz was abruptly and completely sure that Remint was the kind of killer he most feared, the purest and most deadly species of slayer, a man who lived wholly in the moment, untroubled by regret or foreboding. The man moved as lightly as a recent heavyworld immigrant—he gave an impression of irresistible strength, tightly leashed. Behind the mirrored visor, his eyes would be flickering, seeing everything, weighing it on the scales of his purpose. He would destroy without thought whatever obstructed that purpose, instantly and with instinctive efficiency.

Ruiz touched the screen, and the lower left quadrant displayed a still image of Remint's face, as he had appeared on his first visit to the pen. He could see a little of Alonzo Yubere in those features, but the resemblance was obscured by cloned muscle and reengineered bone, so that the expressionless eyes gleamed out of slits cut through a mask of inhumanly dense flesh. If anything, the slayer was more frightening without his armor—he seemed even more truly an engine of destruction.

This was, in fact, himself as he had been, and it was like looking into a smoky mirror and seeing a grinning skull. Ruiz shuddered. Could such a man be defeated? He had never really thought it possible, when he had been such a man himself.

The screen split and began to display another group of armored persons, four in number, tagged: CONFEDERATES OF REMINT Y'YUBERE, IDENTITIES UNKNOWN.

Ruiz touched the forward speed dot on the display, and held it down to cycle past the initial penetration. The two groups of armored raiders converged at a locked ingress to the common area. He saw Flomel, who had evidently been given a ceramic blast pencil during Remint's previous visit, attach the pencil to a security mechanism at the ingress. He watched Flomel trigger a flare of energies that had melted the device, allowing Remint and his people to gain access to the common room.

There was the glare and percussion of weapons, torn bodies, running and screaming. The raiders moved efficiently through the hysteria, cutting down anyone who blocked their path.

They set rip charges at the inner doors of the other Pharaohans' cells, detonated them, swept through. In what seemed an obvious afterthought, the last raiders to leave seized several of the nearest slaves and herded them along.

Ruiz paused the recording, frowned. He was still very tired, but something about the sequence of events bothered him. Why had the attempt to cover their true purpose been so transparently clumsy? In all the other aspects of the operation, Remint had been coldly brilliant, directing the raid with inhuman precision.

An idea bubbled up from some deep layer of paranoia, and Ruiz couldn't help speculating: Was all this an elaborate charade, designed to draw Ruiz Aw into the open?

He shook his head. Even if it was the opening gambit in a clever trap, he would still have to respond. He filed the suspicion away for later examination and allowed the recording to play on.

The pen's security forces had finally begun to react to the raid, and they brought up monomol barricades and heavy flutter guns, trying to prevent the raiders from escaping.

Remint seemed to go into another temporal frame of reference, moving so quickly that he became a blur the camera could not resolve into clarity, no matter how much Ruiz slowed the recording.

Remint flashed forward, ahead of his troops, rolling under the barricades before the guards could react and bring their flutter guns to bear.

Ruiz watched the slow-motion carnage, fascinated and horrified. There was a dreadful beauty in the slayer's movements, as he spun from one guard to the next, slashing with a sonic knife and firing a pinbeam with his other hand. In an instant six guards were down.

One lived long enough to get off a poorly aimed burst. A stream of hypersonic particles scythed through two of Remint's flankers, whose upper bodies dissolved into flying tatters of armor and bone. Only their legs remained whole, geysering blood, held upright by the frozen servos in their armor.

When the gun fired, Ruiz felt his heart stutter for a moment, as though crushed by the pressure of his anxiety for Nisa. But she and the others were in a tight cluster in the center of the raider's formation, and the burst missed them by a considerable margin.

One of the raiders held a neural whip, which he flicked at the prisoner's heels whenever they slowed. Now he touched Nisa with it, and she stumbled, and looked up at the hidden camera, eyes full of shock and pain.

Ruiz froze the image and zoomed it in, until her face filled the screen. His gaze lingered on the clean planes of her cheekbones, the luminous dark eyes, the rich sweet mouth. Even in this extremity of fright and bewilderment, her features projected an admirable strength. Ruiz thought he could almost see the shape of her thoughts. She was thinking about escape, or—if that was impossible—about survival. Then, in a rush of sad realization, Ruiz knew that she was also thinking: *Where is Ruiz Aw?*

He touched the screen and the playback resumed. He watched with a frozen adamant concentration, as the raiders swept through the halls and out onto the quay, where a battered, heavily armed gunboat waited.

The raiders, herding their prisoners, boarded the gunboat. It sped away, powerful engines thundering, throwing up a high roostertail. Hot light lanced from its weapons, destroying the other craft in the lagoon, presumably to prevent pursuit.

The camera's viewpoint flickered and then resumed, following the raiders' craft as it snaked through the twisting waterways.

After a few moments, a weapons pod on the boat's armored transom twinkled orange fire, and the screen went white. A tagline at the bottom read: TRACKING DEVICE DESTROYED.

Ruiz frowned. He wished he were not so afraid of the slayer Remint; that fear would undermine his effectiveness.

Something cold and hard whispered in the back of his mind—words he shut out at first, not wanting to hear them. The whisper grew louder, until he could no longer ignore it. *Leave her; she's probably already dead,* it said. *He'll destroy you; can there be any doubt of this?*

"Probably not," he muttered. But behind his eyes Nisa's

face floated, as he had seen it in the playback: beautiful, tender, true. He couldn't abandon her, no matter how sensible that course might be. She had taken firm root in his heart; if circumstances tore her away from him, he didn't think there would be enough left of his heart to keep beating.

He forced his attention back to the matter at hand, and went through the rest of Diamond Bob's material.

When he was finished, he was no less afraid of Remint y'Yubere, but he knew where to start looking for him.

ALBANY SAT IN the copilot's chair as Ruiz guided the sub into one of the subsurface openings that led to the lagoon at the heart of the stack.

"You're sure you know what you're doing?" Albany was still pale and tense.

"No," Ruiz said, as cheerfully as possible. "But at one time the man spent much of his time and money in the Celadon Wind; maybe I can cut his trail there."

"What makes you think you'll do any better than the lords? They've got good snoops, and snooping's not your specialty." Albany seemed dubious.

Ruiz shrugged. He had explained a bit about their quarry, leaving out the most frightening details. "We're two of a kind," he said. "I understand him better than the pirate snoops."

"Seems thin," said Albany dubiously.

It seemed thin to Ruiz too, but what else could he do?

THE LAGOON WAS a vast black emptiness beneath a high dome of slagged metal, a hollowed-out space a kilometer across.

Ruiz stood on the deck grating of the sub and looked up. Phosphorescent worms slithered across the dome, forming sinuous patterns of cold color; apparently an ancient work of bio-art gone feral.

Across the still water were scattered the riding lights of other vessels. Ruiz couldn't see them well enough to tell if Publius's gunboat was among them. He assumed that the gunboat Remint had used in the raid wasn't here; surely the pirates would have found it, had Remint been so foolish as to come here.

They had picked up an automated mooring buoy. On securing their line, it had summoned one of the robotic bumboats that waited at the quay that circled the lagoon.

It arrived and Ruiz descended the narrow steps set into the sub's bulging topsides. Albany leaned on the sub's conning tower, looking down at Ruiz, his face obscured by the darkness. "I still think we ought to go to ground until this excitement blows over. I know places where we'd keep fat and happy." He spoke in an oddly dispassionate tone. It suddenly seemed to Ruiz that perhaps some vital mechanism had broken down in Albany. He wondered what it might be, and how it had happened—and why it hadn't happened to him, yet.

"You're probably right," Ruiz said. "But I don't think I have any choice. If you want, I'll put you ashore here, no hard feelings."

Albany sighed. "No. I'll stick. You still have your luck, Ruiz Aw. I need something; maybe that's it. Besides, who'd keep an eye on our benevolent employer?"

Ruiz didn't know what to say. The bumboat nudged the sub's flank and beeped insistently. "Thanks," he finally said, and stepped into the bumboat. He looked back at Albany as the bumboat backed water and drew away.

Albany waved and spoke in a low voice that carried across the water. "Good luck, Ruiz. Find what *you* need."

The bumboat beeped again, inquisitively. "The Celadon Wind's ingress," Ruiz told it, and it carried him away.

RUIZ JOINED A procession of odd persons, walking up the ramp toward the Celadon Wind's gate. To his right were a pair of old pirates, much scarred, wearing typically gaudy flamesilk shipsuits, arms affectionately linked, whispering endearments into each other's dirty ears. To his left, uncomfortably close, was some sort of barbarian from a desert world, muffled in black robes, from which came the clink and rattle of many weapons. Ruiz edged away slightly, and slowed his pace so that the man passed him in a waft of ancient sweat and strong hashish. Farther up the ramp was a gang of devolved beasters, a half-dozen men and women with thick, crusty skin and swinish white-tusked faces. They skipped along like schoolchildren on an outing.

Just ahead walked a tall slender woman, naked except for steel-scaled slippers and a great mane of pale hair, confined by a headband set with pigeonblood rubies. In other circumstances, Ruiz might have been distracted by the pleasant rhythms of her movements.

But all he could think of was the terrible efficiency with which Remint disposed of his enemies. It was foolish to worry that he might meet the slayer in the fabularium; no one could be that stupid, or arrogant. But this was the beginning of a trail that might lead to Remint, and Ruiz was growing more and more afraid of the slayer. He felt his heartbeat pick up, he felt sweat break on his forehead, though the ramp was cooled by powerful ventilators, and he cursed himself for this weakness, which might lead not only to his own destruction, but to Nisa's as well—if she still lived.

As he approached the top of the ramp, he managed to suppress the worst of his panic, though he could still feel it at the edges of his mind. He shook his head and tried to unobtrusively shrug some of the tension from his shoulders.

The gate was a tall structure of simulated stone, set against the metal wall of the fabularium. The deeply carved arch displayed elements of a hundred mythic traditions—most of the human persons who might pass beneath it would find some familiar imagery in the carvings. Old Earth gods sported with Jaworld dybbuks and Androsian chickcharneys. Avatars of the Serpent Mystery coiled about icons of the Chlorophyllic Eye. Nilotic succubi clung lasciviously to Dead God saints. The effect was of riotous chaos.

In the center of the arch was an inscription in some archaic Old Earth script Ruiz could not read.

To the side stood a tall Moc bondwarrior in a jewel-encrusted cape—the gatekeeper. A strategically placed spotlight struck an eye-hurting glitter from the cape, but Ruiz noticed that the cape was designed not to hamper the creature's movements. With a carefully proclamatory gesture, it raised a vocalizer and then activated what was obviously a canned speech. "You may keep your weapons," the vocalizer sang in a sweet androgynous voice. "But remember! Within, you are subject to the law of the Celadon Wind. Attempt to maim . . . and you will be maimed. Attempt to kill . . . and you will be killed. We possess the latest semi-sentient security devices, so do not think to circumvent our vigilance."

"I won't," said Ruiz in a wistfully hopeful tone, and passed into the Celadon Wind.

CHAPTER 21

COREAN arrived at the adjacent joypalace just before Ruiz walked up the ramp into the fabularium. The joypalace was a run-down operation, its lobby dirty, threadbare, and at that moment devoid of customers. A person of indeterminate species sat behind a cloudy armorglass security enclosure, reading an ancient printed book. It ignored Corean and her guide as they walked toward the elevators.

Her guide tapped at a scuffed steel door in a long, dimly lit hall, and it opened a crack. An armored man scanned her briefly before admitting her.

Immediately she felt Remint's increased intensity. He was bent over a spyscreen in the darkest corner of the tawdry suite. He ignored her entrance for a moment, then he lifted his passionless gaze. He made no gesture of greeting.

A pair of joyboys huddled together on the greasy plastic-covered bed, their painted eyes huge with terror, arms wrapped tightly around each other. They looked at Corean with an abject hope, as if they thought she might either release them or use them in their accustomed manner. She wondered why Remint hadn't simply killed them and stuffed the bodies in a closet. Perhaps he anticipated a long wait and didn't want to stink the place up. It occurred to her that the joyboys probably thought they were playing some actual part in these events, that their presence here was in some way significant. Something about the thought made her briefly uneasy, for reasons she didn't care to examine.

"He's here," Remint said in his uninflected voice.

She hurried across the room, and tried to shoulder him away from the screen. It was like pushing at a stony mountainside. Then he moved back and she could see Ruiz Aw, walking up a steel ramp behind a beautiful naked woman. His dark face revealed nothing but a calm alertness; she tried and failed to imagine what he was thinking.

"What are you waiting for?" she asked.

"I can't touch him there, or in the Wind. The Wind caters to the most dangerous beings in SeaStack—they're ready for anything. Had Ruiz Aw been smart enough to hide his people in the Wind, I could never have taken them from him . . . though they might have been driven mad by the mythagogues, had he left them there too long."

"So how do you propose to get him out?"

"I believe I know where he will look for me."

"And where is that?" Corean asked sharply. She was feeling a growing impatience with Remint's uninformative pronouncements.

Remint didn't answer for a moment. "In my old dreams. There I have concealed my hook."

THE CELADON WIND was an impressive establishment, compared to other fabularia Ruiz had visited. The entrance hall formed a long narrow amphitheater. Customers strolled along the white-tiled floor, while pale translucent holoimages of thousands of gods and demons watched silently from the tiered seats that rose up to the ceiling far above. At the far end was a white colonnade through which the customers passed into the area of the fabularium they had chosen. The light was dim and red, and the air was doubtless thick with pheromonic influencers; Ruiz felt his mood become darker and more volatile.

As he approached the colonnade, he shook himself, as if to shrug away all those dangerous virtues he had lately rediscovered: mercy, empathy, loyalty . . . love. Remint would know none of these, and now he must become as much like Remint as possible, if he hoped to follow the slayer's path into the fabularium.

Ruiz made his mind cold, his heart small; he tried to turn back time and become again the deadly thing he once had been.

He succeeded, after a fashion.

The colonnade's seven arches were each topped by an animated holoimage that related to the sort of myths to be found within that section of the fabularium.

Ruiz stopped and looked up at the images.

After a bit he found his attention most strongly attracted to the arch that displayed a Kali-like goddess, whose four hands held a knife, a garrote, a graser, and a pulse gun. The arms waved sinuously, tracing a pattern that soon seemed deliciously seductive, and on the goddess's black face was a smile that wavered between sweetness and ferocity. Her features were strong, almost crude, and her eyes bulged with a barely contained mania. Her six dark breasts were exposed and exquisitely shaped. They floated entrancingly with her movements, as though they were made of some lighter-than-air substance, much finer than mere flesh.

He stepped through the arch, and a guidemech emerged from a niche to his right. It offered him a tray of assorted intoxicants, hallucinogens, and mood alterants. When he declined these, it said, "Follow please," and rolled off down the corridor at an easy pace.

"HE SCENTS THE bait," said Remint. "He chooses as I would have chosen."

Corean watched Ruiz Aw, who now moved along briskly behind the guidemech. His face was still unrevealing, but there was now a trace of some additional expression that disturbed Corean by its mysterious familiarity. He seemed even more elementally dangerous than when she had last seen him.

What was the difference? She glanced up at Remint's face, lit by the greenish light of the spyscreen, and saw that Remint wore precisely the same look.

THE GUIDEMECH CONDUCTED Ruiz to a large rotunda, where the lights were even dimmer than in the entrance hall.

In the center of the rotunda was an artificial pool, where luminescent night eels swam beneath cerise water lilies, leaving glowing trails in the black water. The pool exhaled a scent of decay and feverish life. Far above, Ruiz sensed the presence of automated weapons emplacements, tracking the languid movements of the patrons.

"This is the Hall of Pain and Renewal," said the guidemech, and rolled away.

Around the perimeter were a hundred or more trapezoidal openings, each of which housed a mythagogue. Some of the openings were curtained, indicating that the mythagogue was already occupied with a customer or otherwise unavailable. But most of the beings who staffed this section of the Celadon Wind sat at their doorsteps, awaiting a client. A few other potential customers wandered the perimeter, including the tall woman he had followed into the Celadon Wind.

The first mythagogue to his left was an old scar-cheeked man who bore the shoulder tattoos of a Retrantic enforcer and affected a shock of thin white braids. He glanced at Ruiz with an inquisitive expression. Ruiz looked back, waiting for the tug of recognition that he expected to feel from Remint's personal myth-maker. He felt nothing beyond a mild revulsion.

Ruiz began to stroll the perimeter, examining each mythagogue as he passed, still wrapped in the chill purposefulness he had assumed in the fabularium's entrance hall. Some of them met his gaze with a brightly predatory look, some looked away, unease darkening their fey eyes. He passed a spiky-haired woman of the Buffalo Wailers, a blue-scaled Dalmetrian renegade, and a marine-adapted boy with ancient eyes, floating in a giant brandy snifter of murky green fluid—then dozens of others as strange. None of them spoke to him; apparently the management considered the Celadon Wind to be an upscale place and proscribed any undignified hawking of wares.

Still, he sensed a ripple of interest following him around the rotunda, an interest that seemed to be communicated ahead of his slow ambling progress. More curtains popped open in a sudden flurry, and mythagogues craned their necks to get a glimpse of him.

This unexpected attention stimulated him to a higher

level of alertness, and he felt more keenly purposeful, more his former self.

He strolled on. Most of the myth-makers seemed to take great pride in their eclectic eccentricity, as though the quality of their fables had anything to do with the originality of their fashion sense. Decadence was in vogue, Ruiz thought —tiresomely so. Some of the mythagogues winked at him, leered expressively, made silent gestures of welcome. None of them seemed to possess the sort of style that would attract the patronage of a man like Remint.

Ruiz began a second circuit of the rotunda.

REMINT SWITCHED THE spyscreen to a different remote. Corean saw a small man with a face prosthesis of hammered silver, who looked up with unfocused eyes and said nothing.

"He is here," said Remint.

"How will I know him?" asked the man through his metal lips.

"How do you know me?"

The man sighed and nodded. He bent his head for a moment, so that Corean could not see him. When he raised his head, he was wearing a crude skinmask in the likeness of Remint y'Yubere.

Remint switched off the spyscreen. "Now we wait."

RUIZ WAS A quarter of the way 'round the rotunda when a curtain drew back two doors ahead—one that had been closed on his previous circuit.

When he reached the opening and saw the mythagogue, sitting on a tall wooden stool, he felt an unpleasant shock of recognition, and skipped back a step. Above, the automated weapons shifted and whirred, alerted by his too-rapid movement.

Then he saw that it was not his enemy—it was only a small, poorly maintained cyborg, wearing a skinmask. The cyborg took no notice of him; he stared out at the pond, motionless.

Ruiz felt the attention of the other mythagogues and patrons intensify, and he felt a bit unnerved. He stepped closer and peered at the mythagogue, who continued to ignore his presence. What was the proper formula for invoking the mythagogue's services? At first Ruiz could not remember; he had never quite understood the fascination of the synthesized myths available in the fabularia of Dilvermoon, and thus had rarely patronized them.

Then he remembered. "To whom do you speak, teller?"

The mythagogue's face shifted toward him slightly. Ruiz realized that the cyborg was blind, an eccentric affectation indeed, when no pangalac need be sightless, except by choice.

The mythagogue spoke with casual unforced eloquence. "I speak to the wielders of the blade, to the soldiers of the night, to the keepers of propriety, to the righteous scourgers of the flesh. To those who hold murder safe in their hearts."

Ruiz hesitated. His deepest suspicions were aroused. How could he meet a man who masked himself as Remint y'Yubere, without wondering if a trap had been set especially for him? On the other hand, could his enemies be so stupid as to assume that he would enter the mythagogue's den trustingly? That was hard to believe; he had never been a man who attracted stupid enemies, unfortunately.

Furthermore, how could his enemies have known he would appear in exactly this place, so that such a complicated trap could be laid? For all that he thought he understood Remint, he could not bring himself to believe that his motivations could possibly be so transparent to the slayer. *Why not?* asked a small rebellious voice, but he suppressed it and stepped forward with a credit wafer in his hand.

"I'm such a one," he said.

The skinmask was not animated, so there could be no expression for Ruiz to read, but he had the eerie sensation that the mythagogue smiled beneath the dead plastic. "I know," said the man in a soft voice, and held out his hand for the wafer.

He stepped down from his stool and went inside, limping a bit, the servomotors in his legs whining. He paused with his hand on the curtain, and when Ruiz was over the threshold, the mythagogue let it fall shut.

The myth-maker gestured to a straight-backed wooden chair and settled himself on a padded bench. The little chamber was very dark, the walls hung with tapestries so faded and gray that Ruiz couldn't tell what they depicted, though gold thread occasionally threw back a subdued glitter from the light of the single yellow lamp that burned on a small table set to the side.

A narrow door led to the mythagogue's living quarters, and Ruiz stepped to it in one swift stride. He listened at the door for a moment, heard nothing, felt nothing.

"He's not there," said the mythagogue.

"Who?" asked Ruiz, the hair lifting on the back of his neck.

The mythagogue laughed, a dry scratchy sound. "Who else? Remint y'Yubere, whose blood you seek."

Ruiz pressed back against the wall, fighting panic and a curious prideful anger. "How could you know this?"

The mythagogue laughed again, this time more wildly. "It boils off you, your need for him, like a great violent stink —as anyone could tell. Your shadow is full of his shape, as only I can sense. Besides, he told me you would come here, and here you are, unmistakable."

Ruiz drew a pin knife from his boot. "What else did he tell you?"

The mythagogue shook his masked head; once, twice—so violently that the skinmask hung askew, revealing the crudely shaped metal beneath. "He ordered me to hold you here, enthralled by his vast collection of fables, until he could arrange to take you. What else? And I could have done it—have no doubt there! I'd have told you about the Thorn Goddess of Niam and how She found Her heart— rotten though it is. Or why bright flowers spring up in the footsteps of the Cronwerk Demons, and why these cursed blossoms bring madness and death—and why that is good. Or how Thubastable the Loquacious earned His awful name. All of Remint y'Yubere's favorites." The blind head came up. "And you'd have listened, if not because of my grand and glorious Voice, then because you hoped to get a clue to his whereabouts, some bit of information that the lords had failed to extract from me."

A chill moved up Ruiz's spine. He had the feeling that he was out of his depth, treading water in a murky sea of deception—in which swam an irresistible predator. A sensation of helplessness stole over him, and he felt weak and alone, as though all he could do was kick and flail and wait for the crushing grip of terrible jaws.

No. "And what did the lords learn from you?" asked Ruiz.

The mythagogue shrugged. "Nothing of importance. Listen! Go to the curtain and look out, carefully. Do you see her, a woman with steel feet?"

Ruiz remembered the tall naked woman. He stepped across the room and looked out through a tiny rip in the fabric.

She was on the far side of the rotunda, standing still, looking directly toward him across the pool.

"You see her? She's a puppet of the lords. She wears steel on her feet, and smells of sex, blood, and some sweet powder —though I cannot describe her elsewise. What does she look like? Is she beautiful? I think she must be. . . . She was with them when they interrogated me, and I felt her pleasure in it."

Ruiz drew back and went again to the door to the living quarters. He started to ease the door open.

"No!" said the mythagogue urgently. "He has a spy bead within, and one out in the rotunda. He would also have one in here, except the the Wind places a high premium on client confidentiality, and has installed very good antisurveillance tech in here."

"Why do you tell me these things?" asked Ruiz.

"Because I hate him with all the bitter emptiness of my heart," the mythagogue said passionately in a rolling dramatic voice. "He it is who has blighted my life, miserable as it was before he found me. He it is who gave me the neurophage that has forever taken my optic nerve, that still keeps watch, coiled up in my skull, that will never let me see again—for no better reason than his foolish fancy. My blindness gives my tales more 'mystic weight,' he says. As if those great blind mythagogues who served the ancients wouldn't have gone out and bought new eyes in a minute, if they could have." He spit, narrowly missing Ruiz's foot.

"Don't you fear him, as well?" Ruiz was almost whispering.

The mythagogue slumped slightly, as if much of his emotion had suddenly leaked out. "Of course, of course. That's why I didn't help the lords, though at the time I didn't know where he was. But then he came to me, speaking of you and how he would take you. I can't say how I discovered that he was dead, but I knew it, and I wasn't quite as afraid. Not quite. . . ."

"Dead?"

"Dead! He's a machine now, someone's insensate tool. The Gencha have had their way with him, and he is no more. Perhaps you can destroy him, now that he's dead. Can you?" The cyborg jerked his head toward Ruiz, and though his eyes were still unfocused, they burned.

"I must try," said Ruiz.

Somehow the news that Remint had been deconstructed by the Gencha came as no great surprise to Ruiz. The events and circumstances of his visit to Sook seemed to be taking on some great incomprehensible symmetry; he felt like a player in some feverish drama, a performance full of obscure symbolism and contrived irony. "Where is he?"

The mythagogue fell silent for a long minute, until Ruiz began to consider how he might force the information from the man without attracting the attention of the Celadon Wind's security devices. But finally the man spoke in a thin frail voice, completely unlike the declamatory tone he had used before. "If I tell you, and you fail to destroy him, he will punish me in ways I cannot bear to think of."

"I won't fail," said Ruiz in as positive a voice as he could manage.

The man nodded. "Perhaps. You're much like Remint, as he was before they killed him." He seemed to come to a decision; his back straightened and he spoke in a stronger voice. "He told me to call him at the SweetShimmer joypalace, which is just two levels below the Celadon Wind, in this very stack. I can't guarantee that he's there, of course, but . . . look for him in Suite B-448."

"Thank you," said Ruiz Aw, and slipped away.

"A FINE PERFORMANCE," said Remint to the cyborg, who had raised his head inquiringly. Then Remint switched to the outside spy bead, and followed Ruiz on his rapid retreat from the Hall of Pain and Renewal.

Corean shook her head in wonderment. "Doesn't the mythagogue's hatred concern you? The emotion was unmistakably genuine. Is it safe to leave such a virulent creature alive?"

Remint looked at her without expression and did not speak.

CHAPTER 22

As far as Ruiz could tell, the woman did not follow him, though he thought he sensed her interest as he left the rotunda.

He moved as quickly as he could without attracting unwelcome attention. As he trotted along, he gave thought to the spy bead the mythagogue had mentioned. Surely it was still locked on him; how could he rid himself of it before he entered the joypalace?

He left the Celadon Wind by a back way provided for those who wished to keep their entertainments private. As soon as he had emerged from the exit, he turned and reentered the fabularium.

As he had hoped, the parallel ingress was equipped with surveillance stripping gear, available to patrons for a price, and he waited in the security lock while the lock's devices combed three spy beads from the air. A mech arm gathered up the deactivated devices and handed them to him, sealed in a plastic bag.

He examined them with some surprise. Three? He wondered who else was monitoring his movements. Publius owned one of the beads, almost certainly. Perhaps Diamond

Bob was the other watcher. He shrugged, tossed the beads down a disposal slot, and left the fabularium again.

Two levels up from the Celadon Wind, he found a market in a low-ceilinged hall. The floor was crammed with tents and booths and kiosks, selling food, fashion, weapons, and various of the cruder forms of entertainment: drugs, wiregames, flashdeath, personality implants.

Ruiz wandered about until he noticed a booth that purveyed information. There he bought a current map of the stack.

Across the hall Ruiz found a cafe. A dozen small tables were scattered about under a canopy of Old Earth plants, gene-tailored to survive under the bluish artificial light. He sat down close to the solid metal at the hall's perimeter, where he could watch the few other patrons without worrying overmuch that someone might sneak up behind him.

The waiter was a brainchopped woman of great apparent age, who showed him a menu and accepted his order silently, then shuffled back to the little black tent that held the cafe's machinery. She returned with his meal almost instantly; it consisted of a platter of gray textured protein and vatted fungi in various fluorescent hues, sliced into bite-size pieces and covered with a thick bluish sauce. It tasted marginally better than it looked, and he ate it while he examined his map.

The map, installed in a disposable dataslate, allowed him to scroll crudely through the stack, level by level. The major features were represented by wireframe diagrams and touch-dot labels. When he located the Sweetshimmer, three levels below the Celadon Wind, he was immediately struck by its suitability for an ambush. There were only two entries into the joypalace, according to the map, and one watcher could cover both of them. The corridor that led to Suite B-448 served only a half-dozen other suites, and was accessible from a single elevator bank.

He finished his meal and looked out at the people passing through the market. He watched for a few minutes; none of the shoppers resembled the woman with the steel slippers.

He slipped out of the cafe and found a shop specializing in full bodymasks. The shop was housed in an inflatable structure covered with anodized alloy scales, so that it looked like a giant lavender artichoke. The clerk, another elderly brainchopped woman, served him without detectable

interest, and a few minutes later Ruiz left the shop disguised
as a fat merchant. He wore a poisonous-green puffsuit, gold-
mirrored ankle boots, and a stylish pink visor. He'd also
purchased a somatic inductance overlay, which lay against
the nape of his neck and changed his gait into a mincing
waddle, made his arms flip about in a disarmingly frivolous
manner, and raised his voice an octave.

He was confident no one would recognize him, though he
feared that if he ran into one of the muggergangs which
infested the city, he would be attacked. The bodymask restricted his movements and prevented access to most of his
weapons, and the face-covering restricted his vision. Worse,
he had been forced to leave his armor behind, in a public
locker that would surely be broken open and emptied as
soon as he was out of sight. He felt naked and vulnerable,
protected only by a layer of spongy synthetic flesh.

But he could think of no better plan, so he went to the
public lifts and dropped down to the level of the Sweetshimmer.

AT THE MOMENT Remint lay back on the couch, eyes
closed. Corean was reminded of a mech recharging its bat-
teries—the slayer's face seemed even less human in repose,
the grotesquely muscled features even more like some murderous alien mask. She wondered how he could sleep with
Ruiz Aw so close to his trap. Probably, she thought, he
wasn't asleep, but only resting, husbanding his energies in a
wholly logical manner. She wondered what would happen if
she were to go to his couch and touch him. Would she survive the experiment?

She returned her attention to the spyscreen, which now
displayed a view of the corridor outside the suite. In the last
few moments the traffic in the corridor had picked up. A fat
man in a ridiculous green puffsuit simpered and clung to the
arm of a rather homely albino joyboy in a leather whipping
jumper. A few paces behind the fat man, a tall cadaverous
man in the dull black shipsuit of a Dead God acolyte
trudged along, face solemn; he was trailed by a brightly
dressed covey of preadolescent girls, all of whom wore identical looks of unchildlike resignation.

The lights in the corridor went out.

Corean sat in bemusement for an instant, before she realized that something was wrong. She opened her mouth to shout for Remint, when the red emergency lights strobed on, then off. In that blink of time, she saw the fat man moving with astonishing speed up the corridor, a look of wooden calm on his doughy face. The albino sprawled on his back, legs kicking, and the tall acolyte was soaring over the fallen joyboy in a tigerish bound.

She turned and shrieked a warning at Remint, who was already rising from his couch, when the suite's door shattered and the fat man burst through, a splinter gun in his hand.

In that transparent slice of time, she saw that Remint—for all his inhuman speed—would be too slow, that the fat man would kill or disable Remint before the slayer could reach his weapons or get his feet sufficiently under him to take evasive action.

But then a slender hand reached through the shattered door and sank a stun needle into the fat man's neck. The fat man spasmed and flung his arms wide . . . then toppled over, helpless.

RUIZ REGAINED CONSCIOUSNESS as two of Remint's hired slayers were cutting him out of the bodymask. He couldn't completely stifle a groan as his injured nervous system reacted to the rough handling.

Corean's face floated above him, transfigured with vengeful joy. "Oh, how I've waited for this moment," she said, in tones vibrant with pleasure.

He knew better than to attempt speech until he had further recovered from the stun; his muscles were still useless. He looked around, and saw the tall naked woman with the steel slippers removing the last piece of her acolyte bodymask. She favored him with a nod and a cool smile. "Not a bad try," she said. Apparently she was not in the employ of the pirates, as the mythagogue had told him. Other things were also apparent: principally, that Ruiz Aw was an idiot who richly deserved his fate. He sighed.

Remint y'Yubere sat on the couch, hands folded, looking remarkably placid. Ruiz could observe none of the intensity he had expected to see in the slayer's face. The man seemed unaffected by the recent violent events. *Genched,* Ruiz thought, and shuddered. He would be just as placid in a little while.

"That's right," burbled Corean, as if she had added mind-reading to her skills. "You're all mine now." She reached out and touched the madcollar Ruiz wore. "Whose is this? No matter." She clamped a decoupler module to the collar's control linkage, and adjusted the damping field until it resonated with the linkage. The collar clicked open and dropped away. "There," she said brightly. "Remint!"

The slayer looked up incuriously.

"Take us back to your brother's stronghold," she ordered.

Remint nodded. "As you say." He rose from the couch and glanced around the suite. The joyboys, who were still huddled on the bed, both shrieked thinly when his gaze rested on them; he killed them with two brief touches of his pinbeam.

A look of uncertainty flickered across the face of the tall woman; immediately she suppressed it. The other two slayers laughed and brought out a control harness, which they began strapping to Ruiz. It was a device somewhat like the corpse-walker Publius had used; when it was activated Ruiz would be unable to make any movement except those specifically directed by the controller of the harness.

When they had finished fastening the control harness to Ruiz, they rolled him over and sat him up.

"Give me the controller," said Remint.

"Sure," said one slayer, and passed it over. Remint touched the controller's finger pad, and Ruiz's leg and arm muscles locked tight. The intensity of the pain astonished him; his abused nervous system was protesting vigorously. He clamped his jaws shut. For some reason he didn't want to admit how much it hurt.

Remint took one last slow look around the suite, and then he cut down the rest of his people. The two male slayers fell before they could react; the tall woman, who was very quick, had time only to jerk aside slightly as Remint's pinbeam cooked through her breastbone.

Ruiz took a sort of hopeless satisfaction in the terror that filled Corean's face as she waited to find out if she were scheduled to die too. But Remint turned toward the door and said, "Come. Alonzo is waiting for us."

Some sort of terminal bravado caused Ruiz to speak then. "Alonzo Yubere is dead," he croaked.

If Ruiz had thought Remint a terrifying creature before, that pale perception faded to insignificance, seared away by the white-hot intensity that filled Remint's face now. "What?" asked the slayer breathlessly.

Ruiz drew a deep breath. "Yubere is dead."

"Who killed him?" asked Remint, stepping closer and pushing his terrible face into Ruiz's, as if he wished to peer through Ruiz's eyes into the hidden darkness at the back of Ruiz's brain.

Had he not been paralyzed, Ruiz would have flinched away. "I did," he answered.

"Ah, ah. . . ." The slayer rocked back and forth, shaking his massive head, very carefully, as though it might otherwise burst from the pressure of his thoughts. "You killed him? Why?"

"I was paid to do so."

"Ah? By whom?" Remint's lips writhed back and exposed his teeth in a hideous grimace that seemed to carry no identifiable emotional content.

Ruiz could hardly find the breath to reply, but he forced out the words. "Publius the monster-maker commissioned Yubere's death; it was the price of his help, which I needed." At least Publius would not escape unscathed; his machinations had led Ruiz to this sorry ending, and Ruiz found an unambiguous pleasure in the thought of Publius's eventual meeting with Remint.

Remint stepped back, and calm rationality fell over the slayer's features. "Ah. Publius. We know that one, an ancient enemy and colleague." He looked away, and was silent for a moment. Then he asked, in gentle tones, "You would not lie to me, Ruiz Aw?"

"No."

"No, I think not. What would be the point, now?" Remint paused, then spoke in the same soft voice. "You are too much like me, just a tool, sharp steel for the use of weaker hands."

"May I ask you a question?" Ruiz found that he was still driven by his own purpose, even in this hopeless moment.

Remint nodded gravely. "Ask."

"What have you done with my people . . . the Pharaohan slaves?"

"I delivered them to my brother's stronghold. Beyond that I know nothing." Remint turned to Corean, handed her the controller. "You must now proceed as you think best."

Corean recovered her power of speech. "Wait! We still need to get Ruiz Aw back to the stronghold."

Remint shook his head. "My directives in the event of my brother's death take precedence over all other instructions; I must go now to punish his murderer." The slayer started toward the door.

Corean made a serious mistake, then. She stepped in front of the slayer, and, in an attempt to detain him, put a hand on his chest. "Now wait," she said, just before he snapped out his armored forearm and knocked her across the room. She hit the wall with the back of her head, and the controller went flying. She slid down the wall into a boneless heap, unconscious or dead.

Remint was gone, and Ruiz was alone in the suite full of corpses, unable to move a muscle below his neck.

TIME PASSED, AND the agony in his limbs eased somewhat, as his peripheral nerves adapted to the harness. He watched Corean, and wondered if she was alive and if so, how long it would take for her to awaken. The management of the joypalace seemed in no hurry to investigate the trouble in Suite B-448; hours might pass before they sent up a security team.

After a long while, he heard a faint scrabbling sound from an unexpected direction, and he snapped his head around.

To his astonishment, he saw the tall woman attempting to drag herself along the wall. Her face was white, and the wound in her chest made an ugly sucking sound. Apparently Remint's beam had not quite ruptured her heart. It had apparently severed her spinal cord; her legs trailed uselessly. She was making slow progress, pulling with clawed hands at the dirty carpet, her bulging eyes fixed on the harness controller that still lay a good two meters away.

Ruiz couldn't bring himself to hope that she would succeed. His mind seemed to have taken a turn toward cold introspection, and he was unable to take much interest in the woman's efforts.

In a few minutes he fell into a philosophical mood, and

began to examine the woman's continued survival in those terms. At one time, both Remint and Ruiz Aw had espoused a philosophy of Perfect Violence. If he could act with Perfect Violence—he had once thought—then no one could obstruct or withstand him. But here was concrete evidence of the flaw in that philosophy. Not even violence was perfectable . . . not even Remint, as perfect a slayer as Ruiz had ever met, was perfect in his violence. The woman still lived, still hitched her painful way toward the controller!

He began to hope again, faintly—a hope that glimmered away each time the woman paused to gather her waning strength. The pauses grew longer as she approached the controller.

When her outstretched hand was only a few centimeters from the controller, she collapsed and twitched with what Ruiz took to be terminal spasms. He ground his teeth and his eyes filled with hot tears. He thought of Nisa, but only for an instant; his mind was too full of despair to hold anything so sweet.

But the woman's head came slowly up again, and she made one last lunge.

Her trembling finger touched the controller, the harness released Ruiz, and he collapsed backward. The sudden freedom shocked him, so that he lay there for a long moment, mind blank, unable to act.

Then he jumped up and tore at the harness straps, ripping them away joyfully. When he was completely free, he seized the closest weapon, a splinter gun that had belonged to one of the dead slayers—and only then turned to the woman who had released him.

She lay motionless, and only her eyes, which followed him as he crossed the room toward her, showed life.

He knelt beside her, examined her wounds. Her exertions had evidently worsened the damage; bright arterial blood pulsed from the exit burn under her shoulder blade. Her face was bluish; she tried to speak and failed.

"Yes," he said, wanting to comfort her. "I'm going now. I'll put him to death, if I can."

Her eyes showed doubt, but it was a strangely unreproachful doubt. She almost smiled.

Her breathing ceased and her eyes stopped seeing.

He gathered up the rest of his weapons and the madcollar, then ran from the suite, lurching on uncertain legs.

It was only after he had left the joypalace and was on his way up to the lagoon that he realized he had failed to make sure of Corean. He paused, tempted to go back, but if she had recovered and called her people, the suite would still be a perfect trap.

He went on. His head buzzed with bitter thoughts about the imperfect quality of his own violence, and he cursed himself for a fool.

RUIZ WAS STILL busy criticizing his performance as he strode up the ramp toward the quay. A faint unpleasant sound penetrated his thoughts; he stopped abruptly and forced his attention back to the business at hand.

He listened. After a while it came to him; someone was screaming, far across the still waters of the lagoon. The sound was as regular as breathing, as if the screamer paused only long enough to fill his lungs for the next scream.

In all likelihood, the screamer had nothing to do with Ruiz Aw. SeaStack was full of torment. Even so, he thought, he had been gone a long time, several hours, and who knew what mischief Publius might have accomplished in that time?

He touched the madcollar, which he had tucked into his belt. If Publius had arranged a surprise for him, it might involve the collar, which Publius obviously found a demeaning constraint, a severe assault on his dignity. Had Publius given up hope of regaining control of his puppet Yubere? Possibly. . . . Or Publius might consider the situation too volatile, now that Remint was involved. Or he might know of some time limit to his scheme, now passed.

Did Ruiz still need Publius? The stronghold might have fallen into a state of disorganization with Yubere's inaction, which might make it possible for him to sneak in through the same route as before. The possibility of doing without Publius had an undeniable appeal. Ruiz shook his head regretfully . . . he still needed Publius.

Another possibility suddenly occurred to Ruiz. Perhaps the screamer was Publius, perhaps Remint had already found him.

No. No, he was somehow certain that Publius was safely gone, that he had decided to cut his losses and retire from the field.

He took the collar and hefted it, then threw it high into the air, so that at the top of its arc, it cleared the lip of the ramp.

It detonated with a bright flash and a report that made his ears ring. A second later, the sound of another explosion reached him.

He noticed that the screaming had stopped.

LONG BEFORE HE reached the sub, Ruiz knew what Publius had done. Albany's head was a pale splotch against the black metal of the conning tower; his blood made a darker pattern where it had spattered and run down.

When Ruiz drew alongside, he saw Albany's body, floating in the currentless water of the lagoon, the bound limbs still twitching rhythmically in the grip of the nerveburner Publius had attached to him.

Ruiz went aboard. Publius had suspended Albany by his ponytail, which was secured to the conning tower rail with a metal clamp. Then he'd left him to scream out his life, until Ruiz had returned and detonated the collar around Albany's neck.

Albany's eyes were full of blood.

Ruiz went slowly up the ladder. He took out his knife and cut through Albany's ponytail, so that the head fell, bounced once on the deck, and splashed into the lagoon.

Then he went below and set a course for Publius's maze. He still had a use for Publius.

COREAN RETURNED TO consciousness as her Moc carried her from the joypalace. She breathed in the welcome stink of its body, for the moment empty of all emotion but the pleasure of being alive. Her ribs ached; perhaps Remint had broken a couple. No matter; she would heal.

From the corner of her eye, she saw Marmo, floating along silently, holding a graser.

"Marmo . . ." she whispered in a voice that offended her by its weakness.

"Corean?" The old pirate swiveled toward her. "It's almost daylight. I began to worry about you, so we followed."

She smiled fondly at his battered half-mech face. "A good thing you did. Where is Ruiz Aw?"

Marmo didn't answer for a moment. "Your enemy was missing, Corean. There was a disengaged control harness lying on the floor of the suite; it appeared to me that one of Remint's slayers punched it off, just before she died."

The pleasure of survival was suddenly tarnished. "Again?" She could not believe it.

"Never mind. It's time to go to ground, Corean, until this blows over. SeaStack is shrieking; the lords are in a great panic. It is most unsafe. Fensh is waiting above with the airboat, to take us to a secure hiding place until we can leave the city."

She tried to summon enough rage to resist his sensible urging, but between Remint's machinelike ruthlessness and Ruiz Aw's incomprehensible determination, she had somehow been frightened into passivity. She hoped it was a temporary frailty.

"Yes," she agreed, and lay back in the Moc's hard arms.

CHAPTER 23

From the shadow of an adjoining stack, Ruiz analyzed the remaining safeguards at the entrance to Publius's mooring, taking an ironic satisfaction in using the antisurveillance gear he and Albany had brought back from Yubere's stronghold.

He had left the sub some distance away; he must now approach Publius with as much guile as he could summon. From one of the stack-side farmers he had purchased—for an absurd price—a small sampan loaded with crates of vegetables. He wore a stained brown jerkin, tattered shorts, and a large straw hat, all from the same source. He made his movements slow and deliberate, and concealed the readout slate of his sensors beneath a heap of pungent thick-leaved cabbages.

While he considered the indications, he consumed the farmer's lunch, which consisted of a piece of blue-veined cheese, a sweet onion, half a loaf of bread, and a plastic bowl of green-gold spiceplums. It was, Ruiz decided, the best meal he'd had in weeks. He had found an insulated flask of cold water in the bilge, and he took a long swallow, looking up at the green forested ledges of the stack above him. The tide drifted his boat out into the midmorning sunlight for a moment, and the heat soaked into his sore shoulders comfortingly, until he shortened up his lines and returned to the shade. It occurred to him that it was a fine thing to be alive.

The novelty of this notion struck him forcibly—when had he last thought such a thing? On the barge? Perhaps. That joyfully uncertain journey now seemed impossibly distant in time. . . .

He shrugged and gave his attention to the readout slate. Perhaps he was missing something, but he just couldn't find any unambiguous evidence that Publius's security systems still functioned. Either his own gear was faulty—or Remint had gotten here first.

Eventually he finished his lunch and cast off his lines. He lifted the sampan's sculling oar into its fork and propelled the boat across the channel toward the entrance of Publius's mooring lagoon.

Inside, he saw that Remint, or some other hostile force, had indeed been there. The air was still thick with the stink of discharged energy weapons and vaporized metal. Publius's big gunboat was awash in the center of the lagoon, and another gunboat was canted onto the quay near the entrance to the maze.

The place was utterly silent, except for a faint sound of frying electronics, which emanated from the sinking gunboat. Ruiz coasted along, watching his readouts for any sign that he was not alone, but everything indicated that he was. The sampan bumped the quay gently; at the same moment his slate indicated that one close-range detector field remained active at the gate. As far as Ruiz could tell, the field was only able to register the passage through the gate of metal, plastics, or other synthetic materials.

Ruiz sighed. He'd expected worse. He divested himself of all his weapons, which he hid under the vegetables. Perhaps the recent fighting had frightened away any scavengers unambitious enough to be interested in a boat full of turnips and cabbages. He cut the decorative alloy buckles off his canvas shoes. He looked at the buttons that kept his shorts closed; they seemed to be carved from thick fish scales. He picked up the farmer's cudgel, an arm-long piece of dense black wood, capped with a crudely carved margar head. The grip was smooth with use and fit his hand well.

He stepped to the sampan's bow and hitched its line to a mooring ring, then stepped down to the quay.

"You're an idiot, Ruiz Aw," he said to himself. "You're going after the hardest man in the human universe. With a stick." He laughed ruefully.

A smell of recent death came from the mouth of the maze, and Ruiz Aw suddenly wanted very badly not to enter that darkness.

BUT HE WENT in anyway, and found that the maze was now populated only by corpses. He found another one around every corner of the dim passageways—sometimes one of Publius's failed monsters in a pathetic heap of fur and scales, more often one of the monster-maker's Dirm bondguards. The killing, it seemed to Ruiz, had been done with the offhand efficiency that characterized Remint's approach to his trade. Each burn seemed perfectly placed, each dismembering slash seemed perfectly aimed to destroy some vital function. Ruiz examined each Dirm guard for usable weapons, but in each case Remint, in his thorough fashion, had taken the time to put a pinbeam through each weapon's mechanism.

Ruiz found it almost inconceivable that Remint had managed to penetrate Publius's stronghold alone, but the evidence was compelling. He didn't want to think about what it must have been like during the night, when Publius had sent his people into the maze.

Ruiz moved more cautiously as he neared the center of the maze, pausing frequently to listen for any sign that any of Publius's defenses remained active. He detected nothing to alarm him, a condition he found intrinsically alarming.

The devastation at the security ingress was even more impressive. Apparently Remint had fought his way through the maze carrying racks of searbombs and ladder-charges. The ingress was split open, its armor ripped up into long splinters around a hole where the elevator had been.

Ruiz crept to the edge of the hole and peered over. The alloy of the shaft bore the indentations of scaling hooks, which evidently Remint had used to climb down to Publius's labs. Ruiz took a deep breath. He had no hooks; his only way down appeared to be a slender maintenance ladder, severely damaged by the blasts that had opened the shaft. In places it hung loose, twisted and broken. In other places it had half-melted and sagged against the wall.

He wanted to give up, to go back out to the sunlight and the crates of turnips, to forget everything that had gone before, to change his name and become another person, someone who wouldn't have to go down to whatever waited at the bottom of the shaft.

But the way to Nisa led down; Publius was still his prime ticket into Yubere's stronghold. He wondered if she still lived, and if she did, what she thought of Ruiz Aw. Did she hate him, as seemed most likely?

He shook his head, thrust the cudgel through his belt, and started down.

RUIZ COULD SCARCELY believe that he had survived the descent when he finally reached the bottom of the shaft. Twice he had slipped and caught himself after a short fall. Once a section of ladder had broken away from its supports and smashed him against the shaft wall, almost shaking him loose. But none of his scrapes seemed serious, though his injured shoulder was throbbing again.

The shaft wall was ripped open at three levels, as if Remint had set his charges to distract Publius's remaining people and divide their attention. From the perfect stillness of Publius's formerly busy laboratories, Ruiz deduced that Remint's ploy had succeeded.

He began to worry that Remint had already killed Publius, or tormented him into uselessness. "Now you think of this?" he whispered to himself.

Pointless, he thought wryly, *to start relying on logic at this late date.*

So he entered the dead laboratories.

THE SILENCE WAS intimidating. Ruiz moved stealthily through the level, slipping from one place of concealment to the next, pausing frequently to strain his senses for any indication that Publius's security forces were still functioning. He heard nothing.

Here and there he saw the bodies of technicians, who had evidently been armed with makeshift weapons—knives and clubs—and sent against Remint. From one of these he retrieved a knife with a long thin blade, which he bound to his forearm with a rag, so that the hilt lay above his wrist. None of the clubs seemed as suitable as the farmer's cudgel, so he kept it ready in his hand.

A few of these latest victims had lived long enough to drag themselves under lab benches, or behind concealing machinery. Had Remint lost some fraction of his efficiency . . . was he beginning to tire? Might he have taken wounds? This seemed a cheerful conjecture, and Ruiz's spirits rose slightly.

When he heard the ring of steel on steel, he became even more cautious, but he soon discovered that the sound came from the sunken amphitheater that Publius had pointed out on his first visit. The little ursine warriors still slashed at each other with dazzling speed; evidently the events in the laboratory had not distracted them from their inbred ferocity. There were still quite a lot of them; perhaps this was a later generation of the elimination trials.

He looked down at them for a moment, almost envying them their uncomplicated passions.

Ruiz went on a few steps, and then paused by the tanks that held Publius's insurance clones. On an impulse, he slid up the screen that kept the tanks comfortably dark.

The three copies of the monster-maker stirred uneasily, flexing their soft bodies and pawing clumsily at their eyes. Ruiz felt an intensity of hatred that made it difficult for him to draw a breath. That the three clones were in the strictest sense innocent of Publius's crimes seemed an insignificant and abstract fact.

He considered the possibility of taking one of the clones —but the clone would have no knowledge of Publius's current arrangements, nor would it look like Publius. Almost certainly the false Yubere wouldn't recognize the clone's authority.

He bent and touched the control slate, and the nutrient fluid that kept them alive started to drain silently into the sump.

They began to writhe and then to pound at the thick glass that trapped them. The nearest one forced his puffy eyes open and glared at Ruiz, mouthing words that Ruiz could not hear.

He slid down the screen and left them to expire in the dark.

He heard the thud of Remint's boots against the tiled floor just in time to dart behind a nearby lab bench.

From that doubtful concealment, he watched, heart pounding, as Remint appeared from an access corridor, towing a floater on which a man lay, bound with wide straps. Ruiz couldn't identify the man at first, but then the man lifted his hands as high as the straps would permit, and made a theatrical gesture that belonged unmistakably to Publius. So the monster-maker still lived.

Ruiz was pleased to see that Remint appeared seriously battered. The slayer's armor was shattered and bloody over his left thigh, and he walked with a perceptible limp. The armor had separated slightly over his left shoulder, and his left arm hung stiffly, as if the armor had locked at the elbow, though the hand still clutched a splinter gun. He carried a sonic knife in his right hand, and the floater's tow line was hitched to a ring at his armored waist.

Even damaged as he was, Remint still possessed that unstoppable quality. Compared to the Genched slayer, Ruiz felt himself puny, a negligible opponent. What could he possibly do against such a dire creature?

An idea came to Ruiz, just as Remint passed between him and the sunken amphitheater. Ruiz had no time to carefully consider the idea's merits and pitfalls. He had to act instantly, and almost before the idea had fully formed, he sprang from his hiding place and dashed toward the floater.

Remint began to react to his charge when he was still two meters from the head of the floater. The slayer twisted back toward Ruiz, his gun arm rising with only a bit less than his usual uncanny speed. Ruiz ignored the gun and concentrated on hitting the floater with all his power and weight, getting his forearm up to cushion some of the shock of the blow against his shoulder, driving through the floater with his legs even after the blinding pain of the impact.

The floater jolted forward, striking Remint first on his gun arm, throwing off his aim, so that the burst of splinters went wide. Then the floater's chrome chassis smacked into Remint's midsection, driving him back, and his calves caught the low wall around the sunken amphitheater.

Ruiz vaulted onto the floater, swinging the cudgel with all his strength. Remint was toppling backward, but brought the gun down as he fell.

The cudgel caught the back of Remint's hand before he could fire. The gun flew away in a high arc and dropped into the pit.

Ruiz looked into his enemy's face, just for an instant. Remint wore a look of disinterest, his eyes dead and cold and far away.

Ruiz flung himself farther onto the floater, sprawling across Publius, who waved his arms and squeaked. Ruiz squirmed forward.

Remint had finally surrendered to gravity, was falling into the pit. His reaching fingertips had just missed the floater's chassis, or else the blow to his hand had weakened his grip.

When he hit the end of the tether, his great weight overpowered the floater's equilibrium compensators for a moment, and it dipped violently, almost dumping Ruiz off. Ruiz slashed at the tether with his knife, as Remint swung up his good arm and sonic knife.

The tether parted.

Pain seared across Ruiz's bicep, and he looked to see if his arm was still attached to his shoulder.

The floater bucked and leveled. Ruiz flexed his arm in grateful amazement, ignoring the blood that sheeted down.

Ruiz looked down, to see Remint land on his feet among the little warriors. One of them, with a quickness the eye could not follow, turned and drove his long knife through the gap in Remint's left shoulder armor.

Remint flicked his own knife and the small head spun away. The slayer flexed his knees, then sprang upward, gripping the knife handle in his teeth. His good hand caught the rim of the pit.

Ruiz's heart slammed. The man was a monster; nothing human could have made such a leap. He rolled off the floater, his heel aimed at Remint's fingers.

It was almost a fatal mistake. The slayer gave a heave and his hand jumped up off the rim and grabbed for Ruiz's ankle. Only by a great gut-wrenching effort was Ruiz able to divert his kick, so that Remint's fingers only brushed his foot.

"Ah . . ." gasped Ruiz, horrified.

Remint fell back into the pit again, and this time the little warriors were ready for him. Two of them stabbed at the opening in his thigh armor, and the slayer's leg buckled.

Ruiz didn't wait to see what would happen. He scrambled away from the edge, pulling the floater with him, then he began to run toward the exit shaft, shoving the floater as fast as it would go.

"Wait," said Publius in an unfamiliar voice, weak and plaintive. "Who is it?"

Ruiz really looked at the monster-maker for the first time, and saw that Remint had cut away his eyelids, and put some caustic substance in his eyes. He noticed blood puddled under the monster-maker's thighs; perhaps Remint had hamstrung his captive.

"Me," said Ruiz, saving his breath for running.

Astonishingly, a smile spread over Publius's face. "Ruiz Aw? You've defeated Yubere's vengeance? My. God." He coughed and spit up a little blood, prompting Ruiz to wonder what other injuries he had—and if he would live long enough to be useful.

"Maybe," Ruiz said. The dark jagged opening to the shaft was close, and Ruiz slammed the floater inside, scraping the sides. He set the controls to lift and climbed aboard as the floater began to rise up the shaft. He held on tight, his hands clutching the straps that held Publius down, and his heart didn't slow until they were well above the height that Remint had leaped.

"You killed him?" Publius still sounded terribly uncertain.

"Maybe."

"You must have killed him; he'd never have let us get away if he were alive. If he's dead, he can't hurt us. Can he?"

"I'm not so sure," said Ruiz, and found that he was shivering, though the air in the shaft was hot and damp.

"Um," said Publius. "Where are you taking me?"

Ruiz laughed. "Do you really care, as long as it's away from here?" He no longer felt the consuming anger toward the monster-maker that had driven him since he had found Albany. The encounter with Remint had somehow exhausted most of his capacity for emotion, and a dangerous numbness was invading him. He examined the cut on his upper arm, and found it relatively shallow; the bleeding had slowed to a slow seepage. "We still have a deal, don't we, Publius?"

"Oh, yes," said Publius fervently.

"A problem has occurred to me, Publius. How can I be sure Tildoreamors will do as you ask, now that your power is destroyed, and the pirates are in such a froth about anyone leaving the city?"

Publius laughed, a thin mad sound. "Because—oh, this is a ripe irony—Tildoreamors belongs to me wholly, a Genched double, just like my Yubere."

"I see," said Ruiz. "Then we will go to your Yubere and release him and you will instruct him to do my bidding in every respect."

As RUIZ HAD hoped, the sampan was still moored to the quay. He moved a few of the crates, and made a place for Publius's floater.

When he guided it aboard, the monster-maker reached out and patted at the produce with uncertain hands. "Vegetables? This is the best you could do, Ruiz?" His voice was still thin.

"Don't complain," said Ruiz, arranging the crates to hide the floater. "If I didn't still need you to get out of SeaStack, I'd cut your throat and feed you to the margars."

"Would you indeed? I don't know . . . you've changed, gone soft, for all that you've bested Remint. You must have tricked him somehow. . . ."

"How else?" said Ruiz sourly. "How badly are you hurt?"

"I'll live, if you get me to a medunit. Would you moisten my eyes? They feel very strange."

"No."

"No?"

"No. And we'll see about the medunit after you've fulfilled our bargain. Meanwhile, I like to see you suffer."

Publius giggled. "No matter. And even if I die, I have my clones, who'll surely get even for all this destruction. I confess, I'd prefer to keep this old brain; I'm comfortable in it. But times change and we must adapt, eh?"

Ruiz looked down at the blood-smeared face, the dull eyes, the still-arrogant mouth. "Don't be so cocky, Publius. I drained your clones."

A stricken look clouded the monster-maker's face. He clamped his lips shut and said no more.

.   .   .

NISA LIVED IN grayness. Her cell was gray: the door, the walls, the floor, the narrow bench where she sat, the cot where she lay. The light that seeped from the ceiling was gray, neither bright nor dim, except for those times when it grew very faint and she slept. Even the food was gray and tasted of nothing.

She had grown listless in the days since the terrible Remint had thrust her into the cell and locked the door. She had lost track of time, or rather had abandoned it. On several occasions, she had awakened without a memory of falling asleep, and assumed that she had been drugged. She had no way of knowing how long those periods of unconsciousness had lasted, so she stopped caring. She drifted into an almost-comfortable apathy, which was easier than wondering if her mind had been altered in the awful manner Ruiz had described.

She rarely thought of Ruiz and his inexplicable treachery, preferring instead to dwell on happier times on Pharaoh, when she had been the favored daughter of the King. She remembered her father's garden, and the pleasure she had taken with her many lovers, and the various delightful sensations of her patrician station: fine food, the best wines, silks and jewels, the worshipful attentions of her slaves.

After a while Pharaoh seemed more real than her present dull circumstances. It was only when she slept and dreamed that she was unable to maintain her carefully cultivated detachment. In her dreams, Ruiz Aw came to her and pleaded for forgiveness, and she pretended to accept his apologies. In dreaming, she concealed her hatred and led him on skillfully, so that she might make him vulnerable and wreak a dreadful vengeance on him. But the dreams were frustrating because she always woke before she could shatter his heart as he had shattered hers.

The worst thing of all was that she sometimes woke crying weak tears, sad that the dream was over, that he had slipped away again, even though she hated him and hoped never to see him again.

Occasionally she wondered if she were dead and in Hell. Perhaps all that had gone before had been a sort of purgatory. Had she failed that test and been condemned to this eternity of grayness? Ruiz Aw might well have been a demon of destruction, sent to beguile her. It seemed to her there was a good deal of evidence to support such a view.

To escape the dreams, she slept rarely and spent her artificial nights sitting in the darkness, remembering the blazing light of Pharaoh.

It was at such a time that the door groaned and slid back and Ruiz Aw stood there looking in at her.

The lights came up and her eyes watered, so that she could not see him clearly for a moment; he was only a shape against the brighter light of the corridor.

"Nisa?" he said, in a soft uncertain voice.

Her eyes grew used to the light, and she could make out his face. He was shockingly haggard, with thick stubble in the hollows of his cheeks and dark circles under his eyes. He looked much older. He wore the sort of rough garments a slave might wear, and the sleeve of his jerkin was crusted with dried blood.

In that instant of dismayed recognition her heart softened just a bit and she wanted to go to him.

But he held a long-barreled weapon in his hand, so he was not a prisoner. The situation seemed full of dangerous ambiguity. She couldn't imagine where safety lay, here on this terrible world where evil seemed extravagantly magnified and treachery had been raised to a high art. Ruiz Aw had returned, but what did that mean? And was he to be trusted? She feared him almost as much as she loved him—and her heart was still sluggish with some cold burden.

She lifted her chin and did not speak.

WHEN HE SAW her, Ruiz felt an almost-physical pain. She was white-faced and drawn. Her beautiful hair was a wild tangle, and she sat slumped over, as if ill. For a moment her eyes were dull and faraway, but then her head came up and her eyes filled with evaluation. She seemed damaged in some unknowable way—still lovely, but a stranger. His fault.

"Nisa," he said again. "It's all right. We'll be leaving now." He held out his free hand.

She stood slowly. She looked down at his hand, her expression shifting toward a painfully cautious hope. "Where will we be going?" she asked. "Am I allowed to ask?"

"Of course . . . we're leaving SeaStack. We'll find a launch ring downcoast, and get off Sook."

Disbelief fell across her face like a dusty veil. "The others?"

"Them too, Molnekh and Dolmaero. We can't leave them."

She walked past him, her body taut with unhappy expectation, as though she expected him to hurl her back into the cell and laugh at her disappointment. He felt a terrible pressure in his chest, and his eyes watered. How could he explain? There was no time now; every minute they spent in Yubere's stronghold increased the danger that Publius would find a way to thwart their escape.

WHEN SHE CAME from her cell, Nisa saw an injured man on a slab of metal, floating unsupported in the corridor. His wounds were beginning to stink; he wouldn't live long. Standing beside the man was another stranger, a small man with a closed face. The wounded man was whispering urgently to the other, who nodded.

"Who are they?" she asked.

AT HER QUESTION, Ruiz turned to look at Publius and the false Yubere . . . and saw that some murderous plot was being hatched.

A consuming rage filled him, blowtorch hot, fueled by all the awful things Publius had done to him and to others. He felt his vision grow dim with it, and it hammered in his head, demanding some release.

His finger spasmed on the trigger and Yubere's head vaporized. The body fell across Publius and then slid to the floor.

"No," said Publius feebly, wiping Yubere's blood from his face. "Why did you do that? I was just asking him about your slaves . . . what had happened to them. . . ."

Ruiz turned back to Nisa, who had become even more pale. "Always be vigilant around that man. He is the most wicked person you will ever meet; he is as devious as a snake and as cunning as a Dilvermoon herman. Presently he is blind and crippled and chained to the floater—and probably dying—but never forget that he is also the most dangerous person you will ever meet."

She nodded and didn't speak, but he could almost imagine her thought: *Could he be worse than you, Ruiz Aw?*

RUIZ FOUND THE cells in which Dolmaero and Molnekh were being held, and released them. They stumbled into the light, and greeted Ruiz with no more warmth than Nisa had.

What had they been told? He shook his head in frustration. Time was passing, and they would have to hurry or risk missing Lord Tildoreamors's men, who would costume them for their trip on the Immolators' barge.

"Come," he said brusquely, and herded them on their way.

EPILOGUE

ONLY when they were at sea and the peaks of Sea-Stack had begun to drop below the horizon did Ruiz begin to believe that they might escape. The motion of the old barge wasn't too bad yet; the breeze was a moderate offshore one, and they still moved in relatively flat water. No doubt it would worsen.

Publius lay on an improvised litter, alternately raving and torpid. The others were already seasick and spent most of their time at the rail, trying to purge their already-empty stomachs. Their upbringing on a desert world had not equipped them to deal with ocean voyaging. Between the pervasive smell of vomit and the horrible stink of Publius's infected wounds, Ruiz was feeling a bit queasy himself.

Most of the Immolators were in little better shape, and Ruiz could hear the bargemen shouting whenever too many went to the lee rail and their weight threatened to capsize the overloaded vessel. Above the shouts and the sounds of retching came the low buzz of neuro-whips, which the bargemen used to drive the seasick dedicants back into the tweendecks area.

The white robes of the Immolators were not so white anymore, but their dedication was undiminished; the healthier ones sang songs lauding the nobility of suicide and wandered about reading aloud from their sacred book. Though Ruiz fended off their frequent efforts to involve him in this religious fervor, they seemed undiscouraged.

It struck Ruiz that the discomforts of the voyage probably accounted somewhat for the willingness with which the Immolators sought the abattoirs of the Blades.

He hadn't yet explained the events in SeaStack to the Pharaohans, and Nisa still treated him with brittle formality. Exhaustion made him feel clumsy, and he was afraid he might say the wrong thing. Or that she wouldn't understand, no matter what he said. So he kept putting off the explanation and no one pressed him, not even Dolmaero.

Publius woke and thrashed his arms about. "Emperor of Everything," he shouted. "Everything!"

He drew a ragged breath. "Ruiz?" His voice was abruptly lucid. "Ruiz? I know something you don't. Want to know?"

"Why not?" Ruiz said. He hoped Publius wouldn't start shrieking; it undermined their roles as humble Immolators on their way to the suicide fields. Publius tended to shriek in a less-than-humble style.

"Hah! You've never even asked about my secret . . . and a time will come when you'll wish you had, when everyone will wish someone had, everyone. But I won't tell you my Big Secret; you'll find out soon enough, and so will everyone else." Publius smiled with as much malignant relish as ever. "I might tell you a Tiny Secret, if you're a good boy and get me a medical limpet or at least a drink of water."

"No," said Ruiz.

"All right," said Publius. "I'll tell you anyway; why not? My Yubere, before you murdered him . . . he was telling me an interesting thing. He was telling me that one of your slaves had already been down to the Gencha."

Ruiz felt abruptly sick. He shivered, but made his voice light and unconcerned. "Sure, Emperor Publius. Which one?"

Publius stretched his bloody lips in a dreadful parody of a smile. "That's the amusing part, Ruiz. You killed my Yubere before he could tell me which one! Hah! Hah! Hah!"

Then he passed out again.

No, Ruiz thought. It surely wasn't true, just a clever Publius lie, carefully calculated to damage him. It was only Publius trying to get even, in the only way left to him. It was possible the false Yubere might have had time to acquire that information from his people, between the time Ruiz had reactivated him and their arrival in the stronghold . . . but why would he have bothered?

No, it was almost certainly a lie.

ON THE MORNING of the third day, Publius died. Ruiz felt a pang of annoyance at this event, since he had hoped to use Publius's influence among the Blades of Namp to smooth their escape from Sook.

But as he rolled the heavy body over the rail into the sea, his deepest emotion was a vast relief.

HERE IS AN EXCERPT FROM
THE ORPHEUS
MACHINE, BOOK 3 IN
THE EMANCIPATOR SERIES

His situation ever more complicated and desperate,
Ruiz Aw still struggles to hold on to his freedom
and his dreams of restful happiness with the beautiful Nisa. When the final episode of his story begins
(in **The Orpheus Machine**, on sale August 1992),
Ruiz and his band of refugees find themselves ship-
wrecked. . . .

B Y midafternoon, the wind had fallen to a light breeze, barely enough to ruffle the great green backs of the leftover storm swell. The sun had broken through, and only a few wispy clouds marked the verdigris sky.

Ruiz sat in the bow, watching a seabird wheel high above the mast and remembering earlier, less-complicated times: the dusty roads of Pharaoh, the Expiation at Bidderum, the paddock in the Black Tear Pens where he had nursed Nisa back to health and where they had become lovers, Corean's silk-upholstered apartment where he and Nisa had spent their longest time alone together . . . and best of all, the barge trip through beautiful wild country to SeaStack.

It occurred to him that he had never completely enjoyed those sweet lost days—at the time he had been so full of schemes, so taut with violent anticipation, so wary of his enemies, that the best times had slid away from him, leaving only a sketchy residue of memory. Of course, he and Nisa were still alive because of his relentless preoccupations, so perhaps he had made a fair bargain. Still, he wondered briefly if it was the best possible bargain. He thought of that starry night on the barge, when he lay in Nisa's arms. He remembered feeling that if he were to die in that moment, he might never find a more contented moment in which to depart his long strange life, that a measure of safety from future evils could be found in such a death.

Ruiz shook his head angrily. Such thoughts were a slow poison, a weakness that would steal away his future with Nisa. He must cling to his wariness, his treachery, his brutality—until a time came that those qualities no longer served them, until they could finally escape from Sook and return to some less dangerous world.

He looked at her as she slept, her head pillowed on her hands, her features obscured by a tangle of thick black hair. All he could see of her were her slender strong arms and the white vulnerable curve of her neck. He felt an odd constriction of his throat, a mixture of grief and tenderness so powerful that his vision swam with tears. He was astonished; he hadn't cried since his long-ago childhood.

He was distracted by a sudden change in the pitch of the boat's engine, which then rapidly lost speed and began to emit an unpleasant grinding sound.

"What is it?" he asked Gunderd, who had leaped to the nacelle and flipped up the latches.

Gunderd grunted noncommittally and ducked his head into the engine compartment.

The engine fell silent. From the compartment came a series of peevish clatters, and then Gunderd emerged, face blackened with grease. "Dead," he muttered. "Wasn't the fuel cell, after all."

"Now what?" asked Svin the cabin boy, suddenly looking even younger.

"Now we put up the sail and hope this wind holds."

Ruiz helped Gunderd retrieve the gear from the cuddy. They assembled the jointed spars and set the brown lateen sail from the radio mast. Gunderd sheeted it in and the boat moved off, though more sedately than before.

Ruiz looked over Gunderd's shoulder as he fiddled with the boat's minimal navigation module. "Just enough juice left to run this for a few hours," he said, adjusting the scale of a small electroluminescent screen. Gunderd's thin brown finger stabbed at a cluster of wavy lines at the upper right corner of the chart. "Here: the edge of the Dayerak Shelf." His finger moved down. "Here: us." A tiny green dot marked their position, two hundred kilometers off the Namp coast.

Gunderd shut down the display. "We'll save the power until we get into the shoals—that's when our piloting must be accurate." He grinned. "There's not enough juice for the radio—but that's a small loss, since at the moment our only potential rescuers have pointy teeth and big appetites."

Ruiz smiled back. "Have you always been a philosopher?"

"Always. But, back to the matter at hand . . . can you steer a course?"

"More or less."

"Good!" Gunderd patted Ruiz tentatively on the shoulder. "Will you stand a watch at the helm? Jeric and I have been alternating since Loracca foundered, and we're both tired. Svin is unreliable—we might wake to find ourselves sailing back to the Blades—and Marlena seems to be present in body only. Einduix . . . well, he is as he is. Whatever that is."

"I suppose so," said Ruiz. He was tired, too; he had been unwilling to test Jeric's restraint so early in their association. Still, he couldn't refuse to do his fair share; that would only inflame the resentments against him.

He shifted aft and took the tiller from Jeric, who relinquished it with a grimace of barely restrained violence. The seaman went forward, where he glared truculently at the Pharaohans, before settling himself on the floorboards. Dolmaero, who was apparently recovering at last from his bout with seasickness, returned an expression of wary reserve. Molnekh grinned cheerfully and nodded a greeting.

Nisa, who had awakened during Gunderd's examination of the engine, looked bewildered . . . and then disdainful. She rose unsteadily and came aft, to sit near Ruiz.

He couldn't help smiling.

But then his attention was caught by the glitter of Jeric's eyes within his hood, and by the ugly comprehension that came over Jeric's face as he looked from Ruiz to Nisa. A chill touched Ruiz, and he wondered how best to deal with the seaman. Sooner or later he must sleep, and what would happen then?

RUIZ STEERED UNTIL dusk began to shadow the waves. The wind had held steady from the west all day, and the boat had made good progress, cutting a sizzling white furrow through the sea.

When Gunderd relieved him, he took Nisa's hand and led her forward. Dolmaero sat on a thwart, gazing out at the crimson and gold sunset. The Guildmaster seemed much recovered—perhaps the easier motion of the boat under sail had helped. Ruiz was relieved; he would hate to lose Dolmaero's comforting presence.

"So," said Dolmaero, when they had settled themselves. "How are we doing?"

"Well enough," said Ruiz.

"In what way will our situation next deteriorate?" Dolmaero asked. "I don't mean to be ungrateful, but I'd like to know what new torments await us." Ruiz saw that the Guildmaster had yet to recover his equilibrium. Ordinarily Dolmaero would never have spoken so pessimistically.

"Actually, I hope for improvement soon," said Ruiz. "At least we're alive, which is more than can be said for the rest of Loracca's company."

"Yes," said Molnekh. "Let's be thankful for that."

Ruiz nodded. He was very tired; if he did not rest soon, his judgment would begin to deteriorate dangerously. "Listen," he said. "I need to sleep for a bit. You'll have to take turns watching the crew. Especially Jeric. The others may be harmless, but we should take no chances. Dolmaero, you take charge of setting the watches. When Gunderd needs me at the helm again, he'll tell you. You wake me; don't let him or one of the other crew near me."

He settled himself in the curve of the bows and shut his eyes. Almost instantly he slept.

WHEN HE WOKE, it was to a feeling of intense danger and a tumble of unidentifiable bodies, rolling over him in the darkness. He started up, striking at the nearest—but at the last instant he diverted the blow so that his fist clanged uselessly into the lifeboat's alloy. He couldn't tell who his attacker was, or even if he was being attacked. Maybe he was being defended.

Before he could sort out the situation, something cracked into his head from behind, and he fell bonelessly into the boat's bilge, his last emotion an unfocused astonishment that he had been so easily bested.

WHEN HE REGAINED consciousness, he was still astonished—though now the source of his amazement was that he was still alive. He still lay in the bilge, but his head rested in Nisa's lap. She looked down at him with a mixture of relief and apprehension.

Dolmaero leaned over him. "You're awake. Good; we wondered if we might lose you."

Ruiz struggled to raise his head, then looked aft. Gunderd steered; he made a jaunty gesture of greeting. The cabin boy Svin huddled beside the mate, his face white and strained. Ruiz looked forward. Molnekh sat in the bows, grinning with his usual aplomb.

Jeric was nowhere to be seen. Nor was the catatonic purser.

"What's happened?" he croaked.

Dolmaero shrugged. "None of us are sure. But Gunderd has your little weapon, and he took away our knives."

"The crew attacked us? Who was on watch?"

"I was," said Dolmaero. He looked down, clearly ashamed. "But I was looking up at the stars when it happened. Someone threw a canvas over me and knocked me down. By the time I got untangled and stood up, it was over."

"What was over?" Ruiz struggled to a sitting position

and touched the back of his head gingerly. It was crusty with dried blood, but his probing fingers found nothing more alarming than split skin. His head ached horribly, so that he found thought difficult.

"The killing," said Gunderd. "Your crew fared better than mine, Ruiz. Yours are still alive, but two of mine are gone."

"Gone where?" asked Ruiz.

"Fed to the fishes," said Gunderd. "They were thoroughly dead. The purser's guts were lying in her lap. She probably never noticed, but I'd guess Jeric noticed when someone cut his throat. Neat job, too; whoever did it left him on the gunwale so he bled out overboard. Considerate."

Ruiz rubbed his pounding head, trying to massage some clarity back into his thoughts. "Did you see what happened?"

"No." In the cold dawn light, Gunderd seemed much older and more vulnerable, despite the splinter gun tucked into his waistband and his air of nonchalance. "I was asleep. But I can theorize, up to a point. I think Jeric lashed the helm when your man's attention wandered, and went forward to revenge himself on you. Apparently he was surprised by someone. I heard a scuffle—and a classic gurgle—as I was waking. And then you started to get up and I heard the sound of wood on skull. I made a light and went forward cautiously, to find you unconscious and Jeric dead."

"I see," said Ruiz. What had happened? "You found no other indications?"

"No . . . the cutter was very clean. No one had blood on their hands, except for Jeric. His, I suppose."

"Who hit me?"

Gunderd shrugged. "No one will admit to the deed. But whoever did the cutting, the whack was delivered by one of yours. Svin and Einduix were aft when you went down."

Ruiz looked at the others. Nisa wore an expression of frustrated concern. Dolmaero looked embarrassed . . . but Ruiz saw no trace of guilt. Molnekh seemed his usual cheerful self. "Did any of you see anything?" he asked.

No one answered.

"Svin?"

The cabin boy shook his head vigorously. Gunderd laughed. "As well to blame it on sea wights as to suspect

Svin. Remember, the deed was performed with élan and skill."

"Einduix?"

The cook looked up from his seat in the waist, smiling without a trace of comprehension.

Gunderd snorted in disbelief. "Einduix. A remote possibility. He's a butcher, I'll grant you that, but an entirely incompetent one. That he could have made two such neat cuts . . . it seems a foolish speculation."

A silence ensued, during which it gradually came to Ruiz that Gunderd probably suspected Ruiz of somehow engineering the deaths of the two crew members. "Me? Don't be ridiculous," he snapped. "How do you suppose I managed to cut up your people and then arrange to get my head broken?"

"I haven't figured that out—though perhaps one of your confederates assisted you into slumber. But no. Despite the dire reputation your woman gives you, I can't figure out why you'd bother with subterfuge. You had the gun."

Ruiz shook his head and winced. "True. A mystery."

Gunderd nodded. "As you say, a mystery. We'll talk later, when you've recovered your wits."

The morning passed in a dull misery. Nisa bathed away the blood that caked his head, with stinging salt water. He sipped cool water from the boat's recycler and nibbled on a nutrient bar. He slowly began to feel a bit better. He couldn't think of anything to say to anyone.

The beam wind held and the boat made good progress to the northeast and the Dayerak Archipelago. Gunderd steered with the casual intensity of the experienced helmsman, but by afternoon he began to show signs of fatigue. "Come," he said. "Take a turn, Ruiz Aw. I must get my rest before nightfall, I think."

Ruiz made his way aft and took the tiller. Gunderd moved warily away, his hand on the splinter gun. Ruiz could hardly blame him for being cautious, and smiled ruefully.

Gunderd settled himself on the far side of the helmsman's thwart. He watched Ruiz for a while, apparently to judge the quality of Ruiz's helmsmanship. Abruptly he tapped Svin on the shoulder and said, "Go forward with the others, boy. The slayer and I must talk of things which don't concern you."

Svin went slowly, as if reluctant to lose contact with the mate. Gunderd laughed and prodded him with his boot. "Hurry up! Remember, they may kill you, but they probably won't eat you."

Gunderd cast a speculative glance at Einduix. "Hmm . . ." he said. "I would swear the little snake doesn't know a word of pangalac, but why take a chance . . . ? Go forward, Einduix." He made shooing gestures at the cook, until Einduix got the idea and went, still wearing his mindless grin.

"Now," said Gunderd in a low voice. "We must speak as frankly as our hearts permit us to. I don't believe you killed my people; but someone did. If it was one of yours . . . that person is a threat to you as well as me. Someone isn't telling all they know."

"So it seems," said Ruiz. He had been avoiding examining the implications of the past night's murders. His head still hurt, he felt weak and unready for any confrontation.

Gunderd looked away, across the sunlit sea. "I must tell you, Ruiz Aw . . . I think we have a monster among us. I can understand the killing of Jeric, who craved your blood. Whoever cut him was protecting you. But whoever killed Marlena—he was ridding himself of a minor annoyance. True, she stank, and she took up a little room, but she wasn't dangerous to anyone. A cold deed."

Ruiz nodded reluctant agreement.

"Let me tell you what I've thought. The cutter was fairly strong, strong enough at least to pick up Jeric and put him across the gunwale. Probably any of your people could have done it, even the woman. She looks strong for her size. And the fat one might easily have struck from beneath the canvas he claimed was thrown over him. So," said Gunderd. "Let me ask you. What do you know about your people that might shed light on the matter?"

Ruiz took a deep breath. Almost against his will, a memory rose up in his mind's eye: the monster-maker Publius dying. Raving. Telling Ruiz that one of the Pharaohans had been processed by the Gench.

Should he tell Gunderd? In all likelihood, Publius had simply taken one last opportunity to hurt Ruiz.

His mind refused to work properly, he could not foresee the implications of revealing this suspicion to Gunderd. On the other hand, it was very possible that one of the

Pharaohans was no longer his friend, since none of them would admit to striking the blow that had put him down. And none of them had contradicted Gunderd's version of the night's events.

Gunderd seemed as trustworthy as anyone he was likely to meet on Sook; he appeared to have no agenda beyond simple survival.

"All right," Ruiz said finally. "There's a small chance that one of my people—I don't know which one—has recently gone through deconstruction at the hands of the Sea-Stack Gench."

Gunderd's eyebrows rose to the top of his forehead. "Really? And who is the primary?"

"Probably a slaver named Corean Heiclaro. Have you heard the name?"

Gunderd went slightly pale. "Does she own a big Moc and a famous face? Yes? Then I know her." He drew the splinter gun from his waistband and pointed it forward. "Duck, Svin," he barked.

It almost happened too fast for Ruiz to react. He slammed the tiller across just before Gunderd fired, catching the mate in the ribs with enough force to catapult him overboard. The gun flew in a bright arc and plopped into the sea.

Ruiz sighed regretfully.

Gunderd's head popped up in the white wake. The mate was floundering ineffectively, apparently losing the struggle against the weight of his gold chains.

After an instant's hesitation, Ruiz came about and hove to. "Toss him a line," he told Svin, and the cabin boy threw the mate a rescue buoy.

When Gunderd was back aboard, shivering and clutching his ribs, Ruiz let the sails draw, and the boat returned to her course.

Minutes passed in silence, except for the crunch and whisper of the boat, making her way over the waves.

Finally Gunderd raised his eyes and attempted a wry smile. "I begin to believe in your effectiveness, Ruiz Aw. It seems your woman doesn't exaggerate. But I was only acting sensibly. Kill them all and we're sure to get the Genched one. It was a sensible plan."

"Perhaps so," said Ruiz.

"Well, I see that considerations beyond naked pragmatism move you, Ruiz Aw. I should find this reassuring, shouldn't I? At any rate, thank you for fishing me out." He took a handful of clasp knives from his sodden pocket and offered them to Ruiz. "Here. I don't think they give me a significant advantage." His smile grew crooked. "I may as well try to curry favor while I can."

Ruiz took one of the knives and pocketed it. He returned one to Gunderd and pitched the others overboard.

Gunderd quirked up his eyebrows. "Well then," he said. "Let's be allies. I promise to make no more precipitous decisions, if you'll try to do likewise."

"I'll try," said Ruiz, somewhat ambiguously.

Gunderd shot him a sharp glance, but then he smiled and pocketed the knife. "That's as fair as I could ask," he said. "Given the circumstances. I was attempting the direct solution to the problem."

"I understand that," said Ruiz. "But it may not be true, and I value these people."

"Ah," said Gunderd. He lowered his voice to a confidential whisper. "The value of the woman is obvious, even to me . . . though for a fact she seems not too friendly. A lovers' quarrel?"

Ruiz scowled.

Gunderd held up his hands. "None of my business, of course. But after all, even if one of them is Genched, it's not the decay of the universe. I once had a good friend who was Genched."

It was Ruiz's turn to look surprised.

"Oh yes. It was an odd situation, no doubt of that. He was a soldier in the Triatic Wars, outbound for Jacquet's World. He was an assassin, aimed at the High Poet of Bist, and Genched for the part of a talented minstrel so as to gain the confidence of the Poet. The war ended before he was given his final instructions, and then the lander crashed during his recall to Soufriere. They thought he was dead, so no one attempted to retrieve him and he lived out his life there on Soufriere's Midsea. A fine fellow—a voice like sea foam and moonlight. He was a better man than most men, because he acted as he believed he should act, and not as he wanted to."

Ruiz found this an odd story—he thought of Genching as an end to humanity, and of the Genched as organic machines, unalterable and dead. "Interesting," he said. "So you're from Soufriere?"

Gunderd nodded. "Yes. Can you believe it? I was a fisherboy on the warm Midsea; all I knew was nets and longlines and fishergirls. How I ever came to this terrible world . . . well, we all have our stories, don't we? But to return to Genching, do you know of Aluriant the Ambitious, who had himself Genched into a saint? The Gencha will take anyone's money."

"I suppose so. It occurs to me that even if one of mine is Genched, then it's very likely that they've never been in contact with their primary."

Gunderd's eyes brightened. "Really? Then we may have no great problem. The person will have to act as he supposes Corean would wish him to act. Were any of your people close enough to the slaver to have a good idea of what she would wish?"

"Possibly not," said Ruiz. "They were her slaves, kept in the Blacktear Pens with others of their culture."

"Better and better!" But then Gunderd looked perplexed. "Something doesn't fit here. If one of your people is Corean's creature, why did they protect you from Jeric?"

Ruiz shivered involuntarily. "I suppose it seems clear to him that Corean wants me alive so that she can redress the wrongs I've committed against her."

"Makes sense," said Gunderd. "What, if I may ask, did you do to earn Corean's enmity."

Ruiz answered distractedly. "I stole her slaves and her airboat, killed several of her people, ruined her business, stranded her in SeaStack . . . maybe got her killed, though that's probably too much to hope for. This and that."

Gunderd's eyes got big. "Oh. Well, if she's in SeaStack, we won't have to worry about her coming after you anytime soon. The city's in a terrible ferment." He still looked puzzled. "All right. Jeric died because he was about to steal Corean's fun. But why Marlena? She was harmless."

Ruiz didn't answer. He was thinking about that long-ago day in the pens, when Corean had come into the paddock and casually destroyed an incapacitated slave.

Suddenly he found himself believing Publius's dying words. One of the Pharaohans was no longer human.

A terrible pressure squeezed his heart. He looked forward at the three of them huddled in the bows. Molnekh seemed his usual bland cheerful self, which meant nothing. Dolmaero stared at his feet, a dour empty expression on his broad face. Nisa watched Ruiz with an unnatural intensity, her lips trembling between a frown and a smile.

Which one?

Ruiz turned back to Gunderd. "Say nothing that might alert the creature to our suspicions. We may as well try to keep it off its guard."

Look for *The Orpheus Machine,*
available August 1992
wherever Bantam Spectra Books are sold.